DAZZLED

JANE HARVEY-BERRICK

HARVEY
BERRICK
PUBLISHING

First published in Great Britain in 2013
ISBN 9780955315091

Cover design by Hang Le / byhangle.com
Cover photograph: iStock
'Crazy' lyrics © Sam Callahan, with permission

DEDICATION

This book is dedicated to Simon
For his kindness, grace under fire and saxpertise :)

CONTENTS

Chapter One

ONE FLEW EAST, ONE FLEW WEST

Clare

I was late but there he was, waiting for me—my own personal miracle. Well, when I say 'my' he wasn't really mine at all and looking at his beautiful face, I knew he never would be. So I was settling for best friend, which wasn't bad.

He looked miserable, and I felt my face crease in sympathy.

"Hey, Miles. Sorry I'm late. What's up?"

I slid onto the bench next to him and gave him a peck on the cheek; he hadn't shaved and the rough hairs prickled on my lips.

He stared moodily into his beer.

"I got fired. From that job. Kicked out. On the scrapheap. Finished."

"What? Why?"

He sighed.

"Bill, the director ... he said it 'wasn't working'. God, Clare! I was trying so hard—I really thought I was doing something interesting and different. But Bill thought 'interesting and different' was 'bizarre and unconvincing'."

I was outraged! How dare this moron fire Miles? Didn't he realize he was working with one of the finest actors in London?

"The guy's an idiot!"

I almost shouted the words, and a ghost of a smile touched his lips. His shoulders were still hunched defensively.

"Yeah, well..." the words trailed off unhappily. "I don't think I'm cut out for all this. I think I'll stick to the music. Nazzer and Paul have been on about touring the jazz and beer festivals in Germany this summer. I dunno."

Oh yeah, did I mention that Miles also played alto sax like a god?

"Could be fun," I said, non-committal.

He shrugged.

"Yeah, sharing a camper van with two sweaty guys."

I had to laugh. I'd have shared the black hole of Calcutta if it meant being with Miles. Not that I could tell him that.

He smiled up at me.

"Yeah, I know. I'm being a miserable git. The beer festival circuit could be a laugh."

"Jazz and beer—two of your favorite things," I pointed out.

"True. Maybe you could come, too, unless you're working?"

I raised my eyebrows.

"Sharing a camper van with three sweaty guys?"

I'd perfected that casual tone. I'd had years of practice.

Miles and I had grown up together: I was literally the girl-next-door, and as plain as the words suggested.

He was tall and slim, with long, lean muscles, and in the summer, his dark blond hair was streaked with gold. He had the kind of angular beauty that you usually only saw staring out from fashion magazines, but his ready smile was warm and gentle.

The short version: he was out of my league.

Miles was nearly 16 before he finally realized why girls giggled when he spoke to them. But by then, his natural sweetness had become ingrained, and his friendliness a successful mask for his shyness. Then he discovered the magical alchemy of hair gel, and he developed his trademark, just fallen out of bed look.

The first real test of friendship came when our English teacher, Mr. Brady, cast him in the role of Romeo—who else —in the school play. In a panic, he came to me to help him learn his lines. Having not been cast as Juliet, of course, I had plenty of free time.

Then I had to endure the painful spectacle of watching him fall spectacularly in love with his leading lady—and not for the last time.

'Lady' was a loose term for Emma Thomas. She may have had the glossy hair and rosebud lips necessary to play Juliet, and a good memory for lines, which was all Mr. Brady cared about, but I knew that she was a heinous bitch who was so loose she rattled when she walked. No way I was jealous of someone like her. No bloody way.

It came as a surprise to everyone—including Miles—to discover that he really could act. He was good. This was a revelation. Miles wasn't dumb, but he was held back because he was dyslexic. Printed words made him panic.

So every night for two months I helped him learn his lines and helped him to overcome his crippling lack of confidence, or at least to control it. And every rehearsal for two months I had to watch Emma Thomas force her tongue down his throat as she played the virginal Juliet. I wanted to beat her to within an inch of her life. I wanted to swing her around by her hair extensions and toss her into the River Thames. Or face first into the stinking mud. The level of my fury scared me, sending me into the willing arms of Eli Grant, a short and spotty page to Mercutio.

My first sexual encounter was notably disappointing. Perhaps I shouldn't have blinked at the wrong moment. Not even a two pump chump, and not what you'd call a Kodak moment. Even so, I couldn't wait to brag to Miles that I had broken my duck and scored at last. He'd given me a half smile and confided that he and Emma had been sleeping together since the first rehearsal—and that he was in love.

I was heartbroken. More because he hadn't told me than anything else. I knew Emma wouldn't last. I'd describe her as a slutty scrubber, but only if I was feeling generous.

My romance was merely hours long when we broke up. Eli tucked his tiny todger into his jeans, wiped his fingers on his t-shirt and said, "See ya."

Miles dated Emma for the length of the play although, as I'd predicted, by the last-night party she was dancing a tonsil tango with Tybalt. For the first time in my life I'd seen Miles angry enough to want to punch someone. I dragged him home where he hugged me and cried and told me I was his best friend in the whole world. Then he drank half a bottle of vodka and passed out on my mum's couch.

Friend. Strange how that ordinary word pierced me.

And then, two days after Miles' triumph as Romeo, before he was barely sober, Melody Rimes had come into his life. Yeah, I know what you're thinking: what kind of skank has a made-up name like that? Some barely articulate rapper's ho?

Not exactly.

Melody was an agent for a top-class talent agency in town. She'd been dragged along to see the play as someone's unwilling aunt. And there she'd seen my beautiful boy, and there she'd decided she could 'do' something with him.

No, really, I don't think she had any devious designs on his undeniably gorgeous bod; the only thing that turned on Ms Rimes was $$$.

The result was that Miles had a real life, tin knickered, West End agent. Melody started to get him small parts in smaller *made for TV* films and one detective drama where he was brutally murdered before the opening credits. You know, lots of that fake blood stuff they use. You could hardly tell it was him. She even got him to try modeling, but once was enough. He said he hated people staring at him when he was being himself—he was more comfortable playing a role.

The work was steady but the pay was poor. Miles spent most of the cash on CDs. He said he liked the sleeve notes. Whatever. It all ended up on my iPod, too.

Any piece of music that Miles Davis had even breathed on was bought and cherished, along with David Sanborn and Charlie Parker—jazz stuff. Not really my thing but I couldn't help liking what Miles loved. Pathetic.

We had a few epic nights out in Camden, too. Miles was tall, over six foot, so he'd been buying drinks in pubs since he was 15. I had to lurk in the corner, being barely over five foot. I didn't really mind: I was a natural lurker, doing anything to avoid the spotlight. Which is pretty funny, bearing in mind how things turned out.

Our final two years of school followed a similar pattern. Miles would get an acting job, fall in love with an actress, often older, who would turn him inside out and dump him for being 'too nice'. My affairs were less eventful but equally unsatisfying.

We might have gone our separate ways when we were 18 because I had the chance to go to university. The sad truth was I couldn't bear to be far away from him, so I accepted a place at University College London to study History and English Literature. Not that it would be an easy ride—it was a tough place to get into. Miles was so damn proud of my academic achievements, bless him. He could have gone on to college classes too, but he decided he wanted to develop his music and acting. And he'd had enough of studying, he said.

He moved out into a revolting house share in Euston— seriously gross carpets that were *sticky*, and you don't want to know what bacteria had taken up residence in the kitchen. He shared the rent with one of his acting buddies. At least, Jim was supposed to be an actor but I never knew him to have a job. He was a happy-go-lucky no-mark who seemed to spend most of his time smoking weed, drinking cheap beer, and chatting up the slut fest of women who were always hanging around Miles. They were almost always actresses, occasionally singers or musicians, almost always stunning and they hated me. The feeling was mutual.

And then, to my surprise, Melody came up with the goods.

Miles had been so pleased when he'd landed the second male lead in a 'real play'—his words—in a real theater. There was a budget, a lighting department, a costume and makeup department, and a well known TV actor headlining, which meant guaranteed ticket sales. His moment had arrived.

We celebrated with cheap champagne and for the first time we shared a bed. No, not like that. I wish. After a marathon drinking session, Miles had finally collapsed like an exhausted puppy and I had to help him to his room. He hugged me and told me that he loved me and fell asleep, tugging me down onto the bed with him, his strong arms still wrapped around my waist. I was too happy to want to move. I snuggled up to him, enjoying the fleeting closeness, listening to the peaceful sound of his heavy breaths on the back of my neck and knew I was in heaven. And, like a fallen angel, I was soon cast out. Yeah, Literature student.

Miles' phone rang at ten o'clock the following morning, with a demand from the director to attend a pre-rehearsal discussion. He stumbled out of the house pale, shaky and very hung-over. I wandered home, alone with my thoughts.

When I saw him again, his naturally dark blond hair had been dyed a deep auburn on the director's orders, highlighting the tired rings under his eyes in his pale face. It had taken some getting used to. That's a lie—I hated it on sight. No, I didn't say anything.

Three weeks into rehearsals and just two before the opening night, Miles was fired. Which was why I was sitting next to him in a tiny Soho pub, ready to give that short-sighted git of a director a good kicking. Yeah, I was seriously pissed off.

Miles' confidence, fragile at the best of times, and especially when it came to his acting ability, was entirely broken.

"I've got to face it," he said. "I'm never going to make it as an actor. I'm just wasting my time—and everyone else's. What a bleedin' joke."

"Listen to me," I said, fiercely, "just because one dickhead of a director can't see what he's got with you, doesn't mean that you give up."

He shook his head wearily, his wide gray eyes unspeakably sad, his mouth turned down at the corners.

Well, *I* wasn't giving up.

"What did Melody say when you told her?" I demanded.

He shifted uncomfortably and ran his hands through his too-dark hair.

"I don't know. I didn't get the chance. Bill was on the phone to her before I'd got the bus home. She sent me a text—she wants to see me in her office tomorrow." He paused. "It doesn't look good. I think she's going to fire me, too."

"Why would she do that?" I was seething.

He shrugged helplessly.

"She's an agent. If I'm not earning then she's not earning her 15%—she can't go on like that forever with a client."

So bloody noble and self-sacrificing. I wanted to hit him. Or kiss him. Maybe both.

But he was wrong. About Melody, I mean.

Miles

Poor Clare. She spent the next two hours trying to nag me into a more positive frame of mind. So far, it wasn't working. The five pints of beer I sank might have had something to do with it, and I could feel myself sliding into a pathetic pit of despair. In the end, she manhandled me out of the King's Head and force-fed me kebab with curried sauce until I sobered up enough to stumble home. Having Clare around was a bit like having a second mum: a shorter, fiercer mum with a hair-trigger temper. If she was a dog, she'd be a Jack Russell terrier. One of the short legged ones.

She wasn't like most women, thank God. She said what she thought with very little editing. I always knew exactly what she was thinking, and because we had the same sense of humor, I only had to look at her for us both to start sniggering. That had got us into a lot of trouble over the years. She was my best friend.

There was only one subject that we disagreed on: Clare didn't really get the whole acting thing. She put up with it in a way that was kind of patronizing, but she didn't take it seriously. So it was hard to explain to her how I felt when I was fired from *Brief Memories*. Even though the thought of walking out onto a stage reduced me to a shivering wreck, it was something I needed to do. It wasn't about being in the spotlight—pretending to be someone else was the only time I felt like me. I knew Clare thought that because some women were attracted to me that I could breeze through life; she didn't get that it was just skin-deep, and inside I was just as messed up as the next guy. Probably more so. Clare was always confident and clever, always herself—I'd have felt like a moron if I tried to explain it to her. But then again, she was 100% loyal and always on my side, so perhaps I didn't need to.

The next morning I was halfway to Melody's office before I realized I should have tried to tidy myself up a bit. It was too late now. I felt even more self-conscious than usual when I noticed that my jeans weren't the cleanest they'd ever been, and that my Nikes looked like I'd stolen them from some less fortunate homeless person. On the other hand, she might give me the sympathy vote. And I *was* fucking pathetic.

Melody's agency was in a modern, steel and glass building, sandwiched between a Regency townhouse and a Victorian shop front near central London. I pushed through the old-fashioned, revolving wooden door, and the receptionist stared at me. Damn, I knew I looked scruffy and I could feel myself reddening under her gaze, and wishing I'd worn a clean shirt at least.

After a short phone call where she didn't take her eyes off me, probably in case I stole something or carved my name into the desk, she turned and gave me a chilly, professional smile.

"Mr. Stephens, Ms Rimes will see you now. Fourth floor."

I stammered my thanks and shuffled off to the lift, feeling her piercing gaze on my back. It was unnerving. I was glad that the mirrored interior of the lift was dark but then realized I still looked like shit. I closed my eyes until the doors reopened four floors up.

Melody's assistant Daniela was waiting. Luckily, she was smiling at me—she'd always been friendly.

"Hi Miles! How are you?"

"Hey, Dan. Well, okay, I guess. How are you?"

"Just peachy!"

Peachy? Only an American could get away with saying they were 'peachy'. Clare would have laughed. I found myself grinning inanely at Daniela, who tossed her hair over her shoulder and winked.

"Melody's ready for you," she said, bringing me back to earth. "Can I offer you a coffee?"

"Oh, sure, thanks, Dan."

"Black, one sugar. Right?"

I was impressed.

"How do you remember stuff like that?"

I thought she was about to answer when we heard Melody's testicle-tightening voice from the inner realms.

"Good morning, Miles. I'll have tea, thank you, Daniela."

Daniela scuttled off and I peered around the door.

"Uh, hi, Melody."

"Sit," she ordered, waving me to a chair while she scanned a file on her desk. I didn't know if she was waiting for the drinks to arrive or if she was trying to freak me out. Honestly, I was so wound up, she didn't need to prolong the agony just to make a point. Daniela delivered the coffee in silence, throwing me a sympathetic glance. *Uh oh.* Finally Melody glared at me over the top of her glasses. "So, Bill Howden fired you."

"Er, well, yeah." *Shit. This was it.*

"Hmm."

Melody should have been an actor—there was a world of meaning in that 'hmm'. I tried to analyze how she did it. It was the look, definitely: steely but thoughtful. I'd have to practice that one. Crap! I realized I was staring at her. Unemployable and acting like a weirdo—could the day get any worse?

"I *might* have something else for you," she said.

What? That was a surprise. I blinked, my eyes coming into focus as I met her gaze for the first time. She smiled.

"Yes, I thought that might get your attention." *She was laughing at me.* "Do you remember the audition tape you did a couple of months ago?"

I frowned, trying to remember. "Oh, yeah? The American thing?"

"Indeed!"

She raised her eyebrows. Somehow I'd committed a major sin—it must be one of omission because I had no idea what I'd done wrong this time. That was nothing new.

"Yes, *the American thing* is the film script for the bestselling book *Dazzled*: top of the New York Times bestseller list for 31 weeks; translated into 23 languages—yes, that would be *the American thing.*"

She paused for emphasis. She really didn't need to. I got the point: I was a moron with the brain capacity of a flea.

"Well, the director of *the American thing* has seen your tape and she's interested. She wants to meet you."

What? My brain had just gone into freefall.

Melody leaned back in her chair.

"It would mean traveling out to LA and it would have to be on your own buck because nothing's guaranteed. But it would be good for you: get your face out there a bit, meet some people. My colleague, Rhonda Weitz from our Los Angeles office, is willing to schedule some meetings—and she'll put you up at her place for a few nights. I pulled some strings."

Half a beat. I was sitting there with my mouth hanging open. I must have looked like such an idiot.

"I thought you were going to fire me!" I managed to croak out at her.

Okay, so I had more in common with Clare than I thought—I didn't edit much either, although in my case it was less about being candid and more about a brain to mouth malfunction. It's the kind of thing that happens to a guy when he's thinking with his dick, but I *swear* that was not the case with Melody. I mean hell, any guy who got a boner within ten feet of her was risking permanent disfigurement. My dick hid behind my testicles when I was in Melody's office—and then my testicles shriveled to the size of acorns.

Melody smiled again, or maybe she was just baring her teeth.

"No, Miles. If you'd read the contract you signed, you'd realize that *I* work for *you*."

She was definitely laughing at me.

"So, can you get yourself over to LA for Thursday?"

"Yeah! Even if I have to swim."

She snorted loudly and I couldn't help flinching. "Good. Then I'll make the arrangements. Daniela will email the details to you."

She waved a hand, dismissing me, already onto the next job. I stood up, feeling stunned and spaced out—but in a good way—and walked around the desk to kiss her cheek. She looked surprised.

"Thanks, Melody. I mean it. Really. Wow! Thanks."

She smiled thinly. I thought I'd overstepped the mark, but I really did mean it. I was so fucking grateful I could have kissed the ground at her feet.

"Make me proud, Miles."

I was halfway to the lift when she called after me.

"Oh, and Miles, buy a new shirt ... you look like shit."

Clare

Miles was a bag of nerves, that much was obvious. He fidgeted, tugging at his t-shirt, scratching his cheek, running his hands through his too-dark auburn hair. It was hard to say how I felt: excited, pleased, worried and, truthfully, sorry for myself.

When Miles had told me the news, that he was flying out to LA, like a real actor, I felt as if I'd been cut in half. The better half of me was as happy as he was, reveling in the amazing news; the other half was already in mourning, the thought of being without him for three long weeks almost unbearable. But this was his big chance—I couldn't let him see that I was half-hearted about it, even as half my heart shriveled unhappily.

"Have you got your passport?" I asked for the fourth or fifth time. I knew I was annoying him, I just couldn't help myself.

"Ye-es!" he rolled his eyes.

"And you'll text me when you get there?"

"If my phone works. Or I'll email you. Do you think my phone will work? Oh God, Clare, what if I make a complete arse of myself?"

His irritation was suddenly replaced with anxiety. I wanted to hug him, to soothe him. Instead I shoved my hands in my pockets, to stop them reaching out for him.

"You'll be fine," I intoned automatically, while wondering if he really would be okay. He was prone to arseish behavior when he got nervous. Nerves made me mute; they had the opposite effect on Miles. He hated uncomfortable silences, always trying to find something funny to say to fill the gap— sometimes hideously inappropriate things that he later regretted.

His flight was called and it was time for him to go. For a brief moment his eyes were wild with uncertainty, then he blinked and I could see that he was giving himself a mental shake. Finally, now he was going, I allowed myself to reach up and give him a hug.

"Look after yourself," I said into his neck, feeling his warm skin on my cheek. "Text me when you get there." I couldn't help repeating myself.

He nodded wordlessly and hugged me tight enough to

crack a rib. I didn't care. Then he slung his carry-on bag over his shoulder and strode away. He was halfway across the concourse when he turned and yelled, "Love you, Clare!"

People turned to stare; several laughed.

I watched until he was out of sight. It felt like the sun had just gone down—my own personal sun.

"Love you, too, Miles," I whispered.

Chapter Two

BABE IN TOYLAND

Miles

It was nine hours into the 11 hour flight and I could feel my legs cramping up. I shifted uncomfortably, wondering how irritated the woman next to me would be if I asked her to move again, so I could get past her and stretch my legs in the aisle.

"These seats aren't really made for tall people, are they?" she said, sympathetically glancing in my direction. Her voice was low and she had a soft American accent. She must have been nearly forty but she was dead sexy. My dick definitely noticed. Lovely: cramp *and* a hard-on. Her clothes were really cool and trendy, unlike me, and she was totally at ease in her own body. Plus—that voice!

"I think these seats are made for midgets with a bad attitude," I agreed.

She frowned.

"There's no need to be offensive about our vertically challenged friends," she intoned, with an expression that could have frozen oxygen.

I felt my face get hot. Shit! I'd offended her.

"Sorry, I didn't mean ... it was just a joke ... I..."

She ignored my half-arsed apology with a sniff and went back to reading *Vogue*. I sank lower in my seat—she definitely wasn't going to move for me now. Crap.

I stared out of the window, trying to take my mind off my tortured muscles. I couldn't quite believe I was on my way to Hollywood. It felt unreal and I was even more wired than usual—it was a bit like having one of those anxiety dreams where you don't know the answers to a sudden test, or your molars turn to chalk and fall out. Tentatively, I checked my teeth with my tongue. Nope, they were still there. I glanced at the woman in the next seat and caught her staring at me. She looked really pissed off as she turned away. Great.

A long couple of hours later, the plane started its descent. The sun was pouring through my window, and I was looking out onto an ocean of concrete with flotillas of aircraft from all around the world. LAX was beyond vast.

I was feeling a bit spaced out. I never could sleep on planes, so I'd spent most of the night listening to Miles Davis 'Kind of Blue' and some other tracks from the Warner years. My iPod was nearly out of juice and I couldn't remember if I'd packed my charger. I didn't even know if I'd be able to use it out here. Did I need an adaptor? I hated being without my music. The thought was depressing.

First I had to get through Security.

"Passport."

I handed over my scruffy, dog-eared passport. It wasn't my fault it looked like I'd been using it to dig the garden. Nazzer and Paul had dropped it in the Regent's Canal, and it was just luck that a guy had been fishing nearby. I dried it on a radiator and it had gone a bit wrinkly.

The security officer was massive and scary-looking. You know, the kind who probably played American football a couple of decades ago. I didn't want to mess with him—I just had to remember to keep my mouth shut. *No stupid jokes. No stupid jokes. No stupid jokes.* He ran his eyes over me in a way that made me feel like a Colombian drug smuggler. I prayed he wasn't going to get out the rubber gloves. Just the way he was eyeing me made me feel guilty of something.

"Reason for visit."

"Uh, well, I might be here for a job, maybe."

"Occupation, sir?"

Sir! "Er, I'm ... an actor."

I felt like such a fraud saying that, and from the look on his face he could see right through me to the pathetic loser that I was. But finally, after another long gaze, he let me past. Thank God.

At the exit, I followed the instructions Clare had printed out for me (of course she'd printed them out—she treated me like a child sometimes), and I caught the shuttle bus to downtown LA. It felt so surreal buying a ticket for Hollywood. I couldn't get my head around it. Ninety minutes later the bus driver was yelling that this was my stop. Maybe he was yelling because I'd fallen asleep. Crap, I hoped I hadn't been drooling. I wiped my mouth discreetly and hauled my case down onto the pavement.

The bus dropped me off outside the El Rey Theater and I knew I was slapbang in the middle of the Miracle Mile, what the locals called this most exclusive—and expensive—part of Los Angeles. Yeah, I stood out, and not in a good way.

It was everything I'd imagined and more. Skyscrapers were fringed by palm trees, and four lanes of traffic swirled past in a blur of noise and fumes. And the people! It was like London on helium, but with more sunshine: chaotic, alive, frenetic, fucking terrifying.

Bloody hell. I was really here.

And everyone was staring. Talk about conspicuous: I was dragging a wheeled suitcase down Wilshire Boulevard. I may as well have had a screaming neon sign over my head: *Just off the bus! Mug me!* Fuck. I'd have been less conspicuous doing a clog dance.

By the time I'd walked half a mile in the scorching sun, the sweat was running off me and I was pretty certain I must smell like a goat. I'd been wearing the same clothes for 24 hours even before my recent hike. My armpits were wet, my back was soaked and even my crotch was damp—for the wrong reason. Oh joy.

The receptionist at Weitz's office seemed to agree. I could swear her finger twitched toward the security buzzer—before I managed to stammer out Rhonda Weitz's name.

She left me squirming with embarrassment and preparing for humiliation. I didn't know if I was supposed to sit, stand, or wait by the lifts. Inspiration hit.

"Uh, could you tell me where the bathroom is, please?" I choked out.

She frowned, but without speaking pointed down the corridor with a long, creepy, manicured nail. I slunk off, feeling like a criminal. From the look she threw me, she thought I would be shooting up any moment.

Luckily the men's room was empty, so I stripped off my goat-smelling shirt and rinsed my face and armpits in the tiny sink. I rummaged through my case and found a fresh shirt, although it was kind of wrinkled. At least I didn't look so seedy. It was amazing how much more confident I felt once I was less sweaty.

When I got back to the front desk, the receptionist had been joined by a well dressed Latina woman who was clearly irked to be kept waiting. Christ. Were there any women I wasn't going to irritate today? Smart money said no.

"Mr. Stephens?"

"Uh, yeah."

"Follow me, please. Ms Weitz's office is this way."

We took the lift—sorry—we rode the elevator in stony silence. I hated uncomfortable silences and that one definitely qualified, but I knew that if I spoke first I'd start babbling. Clare said I had a chronic case of verbal diarrhea when I was nervous. And I sure as hell was nervous going into that meeting.

Rhonda Weitz was short and round with a brisk, no-nonsense attitude. She reminded me of my old high school principal. I liked her on sight and felt some of the tension leak away. But not all.

"Hey, Miles, good to meet you."

She held out a meaty paw and inadvertently crushed my knuckles as we shook hands.

"How was the flight? Hell, right?"

"I've had more fun sticking lit matches under my fingernails in a Swedish massage parlor."

She fixed me with a stern look.

"Er, well, not really. That was, er, a joke."

"I'm thinking you should talk less," she snapped.

Shit. "I know. I get told that a lot. Sorry."

She smiled, briefly.

"Don't worry about it. That's what I like about you Brits —you can't sell the bullshit. So, to business. You're meeting Jo-Anne Moody, the director, at five..."

"Today?"

She pierced me with her gaze, and I swallowed nervously.

"Problem?"

"No, I just ...er ... no, no problem."

"Well, Jo-Anne, she just wants you to read through a few scenes with Lilia, film a couple of tests with the two of you ... I'll be straight with you, Miles: this is a long shot. The studio wants a name to play alongside Lilia. But Jo-Anne is pushing for an unknown. If she likes you, and if she can persuade the studio... maybe. But if not, I'll set you up with some other meetings. Melody Rimes has great things to say about you."

That made me smile: normally Melody just told me I looked like shit.

"Yeah? She told me to buy a new shirt."

"Shoulda listened to her," said Rhonda.

Clare

I sat in my room chewing a nail. I was supposed to be reading Bacon's 'New Atlantis' but my mind was 6,000 miles away. I was anxious that Miles hadn't texted or emailed. Surely he should have arrived by now? *Don't be so bloody pathetic*, I told myself fiercely. *You're not joined at the hip—go out and have a life—at least pretend that you've got one. That's what Miles is doing.*

Now I was irritated with myself, too. I threw down my book, stuffed my wallet in my pocket and headed out.

Miles

"Here y'are, man."

The taxi driver had pulled up at the gate of a stunning beach house half hidden by palm trees, with a hot Mercedes Coupé sitting in the driveway.

"Er, are you sure?"

I eyed the mansion doubtfully. The audition was *here*?

"Sure, buddy. Thirty-seven ninety-three, like you said."

I pulled out my wallet and handed over four, crisp ten dollar bills. I was still unfamiliar with the all green currency. As I stumbled out of the cab, I could feel the heat from the road radiating upwards through the soles of my shoes. At least I'd been able to leave my suitcase at Rhonda's office.

I was feeling wired and sleep deprived at the same time—and, if I was honest, the three vodkas with Red Bull that I'd drunk on the plane hadn't helped. Even so, I felt the familiar nervous tensing of muscles that always accompanied me to auditions. I'd flown all this way—probably for nothing—but suddenly I really cared that this went well. I couldn't face the thought of slinking home with my tail between my legs.

Okay. I could do this.

I took a couple of deep breaths, pushed my way through the unlocked gate and crunched up the gravel driveway. I was about to knock on the door when it swung open, leaving me standing stupidly with one hand in the air.

A tanned, athletic woman of about 50 smiled at me.

"Well, hey, you must be Miles. Come on in. I'm Jo-Anne Moody, the director. Lilia is just taking a break. She'll be along in a minute."

She paused, still smiling, giving me a chance to say something. I wracked my brain but it was a thought-free zone. She cocked her head to one side and gazed at me as I struggled to find something, anything to say.

"Hi," I croaked, staring stupidly at her feet. She was wearing Nikes.

She stepped back into the impressive entrance and waved at me to follow her. She didn't seem fazed—perhaps she was used to monosyllabic morons knocking at her door asking for an audition.

I was distracted by the enormous chandelier hanging from the ceiling. Wasn't it a bit weird to have a chandelier in a beach house? Maybe it was just a house by the beach rather than ... I thought of what Clare would say if she could see it and it made me smile. Uh oh. Jo-Anne was staring at me, a quizzical look on her face. Oh, crap! She was still waiting for me to say something. She was probably beginning to wonder what a mute actor was doing standing in her hall. I swallowed but my mouth had gone dry.

After an uncomfortably long pause, she took pity on me. "So, it says on your profile that you're 20 years old, Miles?"

Finally a question—and one I could answer.

"Yeah, that's right."

"And you've done some TV work and stage work?"

"Yeah, some. Not much."

She smiled pityingly.

"That's a very British answer."

I didn't know how to reply to that, so I just stood there like a gormless twerp. It was becoming a theme. I shoved my hands in my pockets just to have something to do. Christ! I must have looked like a complete idiot.

"What the hell happened to your hair?" She was frowning at me, and her tone took me by surprise. "It says on your profile that you're a blond."

Since when? Bloody Melody!

"Really? Well, more light brown, I guess. It was dyed for a job. I was just letting it grow out..."

God! Stop talking, moron!

"Hmm."

Again with the 'hmm'.

"We're in my bedroom," she said, casually.

!!!

She walked off briskly, and I followed pathetically through her amazing house. It was full of modern, abstract artwork—probably the real thing, unlike the posters of Klimt that I had in my bedroom at home. Then she led me up the wide, oak staircase into a sort of upstairs conservatory area, and my anxiety level climbed a couple more notches. But the view was stunning and for a moment I was lost in the horizon, the ocean pounding over the stony beach. What would it cost to live in a place like this? It was almost painful even to imagine. More than I'd ever earn, that was for sure.

Jo-Anne handed me a script with some passages highlighted.

"Just give this a read through. I'm not expecting you to memorize it—just get the general feel for your character, Nuriel. And take your shirt off when you're ready."

What?!

"Is that a problem?"

She looked at me curiously and I could feel my face getting hot.

"Uh, no. That's fine."

What the hell?

God, I really wished I hadn't had all that beer and kebabs over the last couple of weeks. It never occurred to me that anyone would ask me to take my shirt off in an audition. I could have cursed Melody for this. Ironically, I'd have killed for a beer right then.

Okay. I'd focus on the script. *Yes, concentrate on that.* I did remember it. It had seemed kind of dumb when I did the audition tape—definitely a chick flick. I was supposed to play an angel who had come to earth to help the citizens of a community in small-town America. And, of course, I'd fall in love with a human girl. So I was a perfect being. Great. How the hell was I going to play perfect? I was vaguely aware that angels were asexual beings—at least I thought they were.

Suddenly I wasn't so sure of anything. Shit. Maybe they thought I was gay.

Feeling pale and definitely not toned, I pulled off my shirt and stood self-consciously looking out toward the ocean. At least there were no mirrors. Thank God I'd had a quick wash at the agency. *Shit! Did my breath smell?* I rifled through my pockets and found a packet of mints. Would three be enough? I tipped them into my mouth and started chewing.

Jo-Anne leaned through the doorway. She was staring at my chest, a frown on her face. I guessed that wasn't good.

"Hmm ... I think we can do something with that. This way, Miles."

Do something with what?!

The room next door was set up like a small studio with bright, halogen lights, a video camera and a very large and obvious bed in the middle of the room.

What the hell was going on here? Were they making a porn film? Was I making a porn film?

Jo-Anne smiled at the expression on my face. I must have looked like a deer gazing down the barrel of a hunter's rifle—or possibly more nervous than that.

She answered my unspoken question.

"I prefer not to use the studio's casting suites—they're so cold and impersonal. I find I get a better idea of an actor's range if it's in a more neutral environment."

She thought her bedroom was 'neutral'?

"Try and relax, Miles, it's not the orthodontist." Then she muttered to herself, "Although as you're British that might come later."

Huh?

I stood awkwardly, wishing I at least had my shirt to hide behind, trying to scan through the script and make some meaning from the words swimming in front of me. But my brain was having a serious meltdown. *Oh no, not here. Please!* Usually Clare helped me prep for script readings. The dyslexia always got worse when I was nervous—like right now. I tried to calm the fuck down and ran my finger under the lines as I tried to read through them slowly. They didn't seem to make much sense—I started to panic.

"Okay, Jo-Anne, let's do this, if we have to, although I don't see the point ... oh!"

I heard the sullen tone floating up from the hallway. I turned around and found myself staring into the eyes of one of the most beautiful women I'd ever seen. Long, glossy hair, jade green eyes, fan-fucking-tastic skin, and oh, so familiar. Shit! Shit! Shit! Lilia Purcell, a bona fide film star since the age of 12. And she was staring—at me! Why hadn't I put two and two together while I was in Rhonda's office? Lilia ... Lilia Purcell!

Then her words sank into my numbed brain ... *if we have to ... I don't see the point ...* She didn't want to be here. That much was obvious. I was wasting my time. Wasting *her* time.

I felt sick. Then I felt fucking angry, disappointment and frustration crashing through me. Twenty hours and six thousand effing miles. For this.

Lilia's look of irritation was replaced by her famous 100 mega-watt smile. I had to hand it to her: the bitch could act.

"Hi! It's great to meet you. I'm Lilia."

Amazing! As if she'd never said a word, as if I hadn't heard her casual dismissal of me.

She held out her hand and automatically I shook it quickly. Her skin was soft and cool. It occurred to me, in a vague way, that she was smaller than I'd imagined; smaller than she looked on screen—actually quite tiny.

I realized I was still staring, and that she was waiting for me to say something. I felt so fucking inadequate and that made me even more furious. I couldn't help glaring at her and I was pleased because her fake, fucking smile faltered slightly. *Good.* In my peripheral vision I could see Jo-Anne raise her eyebrows.

Oh yeah. Great start to the audition. They were looking for chemistry, *damn it!*

"Okay, guys, we'll read from page 17. This is where Esther

first begins to suspect that Nuriel is more than just another student at college."

Lilia strolled over to sit on the bed facing the camera, looking totally at ease, flicking her long, shiny hair over her shoulder. I was still staring down at the script, trying to find my place. Trying to remember what I was supposed to be doing. *Yeah, acting. Right.*

"Miles, when you're ready," said Jo-Anne, not unkindly. "I need you in camera shot: sit next to Lilia, please."

Shit. Of course. This was a film test. Was there anything I could do today that wasn't moronic? Probably not.

Jo-Anne turned on the video camera.

"Three, two, one..."

"You don't sound like you're from around here..."

Lilia's voice was softer now. I looked up. Jeez! Her eyes were really green.

"Um, Miles?" Jo-Anne's voice broke into my dreaming.

I scrambled to find my line.

"How do I sound?" I mumbled. *Idiotic—that was how.*

Lilia laughed, natural and carefree. I felt like she was laughing at me. I couldn't help scowling at her again.

"Other than like you're from another planet?"

"I'm trying ... to fit in ... but it's harder than I thought." Too bloody right.

"Why is it so hard?"

The next line stuck in my throat. *"The people here are so ... different. It's different from what I thought it would be ... I feel ... different..."*

Lilia leaned toward me, staring into my eyes, her forehead wrinkled with concern. When she put her hand on my knee I nearly jumped. Bitch! She knew what she was doing.

"Why do you feel different?"

"Okay, that's great, guys," said Jo-Anne. "Miles, good intensity but could you try it with an American accent this time?"

Fuck. Of course.

. . .

Clare

"Oh, come on! Lady Macbeth is just a cipher for Shakespeare's misogynistic views: all that 'unsex me' stuff!"

I was vaguely aware that Tasha was on a roll. Ever since she'd read 'Man Made Language' she saw sexism everywhere. If it was the 70s, she'd be burning her bra, although she'd have to take out the padding first.

The tutorial room was hot and stuffy, typical of London during a late Spring morning. My jeans were too thick and heavy for the unexpected heat wave and my armpits were already damp. But instead of nodding off while Tasha sparred with Professor Herring, I felt anxious. Miles had emailed me during the night to say that his phone didn't work and that he was going straight to an audition. The bastards hadn't even let him recover from the journey. In fact, he'd have had the audition by now and was probably in bed. I tried not to dwell on that tempting image.

It was really unfair to expect him to perform when he'd been traveling for the best part of 24 hours. He'd said LA would be tough; I just hadn't realized it would be inhuman.

"And what is your opinion, Clare?" said Professor Herring, inconsiderately breaking into my worrying.

Miles

Second time around I nailed the American accent. Lilia blinked in surprise. I couldn't help a small smile. Yeah! Bring it on!

"That was good, Miles," said Jo-Anne. "Lilia, could you just try your part again: try to sound more concerned and less smug."

Smug! Yeah, bitch!

Lilia frowned. I was liking Jo-Anne a lot at this point.

We went through the scene one more time. I nailed it again. *Yes!*

"Okay, good, you guys," said Jo-Anne. "Let's just do the scene in Esther's bedroom. Page 35, Miles."

Bedroom scene? What? Oh, shit. I struggled to find the right page, feeling sweatier and more uncoordinated by the second. What happened in that scene? Fuck—we had to kiss. Thank God for the mints.

I hated kissing people I worked with. It was so weird, being that intimate with someone you didn't know—especially sober. It was almost more intimate than getting naked—not that I had a lot of experience of that when it came to acting for a film. Okay, well, none. I wondered what it must be like to have to do a love scene—that must be ... *focus! Kissing scene!* I just had to remember: no tongues.

Lilia shimmied up the bed, sitting cross-legged. I sat awkwardly on the corner, trying to avoid impaling my balls on the short bedpost. But at least it helped me to focus. *Concentrate, you moron!*

"Okay, Lilia," said Jo-Anne. "Three, two, one..."

"*Nuriel! What are you doing here? If my mom catches you...*"

"*She won't. She's sleeping. Esther ... I had to see you. There's something I have to tell you ... about me...*"

"*I don't care! It doesn't matter ... not to me...*"

Lilia crawled toward me across the bed, looking as sexy as hell. I couldn't take my eyes off her. Her mouth was slightly open and she was staring into my eyes. Then her arms were around my neck and I could feel her breath on my face. She even smelled good. And my stupid, fucking, moronic body took over. I dropped the script and kissed her hard, pushing her back down on the bed.

"Okay, you guys," said Jo-Anne, bringing me down to earth suddenly.

I opened my eyes. Lilia was lying on the bed, a look of astonishment on her face. I flushed. If I was lucky they'd just kick me out; if I wasn't, Lilia would be calling the cops and I'd be charged with assault. Any second now...

"Well ... let's try that again," said Jo-Anne, mildly. "Nice improvisation, Miles, but see if you can stick to the script."

From the corner of my eye I saw Lilia smirking at me.

I shook my head, trying to clear the sensation of kissing her soft lips. *Concentrate!*

"Three, two, one..."

"*Nuriel! What are you doing here? If my mom catches you...*"

"*She won't. She's sleeping. Esther ... I had to see you. There's something I have to tell you ... about me...*"

"*I don't care! It doesn't matter ... not to me...*"

She stared at me and I stared back. I raised one hand to her cheek and let it hover there. She sighed and leaned her head into my hand. I felt like I'd been stung. I jerked my hand back and frowned at her. Lilia looked puzzled and then —pain flared briefly behind her eyes. I'd hurt her feelings. Or maybe she was acting. How the hell was I supposed to know? Maybe that was what drama school taught real actors. It was so confusing. I'd never behaved like this in an audition before. Damn, Lilia was good.

"Interesting, you guys," said Jo-Anne, with a straight face. I'd no idea what she was really thinking. "I like what you're doing there, Miles. Okay, let's do it one more time."

I took a deep breath.

"Three, two, one..."

"*Nuriel! What are you doing here? If my mom catches you...*"

"*She won't. She's sleeping. Esther ... I had to see you. There's something I have to tell you ... about me...*"

"*I don't care! It doesn't matter ... not to me...*"

I raised my hand to her cheek again and her look was blazing. I blinked and closed my eyes. Maybe that would make it easier. But I opened them too soon and she was staring at me again. *What the hell?* I tried to remember the script. *Kiss her! Kiss her!* I leaned in, my eyes still locked on hers and very slowly, our lips touched for the second time.

Lilia launched herself at me, and this time I was the one knocked backward onto the bed.

"Fuck!"

"Cut!" said Jo-Anne, laughing.

Lilia giggled at my expression, and I felt a smile steal

reluctantly across my face.

"That's great, you guys!" said Jo-Anne.

Chapter Three

THE AWAKENING

Miles

The light was too bright. I struggled to wake up. Where the hell...? Then I remembered. *Oh.* I'd forgotten to pull the curtains and daylight was flooding into Rhonda's guest room. *Daylight?* I sat up blinking, feeling confused, and the memories of the day before—days before—came flooding back. Yes, I'd really met Lilia Purcell and she'd been ... okay. Nice. I mean, God, she was gorgeous. Just thinking about her pushing me back on the bed during the audition started a train of thought that was definitely not conducive to getting up. Well, not all of me.

I frowned at the tent that I was pitching under the sheet and tried to ignore it. I looked at my phone to see what time it was. Oh yeah, I'd turned it off. I needed to get an adaptor for my charger if I was going to be able to use it, and I needed to find an internet café so I could email Clare again. She'd be sending out search and rescue if I didn't stay in touch regularly. I rolled my eyes—her over-protectiveness could be really irritating sometimes, even though I knew it came from a good place. I wondered what she was doing now. What time was it there? I didn't know. It was eight hours difference, but I couldn't remember if London was ahead or behind. Whatever.

I sat on the edge of the bed and watched the room spin slowly—I must have had too much of Rhonda's expensive bourbon last night—by which point I'd been awake for about 36 hours. I fumbled for my jeans. They were lying in a heap on the floor where I'd dropped them last night. My case was in the corner, still packed, so I rifled through it and found a black t-shirt that was slightly less creased than the rest. At least I wasn't going to need a jacket—it was a balmy seventy degrees every day. I didn't have any particular plans but I thought I'd head into town—wherever that was—maybe do some sightseeing while I was there.

Rhonda said she was working on getting me some more auditions, but for now I was free of responsibility or commitment. It felt good.

It was exciting, too, the thought of being on the loose in Hollywood, home of the world's hottest women—and Lilia Purcell. Hmm, best not to think about her—stick to reality, not fantasy. I suddenly realized that I was starving. I wondered what the protocol was for rummaging through my agent's fridge. Maybe I should find a coffee shop instead.

But more than food, I wanted a shower. I pulled on my jeans, not bothering with the buttons, and stumbled off to the bathroom.

"*Dios mio!*"

A short, dumpy Hispanic woman was staring at me in horror. *What?* I didn't know who was most shocked but when she started to back away from me, crossing herself as she went and clasping her hands in prayer, I reckoned it was probably her. Shit! She must have thought I was some sort of intruder!

"No! Wait"

She turned and ran, screaming as she went.

Shit! What if she called the police?

"What the hell is going on here?"

Rhonda. Thank God.

She strode up the stairs and gaped when she saw me.

"Miles! What are you doing?"

"I ... I was just going to have a shower. And ... and she ... that woman ... she just started screaming!"

Rhonda looked bemused for a second and then smiled.

"Adelita," she called to the quaking woman hiding behind her, "this is my house guest Miles. Miles, meet Adelita, my housekeeper."

"Er ... hi. Nice to meet you," I stammered. Could that have been any more embarrassing? I made a grab for my jeans before they headed further south and I caught the fearful look Adelita threw at Rhonda before she mumbled something in Spanish. Rhonda replied and Adelita's stance relaxed. She nodded at me, smiled shyly then wandered back down the stairs muttering to herself.

I was still holding up my jeans and feeling like a complete twat.

"Er, is everything okay?"

Rhonda smiled broadly. "Oh sure! First she thought you were a rapist and then she thought you were my lover..."

I was pretty certain my face was the color of a London bus.

"Which surprised her considerably since she knows I'm a lesbian."

"Oh!" I croaked, my voice unrecognizable to my own ears. "Right."

"Go take a shower, Miles, we need to talk," said Rhonda, still smiling to herself.

Shit. That was embarrassing.

I stumbled into the bathroom and let the shower ease some of the sudden tension in my shoulders. I leaned my hands against the cool tiles while the water poured over my head. It was soothing. And Rhonda—or probably Adelita—had left out some expensive-smelling bodywash.

I didn't know how long I'd been standing under the hot jets but I felt a whole lot better when I staggered out. I caught a glimpse of myself in the mirror. It wasn't steamed up: Rhonda must have had one of those fancy, heated mirrors —not that I was planning on shaving today.

Yeah, this place screamed serious money: like Jo-Anne's place. The thought made me frown—and what did Rhonda want to tell me? If it was good news she'd have just said, wouldn't she?

Rhonda was waiting for me in her home office.

"Miles, take a seat."

Her voice was clipped and cool. I wondered if agents practiced that. She waited, her face closed and unreadable, while I sat on the hard leather chair next to her desk. Everything was happening in slow motion, my career, my life, unraveling in bullet-time—cue the extreme close-up of my nervous twitch. Just to add to the impending humiliation, my stomach rumbled loudly, and I remembered I was hungry. I hadn't eaten much yesterday—probably the memory of having to take my shirt off in front of Jo-Anne and Lilia.

Rhonda raised her eyebrows but I was grateful she didn't mention my gut's audible interruption.

"Sooo," she said, stringing out the tension. Maybe the woman was a sadist. Maybe she had handcuffs in her drawer —with a basement full of whips and stuff.

Automatically my eyes sank to the floor. I wished she'd just let the axe fall.

"Jo-Anne called..." *Get on with it.* "She was very impressed with you."

What? I looked up, thinking I'd misheard.

"She wants you for the part, Miles, and Lilia is championing you, too. Apparently the chemistry was ... how did Jo-Anne put it ... sizzling."

I stared at her open-mouthed. *Is this a joke?*

"There's just one problem..."

Oh, here it comes.

"The studio heads still need some convincing. They want to make sure you can sell the look. You know, clean cut— angelic."

She rolled her eyes when she saw nothing but a blank expression on my face.

"Jesus, Miles! You're scruffy, your hair's a mess, your

eyebrows need plucking, your teeth are obviously British, you're gonna have to start working out and damn it, stop chewing your nails!"

What? Crap! Was I?

"Sorry," I mumbled. God, I sounded pathetic. I think she took pity on me because she stopped yelling.

"So, the plan is to get you suited, booted and beautiful, okay? But they liked the fact you're pale. After all, whoever heard of an angel with a tan?"

Yeah, and whoever heard of an angel with plucked eyebrows?

"I've booked you in at a beauty salon the agency uses. They'll take care of you."

I didn't like the expression on her face—it all sounded ... painful.

"The car will be here to pick you up in 10 minutes. After the salon, I'm sending you to Bradley, my personal shopper. He'll dress you..."

Rhonda fixed me with her gimlet eye.

"This will all come out of your future salary, so you'd better nail this, baby." She softened slightly. "Later, you'll be meeting the studio heads, casually, of course, at an event dinner—the Metron Awards. I'll be there."

Then she handed me a folder.

"This," she said, slapping the flat of her hand onto the desk between us, "this is a list of the studio heads. Study their faces—learn their names. There'll be a test later." She frowned at the folder, then at me. "Don't fuck up."

And I was dismissed.

This was so bizarre. I didn't know what to make of it all. I guessed I should go with the flow ... like I really had a choice ... and Rhonda was bloody intimidating. Even more so than Melody, and she was a double-hard, take-no-prisoners bitch-on-wheels.

The car—*my* car, turned out to be a flashy four-by-four ... oh, sorry, SUV. The driver was a tall, thin black guy with hair graying at the temples. He was wearing a uniform. I mean seriously, jacket, peaked cap—the whole thing made me feel like an impostor. The driver gazed at me coolly when I automatically went to sit in the front passenger seat, and patiently held open one of the rear doors.

"Perhaps you'd be more comfortable in the back, sir, where there's more room."

Sir?!

God, this was embarrassing.

I slid into the back seat as he suggested—instructed—and stared out of the window. Nobody seemed to walk anywhere, and I realized that it was probably because there were hardly any pavements. I wasn't used to being driven either. There wasn't much point driving in London, in my opinion, what with the congestion charge, council permit parking fees, and the cost of petrol. I hadn't even bothered to take my driving test—mostly because I couldn't afford the lessons. At home I had an Oyster card for traveling on the Tube and buses or, if I wasn't working, which was most of the time, I saved money by walking. You see a lot more of a city when you travel by foot, and I knew all the alleyways and shortcuts in London. Out here, I was lost. I had no sense of direction, no sense of how LA fit together as a city—it seemed all so strung out. A bit like the people.

The buses even carried adverts for the latest must-have plastic surgery. *What was this place?*

I was feeling tense again. I needed music but my iPod had died. Nervously, I glanced at the driver.

"Er ... would you mind putting the radio on, please?"

"Yes, sir. What would you like to listen to? The news?"

"No, not news. Music ... are there any good jazz stations?"

"You like jazz, sir?"

I could guess what he was thinking: *white boy likes jazz?*

"Yeah, I do."

"Hmm..."

I watched him punch buttons on the car stereo.

"Do you like jazz?"

His eyes met mine in the rear view mirror.

"Brought up with it. Ma daddy played with Chet Baker and Stan Getz."

No bleedin' way! "You're kidding!"

"No, sir. 'It could happen to you'."

"Wow!" *This place was amazing!* "Do you play?"

"Naw. Talent skipped a generation. You?"

"Alto sax. But I'm no Everette Harp."

He smiled at me and shook his head. "Bit on the pale side for that, son."

Then he pushed another button and the surround sound speakers bathed me in music. I recognized the tune: Brubeck's 'Take Five'. And I started to relax, my fingers drumming to the music. I opened my eyes and saw the driver watching me. His eyes crinkled slightly and I thought he was smiling. I smiled back and he turned up the volume.

"Name's Earl," he said.

"I'm Miles. Good to meet you, Earl."

"Miles, huh? That's a fine name, boy."

"Thanks. Named after Miles Davis."

"You don't say!" he laughed.

Cocooned in the music, I leaned back. Maybe today wouldn't be so bad.

Or maybe it would be exactly as bad as I was expecting. The car pulled up in front of a swanky beauty salon. I stared at it in horror. Through the lightly tinted window I could see a row of helmet-haired women getting their claws filed. Surely this couldn't be the place?!

I realized Earl was watching me, his expression sympathetic.

"Here?" I managed to croak.

He nodded.

"Oh, shit!"

That made him smile broadly. "I'll pick you up in two hours, sir."

Two hours?! What the fuck were they going to do to me for two whole hours?

Earl started to get out of the car and I realized he was

about to open the door for me. Hurriedly, I flung the door open and almost fell onto the street. I saw him cough and I knew he was trying not to laugh. I'd be laughing if I were him; but I was me, and my mouth was dry with terror.

Earl watched as I walked slowly toward the salon's entrance. Was this how prisoners felt, walking to their execution?

A scarily blonde woman of about fifty was sitting at the reception desk, dressed in a navy blue uniform. If she hadn't been so full of Botox, her eyebrows would have gone through the roof as she glanced up and saw me. She gathered her wits more quickly than I did.

"How may I help you this morning, sir?"

"Er ... Rhonda ... er, Miss Weitz ... er ... she booked me ... I'm..."

"Mr. Stephens?"

I nodded, suddenly mute.

"Ms Weitz's assistant called ahead. My name is Casey. If you'll follow me, Mr. Stephens, our Executive Colorist, Sonia, will be with you shortly."

Color? Oh yeah. They didn't like the auburn. Neither did I, much, but I had just planned on letting it grow out or shaving it off.

She directed me to a plush, leather bench seat.

Another woman in the same navy uniform approached me. She was thin, with bony shoulders, skinny tits, and shiny dark brown hair.

"Hi there, I'm Sonia. How are you today, Mr. Stephens?"

Before I could reply she was running her fingers through my hair with a critical eye. She shook her head. People seemed to do that a lot around me.

"Well, I'm going to have to strip out this color first, Mr. Stephens, before I can put the blond in."

"Blond?"

"Yes. That's the instruction Ms Weitz has given. Between light blond and gold blond." She hesitated for the first time. "I understand it's for a film role?"

"Er, yes, I guess. Okay, then."

She smiled. "Right! I'll go mix the colors. Can we offer you a beverage? We have a range of herbal teas..."

I noticed she dropped the 'h' on herbal. It sounded foreign, very sexy.

"Or skinny latte, decaffeinated Americano, mineral water—still and sparkling, freshly squeezed pomegranate juice..."

Bloody hell. It was all so healthy. It made me want to ask for a double cheeseburger, fries and enough caffeine to stun a bull elephant. I settled for water.

I was so pathetic.

Ninety minutes later, I'd been dyed, manicured, shaved and had my eyebrows threaded *and* waxed. God knows how women put up with having their legs waxed. It was uncomfortable, painful even. My eyelids were pink and I looked kind of startled. I had an American girlfriend once who'd had a Brazilian: it was ... interesting. My mind drifted, wondering why women would want to have their pubes ripped out using hot wax ... even though the result was... an experience. Sensual, but a bit weird; I mean, she was a grown woman, after all. But this was America and things were very different ... as I was learning.

The manicure was okay and my nails were clean, even, and very shiny. And I'd definitely have that wet shave again—the hot towels felt amazing.

I was hustled to the sink for the hair dye—or was it bleach—to be washed out by Paulo. Yet another navy-uniformed staff member. Paulo was short, über-trendy and ultra gay. From my peripheral vision I could see him running his eyes over my scruffy clothes. For once, I felt irritated rather than intimidated. I didn't say anything—the guy was only doing his job. Sort of. Instead my irritation was aimed at Rhonda. I knew I wasn't being fair. But I was royally pissed off.

Paulo yakked away but I didn't have to do much more than mumble 'yes' or 'no' at intervals.

Then I was wheeled over to Raquel, the stylist. I looked in the mirror and blinked, shocked.

Jesus! My hair hadn't been that fair since I was about five years old. It looked ... odd.

"Oh! That is such a *fun* color on you!" said Raquel, beaming.

I grunted. I couldn't see what was fun about it—I looked gayer than Paulo.

I closed my eyes and let her get on with it. I had no idea what she was going to do and I was past caring. I thought I was having an out-of-body experience and I still felt jet-lagged.

Thirty minutes later I was done. At last. I didn't recognize myself in the mirror. I'd got used to the auburn. My hair was short at the back and sides and spiky on top. She'd used a ton of hair gel.

I wanted to slink out the door but to my utter horror, all the staff gathered around and applauded.

"Oh, he looks so cute!" gushed Paulo, and kissed me on both cheeks. Sonia looked like she was about to cry. Happy tears, I hoped.

Was I supposed to make a speech?

"Thanks," I muttered.

"Have fun tonight!" said Raquel.

"Come back and see us soon," called Paulo.

I bolted for the door. Earl was waiting. His expression was carefully blank but I could tell he was amused. I climbed into the car wearily. I could see he was studying me in the mirror.

"How you doin', son?"

"Wishing I'd stuck to playing sax, Earl."

He nodded solemnly. "Ain't it the case."

Next stop was a large department store. I was directed up to the personal shopping reception to 'await Bradley's assistance'.

I was expecting another version of Paulo, but Bradley was a guy in his late fifties. Definitely gay but with a quiet, professional air.

"Good afternoon, Mr. Stephens. How are you today?"

That was one of the strange things I'd noticed about Americans: in one way they were much more relaxed about stuff than we were, but in another, so much more formal.

"Yeah, good, I think. Thanks."

It was a lie. I felt like shit, despite the primping and preening at the salon.

Bradley raised an eyebrow, but didn't comment.

"So, I understand from Ms Weitz that you'll be requiring a suit and accouterments for an event dinner tonight?"

Accouterments? What the fuck were they?

"Yeah, that's what she told me, too."

I tried to keep the censure out of my voice; after all, everything Rhonda was doing was for my benefit. I was just feeling a bit like a puppet—someone pulled a string and I danced to their tune. It was uncomfortable.

"If I may take your measurements, I'll bring some suits and shirts for you to try."

Bradley did his thing with the tape measure and left me brooding over a glass of sparkling water and orange juice. I could have had champagne, but my head was already fuzzy enough. I still hadn't eaten anything—I was seriously starving.

He arrived back with half a dozen suits in a variety of colors including—bloody hell—burgundy. He had to be kidding!

"Any preference as to color, Mr. Stephens?"

"My name's Miles."

He hesitated then smiled more naturally. "Miles."

"Well, er ... black ... or gray..."

"Classic colors."

"I guess."

He handed me the first choice: a suit in charcoal gray, a simple white shirt and pewter tie. It seemed fine to me but Bradley insisted I try everything he'd brought over.

An hour later I emerged, suited and booted. Bradley beamed at me.

"Your driver is outside with Ms Weitz, sir—Miles. Have a good evening."

Showtime.

Rhonda's eyes narrowed as she ran her razor gaze up and down me. I'd seen the same expression on one of the raptors in *Jurassic Park*. But she nodded. I'd passed the test.

"You clean up good, Miles," she said, somewhat grudgingly. "Now, try to keep your feet out of your mouth this evening. In fact, try not to talk at all."

"I'm not that bad, Rhonda!" I bleated.

"Miles, just don't fuck up."

Her voice was more than a warning—she was friggin' scary.

The car stopped at an expensive-looking hotel, complete with palm trees and liveried doorman.

"This is where we pick up Lilia and then you both change to the limo," said Rhonda, daring me to argue. "We want the studio bosses to see how good you kids look together."

It was the first time anyone had mentioned that Lilia was going to be there. Or that there was going to be a limo. I should have been excited but I reminded myself it was just another part of the audition—not a date.

Rhonda escorted me into the hotel, greeting the doorman by name.

"Wait," she barked at me, pointing at a low chair next to a potted plant.

Yeah, I can sit up and beg, too! Christ!

She was gone for what seemed an interminable length of time. I caught myself chewing on a nail out of boredom. *So much for the manicure.*

"Hi there!"

I looked up, and a beautiful woman with short, sleek red hair was smiling down at me.

"Great to see you again!"

I gaped at her. "Er..."

"Didn't we meet at CJ's party? He throws the best parties!"

I stood up awkwardly. "Er, sorry, no. I don't think so."

"Oh, you're British! I just love British accents! They're so sexy! I'm Sabena, by the way."

She held out a hand with long, square nails that look like they could hook out an eyeball from ten yards.

"Miles. Er, pleased to meet you."

"Well, Miles, my date hasn't shown so it looks like I've been stood up. Do you want to buy me a drink?"

God, she was gorgeous!

"I'd love to, but..."

"Great! I'll have a Cosmopolitan."

"Miles! What the fuck are you doing?"

Rhonda was bearing down on me—it wasn't a pretty sight. Automatically, I took a step back.

"Oh, sorry, I didn't realize you were with your *grand*mother!" said Sabena, rather waspishly. "You really should have said you were working—time is money, you know."

I watched, bemused, as she strolled away, flashing an almost indecent amount of thigh. My dick woke up.

Down boy.

Rhonda stared at me, her arms folded. "Would you like to explain what's going on, Miles?"

Suddenly, I didn't have a problem with a trouser tent.

Reluctantly, I turned my gaze from Sabena's mesmerizing legs and blinked guiltily. "Search me, Rhonda. I have no fucking clue what's going on."

I ran my hands through my hair in exasperation and was relieved to see her smile.

"Well, Miles, she was a hooker."

Uh oh. Hadn't expected that.

"But ... but she was beautiful!"

Rhonda sighed. "They wouldn't let her into a classy joint like this looking like a streetwalker, now would they? And by the way, when I arrived, she thought you were my rent boy."

What the fuck?!

She smirked at me. *Bitch.*

I was distracted as a soft crescendo of voices rippled across the lobby: Lilia had made her entrance. She glided across the floor, stunning in a floor length, emerald green gown, and as she passed whispers followed her like a breeze through a reed bed.

"Hello again," she said, softly.

"Er, hi."

Rhonda trod on my foot hard. I took that to mean that she wanted me to say something else. I just didn't know what. Or, maybe...?

"You look nice," I stuttered, trying to smile at Lilia.

I heard Rhonda's groan beside me.

"You look stunning, Lilia, as always." Rhonda filled in the gaps of my dismal Hollywood etiquette.

"Why, thank you, Rhonda. Always lovely to see you."

They air-kissed while I tugged at my collar.

"Yeah, you look great, Lilia. Very ... green."

Very green? Oh crap!

Lilia raised her eyebrows and seemed to be trying to rein in a smile. Rhonda's mouth snapped shut so hard I thought she'd break a tooth. Or a tusk.

"Shall we go? Miles?"

Lilia was waiting for something, staring at me expectantly.

"Miles," snarled Rhonda. "I think Lilia would like to take your fucking arm!"

"Oh, right. Sorry."

"Now listen: when you get to the venue, get out of the car first then stand aside and let Lilia get her shots on the red carpet. She'll let you know when she's done, then you'll offer her your arm and escort her inside. Got that, Miles? It's not rocket science. Follow her lead: at least Lilia knows what the fuck she's supposed to be doing."

"Yeah, yeah, I've got the picture."

She softened slightly. "I know you haven't done this before, but you'll be fine."

"You're not coming with us?"

Suddenly, I felt panicky.

"I'll meet you there, Miles. No one wants pictures of my wizened ass."

Which was true. I'd actually pay money *not* to see photos of Rhonda's ass, in any state.

We walked to the hotel entrance and I could feel every eyeball staring, or popping, possibly. Several flashes of light followed us as people took snaps with their camera phones. I couldn't help tensing up.

"Just keep smiling, Miles," whispered Lilia, out of the corner of her mouth.

Easier said than done when I felt like puking.

I helped her into the limo that was waiting for us. I found myself missing Earl. The new driver didn't speak, just pulled out into the evening traffic. My stomach rumbled again, and Lilia looked at me quizzically.

"Yeah, sorry. I haven't had a chance to eat today. I'm starving."

"Hmm, they probably want to keep you mean and lean. There'll be canapés tonight, but nobody ever eats them."

"Why not?"

"Well, the whole possibility of getting caught on camera with food in your teeth or crumbs on your clothes; plus, everybody is on a diet."

Oh.

"Except you."

Oh.

The journey was short, mercifully, because I had no idea what to say to Lilia. She stared out of the window, frowning slightly, and I really, really wished the limo had a drinks cabinet.

As we approached the hotel hosting the awards ceremony, the sound increased block by block. Soon, the yelling was appalling and I was on my last nerve by the time the limo slowed to a halt. Plus, driving up to a face full of flashing cameras was just damn scary. I felt like a Christian arriving at the Coliseum. Lilia was relaxed, but my heart was racing like I'd just met scary Miley Cyrus in a dark alley.

Lilia leaned over and kissed me on the cheek. "You'll be fine."

And with the touch of her lips, my heart rate spiked. It was possible I'd have a stroke, right there on the red carpet. I wondered how much the paparazzi would get for photographs of that. I guess it depended on whether or not Lilia would give me mouth-to-mouth resuscitation.

A valet opened the door and I stepped out first, then turned to help Lilia. I was nearly blinded by all the camera flashes. I tried to smile, but my face was impossibly frozen.

Lilia posed and pirouetted for the cameras, and I stood there, as useful as a ham sandwich at a Bar Mitzvah.

Eventually she signaled for me to join her. Another barrage of lights flashed our way and this time the paparazzi yelled out.

"Who's the guy, Lilia? Are you two dating? What's the story?"

She smiled without replying, and towed me into the hotel, then turned and waved to her adoring public. And right then, with my cheek still burning from her kiss, I was one of them.

Inside we were met by Rhonda. She must have come in the back exit. Her and her wizened ass. I really wished she hadn't said that: I just couldn't get the picture out of my mind. It was going to give me nightmares.

She escorted us toward a group of well-oiled men poured into expensive tuxedos. I recognized Donald Hyde from Rhonda's quick show-and-tell, and I guessed the rest were the other studio chiefs.

Lilia air-kissed them all and soaked up the compliments. *I was really going to have to learn how to do that.* Then it was my turn. I didn't air-kiss, of course: I wasn't that much of a moron. I shook hands in a manly way.

"This is our young British star, Miles Stephens."

That was fucking funny! Star? HA! Rhonda really knew how to talk the talk.

We chatted superficially and I managed not to open my mouth to insert a foot. Rhonda gave me a small nod: it had gone well.

I would have loved to say I relaxed after that, but once I'd been paraded, I was left by myself—Johnny no mates. In other words, I was completely ignored. Lilia was off being, well, Lilia—movie star, and Rhonda was schmoozing. Occasionally, she marched over and trotted me off to shake hands with some other suit, or kiss some woman with the shiny, stretched face of the over-botoxed brigade, which I was beginning to recognize.

It was pretty cool though, for a lad from the wrong part of north London. I mean, there were a lot of serious stars there. I felt like I'd walked into a Hollywood who's who of living waxworks.

I swiped a passing glass of champagne and knocked it back. Big mistake. It went straight to my head, reminding me I hadn't eaten for 24 hours. Lilia was right about the canapés: they were thin-looking things, the size of a dime, and designed to be eaten in one go. I vacuumed up half a tray, ignoring Rhonda's warning stare then made my way to the men's room. I was pretty sure she wouldn't follow me.

I pushed open the door and wandered in, one hand already on my zipper. My eyes bugged out and I think I spat out a few crumbs. *Fuck me! I could not believe I was seeing that! And I really wished I hadn't!*

A Very Famous Actor, well known for his 'warm and affectionate marriage' to a TV starlet, was in the throes of getting a blow job from a young, skinny woman in a shiny, sequined dress. Yeah, I noticed the dress.

He came loudly while I was frozen to the spot. He opened

his eyes and saw me. He gave his trademark, white-toothed grin.

"Sometimes it's great being me!"

And then he winked.

I tried to smile, backed out still apologizing, and reversed into Lilia.

"Ouch! Watch where you're stepping, Miles! Wow, you look pale—I mean, even paler than usual. Are you okay?"

I couldn't speak, and then the Very Famous Actor walked out followed by the skinny woman who looked like butter wouldn't melt in her mouth, *or anything else.*

"Oh," said Lilia, a smile of understanding crossing her face. "Yeah, he does that. He's known for it: it's kinda his thing. Don't worry about it."

I wasn't worried—just in awe.

I shook my head and she smiled at me sympathetically.

"You having fun?"

"Truthfully? Not as much as I thought I would. You know, meeting all these celebrities. No offence."

She laughed. "We're just people, Miles. No more or less interesting than anyone else—just more famous. Sometimes it's a real drag. I mean, we're all so damn conservative. We can't be seen to put a toe over the line or it's professional suicide."

"Mr. Joe Blow doesn't seem to care about that."

She smiled.

"He's a nut job. It'll catch up with him one day—then all the rats will come out of the sewers. You'll see. It's all about how long you can get away with it. It's a game for people like him. But no one gets away with it forever."

I found her words faintly depressing. Nothing was real here—especially not the smiles.

And I was still hungry.

Chapter Four

HOME ALONE

Clare

I was trying hard to concentrate on my studies and the two essays I had to write: a structural comparison of Austen and Brontë, Charlotte; and ... well, I won't bore you with all that.

Jess and Colin were sitting with me in the cafeteria drinking coffee. She was on the same course as me and Colin was studying ... actually, I had no idea what he did. Mostly, he was a lazy tosser.

It was supposed to be an informal study group, me and Jess, but we weren't doing much work. It was near the end of term and we didn't have exams, just those damned essays. Instead, Colin was editing Jess's Facebook page with fictional updates and she was squawking away and giggling. It was irritating, you know, to be the third wheel. Again.

I tried to find a more comfortable way of sitting on the hard chair and to lose myself in 'Persuasion'. It was my favorite Jane Austen—about second chances, love second time around.

"Hey, Clare!" Jess's shrill voice set my teeth on edge. "Isn't that your mate, Miles? Wow! He looks ... wow! I mean, more than usual!"

"What?"

Jess's eyes were nearly popping out of her head and even Colin looked slightly stunned—although he may have been slightly stoned; it wasn't always easy to tell the difference, and what's a vowel between friends?

Jess swiveled her laptop around so I could see the video clip. It was some sort of Hollywood film awards. There was a red carpet, camera flashes going off and ... holy shit! She was right. It was Miles—looking unbearably suave in a sharp, gray suit, polished shoes and ... very, very blond. He was smiling, although I could tell he was uncomfortable, and he was leaning in toward some size zero airhead who was showing too much of her cleavage—what she had of one. Tramp.

"That's Lilia Purcell he's standing next to!"

Jess's voice was awed.

What? Who? What!

Even I'd heard of Lilia Purcell.

"You didn't mention anything about this." Jess's voice was accusing.

I was too hurt to tell the truth—that I hadn't known—so I adopted a dismissive tone.

"I wasn't allowed to say anything. All very hush-hush."

"So, are they, like, dating?" Jess cut to the chase.

"No!" My voice was too loud, and Jess blinked. "They just met ... at some event. Miles is out there auditioning for a film part."

"Cool! She's a babe."

That was Colin's contribution to a conversation that sliced through me. Why didn't Miles tell me? Why hadn't he been in touch again?

Because his life is a damn sight more interesting that yours. I couldn't help thinking that. Sod it. Sod him.

I made my excuses and left them drooling over the short clip and scanning websites for further information. I didn't want to know. That was a lie. I did. *Very much.*

Back home I turned on my laptop and decided to torture myself by Googling everything I could find about Lilia Purcell and watching *that* clip over and over again.

I scowled at the screen and felt like slamming the laptop shut, unable to bear the way the slut had her arm hooked around Miles' waist. But taking out my pique on a piece of harmless technology wasn't really the answer.

Suddenly an email dropped into my inbox. It was from Miles. My stomach jolted pleasantly and I felt like all my innards had been rearranged. I was irritated by my own reaction: Miles isn't, wasn't and never would be mine. *Get over it!*

To: CMilton93
From: Milesb4isleep
Sent: Tuesday 3 PM
Subject: Holy Shit!
Hey hon!

His casual use of that endearment both thrilled me and chilled me.

So I got around to using the email you set up for me. Im here in la-la land hanging out with the rich and famous. Seriously! Can you believe it? Ive attached a foto from last night. My agent got me an invite to this swanky awards thing and it was unbelievable. A real red carpet—the works! You have no idea how short so many famous people are in real life. And the women!

I'm not sure I wanted to read the next sentence.

They take the whole size zero to a new level—there all skin and bone and up close its really unattractive. I wonder if they ever eat? Im starving—there wasn't any real food at this thing. You would of hated it.

I breathed a sigh of relief. Then I wondered if he thought I was fat. Well, I was fat—compared to the lollipop-head clones. I hated diets—they made me depressed, and hungry.

> *Rhonda, my LA agent, made me spend the whole afternoon in a effing beauty salon. Can you believe it?*

Not really. He was so beautiful already…

> *Ive had my first ever manicure…*

I've *never* had a manicure…

> *And they even waxed my bleedin eyebrows!*

What?!

> *But I got a wet shave and hot towels, too, which was flippin fabulous. Oh, and they dyed (sp?) my hair blond. It feels wierd but I dont have to look at myself so Im not gonna stress it.*

I could look at him all day.

> *But the best thing—the most amazing thing—is that I met Lilia Purcell. I had my audition with her. She was a bit of a cold cow at first, but she really liked what I did in the audition and shes told the studio heads that she wants me for the role! Can you believe it?*

Yes. Harlot. And I bet that's not all she wants.

> *And I really liked Jo-Anne Moody, the director. The whole idea of the makeover was to show that I scrub up okay, I think. If I get this job Ill have to shave every day. What a pain.*

> *Do you shave every day? ;)*
>   *Love ya!*
>   *Mx*

I love you, too, Miles, you annoying, irritating, stupid, stupid man! *And when are you going to learn to spell?!*

Miles

Day four in LA.

I was woken up by Adelita, Rhonda's maid, banging on my door.

"Mr. Miles! Mr. Miles! Telefon! Telefon!"

She opened the door and peered in. *Shit! I was sleeping naked. Some privacy, please!* She crossed herself *again* and scuttled out, pulling the door behind her, but it was still ajar and she was still yelling at me. I scrabbled around in a heap of clothes and pulled on a pair of jeans.

Adelita was waiting at the door, clutching a cordless phone. She shoved it into my hand and backed away from me, looking as if she thought I might assault her virtue, or that my head might start revolving.

"Hello?"

"Miles. Get your pale, limey ass over here *now*," Rhonda bawled down the phone. "I've sent a car for you. Take a shower. Wear the suit. You've got four minutes. And have a fucking shave!"

The phone went dead and I was still trying to think what came after 'hello'. Finally my brain connected with the parts that moved and I hustled. Rhonda sounded as cheerful as a hungry grizzly with poison ivy up its jacksy.

Earl was waiting for me with the same sardonic smile on his face.

"Hi, Earl," I wheezed, skidding to a stop at the car. *Nine minutes, and I didn't cut my throat shaving—not bad.*

"Another day in Paradise," he said, holding back a smile.

I smirked and climbed into the back seat.

"Got something special for you, son," he said, and pressed a button on the steering wheel.

I listened for a moment.

"Bud Shank?"

He chuckled quietly. "White boy—like you."

Ten minutes later, we were pulling up to the security gate at the studio. Earl flashed some ID, the barrier was raised, and we were through. I felt the familiar tensing of my stomach muscles, the tremor of nerves, and I had to remind myself, *don't talk shit, don't talk too much.* I wished Clare was here—she'd say something to help chill me out. But she wasn't. There was no one. I had no friends in LA, only people I worked with, or rather people I *might* work with. And that was a whole different ballgame.

Earl was cool. So maybe...

Perched at the reception desk was a permatanned woman with a cloud of peroxide hair, and candy pink fingernails that flexed like talons. Despite her seriously scary appearance, she gave me a reassuring smile. It reminded me of Mum.

I tried to smile back but my face was frozen in what was probably an expression of abject horror. Or maybe I just looked like my usual moronic self.

A size-ooooooo assistant, who had overdone the perfume big time, showed me up to 'Mr. Hyde's office'. I wondered, absently, if Mr. Jekyll was in the room next door. *I must NOT say that out loud.*

"There he is! Come on in, Miles."

Rhonda welcomed me warmly. It was unnerving. She seemed ... what was the female of 'avuncular'? Aunticular? Clare would know—but I didn't. I realized that the thought alone meant that half my brain was in terrified denial. I tried to tell myself, *it's just another fucking job,* but I was a sodding awful liar. *Yeah, and a third rate actor,* my Id spat at me, the sour-faced git. My balls had shrunk in terror at the sound of Rhonda's not-so-dulcet tones.

Donald Hyde stood and offered me a firm, practiced handshake. He'd had a manicure, too.

"Welcome, Miles. Good to see you again. I hope you had a pleasant evening last night. Please, take a seat."

Rhonda was beaming. It was eerie. Then I spotted Jo-Anne Moody on the other side of the room, and she winked and gave me the international hand gesture where her thumb and forefinger made a circle. I thought it meant 'okay'—either that or 'butt monkey', depending on which country you were in.

"So, we've reviewed the screen test," said Hyde, "and we think you're the guy who's gonna bring Nuriel to life for us. Congratulations, Miles, I think you'll *dazzle* us!"

I stared back. Was it possible to be recklessly speechless? *Oh, he made a joke—I should laugh.*

"I think you could say he's a little overwhelmed," said Rhonda, kicking my ankle hard.

Rhonda's sudden assault took me by surprise. It must have looked like I'd just tried to dive onto the floor.

"Er, thanks," I managed to cough, while rubbing my ankle. "That's ... really..."

Disbelief, gratitude, awe and sheer blind panic flooded through me.

"Well done, Miles," said Jo-Anne, strolling over and smiling down at me. "I'll be finishing pre-production this week and we can start shooting in a month. We've really taken it to the thirteenth hour trying to find our Nuriel: I'm glad we got there at last! I'll messenger over a copy of the final script this evening."

"Subject to his signing the contract, of course," said my own personal Rottweiler.

"Naturally," replied Hyde, and they all gave this fake laugh. "We'll have the paperwork emailed to your assistant, Rhonda. I'm sure it'll all be in order, as discussed. And, ahem..." he glanced at me, "...and the other ... *details* we discussed?"

I felt like I'd entered an alternate reality: they'd made their acquisition and I was just dancing to their tune. I wasn't entirely sure which of them was pulling the strings—the one with the most money. So that would be Hyde then.

Rhonda nodded. We all shook hands, and then she hauled me out of the office before I could speak, which was probably her plan.

As soon as we were alone, she dragged me up the corridor and into the first empty room she could find: the men's room. The urinals were the clue.

"What the fuck are you playing at, Miles? Are you deliberately *trying* to blow this deal?"

I took a wild stab and guessed she was mad at me. *I had no fucking idea why.*

"No!"

"Well, you goddamn sound like it! Have you no concept of how to ass-lick?"

Her words, intense expression, delayed shock and the fact we were standing in the men's bogs suddenly tipped me over the edge. And I couldn't help keeling over with laughter.

Rhonda's face turned purple and I thought she might actually hit me, but a reluctant smile oozed across her face.

"Jeez, Miles. You're one crazy fucker, you know that, right?"

"It's been mentioned," I coughed, trying to pull myself together. "Sorry, Rhonda, but you might have warned me. I mean, it's fucking fantastic news."

"Yes, it is, my friend. Now let's get out of the john before we start off an interesting line of gossip. Come."

"Where are we going?"

"My office: you've got a contract to sign."

We were sitting in Rhonda's swanky-danky office and all the blood left my face.

How much?

I couldn't believe the figure that she was showing me, even though it was there in triplicate.

"One ... one *million* dollars?"

I counted the number of zeroes again.

"You okay, Miles? You look kinda pale?" Rhonda sounded concerned.

"Fuck me!"

I realized I'd spoken out loud. "That's ... that's a lot of money."

Rhonda nodded. "Serious shit now, Miles. The big time. Of course," her voice was ironic, "you won't get anything like that amount."

Oh?

"Well, you gotta pay your tax, baby. That'll knock off $350,000. Then there's my 15 per cent, plus something for Melody. The US and UK have a double taxation treaty so you won't own tax on your income twice."

I had no idea what she was talking about.

"Well, the small print, Miles, is that you'll take home about $450,000—or about £290,000."

That was one shed load of money. I gaped at her. My jaw was on the fucking floor.

"Still with me?"

I shook my head. Nope. I was in cloud cuckoo land. I was so far off the planet I could see the rings of Saturn.

She told me to read the contract first, but my head was spinning and the words spilled across the page in an unrecognizable vomit of letters.

Rhonda smiled. "Yeah, it'll take some getting used to, but trust me—this is just the beginning. Now, sign here ... here, here and here."

She pointed. I signed.

"We'll fix you up with a furnished rental space—you can't camp out in my guestroom forever, Adelita will have an aneurism, the way you walk around with your ass hanging out. I've got you a monthly cell," and she passed me a top-of-the-range Smart phone. I'd never learn how to use it. It probably had more computing power than they had on Apollo 11.

"And you'll need a car. Oh, and a personal checking account—so we can pay you."

Finally my brain caught onto something. "Actually, Rhonda, I can't drive."

She stared at me uncomprehendingly: guess we had something in common after all.

"Are you shitting me?!"

"Er, no. I never took my test."

"You realize you have to drive in the movie?"

No. Crap.

She shook her head. "I do not get you Brits. How the hell do you ever get anywhere?"

It was a mystery. Oh wait, didn't we colonize America 400 years ago?

"You'll have to learn. I'll add it to the list." She sighed.

I stood up suddenly. I couldn't sit there anymore—my head would explode. I was on the verge of losing it, big time, overwhelmed with this assault of unfamiliar emotions.

"Where are you going?"

"I ... I need to get some air," I muttered. "I'll see you later."

She frowned but didn't try to stop me. "Okay. *Try* to stay out of trouble, Miles."

I nodded, barely aware of what she'd said.

I took the stairs, unable to bear the thought of being in a lift with people who might want to talk at me. I needed to get my head together and fight down the panic that was threatening to engulf me. And I needed Clare.

Clare

I'd just started my shift at the local pub when my mobile rang. Or, more accurately, it buzzed against my arse, which wasn't as much fun as it sounds. But it was enough to make me slosh bitter ale all over the front of my jeans. Oh great—a really unattractive wet patch. And now I'd smell of stale beer all evening. *Fun.*

There was no caller ID, so I assumed it was probably one of those marketing calls, but I took it anyway, planning to tell the caller to sod off.

"Yes?"

"It's Miles! How are you?"

I swear my heart stopped beating at the sound of his voice.

"Great! I mean, great!" I stammered. "How are you? It's great to hear from you." *Oh, please God, give me another adjective!*

"Clare, you're not going to fucking believe this—but I got the job! That film part I was going for. I've just signed the contract!"

Oh gawd and does your granny gallop?! He'd done it!

"That's ... that's just *brilliant*, Miles. I'm so proud of you—I *knew* you could do it. I mean, it was a foregone conclusion: they weren't going to let you get away that easily. And..."

"Yeah, thanks. Thanks. Look, I know it's a really big ask, and you can say no and that'll be cool, but it would be so fucking amazing, I mean really great if you could."

"Could what?" I said, puzzled.

"Oh!" I could hear him taking a deep breath and my desiccated heart jolted into life. "Come out to Los Angeles. I could really use a friend out here, Clare. I'm really out of my depth. I'll pay for your ticket—I'll have money. Please say yes, Clare. Please!"

My heart stuttered again. He wanted me. Me. Yeah, I know, just as a friend. But that was enough.

"Are you kidding, Miles? You and me in LA? *Of course* I'll come! Just try keeping me away!"

There was a long silence and I wondered what it meant.

"You. Are. One. Awesome. Fucking. Friend."

He yelled down the phone so loudly, I had to hold it away from my ear.

"Yeah, and don't you forget it!"

I can't help laughing—for pure, bloody joy.

Chapter Five

NEW MOON

Miles

There was a woman staring at me. I had no idea why, but it was unnerving. I was at LAX, waiting for Clare to talk her way through immigration, and this woman was just staring at me. I shoved my hands in my pockets and shuffled from foot to foot but I couldn't act casual. *How fucking pathetic was that?* I was an actor, for God's sake, and I couldn't even *act* casual.

I tried ignoring her but eventually she walked over.

"Hi! Can I have your autograph?"

What?

"Er..."

"You were with Lilia Purcell at the Metron Awards—I saw your picture."

"Er..."

"You make a really cute couple."

"Thanks." I didn't know what else to say.

She handed me a chewed biro that was leaking green ink, and I signed my name on the scrap of paper she held out for me. I think it was the receipt for her grocery shopping. I could see her squinting at my horrible handwriting, trying to work out if she recognized my signature. She looked vaguely disappointed but smiled and thanked me anyway.

That was *weird*. And now my fingers were covered in green ink.

I didn't really get the chance to process what had happened ... or even to enjoy the experience. It would be something to tell Clare. No doubt she'd laugh her arse off.

And then I saw her—the surly expression that I'd missed so much. I couldn't stop smiling. It felt like months since we'd been together, not just a few weeks.

I caught her eye, and she grinned at me. It was like coming home, having her here, and I felt myself relax properly for the first time since I'd landed in LaLaLand.

"Wow! Look at you! Mr. Movie Star!"

I scooped her into my arms and hugged her tightly.

"Bloody hell, it's good to see you, Clare! I've really missed you."

"You big lug! You've been too busy wining, dining and smooching with the glitterati to worry about me."

"Not true. I'm wounded! I've thought about you ... at least twice."

She thumped me on the arm.

"Ow!"

"Wimp!"

I'd forgotten how strong she was—for a short-arse. I grabbed her case. Jeez! What had she got in there—the Encyclopedia Britannica?

It was so easy being with Clare. We talked all the way, catching up on what I'd missed. Not so much by the sound of it, although Paul and Nazzer had taken the VW camper and gone off to some beer festival in Prague. I felt a twinge of sadness that I wasn't with them. But Clare was totally jazzed to be here in Kal-e-forn-ia.

"You remember my friend Jess? Her of the motormouth ... She was speechless when I told her I was coming out here—and you know how rare that is!"

She laughed and it was so good to hear.

"So what've you been up to—apart from landing mega film roles and dying your hair."

I laughed a little uncomfortably. "It's hardly a mega film role, Clare."

She frowned at me.

"Okay, well maybe it is, for me, but..."

"But what?"

Truth or dare time.

"I am absolutely bricking it."

She rolled her eyes. Not the reaction I was expecting: sympathy and support would have been nice.

"Oh come on, Miles. Don't be so ... you're *always* like this —every time you get a job we get the whole spiel about what a terrible actor you are and what sort of retard would give you a job. That you're not a real actor, that you'll be found out because you're a fraud. Heard it all before, mate."

Wow. I'd forgotten how *surgical* she could be. Clare took no prisoners.

I was quiet. "This is a really big deal for me."

She sighed. "I know. You'll be great." She took my hand and squeezed it. "I mean it. It'll be okay."

"I'm so glad you're here."

She smiled, but for the briefest moment there was a look I didn't understand flickering across her face. It was gone before I could identify it.

Clare

Miles had gone to the trouble of booking a taxi to take us back to his place. No waiting for the bus for Mr. Movie Star. I wanted to tease him but I thought it was too soon for that. He was even more on edge than usual—which was saying something. But damn, he looked good! I was getting used to the blond hair, and he was looking pretty buff in his white t-shirt and black jeans.

Don't think about that.

His flat was about a minute from Hollywood Boulevard—how cool was that?!

The taxi pulled up outside a small, neat, blue painted

house with a black door and a neon sign that flashed the name 'Dorothy'.

"I know, I know," grinned Miles, looking embarrassed. "But it's a great apartment: that's mine up there—the one with the balcony."

I was still stuck on the name. I mean, who names their house 'Dorothy'?

Miles was gazing up at his new home with quiet pride. Neither of us had ever really had our own place before, and I knew it was a big step for him. I hesitated to ask whether or not it had two bedrooms. And despite my best efforts, a small, quiet, but increasingly desperate part inside me was hoping that there was only one.

"It's fully furnished and it's got cable and internet. Rhonda got it for me because they don't mind short-term rentals. Come on in."

He lifted my case, and carried it easily up the steep flight of stairs to the first floor.

"Have you been working out?" I asked, accusingly.

"Er, well, yeah. It's in the contract. Two to three hours a day, six days a week."

"You're kidding me?"

Miles shook his head. "Nope. Wish I was. I fucking hate the gym. My trainer's a fascist bitch. I reckon she's an ex-Soviet shot-putter or something."

I refrained from pointing out that Soviets and fascists probably weren't best buddies. But this was Miles we were talking about. Bit challenged on the whole world history thing, unless it was to do with jazz.

"They've given me a diet plan, too."

His voice dropped to barely a whisper. I could tell by his face that he was mortified. I managed to clamp my teeth shut to stop from saying something we'd both regret.

"Oh. They think you're ... fat?"

I could hardly bear to say the words—he looked perfect to me.

He shrugged. "I guess. And they want me to see a dentist."

That really was the bloody limit!

"Miles, you have great teeth. What on earth would they want to mess with that smile for?" I tried to keep it light, but really I was seething. Who were these people? What sort of bland, generic automaton did they want? "Tell them to piss off!"

He smiled, but he still looked worried. "I don't think I can. The contract..."

"Look, give me the damn contract and I'll tell you whether or not you've signed up for this shit. Okay?"

Without warning, he wrapped his arms around me and hugged me to within an inch of my oh-so-confusing life.

"I'm really glad you're here, Clare. I guess I've been going a little crazy."

I wanted to think of a witty rejoinder, but my lips couldn't form the words. Not while his arms were wrapped around me.

He held me for a few precious moments, and I could feel his warm breath on my cheek, and his hard body pressed against mine.

I'd begun to believe that after three weeks apart, after three weeks going cold turkey, that I'd have some immunity to how he made me feel.

Yeah, dumb, I know.

He let me go with a grin and pulled a door key out of his pocket.

The hallway outside the apartment was stylishly decorated for someone of Donald Trump's subtle tastes, but at least it was clean and nearly new.

Miles pushed open his front door with a flourish and sweet, shy smile.

"Enter, m'lady."

"Thank you, kind sir, I ... Bloody hell!"

The apartment was lavish—one huge room hung with an enormous, crystal chandelier.

"Jesus, Miles! How much is this place costing?"

He frowned then shook his head, bemused. "I don't know. Rhonda arranged it all. I love it—it's ... big."

"Big? You could park Mum and Dad's whole house in here!"

"Yeah, I know. Cool, isn't it?"

He winked and gave me a sly glance. Oh, what the hell. Why shouldn't he enjoy it all? Sadly, I noted that there were two bedrooms. Thankfully they were both calm, white spaces with vast beds and polished dark wood floors. No more chandeliers. Nothing too over the top.

"I had to take down most of the mirrors," said Miles, apologetically. "There were eight of them! I've shoved them in your closet."

"Closet? Wardrobe, methinks. Get a grip, Miles, or you'll *turn into one of them*."

He grinned at me. "Yeah, can't help it. I've been tuning into all the different accents you hear out here—kind of research for my part, y'know."

I didn't know, but I could imagine. "Whatever: just don't go getting all mid-Atlantic on me."

"I'll try. No promises. Come on, I can't wait to show you around. Let's hit the bars—if you're not too tired."

Miles

I didn't know why it felt weird showing Clare my new place. She looked so overwhelmed. Maybe that was how I looked when I first came here. I'd gotten ... become used to it, I guess.

We strolled out to Hollywood Boulevard and I pointed out all the sites: the Walk of Fame; Grauman's Chinese Theater; Drai's at the W hotel.

She picked a quiet bar in a trendy area, and we sat down in a booth with a beer each. Clare ordered us nachos. I didn't say anything but I wasn't supposed to eat them on the special diet that had been planned for me. I knew Clare would laugh, but she wasn't the one who was going to have to take her shirt off in front of film cameras, let alone in front of Lilia Purcell. I didn't want to feel like I did last time. But I couldn't say this to Clare. The thought depressed me—I used to be able to tell her everything.

She slept late the next morning—jet lag. I was up at six to get to the gym. I didn't mind running so much, but the reps and weights were tedious enough to make me feel like chewing my foot off just to alleviate the boredom.

"Come on, Miles! Keep going! Push it, baby! Push it!" Hilda, the Soviet Nazi fitness fascist, was in cheerleading mode today. *It was so fucking irritating.*

I almost expected her to yell, 'Feel the burn!' but that wasn't part of her motivational speech, apparently.

Sweat was pouring off me and I was red in the face, every muscle glowing with effort. But I also felt stronger and I liked the leaner, harder look that was beginning to develop. I still needed to go further. What was it they said, the camera added 20 pounds? Pity it wasn't going to be 20 pounds of muscle.

After another hour of encouraging, cajoling, mocking, jeering and bullying, Hilda called a halt.

"You're getting there, Miles. We'll make an athlete out of you yet!"

Yeah, right.

"You're gonna look great, baby. You got my gold seal promise on that." She paused, her eyes raking up and down my body, making really fucking uncomfortable. "So, you got plans for tonight? I thought we could maybe catch a few veggie juices. Whaddya say?"

Veggie juices?! Seriously?

"Er, thanks, Hilda, but my friend just flew in from England and I promised I'd take her around and show her the sights."

"Your girlfriend?"

"Well, she's a girl and she's a friend, but ... no, not a girlfriend."

"You can ditch her for one evening."

It dawned on me that Hilda was making a pass at me. How the hell was I going to get out of this one without the Soviet Nazi in her having a meltdown?

"No, sorry. I promised. Like I said."

"Raincheck?"

"Sure." I agreed, even though I had no intention of following through. I had two more weeks of pre-prod, so only two more weeks of Hilda's nagging. If I lasted that long.

I jogged slowly back to the apartment. Clare was still asleep so I took my time showering. I was just drying off when she banged on the bathroom door.

"Miles! Hurry up! I need to have a pee!"

"Okay, okay," I grumbled. "Keep your hair on."

I stumbled out of the bathroom as she pushed past me and slammed the door. Charming.

Rummaging through the closet I found some jeans and t-shirts, all clean and folded up. God, I loved this. The apartment came with a housekeeper who did all the laundry. It was going to be hard going back to the squalor of my flat in Euston with Jim the Unwashed when this ended. I didn't even have to do grocery shopping here—everything was taken care of. I knew there was a price, but right there and then, I didn't care.

I heard the toilet flush and a grumpy-looking Clare shuffled back out into the main room, her hair a lopsided bird's nest.

"God, I'm starving. I don't know if I want breakfast or chocolate—my body clock is all over the place."

"It'll wear off in a few days," I offered.

"Huh, listen to you. Suddenly you're Mr. Jet Set."

I frowned, annoyed. *What was eating her?*

My phone rang, saving me from saying something I might later regret when used in evidence against me. There was nothing wrong with Clare's memory—only her temper.

The caller ID showed Rhonda's name.

"Hey, Miles! How's the diet going?"

God! Was everyone *on my case about this?*

"'S'okay. What's up, Rhonda?"

"I've organized a driving lesson for you at 1 PM and then at 2 PM you've got media training with Gayl Lemon."

"Media what?"

"Miles, you've gotta know how to talk to the Press, how to do interviews. I mean, face it, right now you only open your mouth to change feet. You make the studio guys nervous. Gayl will help you with all the usual stuff."

"Such as?"

"You'll see. And after you'll be seeing Natalia Da Silva."

"Who?"

"Keep up, Miles—your stylist."

"Er, but I already got a suit and..."

"Jeez! Your whole wardrobe looks like it came from a disaster movie! You need to look good *every* time you leave your goddamn front door. I've *explained* this to you."

"Er..."

"The driving instructor will drop you at Gayl's offices and *then* I'll send the car to take you on to Da Silva. Capiche?"

It was easier to agree.

"Yeah, sure, Rhonda."

"Ciao."

And she was gone.

I stared sourly at the phone.

"What was all that about?"

I sighed. "We won't be able to go to the beach this afternoon. I've got a driving lesson and media training. Apparently the studio bosses don't think I'm competent to speak for myself."

Clare looked at me evenly. "They've got a point, Miles. It's not really your thing, is it, talking off the cuff? You know what Americans are like—they're so literal and you're so weird ... I mean, it could be useful. You should be more open-minded."

"Bloody hell. If I was any more open-minded my brains would fall out," I muttered, so she couldn't quite hear.

Her words had cut me, but I knew she was right. I

thought back to the woman on the plane—I'd managed to offend her in one short sentence.

I really couldn't wait for the production to get under way then all this shit would end. I just wanted to *work*.

"So," said Clare, "can I come with you? I don't want to hang around here by myself. And if I'm going to be your assistant," she laughed, "I need to know this stuff."

"Fine. Fine. Come. Why not," I snapped, annoyed that it was just a good laugh to her.

She looked surprised. "What's your problem?"

I ran my hands through my hair in frustration. "It's just..."

"What? Tell me?"

"They hired me to do a job and they want to ... change everything about me. They're even sending me to a bloody *stylist* to tell me what clothes to wear. I feel like I'll forget who I am."

"Oh, please! As if."

She didn't understand. She couldn't see how hard it was when pieces of me were being chipped away: the way I spoke, the way I smiled, my hair color, the shape of my body—all changed, or being changed. I felt like I was being swallowed up by the studio machine. It made me anxious. But Clare thought I was being a diva—I could see it written all over her face. I was beginning to regret asking her to come out here.

In silence, I fried a couple of eggs and toasted some bread for an egg sandwich. For her. Not me. Obviously.

"Do you want ketchup with it?"

"No, thanks. Just as it comes. Aren't you having one? I thought you'd be starving after all that gym rubbish."

My temper exploded. "I know this is all a big fucking joke to you but I'm the one who's ... who's got to go out there and put myself on the line. Everyone's telling me I'm too fat, too ugly, too stupid, too badly dressed—and ... and there's all this pressure ... and now my best friend is just pissing her pants laughing at me!"

I was staring at her, panting, my hands clenched into fists. I couldn't look at her shocked expression, so I shoved the plate at her and stormed off into my bedroom, slamming the door. I felt as if I'd reverted to being 12 years old and arguing with my mum about playing my music too loud. I leaned my head against the cool glass of the window, letting the fury pulse through me.

I ignored her tentative knock, but she opened the door anyway. How very Clare.

"I'm sorry, Miles. I was just trying to ... be funny. You know, make light of things. I'm sorry if I made it sound like I don't care. I do. You know I do."

Clare

I wound my arms around his waist and rested my head on his back. I'd never seen Miles so tense—it wasn't like him to lose his temper. And he'd never shouted at me before. Never.

He was holding himself tightly, as if he was afraid he'd explode again. I could feel the tension radiating out through his rigid muscles. *Shit! He was really losing it!*

"I'm sorry, okay?" *Please tell me you're not mad. Please!*

He turned around and kissed my forehead.

"I'm sorry I yelled. It's just..."

He let out a long breath and rubbed my arms gently.

"It's okay," I said, quietly. "Don't worry about it."

Below us, a car horn honked. Miles threw an irritated look over his shoulder.

"Oh, crap! My driving lesson—I'd forgotten. Sorry, I've got to go. Do you still want to go to this media training thing later?" he asked, looking harassed.

"Yeah, should be a laugh."

He flashed me a grateful smile, and then he was off. I could hear him running, taking the stairs three at a time. He sketched a wave and I watched through the window as he had a short conversation with the instructor. A tall, glamorous looking blonde woman.

Bloody hell: wasn't there anyone out here who didn't look like a film star? And then suddenly a light went on in my head

—I got what Miles had been trying to tell me: everyone out here was judged on their looks. HD TVs were the new high court and the jury was still out. Every wrinkle, every spot, freckle and mole, highlighted for everyone to see. Yeah, I sort of got how Miles must be feeling. Sort of. But he was right—I had no clue how it must feel to stand in front of a film camera, every blemish recorded for posterity.

I really wanted to rewind this morning, press the delete button and start again. I'd go right back to the moment that Miles came out of the shower with just a small towel wrapped around his waist. I mean, wow! I'd seen Miles without his shirt on before—wandering around the flat, playing football in the park, the summer we went to the beach at Brighton—but I'd never seen him look so well muscled. Did I mention wow? The Nazi Soviet personal trainer must really know her stuff. Bitch.

But after the ogling, I really hadn't meant to wind him up. I just wanted to make light of it all. Well, that backfired—big time. Worse still, he thought I was being insensitive. As if he wasn't at the forefront of my mind almost every waking minute, to the point where I disgusted myself.

I spent the next hour wandering around the apartment, unpacking my case and dressing with more care than usual. I put on my best jeans, the ones I usually saved for dates—which meant they'd only been worn once—plus a new t-shirt that was slightly more girly than usual. I wondered if mascara was appropriate for media training and figured in for a penny, in for a pound. It felt weird wearing makeup in the daytime.

By the time Miles returned, I was feeling as tense as he looked, but I tried very hard to act chilled. I ran down and jumped into the back of the car. Thankfully, Miles wasn't driving.

"How was the lesson?"

"Okay, I guess. I've done nearly all the practice hours and I've watched Drivers' Ed videos and that. The learner's permit should be here any day." He sighed. "It's pretty easy driving out here, I think. Compared to London anyway."

The instructor raised a plucked eyebrow and glared at me in the rear view mirror.

I didn't know what to say to that, having never bothered about driving. Even if I bought a car for a few hundred quid, I couldn't possibly afford the insurance.

The driving instructor smiled insincerely and dropped us at the offices of Lemon Inc. Time to find out what media training was all about.

Miles

"Hi! My name is Gayl Lemon and I'm here to show you how to do awesome interviews! Yay!"

Next to me, Clare stifled a laugh and suddenly I was glad she was here after all. The studio had sent three other actors on the course and there were some money types in suits. Altogether there were eight of us, including Clare.

Ms Lemon was pencil thin and wearing the kind of pale green power suit that I thought went out with Jackie Kennedy. Although apparently not. It looked a bit odd. Her face said forty, but her hands said sixty.

"You'll learn the art of meeting the press: how to talk to reporters and to give them what they want, including sound bites; we'll practice different kinds of interviews, including junkets with multiple questioners; on- and off-the-record comments; and for those of you in the moviemaking business, how to handle the Red Carpet."

She said 'red carpet' in a way that clearly demanded Capital Letters.

"We'll start with some basic principles: firstly, and most importantly—prepare, prepare, prepare. Don't wing it, people, even if it's a subject you know well—and don't assume an audience will know the subject at all. Practice those sound bites. Now, you might get someone trying to provoke a reaction out of you: well, make sure *you* set the tone. Don't vary your message because the questions are hostile or provocative. Decide what you want to communicate—and keep that in mind throughout an interview. If questions don't lead you there immediately, take a detour in your answers—this is what we call 'bridging'. And golden rule time, people: nothing is 100% off the record. Ever."

By this time, Clare's eyes were as round as billiard balls and I could see her glancing at me anxiously. I knew why—she thought I couldn't hack it. That really pissed me off, especially because I knew she was right. How the hell was I going to learn all this corporate bullshit?

"Okay, lovely people: media training 101. When dealing with journalists—and this fact is true for the general public, too—try to use their names once in every sentence. It makes them feel special. Always remember to ask at least one question about them. For example, if they're wearing a wedding ring, ask how long they've been married. If they mention they're a mommy or a daddy, ask their child's age or name. And never, ever underestimate the value of a compliment. Everyone loves a compliment, and if you're the one handing it out ... everyone's going to love you. Make them feel good about you."

This was so un-British. I knew if someone gave me a compliment I'd just try and turn it into a joke. But this was serious. Gayl was serious.

"We'll start off easy and fun: practice that Red Carpet moment. The four key things you Must Remember about the Red Carpet are: answer every question as if you've never heard it before—even when you're answering for the fiftieth time. No reporter wants to feel second rate and we sure don't want a Bad Review because of that, do we, people!"

"No, ma'am!" they chorused, much to Clare's continuing amusement. I stuffed my fist in my gob to try and stifle the hysteria that threatened to overtake the few senses that were still in working order.

"The second Red Carpet Key is to Enjoy Yourself! Smile, people! That's the name of the game! Thirdly, speak slowly and clearly—and never, ever, EVER give 'yes' or 'no' answers! What do we Never Do?"

"Give 'yes' or 'no' answers," we parroted back.

Gayl beamed.

"And fourthly, Eat Something! You sure don't want to be Passing Out on the Red Carpet!"

She droned on. We learned how to 'pitch it, promote it, tell it and sell it', and she talked about the importance of not dissing the fans. This was one thing I could really relate to. I remembered when I was 13, waiting for hours outside Ronnie Scott's jazz club just to get David Sanborn's autograph—and the disappointment I'd felt when his chauffeur-driven car left by the by the back entrance.

"As the great Jack Nicholson says, people, 'it's easy to forget how meaningful these encounters are for fans'. And we don't want to let them down. What don't we want to do?"

"Let them down," I muttered, avoiding Clare's accusing gaze.

"Now, something else to remember: no matter what you think of your coworkers on a movie or at the office, when you're asked you say, 'What a great guy!' Okay? Let's practice those Red Carpet Keys in pairs. Miles, why don't you practice with me?"

Oh, crap.

"Now then, you're on the Red Carpet and I'm An Interviewer, okay?"

"Yep, got it."

"Miles Stephens—can you tell us who dressed you tonight, Miles?"

"Er ... myself. I was by myself ... er..."

She sighed. "Miles, focus! I'm asking you about which designer provided your clothing. I talked about this—point three in the seminar introduction!"

Oh, great. Public humiliation.

She huffed loudly and tried again.

"That's a fabulous suit, Miles. Where's it from?"

"I dunno. From a shop. Er..."

"No, Miles, no! You must know these things. And if you get brain freeze," she sighed again, "just say, 'Oh, they did a great job!' and move on. Okay? Okay, let's try again. So how did you get on with your costar, Lilia Purcell?"

"She's a great guy ... I mean, great girl. She's great."

Gayl's Daz-white smile slipped entirely. I thought she was going to cry. Out of the corner of my eye I could see Clare, helpless with laughter.

The rest of the training was excruciating—mostly for Gayl, because I was so bad at it, and the studio had obviously told her that I had to pass this shit. I hoped it was like puppy training classes—no matter how badly behaved your pooch, everyone got a certificate at the end. I really fucking hoped so. At least I hadn't pissed on the floor. Yet.

Clare was enjoying herself, quietly winding up the guy she was practicing with. She caught my eye and wrinkled her nose. I smiled back weakly. Yeah, big fucking joke.

After another gut-churning hour, Gayl released us. She looked slightly frazzled and when she smiled at me, I thought she was going to pull a muscle.

I was shocked when two of the women attending the media training asked for my autograph. I think it was because Gayl had dropped Lilia's name a thousand fucking times. Clare looked royally stunned so it was worth it just for that.

When we finally got out of there, Clare was quiet.

"I'd better read that contract tonight," was all she said.

I recognized the SUV that was waiting, relieved it was Earl who'd be driving us.

"Hi, Earl. This is my friend, Clare."

"Good evening, miss," he said, smiling at her.

"Oh, hiya. You're the one who's actually got some taste in music—Miles told me about you."

Earl grinned at her and tipped his cap.

I was sort of jealous—Clare got on with everyone. She was so much better at all of this than me. Without even knowing it, she'd done just what Gayl had told her—started off talking to Earl with a compliment. Fuck. How was I ever going to learn that?

But if I'd thought that three hours with Gayl Lemon was

hard going, her brand of humiliation was nothing compared to my first visit to a stylist.

Earl drove us to a discreet four-story building and a man sitting in the foyer directed us to the top floor.

A bombshell blonde who was a dead ringer for Veronica Lake, met us as we got out of the elevator. I swear I was trying *not* to look at her tits. Honest.

Clare elbowed me in the ribs, and my head jerked up.

"Good afternoon, Mr. Stephens," said the blonde. "I'm Wendy Deluth, Miss Da Silva's personal assistant. And you are...?" she turned to Clare.

"Clare Milton," said Clare, stretching out her hand. "Mr. Stephens' personal assistant."

Wendy looked disbelievingly at Clare, running her eyes over the jeans and t-shirt she was wearing. I glanced over—Clare looked fine to me. Her tits were nice, too.

"I see," said Wendy, tightly. "I'll inform Miss Da Silva that you're here."

She wore her air of disapproval like body armor.

Clare pulled a face behind her back. I couldn't help sniggering, and I saw Wendy's shoulders twitch with irritation.

She led us into a large, hotel-like room. I looked around, expecting to see racks of clothes, but there was nothing. *Weird.*

Wendy brought us water, juice and bagels. Clare tucked in. I looked longingly at the bagels, but poured myself a glass of water and imagined taking my shirt off in front of the studio cameras. Yeah, they should patent that as a damn diet —Weight Watchers would be out of business.

Natalia Da Silva swept into the room. She was a well dressed woman in her sixties and her hair looked like it was made from steel wool. I stood up, nervously shifting from foot to foot. But instead of shaking hands, she cast an expert eye over my clothes and I felt my face getting hot.

"Good afternoon," she said, a slight accent coloring her voice. "I am Da Silva."

She said it just like that—like she was a brand of car, or Madonna or something.

"Avanti. We will begin," she said, waving a skinny claw at Wendy.

Immediately, the double doors swung open and a procession of female helpers marched in, pushing waiting racks of clothes. I mean, like *thousands* of items. Holy shit! Then they did a sort of little curtsey to Da Silva, and sashayed out again.

I felt like such a yokel, with straw still stuck in my hair, dazed and confused in the big city.

I glanced over to Clare—she looked thunderstruck.

"First, I'll have Wendy establish your measurements," Da Silva said, with authority. "We'll need to get some suits made, of course."

"Er, okay."

She waited. I waited. Clare raised her eyebrows, and Da Silva pulled a tape measure out of her bag, passing it to Wendy. Then we all waited.

"Is there a problem?" said Miss Da Silva, looking puzzled as she stared down her long nose at me.

"Oh, right."

I held out my arms, thinking Wendy would want to measure me or something.

Miss Da Silva gave an amused smile.

"We need to measure you accurately, Mr. Stephens. If you could take off your clothes, please."

Oh, hell, no!

Clare snorted, and managed to turn it into a strangled cough when everyone looked at her.

"Mr. Stephens?"

This was so fucking embarrassing!

"Er, um, I ... I'm not ... I'm not wearing any underwear," I managed to choke out at last.

Clare had to turn away to hide her laugh as the two stylists stared at me disbelievingly.

"Sorry," I mumbled. "I thought I'd just be, you know, looking at clothes."

"Well," said Miss Da Silva, attempting to retrieve the situation, "I was going to mention underwear anyway."

Yeah. Imagine hearing that in a sentence.

Clare stuffed her fists in her mouth and appeared to be chewing on a knuckle, but it was clear to everyone that she was on the verge of hysterical collapse.

"Si," continued Miss Da Silva, "we always recommend to our gentleman clients that they wear boxer briefs. It gives a much more flattering line than boxer shorts as those can bunch up most unattractively." She looked me up and down appraisingly. "I'd say you're a medium."

And she nodded at Wendy, who passed me a pair of black boxer briefs.

"If you'd like to change behind the screen, we'll wait here."

Great. So now I was going to be standing in front of three women—two that I'd never met before—in my underwear. I took a deep breath. At least it was *new* underwear. And clean.

I walked behind the screen Wendy pointed toward, and undressed. Fuck, it felt weird.

Clare

I almost stopped breathing when Miles walked back out. He looked so amazing I wanted to just sit and drool, enjoying the view. But I felt really bad for him, too. He looked so embarrassed, his eyes flicking everywhere but at me or the two hags at my side.

But you know, wow! That boy had *nothing* to be embarrassed about. All the gym time had really honed and toned everything he had. I just wanted to sit there and look. Or maybe lick him all over, starting with that amazing chest.

The black boxer briefs clung to him, showcasing his gorgeous arse, and bugger me if the front view wasn't even more ... impressive.

The Da Silva woman raised a tweezered eyebrow as she glanced at Wendy, who seemed to be having trouble breathing. Yeah, I knew how that felt, but then again, she must have seen a load of naked or half naked men in her job.

"If you could just stand in front of the mirror, Mr. Stephens," said Da Silva.

He did as she instructed but I knew he wouldn't be looking at himself—Miles wasn't like that.

He was shifting from foot to foot as Wendy wielded her tape measure, starting with the length of his arms, his height from neck to waist and neck to hip, the width of his chest.

"Allow an extra three-quarters of an inch there," instructed Da Silva. "He's still working with his personal trainer."

"Yes, ma'am," said Wendy. Then she knelt down so her head was about level with Miles' crotch. *Lucky cow.*

He jumped as she tried to measure his inside leg.

"Miles! Stand still," I barked at him.

His eyes looked at me piteously.

"Her hands are cold," he whispered.

Wendy looked embarrassed and rubbed her fingers to try and warm them up. At least she wasn't rubbing them on *him* to warm them up, although I wouldn't have been surprised if she wanted to. I wouldn't blame her—but I'd rip her arms off if she tried.

Miles took a deep breath and stood stock still, but he jumped again when her hand brushed against his balls.

That was no accident, bitch!

My eyes narrowed as his widened, and I saw his familiar blush start to creep up his neck. And there was no doubt it wasn't just a rush of blood to the head. I *definitely* saw his dick twitch.

He stepped away quickly, utterly mortified, and his hands automatically swept down to cover himself up.

"Sorry," he muttered again. "Sorry."

Da Silva coughed. "It happens all the time."

I looked up at her. "It does?"

She smiled at me, a surprisingly naughty expression on her face. "Yes." Then she turned back toward Miles who looked as if he wanted to be buried on the spot where he stood, mostly naked and semi-erect. I mean, that's how he stood—not how he wanted to be buried.

"Do you dress left or right?" she said.

"What?" said Miles.

"What?" I said, at the same time.

Da Silva tried to hide another smile. "Your suits will be bespoke, as I said, Mr. Stephens. When the trousers are tailored, we allow a little extra room on one side. It gives a better hang."

"Left," he choked out, then almost ran behind the screen.

I couldn't blame him. It was what you'd call a pretty damn personal question.

Chapter Six

BRIEF ENCOUNTERS

Clare

To be honest I was expecting the media training to be a bit of a joke, but it was actually quite useful—especially for someone like Miles, who seemed genetically unable to edit what came out of his mouth.

Of course, I teased him about it because he really needed to lighten up. I was worried about how stressed he seemed. The incident at the stylist hadn't helped and he refused point-blank to discuss it. Yeah, well, I was thankful that I had my bits all tucked inside so that the only person who knew I was having a fantasy moment was myself.

I really hoped Miles would be able to relax once filming started, or at least to be able to focus on the job he wanted to do instead of all the peripheral bullshit. But, I spoke too soon, because, like rock opera, it got worse after the interval.

Miles' cell phone rang while we were having breakfast the next morning: a bacon sandwich for me; fruit with yoghurt for him. Honestly! He was going to fade away.

"Hi, Rhonda!"

His eyes widened and his expression became ghostly. *What had happened?* I was on edge, waiting anxiously.

Miles ended the call, but continued to sit at the table, staring with horror at something I couldn't see.

I counted to 15 ... well, almost five. I couldn't bear it any longer.

"Say something!"

He shook his head, as if trying to wake from a bad dream.

"The Press have got hold of the news that I'm going to play Nuriel and..."

His voice was soft and halting.

"And what?"

"It's all been pretty negative stuff. Apparently the message boards for fans of the book are all campaigning to get rid of me—there's even a petition. Sixty thousand people have signed it already."

Holy shit! Sixty thousand?!

"The studio chiefs are tripping out. They're sending a car for me." He paused. "Rhonda's meeting me there. I think they're going to fire me."

"Can they do that?"

He shrugged. "Yeah."

Oh no, that was so unfair! I couldn't say the words out loud because they wouldn't help.

"I'm coming with you. Don't argue, Miles."

And when he didn't, I knew he was really worried.

As we waited on the front porch for a studio car, Miles' anxiety was contagious. I was chewing my way through a third nail when Earl pulled up at the curb. I was grateful it was him—he had this really calm quality. It helped Miles. A bit.

"Hey, Earl."

"Morning, Miles, Miss Clare. Something soothing to listen to?"

He nodded and soon I recognized the sad, soulful notes of Miles Davis playing 'I Fall in Love Too Easily', drifting through the speakers. I wasn't sure it was music designed to lift the spirits, but Miles leaned back on the seat and closed his eyes. I said nothing.

Earl didn't speak either, just nodded in time to the music.

When we arrived, a pretty assistant hustled us up to see

the studio head—some guy called Hyde. I mean, she was practically running and looked almost terrified. Whatever was cooking, they were taking it seriously.

As we stepped out of the lift, angry voices echoed along the corridor.

"This is a complete fuck up! How in the name of all that's holy did the Press get hold of..."

A woman's voice: "It was your genius idea to have him on the red carpet with Lilia. What did you *think* was going to happen? You *wanted* this to happen—test the water, see how the fans would react ... Well, now you know!"

The man: "That's irrelevant."

The woman: "The hell it is! I'm not riding the studio's shit list because of you. We have to manage the situation."

The man: "Fuck that! Manage it how?"

The woman: "Get the Press onside. Look, I can get him on *Ellen* tonight."

The man: "He's not ready for that! Have you read the feedback from Gayl Lemon? He's a fucking disaster. We'll have to recast."

The woman: "Give me 24 hours to turn this around."

The man: "I know you think you can walk on water but..."

The woman: "Twenty-four hours. At this point you've got nothing to lose."

The man: "So help me..."

The woman: "Ah, just grow a pair, wouldja?!"

Miles' face was grim. The assistant tapped on the door nervously and the voices paused.

"What?" yelled the man, stress dripping from the single syllable.

The assistant opened the door warily as if afraid she might need to duck quickly.

"Mr. Stephens and his friend are here, sir."

"Friend? Who the fuck?!"

Miles surprised me by striding in purposefully. I trailed behind, wondering if I should wait in the corridor. But no: Miles needed me.

He surprised me again, his voice was cool and steady. "Mr. Hyde, Rhonda: you wanted to see me."

"Who's your friend, Miles?" said Rhonda, icily.

Instead he turned to me.

"Clare, this is Rhonda Weitz, my agent, and Donald Hyde, the head of Dark Moon Productions: my friend and assistant, Clare Milton."

You could have knocked me down with a feather—he sounded so calm!

"I see," said Rhonda, her eyes measuring me. I was sure I was glaring at her. "Well, we have something of a situation here, Miles. The Press have gotten a hold of the news that you're playing Nuriel—and they want your balls on a plate."

"But why?" I couldn't help butting in.

She spoke slowly, as if to a particularly dim child, while her glacial eyes remained fixed on Miles. "Because he's a Brit and the role is American; because fans have a preconceived idea of how Nuriel should look—and the photos that the papers have gotten hold of are less than flattering."

For the first time I caught sight of the newspapers scattered across Hyde's desk. Miles blanched when he read the headlines:

'Back off, Brit!'

'Miles Behind!'

'He's No Angel!'

There was an old publicity still from one of Miles' minor theatrical roles—oh, they would pick the one where he played a drug addict.

"So the sitrep is this, Miles..." Rhonda's tone was businesslike and unemotional, as if she was a vet talking to the owner of a dog she was about to put down. "We have to manage the negative output. First, we're going to get the author of *Dazzled* to throw her support behind you; and secondly, I've been able to get you a slot on *Ellen*. Charm her, which you will, and half the battle is won."

"Does the author really support me?" Miles said, quietly.

"I have no idea," Rhonda replied, bluntly, "but she will.

Don't worry about that—I'll take care of her. Right now you have to prepare for *Ellen*."

"Who's she?"

"Jeez, Miles! Are you really that clueless?" she snapped, her calm mask falling away. "Ellen de Generes' talk show is one of the most watched in the continental US of A. We're talking 2.74 million viewers with more on the internet later." She took a breath and spoke in a more measured tone. "Filming will be at Burbank this evening. And Miles, it goes out live, so don't fuck up."

My stomach lurched unpleasantly. How the hell was Miles going to cope with that? How would anyone? His face looked blank with shock. I thought I was going to be sick on his behalf. What were friends for, right?

He looked at Rhonda. "What do you want me to do?"

A small smile chipped her concrete expression. "Suited and booted, Miles. I'll have Bradley send over another outfit. Now, we need to run through the probable questions."

Miles

In less than ten minutes, I was going to be going out on national television—*American* national television. I was so far beyond stunned that it seemed incredible my lungs continued to fill with air and blood still circulated in my veins.

I'd spent the day being prepped by Rhonda and the studio's PR team. Clare had been holding my hand, metaphorically speaking, but even she looked dazed and had little to say other than repeating the words, "You'll be great." I wished she was a better actress.

A suit and tie had been delivered in record time and a new white shirt still had razor-edged packing creases in it. Some poor gofer had shined my shoes and the hair and makeup artists had been summoned to 'gloss him up', as Rhonda so frankly put it.

I even met the author of *Dazzled*. Laura Dorien was kind. Rhonda introduced us.

"So, Laura, I'd like you to meet your Nuriel, Miles Stephens. Miles, this is the fabulous bestselling author, Laura Dorien."

We shook hands and Rhonda left us alone 'to talk'.

Laura smiled pleasantly, although her eyes swept over me first. *Jeez*, I couldn't get used to women doing that so blatantly. It was embarrassing. But I guessed that in her case at least, it was to see if I measured up to the character she'd created. Eventually, she nodded so I supposed I passed the test, whatever it was.

"So, Miles, have you read *Dazzled?*"

That was even more embarrassing.

"Um, no, sorry. I've read the script though." *Mostly*.

She inclined her head to one side, looking neither upset nor surprised.

"And did you like it?"

"Um ... yeah ... it was ... great. Really great."

She smiled.

"It's okay, it's not really written for your demographic," she said kindly, patting my knee. "Well, here's the outline: Nuriel is an angel who believes that he can easily influence people to do good. God is offended by his arrogance and to punish him for his presumption, God sends him to Earth to do exactly what he said—influence people to do good. Of course, Nuriel finds it much harder than he thought he would. He finds people fickle, complicated, hard to understand—especially coming from a being who has never suffered hunger, pain or loss. And then..." her eyes crinkled in a smile, "you fall in love with a girl—and that's where the trouble really starts."

She talked me through the rest of the main points of the plot and my character. She understood how I felt, I think, because she said her own sudden fame had felt like a physical assault—her words—and she'd had negative press, too.

"I'm really sorry the book's fans have given you a hard time, Miles. I won't kid you—you'll have a lot of expectations to live up to. And, after all, it's not going to be easy to play the perfect being, is it? But if it makes you feel any better, I saw what you did in the audition and now, having met you in person—I think you'll be perfect."

"Um, really? Wow, thanks, Laura. I appreciate that. It'll be nice to have one person not yelling at me."

She laughed, and it sounded real.

I felt a bit better after talking to her, one human being to another, but her good work was undone when she said to me, "Are you ready to be the new It Guy?"

"Pardon?"

She sighed. "Miles, I don't think you realize how this is going to affect you. This role will change your life. Are you ready for that?"

My throat went dry. I couldn't speak so I just shook my head. Her pitying look told me more than her words.

We were interrupted by the assistant producer's voice, which seemed to come from a long way away.

"Two minutes, Mr. Stephens."

My hands were ice cold. I noticed, dispassionately, that Rhonda looked worried. I guessed that wasn't good.

The AP was waving at me to follow her, and I vaguely heard my name across the set's microphones. Ellen was doing her intro.

"We're about to meet the guy who's going to bring us heaven on earth—or not, if the fans have anything to do with it. He's no angel ... he's Miles Stephens!"

I walked forward, somehow my legs responding to the distant commands of my brain. Suddenly Clare grabbed me and kissed me.

"You look effing hot, Miles!"

Her words made me smile as I walked out onto the set, and I held them as a talisman against making a complete sodding arse of myself.

As I approached the stage, I could hear a few cheers and a lot of booing and catcalls. *Bastards! How would they feel walking out to that?* Hellfire! There were a lot of people in the audience.

Ellen gave me a big, friendly smile, and reached up to kiss me on the cheek. I half-fell into the armchair next to her and couldn't help returning her grin.

Ellen: [*ironic tone*] I hope you enjoyed our warm welcome here, Miles!

Miles: Kind of reminds me of my last job.

Ellen: Oh really? How's that.

Miles: I was fired.

Ellen: [*laughs*] Well, congratulations on the new film role—the male lead in Laura Dorien's bestseller, *Dazzled*. Are you nervous? Playing Nuriel is a pretty big deal for the fans of the book.

Miles: I wasn't, but, yeah, I'm pretty nervous now.

Ellen: The fan sites haven't been very complimentary—how much does that bother you?

Miles: Usually people wait to see me act before they hate me. But no, I get it: everyone has their own view of what Nuriel should be like.

Ellen: I understand that Laura Dorien is a fan of yours?

Miles: I met her today for the first time and she was really nice. She talked to me about the book and my character ... yeah, it helped a lot. She was great.

Ellen: There's been quite a lot of negative press —you being a Brit, for one thing, and for not being pretty enough, which seems bizarre now we've met. How do you feel about that? I mean, it must be kind of upsetting.

Miles: Yeah, but there's nothing I can do about

it. I'll just play the role as best I can and hope the fans like it.

Ellen: And I believe Lilia Purcell who's playing Esther is supporting you?

Miles: She's great. I mean, I only met her at the audition, and once since, but I've been told that she said she wanted to work with me, which is pretty amazing. So, yeah, she's ... great.

Ellen: I have a feeling that when this film comes out a lot of women are going to be throwing themselves at you.

Miles: That would make a nice change. They usually run in the opposite direction, screaming.

Ellen: [*laughs*] Oh, I think there'll be a lot of screaming.

Miles: I'm used to women screaming at me—I mean, in relationships I always seem to have a woman scream at me. Quite often they throw stuff, too. I've learned to duck.

Ellen: [*laughs*] I don't think you'll need to worry about that! And I think we should just get some details here—are you single?

Miles: Yep. Definitely single.

Ellen: Oh? *Definitely* single. Not just a *little bit* single?

Miles: I can't remember the last time I had a date.

Ellen: I find that hard to believe. You're not a relationship kind of guy?

Miles: Oh, yeah! I just can't find anyone to commit to me. But then again a woman who commits to me probably should be committed.

Ellen: Well, just in case there are any ladies out

there who'd like to commit, are you living in LA now?

Miles: I guess, sort of. I mean, everything is rented, even my phone. Oh yeah, even the sheets on my bed. I don't own anything.

Ellen: Wow! That sounds kinda sad. Do you rent your car?

Miles: Actually, I'm still learning to drive.

Ellen: Seriously?

Miles: I never needed to before.

Ellen: So, what ... you get the *bus*?

Miles: Sure ... Oh, you think that makes me sound like a total loser?

Ellen: [*laughs*]

Miles: In London there's no point having a car. I walk, get the bus or take the Tube. But I'll definitely need to drive, living out here.

Ellen: Don't take the bus, man! You need to try and, you know, *own* some stuff!

Miles: I haven't even got an adaptor for my iPod yet. That's the first thing I've got to do.

Ellen: What sort of music do you like?

Miles: Lots of things, I'm pretty eclectic when it comes to music, but jazz, mainly.

Ellen: Like Miles Davis, by any chance?

Miles: Oh yeah! My mum named me after him.

Ellen: That's great. Your parents must be really proud of you.

Miles: I don't think Mum really knows what I do. She's a bit bemused by it all. Mind you, so am I. Just generally dazed and confused.

Ellen: Or maybe *dazzled*? [*laughter*] I feel like that every morning when I wake up. [*laughs*] Well, Miles, I've got some questions here for you that viewers have emailed in. Mercedes from San Diego wants to know, 'What is your idea of the perfect date?'

Miles: Anyone who'll go out with me, pretty
    much. [*laughter*] Er, somewhere with music
    —and food. I'm a big fan of food, although
    I can't cook.

Ellen: [*laughs*] Who's taking care of you, man?

Miles: I don't know! No one—oh, my best
    friend flew out for a few weeks. We'll get
    takeout.

Ellen: Okay, here's another one. Gina from
    Cleveland says, 'millions of teenage girls
    have a crush on Nuriel: who did you have a
    crush on when you were 15?'

Miles: Hermione from the Harry Potter
    films.

Ellen: You like brainy women?

Miles: Definitely: someone has to have the
    brains in a relationship, don't they?

Ellen: [*laughs*] That's the rumor—works for me!
    [*pause*] Well, we have a tradition on *Ellen*
    that everyone gets a gift of Ellen
    underwear.

Miles: You're kidding? Fantastic! Even my
    underpants are rented.

Ellen: Wow! Too much information! Well, these
    will come in handy. [*Hands Miles a pair of
    Ellen boxer briefs, with the words 'I'm no Angel'
    printed on the ass end.*]

Miles: Those are wicked! I mean, they're great!
    Thank you very much! I shall wear them
    always.

Ellen: [*laughs*] Miles, it's been a pleasure. You
    are one charming guy! I hope you'll come
    back and talk to us once *Dazzled* has been
    released. Miles Stephens, ladies and
    gentlemen!

[*Applause. Go to commercial.*]

. . .

Clare

I was so proud! Miles had charmed the pants off Ellen (pun intended). His agent, Rhonda, was beaming with relief, and there were no more boos as he left the stage.

"Miles!" Rhonda was bellowing and rugby tackled him when he walked back into the green room. "You nailed it, baby!"

Suddenly, everyone was smiling and relaxed. Miles looked slightly dazed but delighted with his free gift. I tried to banish the thought of what he'd look like wearing them. Just them.

Rhonda's phone buzzed. She had an intense conversation that seemed to consist of 'Uh-huh'.

Miles watched her anxiously.

Finally, she ended the call, closed her eyes and sighed. When she opened them again, a broad grin stretched across her face.

"Miles, that was Hyde. You aced that interview: the studio is pleased. Twitter is trending that the audience loved you. Well done."

Relief.

[*Fade to black.*]

Chapter Seven

THE COLOR OF MONEY

Clare

We celebrated with beer at a small bar not far from the apartment. It was one where they didn't check ID until later on in the evening. I just couldn't get used to that—back home, we'd been sneaking into pubs since Miles was 15. And it had been legal since we were 18. I would be legal to drink in the US just before Christmas, but Miles' 21st birthday wasn't until Easter next year. We were way underage. Oh well, I'd always wanted to be a bad influence.

The hostess greeted Miles by name, a hungry look in her eyes. As usual, he didn't notice. As usual, I was amused and irritated.

And jealous.

As usual.

Then two hideously underdressed women of about my age came over 'to say hi'. *Yeah, right.* They were all miniskirts, strappy t-shirts and enough mascara to make a drag-queen blush. Tramps. Oh, and they were fans of the *Dazzled* books and had just watched Miles' interview with Ellen. They couldn't wait to tell him that he'd won them over.

"You're so cute! I love your accent!"

"Oh, me, too! It sounds so gentlemanly!"

Miles smiled shyly and they melted. *The Miles Stephens' effect, ladies. Join the queue.*

Do women still swoon? I didn't know—I was having a Mr. Darcy moment myself.

Miles hadn't changed out of his sharp interview suit, although he'd loosened the tie and rolled up the shirtsleeves, exposing his muscled forearms. The women insisted on having their photos taken with him and, of course, Miles obliged, because he really was a gentleman. He couldn't help it, bless him. My job, naturally, was to take the photos— otherwise I was wallpaper as far as those hideous hags were concerned. Eventually even their pea-brains seemed to realize that Miles wasn't encouraging them, and they stumbled away on their sky-high heels that made their feet look like pig's trotters. They seemed star-struck and were giggling to themselves.

Rhonda was uncharacteristically fuzzy. She kicked off her Manolos and was drinking beer from a bottle. I liked her a little bit more.

She peered myopically at her iPhone when it buzzed gently.

"I've had a text from Lilia's agent, Todd Williams. You're invited to a pool party at Lilia's tomorrow. That's good—give you kids a chance to get to know each other a bit more before filming."

Miles looked surprised but pleased.

"She's got a swimming pool?"

Rhonda sighed and shook her head, but she was still smiling.

"Miles, even janitors have pools in LA."

"Yeah, but it's cool! What time does she want us there?"

Rhonda frowned. "The invite is for you, Miles." She threw a chilly look at me, "Not your friend."

Okay, not liking her as much now, frosty faced troll.

Miles pouted. *Damn, that was sexy!*

"I'm not going without Clare."

Really? Wow!

Rhonda was instantly back into pit bull mode.

"Look, Miles, you have to think of these opportunities as work. I'm serious—this movie is a multimillion dollar deal. Every time you leave your apartment, you're on show. Get it?"

He started to protest, but she cut him off.

"Don't be naïve. This is how it is. Just get your ass over there—and make sure you look good."

He folded his arms and leaned back in his chair.

"No. Not without Clare."

I couldn't help a small smile, and Rhonda scowled at me.

"Don't blow this deal, Miles."

Her voice was low, the warning implicit.

"Don't tell me who I can have as a friend, Rhonda."

Miles' voice was quiet but authoritative, and Rhonda's eyebrows hit her hairline. *I could hug you, Miles! And kiss you. Maybe also...*

Rhonda flung me an angry look.

"Fine. Fine. Just don't get in his way, Clare. This is Miles' chance—don't screw it up for him."

"As if I would!" *Hairy-arsed hobbit!*

"And for crissake, dress the part, can't you?"

"It's a fucking pool party, Rhonda, not a fashion shoot," said Miles in a milder tone, his anger evaporating with her tacit agreement.

"My way or the highway, Miles. Clare needs to look the part—as much as she can."

Cheek! What was I—chopped liver?

"That means a morning in the beauty salon, at least," Rhonda growled.

A wicked grin spread across Miles' lovely face. "Yeah! The beauty parlor! Payback time, Clare!"

"No bloody way!" My protest was rather overly loud, and several people turned to look at us curiously. But Miles wasn't backing down.

"I had to do it, Clare, and you told me I was being a wuss. Aren't you up to the challenge?"

Bastard. He knew me so well.

"Fine. I'll do the bloody salon. But nobody, *nobody*, can make me wear a bikini!"

"Trust me, honey, we'll all be grateful for that," said Rhonda.

Snarky bint.

I was splayed out, legs open wide and feeling more than a bit vulnerable.

"Aaaaaaaaaaaaaagh! Bloody hell!"

"Are you okay, ma'am?"

I leaned up on my elbows, pain pulsing through me.

"Am I okay? Do I bloody sound okay?! I thought you were waxing my legs? Not..."

I couldn't continue. The salon beautician was looking at me in complete bemusement. The sadistic bitch had just poured hot wax over my pubes and she was asking me if I was *okay*?!

"Do you want me to continue now, ma'am?"

"No! I only wanted my legs waxed! Can you just get it off?"

She sucked her teeth. "I don't know: no one has ever asked me to."

Bloody, bloody hell!

"Oh, for God's sake—just rip it off then."

She pursed her lips, applied the gauze and...

"Aaaaaaagh!"

I looked down at myself. It was a bizarre sight. Half my thatch had been shorn, the other half was as luxuriant and wayward as ever. Half my nether regions were glowing pink, unattractively speckled from having the pubes torn out, and as hairless as the day I was born.

"Do you want me to finish your Brazilian, ma'am?"

The cow was laughing at me.

"Well, I can't go around looking like a monk with a bad tonsure!"

She smiled icily and ripped off another patch of hair. The pain was off the Richter scale. It was a Brazilian all right—a bloody Brazilian rainforest where there'd been illegal logging. I couldn't *believe* men were turned on by this. Bloody perverts! Men didn't go around having their balls waxed ...or did they? Suddenly I wasn't so sure—this was LA after all. I made a mental note to ask Miles, although he might not tell me. Hmm.

When I limped back into the reception area, walking like I'd just got off my camel, Miles was lounging in a chair reading a paperback, *Running the Voodoo Down*. About jazz. Again.

His eyes opened wide when he saw me.

"Blimey, Clare! You look..."

"I know, I know. You don't have to rub it in."

I'd been cut and styled, highlighted and blow-dried, primped, preened, spray-tanned and subjected to torture that ought to be forbidden under the Geneva Convention.

"No, no! You look ... good!"

I blinked at him a few times. He seemed serious.

"Good?"

"Yeah, not like yourself at all."

I watched the sudden color rising in his cheeks as he realized what he'd said.

"Thank you, Mr. Tact and Diplomacy."

He winced.

"Oh come on, I didn't mean it like that."

I wished I could say that I swanned out of the salon, my head held high. The truth was I could barely walk without feeling an unpleasant burning sensation.

Miles frowned.

"What's wrong with your feet?"

I stared down at my pedicure. "Nothing. Why?"

"You're walking funny."

I said nothing, but blushed the color of a fire hydrant.

Miles hailed a taxi and I climbed in awkwardly. I was wearing an unaccustomed dress. I mean, I wasn't used to wearing a dress *and* it was a new dress: unaccustomed times two. So, what with the dress (unaccustomed as I was), and what with my recent deforestation, I was feeling more exposed than usual. I knew I was going to look plain and dumpy next to every woman at that pool party, and I hated the fact that I'd been forced to 'make an effort'. I felt fake and irritated with myself and everyone else. I envied Miles his casual t-shirt and board shorts—damn he looked good. But it was really beginning to sink in now, what he'd been trying to tell me about living out in this weird fishbowl: the show was everything.

"What's the matter?"

"I look like a friggin' cupcake in this dress!" I snorted, tugging at the too-short, frothy skirt.

Miles smirked at me. "Nah, you look fine."

Well, he would say that, wouldn't he? If he wanted to keep his teeth attached to his jaw.

The taxi wound its way into the hills until it pulled up at the gates of an enormous faux chateau. You know the kind, you've seen it on *Homes of the Stars*: huge, synthetic, utterly tasteless. A bit like Lilia herself, now you mention it. Okay, okay, so I may have been a touch jealous of the frowzy mare.

Miles

It was weird seeing Clare dressed like such a girl. I knew she was a girl, obviously, but she'd always been like another mate. My best mate, but an honorary bloke. I couldn't get over seeing her all girly—it just ... *wasn't right*. And I could tell it made her uncomfortable because she'd been twitching and shifting around in her seat the whole journey. Thank God we'd arrived—she was making me nervous.

Lilia's house was a-ma-zing! It was huge, surrounded with palm trees, and looked like it just floated off a movie set. I loved it. *This was living!*

An equally enormous security guard stood at the gates, checking names off against a list. It must have been hot in that suit. I wondered if he had a gun. I suddenly noticed that he was wearing one of those FBI-type earpieces, and Rhonda's words about 'the big time' came back to me. What was it like to live like this? I mean, it was better than just about any other job I could think of, but that didn't mean to say it wasn't without cost—personal cost. Needing a security guard for a house party was only one example. Back in London, parties were three mates with a six-pack of beer, and pizza for a touch of class.

"Man! Look at this place!" The taxi driver shook his head in awe. "Who you gotta sleep with to live in a place like this?"

That seemed a bit unfair. I mean, Lilia was really nice and not at all starry. But I guessed there would always be people who'd think that sort of shit. I wondered vaguely who they'd be saying I slept with to get this gig. Rhonda? The thought made me laugh, and Clare looked at me curiously.

I paid the driver, remembering Rhonda's advice to tip well. Clare raised her eyebrows at my largesse. Okay, maybe I overdid it. I wasn't used to having money—it was hard to get the balance right.

Clare stumbled slightly as she climbed out of the taxi, so I took her hand, all small and warm. She scowled at her sandals, and I glanced down at them in surprise. She normally wore sneakers—and I'd never seen her wear girly stuff like that, strappy and high-heeled. Perhaps that was why she was all over the place in them. It was pretty funny really, but unless I wanted her to punch me in the face, I decided it would be better not to laugh.

"Come on, then," she muttered. "Let's meet the great and the good—or the famous and the wealthy."

I couldn't help rolling my eyes—there was a bit of inverted snobbery going on. Ah hell, she'd be cool when she met Lilia.

But when uniformed staff greeted us at the front door,

Clare wasn't the only one with nerves. Holy shit! This was seriously rich. Lilia had a butler?!

"Miss Purcell is by the pool, madam, sir. This way."

Clare threw me a look and tightened her grasp on my hand. For someone pretty small, she had a grip like a WWE wrestler. Same sort of personality, too.

The house was jammed with people, and there were some seriously hot women there. I started getting a bit warm under the collar trying to work out who'd got fake boobs and which ones were real.

"Miles, you're drooling!" hissed Clare, and I snapped my mouth shut.

But, I mean, come on! Some of those bikinis were so skimpy they may as well not have been wearing anything. Oh hell, I was going to have a problem in a minute. I hoped the water in the swimming pool was cold—I was going to need it.

But poolside, things got even hotter. Or rather, the women got even hotter. Maybe it was like the Elizabethan royal court that Miss Delaney used to try and stuff into my brain during history lessons: the closer you were to the Queen, the more important you were. Minions had to loiter in the outer areas—and then I realized we were being ushered straight to the queen herself: Lilia Purcell, A-lister. Goddess.

She was lying on a sunlounger under an enormous palm fringed parasol. Her bikini looked like it had been spun from pure gold, and her lightly tanned skin was flawless. Oh my fuck. She was gorgeous.

"Hey, Miles! You made it. And you brought a *friend?*"

Even though I was concentrating on trying not to stare, I could still hear the slight inflection on the word 'friend'. I guessed she was asking me if Clare was my girlfriend. Did that mean anything?

"Hi, Lilia. Thanks for inviting us. This is my friend Clare, from England."

"How nice," said Lilia, frostily.

"Charmed," replied Clare, raising an eyebrow.

Oh, not good. I was waiting for a referee to call, 'Seconds out!'

The women eyed each other up, and the temperature dropped to just above freezing. Their body language reminded me of two cats on a fence—and they were stretching their claws.

I shuffled nervously from foot to foot, not sure what to do to calm the situation. Then Lilia sat up and inadvertently gave me an eyeful straight down her cleavage. *Fuck.* All rational thought was impossible.

"Miles, I need to talk to you about the script. Walk with me."

It didn't sound like a request.

Clare narrowed her eyes, and I shook my head at her slightly. I was trying to tell her, *This is work—I have no choice*, and I hoped she'd get the message. Wow, she looked pissed off.

Lilia grabbed my arm and led me away. Immediately, I was overheating just from the touch of her fingers. *This woman was hot!* And then I remembered that we were going to be filming sex scenes together. Yeah, I knew it would be PG13 but even so: her, me, bare flesh. *Shit!* How the hell was I going to deal with that? I knew my face was flushing and Miles Junior wasn't exactly impervious to Lilia's serious charms.

But before I knew it, she was introducing me to her friends and it gradually dawned on me that a good number of them were well-known—you know—famous. Not real stars like Lilia, but respected actors from TV. *This was so damn weird—me, here, with them.* I wondered vaguely where Clare was. Probably off having a good time somewhere. She knew how to enjoy her own company—always had. I kind of envied that.

"So, this is Miles Stephens, my new costar," cooed Lilia.

I knew that my face had reddened further. I felt so fake, her calling me that. Of course, she knew it was bullshit; there was only one star here—and it wasn't me. But it was cool of her to say it. That was Lilia: cool. Really fucking cool. And hot.

And then she rested a hand on my chest and my cock leapt to attention.

Clare

That Lilia was a complete bitch. She looked at me like I was some kind of slime on her fancy shoe, and then separated me from Miles with ridiculous ease. With those skills, she'd have aced any sheepdog trials. He didn't even realize it was happening. That didn't surprise me—he'd always been dense around women, bless him.

Actually, no. Not 'bless him'! He'd abandoned me here with a bunch of vacuous strangers who all looked as if they were in need of a decent meal.

"So, what are you?"

"British!" I squawked, as an implausibly gorgeous guy leaned against the wall next to me. He wasn't even wearing clothes. Well, swimming trunks, but that was all. He looked like a model—he probably *was* a model. And he'd waxed his chest. Mmmm, nice tattoo. Wonder how far down it went?

He smiled, and I was nearly blinded by the whiteness of his teeth.

"I guessed that," he grinned.

How? What?

"I meant, are you an actress—or something?"

"Oh. Right. No, I'm a student."

"Training to be an actress?"

"No, History and English Literature, actually."

"Huh?" he sounded puzzled; he looked bloody gorgeous. Not as gorgeous as Miles, of course, and there was something calculating about his expression.

"How did you swing an invite?"

"I came with a friend. Lilia invited us."

His eyes lit up like the Chrysler Building. "Cool! You know Lilia?"

"Not exactly. Rhonda Weitz is my friend's agent—she talked to Lilia's agent. Or something."

"Wow! *The* Rhonda Weitz—can you hook me up with her? I'm looking for new representation."

"Er, I don't think so because..."

I didn't get the chance to explain further because he shrugged and walked off, flinging a "Take it easy," over his shoulder.

How rude!

But as the afternoon wore on, the rubbernecking became of epidemic proportions. Every time I thought I was having a conversation with someone, the moment they found out that I wasn't 'in the biz', they lost interest. It dawned on me that this wasn't a social event—it was networking. Everyone wanted something. Were these really Lilia's *friends*? Suddenly, unexpectedly, I felt sorry for her.

Now where the hell was the barbecue, where could I get a drink, and what had that maneater done with Miles?

Miles

Everyone was *so* friendly—Lilia's friends were totally cool. They were all really interested, asking questions about the film: when would we start shooting; who was the cinematographer; what the schedule was—stuff like that. Luckily, Lilia fielded all those questions which was a good thing, because I was starting to feel buzzed by all the champagne. Every time I turned around, a waiter had refilled my glass. I didn't even know how much I'd drunk. God, I hoped I didn't say or do something stupid.

I wished Clare hadn't buggered off and left me alone. I knew I'd said to her that this was mostly work—did I say that to her? Well, I was sure she knew, but I was starting to feel overwhelmed. All the people I'd met knew so much more about 'the biz' than I did. Everyone was either an actor or working on a script. They all had something 'in production' and everyone was dropping names like it was going out of fashion. They acted like they owned the world—and they all had great teeth.

Plus, they all seemed to know each other. I was beginning to feel as on-trend as a Betamax video in a Blue Ray world.

When Lilia took yet another phone call, I was relieved to slink away and take a breather from the intensity of the *niceness*. Everyone had been great—so why did it feel so fake? Maybe because *I was* the fake. Compared to everyone here, I had almost no credible experience, and that little voice of doubt that told me I was a talentless tosser was becoming deafening. I was regretting signing the damn contract—I was going to look such a bloody idiot.

It felt like everyone was staring at me, wondering what sort of loser Lilia had hooked up with; probably feeling sorry for her having to work with such a rank amateur. Fuck—I was losing it.

When my hands started to shake, I knew I had to get a grip.

Where the hell was Clare?

Then I spotted her by the buffet—of course. The amazing spread had hardly been touched. *Did anyone here ever eat?* I knew I should probably get some scran to ease up the effects of the alcohol but I was aware that filming was due to start in ten days and, according to both Hilda and Rhonda, I still need to lose more weight. *The camera adds 20 pounds.*

But I could enjoy watching Clare eat.

"Hi, hon. Having fun?"

"Oh, just wonderful," she snarled.

I was taken aback.

"What's wrong?"

"How can you stand it?" she huffed at me, and I immediately felt irritated. *What was her problem?*

"What do you mean?"

She waved her arms around. "This! They're all so ... so ... *actory.*"

I couldn't believe she was being so snooty. *This was my work.*

"*I'm* an actor, Clare." *Trying to be.*

She raised her eyebrows. "I don't mean you, Miles. Obviously. It's just that ... oh well, never mind. How are you doing with Miss High and Mighty?"

"Lilia's been really nice to me," I said, my voice warning her off the bulldog routine. "It was nice of her to invite us."

"Oh yes. Very *nice*," she replied in a snarky tone.

Okay, now she was pissing me off.

"What's your problem, Clare?"

"My problem, Miles," she spat out, "is that this is all so fake and you're just lapping it up. This place is really changing you—you used to laugh at people like this. Now you're all..."

She stopped suddenly.

"I'm all what, Clare?"

I was breathing hard and glaring at her.

"Never mind."

"No, go on. Say what you think—you always say what you think, don't you? That's your *thing*, isn't it, honesty? Come on, Clare, be honest with me ... I'm all *what?*"

She scowled. "You're not *you*."

What the fuck?

"What's that supposed to mean? Or maybe you mean I'm just not that pathetic loser I used to be. Except that I am, aren't I. Don't you think I don't know that I don't fit in here? Everyone is *somebody* and I'm just a nobody with big dreams. If that's what you wanted to say, *friend,* then feel free."

Her face went red, and I didn't know if she was angry or upset.

But then she went in a different direction.

"What did Lilia have to say about the script?"

"What?"

"She said she wanted to talk to you about the script?"

Oh, yeah. "We didn't get to that."

She raised an eyebrow and crossed her arms, a mulish expression on her face. "What a surprise."

"What's that supposed to mean?" *I sounded like a fucking broken record.*

She rolled her eyes.

"Well?"

"Oh, come on, Miles! It's just so obvious."

"Not to me."

"She wanted to get you away from me. She fancies the pants off you. She looks at you the way I look at chocolate."

"She doesn't."

"Yes, she does."

I ran my hands through my hair in frustration. "She's a fucking film star, Clare."

"Yeah, and? Miles, you're co-starring with her in the film version of a book that was in the New York Times bestseller list for a year or something. *You'll* be a film star, too, after all this."

"That's not going to happen."

She sighed and I didn't know if it was in frustration, irritation, or both. This was Clare, so it was probably both.

"Didn't you listen to what Laura Dorien said to you: 'Are you ready to be the next It Guy?' Remember?"

"Don't do this, Clare."

"Don't do what?"

"You're freaking me out."

"*This* is what you said you wanted, Miles. Perhaps you should just make up your bloody mind and stop being so..."

I didn't know if I wanted her to finish that sentence or not. We stood glaring at each other, until she said, "I want to go home."

I was so fucking furious with her right then. "Fine. I'll call you a cab."

I turned my back on her and pulled out my cell phone, dialing quickly.

"The taxi will be here in 10 minutes."

She stared at me, biting her lip. "Are you coming with me?"

"No."

I knew I was being a dick, but I thought it was best if we just kept some distance from each other now. God, that sounded so weird—I'd never wanted to keep my distance from Clare before.

A hurt look flashed across her face but then her naturally pugnacious expression was back.

"Please yourself. I'll wait out front."

"Fine. Just don't wait up."

"I won't."

"Fine."

"Fine."

And she stormed off.

I was thinking about going after her when I felt a soft hand on my shoulder and nearly jumped.

"Hi, I'm Colt."

Colt?

"Er, hi. I'm Miles."

"I know."

Huh?

"You're going to be Nuriel, right?"

I nodded, frowning slightly.

"Yeah, so I was wondering, could you get me a part in the movie? Something small, I don't mind. I'd be very ... grateful."

Colt was hanging onto my shoulder and I had to admit she was fucking gorgeous. Well, all the women at Lilia's party were hot.

She traced her nail down my arm and stood so close, she was rubbing her tits against my chest.

Guys are supposed to like that, right? Easy, uncomplicated sex. But truthfully, I was a real *girl* about sleeping with someone—so Clare said. Feelings, all that stuff, although right now my cock was having difficulty remembering it. I had to admit to myself that I was tempted—this woman was off the chart beautiful. But you know what stopped me? It wasn't any sort of sense of chivalry, or the fact I had no power to get her on the film; it wasn't even because I didn't see myself as a manwhore. What stopped me was a sudden image of Gayl Lemon's face.

Yeah, okay, that sounded weirder that even *I'd* like to

admit. Maybe Gayl was hot in her day, I couldn't say, but she was old enough to be my *grandmother*. My dick shriveled at the thought. But Gayl had talked endlessly about the *image*—how people see actors as role models. If this film went the way they were saying, it wasn't just me who was going to care who I slept with. I couldn't imagine what it would be like to wake up one day and see my face plastered over the newspapers with some skank talking about the night we'd spent together. I definitely didn't want to be like Mr. Joe Blow.

And I didn't want to be like *him*—my hole chasing fucking father.

"Sorry, Colt. I don't have any say about casting."

"You wanna party?"

God, she wasn't making it easy for me to say no, especially the way she kept pushing her tits against me.

"No, I'm okay, thanks."

"Well, call me, if you change your mind."

"Er..."

She walked away. *How was I supposed to call her—she didn't give me her number?* Whatever. I didn't want to call her.

I headed for the front door.

"Miles? Where are you going?"

Lilia's voice stopped me in my tracks.

"Oh, hi ... I thought I'd head back now. I've got some things to do, y' know."

"Such as?"

I decided to come clean.

"It's a great party, Lilia, I'm just feeling a bit freaked. I need to get some head space."

She smiled.

"I remember that feeling. Sure, fine, but we need to get our shots first."

Shots? What, injections?

"Of you and me, Miles, enjoying this wonderful party."

I frowned at her and she sighed.

"Look, the studio paid for this party. It's publicity, right?

They want some pictures of us together." She saw the look on my face. "Think of it as work, that's all."

I felt so incredibly stupid. And out of my depth.

"Okay, sure."

When Lilia took my hand, I followed.

"This way."

Back at the pool, a photographer with an impressive paunch was snapping shots of the partygoers. Even I could tell that the level of excitement had gone up a notch. But his eyes brightened when he saw Lilia. The money shot. Right.

"Hey, Louis," said Lilia. "Where do you want me?"

The guy licked his lips, and I felt an urge to punch him.

"Sitting by the pool, honey. Tell the guy to take his shirt off."

"I've got a bloody name," I muttered, so only Lilia could hear me.

She patted my arm. "It's just business, Miles. Don't take it personally."

Whatever.

Feeling even more self-conscious, I pulled off my t-shirt and threw it on a chair. Lilia smiled.

"You've been working out. Looking good, Miles."

I felt my face flush, although whether it was more with pleasure or embarrassment, I couldn't say. I felt so uncomfortable posing with Lilia that I had to pull my sunglasses out of my pocket. I told myself it made it easier.

After 17 excruciating minutes, we were done. God knows what I'd look like in the pictures. Lilia had been cute and flirty: touching my arm, resting her head on my shoulder—completely relaxed and smiling. Yeah, she was an actress, all right.

I headed for the open bar, planning on getting wasted. Colt was there, sitting on some guy's knee. He had his hand on her thigh, like really high up on her thigh.

I started feeling nauseous. All I could think about was going home, but I wasn't ready to face Clare.

Chapter Eight

THE LAST PICTURE SHOW

Clare

Stupid bloody dress! It had a zip up the back. How the hell was I supposed to undo that by myself, not being a contortionist? Shit, I knew I should have tried yoga lessons.

I was so furious when I got back to Miles' apartment. I couldn't believe he'd dumped me at that stupid party. Or had I walked out? I wasn't sure. Either way I was hurt and angry and not entirely sober. I needed chocolate. I didn't care about that whole 'moment on the lips, lifetime on the hips' thing. Everyone knows that if you break the chocolate first, the calories fall out. Right?

I changed into my jeans and then thought better of it. That bloody Brazilian. *Never again.* I was limited on leisurewear, so I marched into Miles' bedroom, ignoring his sheets that smelled faintly of spice, and rifled through his closet. After a moment, I pulled out a pair of sweatpants—I really hoped they were his favorites because I had plans for them.

I found scissors in a kitchen drawer and hacked off the legs, which went some way to venting the violent impulses I was having. Then I stomped out to find a shop that sold chocolate. Candy. Whatever. I needed sugar, fat, and cocoa beans—or any combination of the above.

Half an hour later, I had fifty bucks worth of sugary delight and a $2.99 DVD of *Dirty Dancing*. Perfect.

When I found a bottle of vodka in the freezer drawer of Miles' refrigerator, my evening was officially 100% improved.

I'd just got to that iconic passage where Johnny says, "Nobody puts Baby in the corner," when I heard the apartment door open.

I tried reeeeally hard not to look, but I couldn't help glancing up.

Miles was standing there, so damn cute and sort of rumpled. He seemed sober, too, which surprised me.

"Sorry," he mumbled.

I waited for a moment to see if I felt like accepting his apology. His gray eyes were so serious and sad, that I couldn't hold out a second longer. Pathetic, I know.

"Yeah, me, too."

He slumped down next to me and stretched out his legs.

"What are you watching?"

"Quiet."

"Oh, God, not *Dirty Dancing* again. I must have really pissed you off."

"Ssh."

He spotted the vodka and took a swig, pulling a face as he swallowed.

I wanted to lick that Adam's apple as it bobbed in his throat. I sighed. *Never gonna happen.*

"Are we okay?" he said, quietly.

"Yeah. You're a dickhead, but we're fine."

He gave a small smile. "I know. Must be genetic. Sorry."

"So, how was the party?"

I knew I was pushing it, but I couldn't help asking.

He scowled. "Crap. You were right about that. It turned out that it was just a fucking photo op. Lilia told me that the studio paid for the party. Can you believe that? Hell, for all I know, everyone else was paid to be there. Nothing in this city is real."

"Why did you stay?"

He sighed. "I didn't. I did the shoot and left."

"But you've been gone ages?"

"Yeah, well, I was going to tell you about that..."

I turned to look at him. He looked slightly happier—shifty—but definitely happier.

"What did you do?"

He leaned forward and dragged out a long, black case from the side of the couch. I hadn't noticed it when he'd walked in—I was too busy looking at *him*.

His fingers stroked the silk as he opened it.

"Blimey! You bought a sax!"

I watched as his fingers traced the delicate filigree engraving, some sort of trailing flower, winding its way up the body of the instrument.

"Yeah, she was so fucking gorgeous, I couldn't resist."

Yep, I was jealous of a piece of bloody silver painted brass. I wanted his fingers tracing over *me* like that. I wanted his eyes to be filled with lust when he looked at *me*. Bloody, bloody hell.

"Selmer soloist mouthpiece," he drooled. "Hemke 3 reeds, and she sounds sooo sweet—perfect."

"Where did you go to get her, I mean, it?"

"After you left," his eyes flicked to me, a guilty expression on his face, "after the photo shit, I called Earl. He knew this cool music shop and ... I couldn't resist. If I'm staying here, I need my music and..."

"Hang on, you called Earl on his day off just to give you a ride? He probably works all hours as it is! Why didn't you call a taxi?"

"Ah, crap. I didn't think."

Huh, typical.

"I think I just wanted to talk to someone, you know."

"And you couldn't talk to me?"

"You'd gone."

"Did I mention that you're a dickhead?"

"Yeah. It's a recurring theme. Reminds me of home."

I elbowed him in the ribs and he pretended to be hurt.

Oh well, at least he hadn't spent any more time than he had to with that skeazy actress. I really liked that word—*skeaze*, it was almost onomatopoeic.

He rested his hand on my knee and I looked up in surprise, but his eyes were focused on the cut up sweatpants, a quizzical look on his face.

"Do you want to work on your script?" I said, changing the subject before he could start it.

He shook his head, smiling, because he knew exactly what I was doing. "Nah, I want to get drunk and pass out on the couch."

"That brings back memories."

He smiled at me and reached for the vodka.

"Okay, you can have tonight off, but only because it's been a shit awful day. Tomorrow, we work on your lines."

"Yes, boss," he said.

"That's right! And don't you forget who's on top!"

As I said the words, my face flushed and Miles smirked.

"Do you like being on top, Clare? I never knew that. Figures, though."

"Shut up!" was my genius reply.

"I don't think so, because I have this image in my head now. Are you into whips and chains and all that kinky shit, too? Do you handcuff your guys?"

I knew he was teasing me but suddenly the thought of having him tied up at my mercy was very appealing.

"Why?" I said. "Are you offering?" *Please say yes. Please say yes.*

He laughed. "Nah, you're too scary."

And that was the end of that conversation.

Shit.

"Hey, Miles! You made Perez Hilton's page!"

He looked up from the script, and momentarily paused, his fingers still twisting restlessly in his short hair.

"Who?"

"He does this big celeb gossip website. He's published the photos from Lilia's party." *And you look so fuck-me hot, I'm drooling enough to need a bib.*

Miles frowned.

"Oh," he said, and buried his face back in the script.

I felt sorry for him. It was such a struggle for him to learn lines. I'd Googled some stuff on dyslexia and decided that he suffered from 'stress spirals'—you know, when you do okay at something some of the time, but getting stressed means your confidence plummets and you give up in anger and frustration. That was definitely Miles.

It helped that the script was set out in short chunks of narrow text across a whole page, but at school they used to clip a sheet of yellow cellophane over the top of his textbooks to sort of calm down all the white paper. I'd found an art shop in the neighborhood, and bought some of that cellophane for Miles. It helped. Mostly it helped if we read the lines together over and over, but it got pretty boring and I knew the damn speeches better than he did.

But he was loads more patient than me and he didn't complain. What with that, his gym time with the fitness fascist, costume fittings and publicity stuff, he barely had time to breathe.

I'd taken on various aspects of his life, like a real PA. I even reminded him to call his mum on her birthday, bought a card, wrote the address on the envelope, put the pen in his hand to sign the card, and stuck it in the mail. I was good at that shit—being organized had never been a problem for me. Mind you, I would have let him lick the stamp because— whoa, lookin' hot—but sad to say, the stamp was just peel-and-stick. Sigh.

I printed out a schedule for him and taped it to the fridge so he knew what he was doing each week, but today was the last day I'd have to do that—tomorrow we were moving to the film's location.

I was excited. Miles was panicking quietly.

We were heading north to the small town of Petaluma, in Sonoma county. It was standing in for the fictional town of Flatrock, and we were staying on some private estate to make security easier. It was about 50 miles from the wineries of the Napa Valley, and 50 from San Francisco.

It was a bit freaky to think that professional bodyguards would be needed. Although I couldn't stand the skank bitch, I felt sorry for Lilia for needing them. Mind you, if she caused Miles any problems, she'd need a bodyguard to protect her from me. *And that was a gold-plated, um, solid gold promise.*

She'd texted him a couple of times over the past week, but they hadn't seen each other. Not that I knew of. I was dying to see what he'd put in his replies to her. I *nearly* checked his phone while he was in the shower, but I didn't want to start acting like a bunny boiler. I had tried to justify it on the grounds that I was his personal assistant and therefore ought to know, but I couldn't quite bring myself to do it. Miles was my friend, and you don't do that to your friends. Instead, I printed out my summer reading list that the university had sent me, and downloaded everything onto my new Kindle, a really great gift from the newly minted and gratefully well off Miles, bless him.

I toggled back through the photos from the pool party for the ninth or tenth time. Miles still looked hot—yeah, like a real film star. *She* looked like a skinny skank. *Note: smiley face to self.*

She really pissed me off.

And then Miles and I had started the script read-through. I nearly freaked when I realized that he and Lilia had a couple of sex scenes, but Miles' face drained of color when he saw what he was going to have to do in front of an audience. He was so obviously unhappy at the idea, that it helped me man up, so to speak. And I couldn't help imagining my own sex scenes with Miles—it was going to kill me seeing him get naked with the bony hag.

Ugh.

At least he wasn't looking forward to it either.

They would have three days of rehearsals on location before the 40 days of 'principal photography' started. It didn't seem like much to me, not compared with the preparation time for a stage play, but what did I know. I supposed the difference was that if anybody messed up, it could just be reshot.

"Holy, fuck! What time is it?"

Suddenly, Miles leapt to his feet, nearly giving me a heart attack.

"Seven, you dill! Bloody hell, my ears are ringing."

"I'm supposed to be at the gym with sodding Hilda!" he yelped.

Oh. Yeah, the PA should have been on that. I'd have to have a word with her.

Miles dropped the script on the couch and ran to his bedroom. I followed at a more leisurely pace, not being particularly bothered that he was going to be a few minutes late. I mean, it was his last session with her, so it hardly mattered.

I opened my mouth to expound on that theory, when the words dried in my throat. He had his back to me, and was naked except for a pair of tight fitting boxer briefs with the word *Wicked* printed across the backside. *Thank you, Ellen.* God, I wanted to pinch that pert arse, run my hands up the hard lines of his back, and massage his defined shoulder muscles. Then lick them. Maybe nibble a little. Or a lot.

"She's going to kill me," he muttered to himself.

Oh, you'd better believe it, baby! I'd ride you till you passed out from exhaustion, feed you a bacon sandwich, hose you down and start again.

Oh ... he was probably talking about Hilda, not me. Bloody hell. I really needed to get my head in the game. I was here to help him, not ogle mindlessly, although...

"I'll come with you," I said.

He jumped slightly, not realizing I was standing in the doorway, then frowned.

"It'll just be sweaty and boring," he replied.

Yeah, hate that ... Miles, all sweaty. Mmm. *Get a bloody grip. No! Not like that!*

"And, um, I jog to the gym."

"Bugger that!"

He grinned. "I thought that's what you'd say."

I watched as he pulled on another pair of sweatpants that hadn't felt the wrath of my scissors, an Al Stewart t-shirt with cover artwork from *Russians and Americans*, and his running shoes. He winked and ran out of the door.

Miles

I thought Hilda would take it easy on our last day. Yeah, I was wrong about 180 degrees.

"Come on!" she yelled. "Move your ass! Faster!"

Fuck, I was really glad I'd brushed off every offer she'd made for us to get together. I mean, hell, I could just imagine her shouting stuff like that during sex—it would really put a man off his stride. But whatever I thought about her personally (and not much of it was good), she was one helluva fitness trainer. Although, maybe wanting to do the work just to get away from her was not the kind of motivation most trainers used. I hoped.

One hundred and fifty excruciating minutes later, we were done. I was definitely done. I wasn't even sure how I was managing to live without a life support system, or oxygen at the very least.

I was nearly on my hands and knees as I hobbled toward the men's locker room. My t-shirt and sweatpants were ringing with sweat and I probably smelled like a skunk.

I set the shower to lukewarm and let it pour over my head ... until I heard Hilda's voice a few feet away.

"So, Miles. Last day an' all. How about that veggie juice?"

What the fuck?

"Jeez, Hilda, I'm naked in here!"

"Oh, get over yourself, Miles. I've seen it all before, baby. I used to physio for the Oregon Ducks."

Who? What?

"When you've seen one dick, you've seen them all."

Did she say 'dick' or 'duck'?

"Um, right."

"But I prefer one-on-one these days."

Holy crap!

She paused. "So, get your pale ass out of the shower and we can head on out."

"Actually, Hilda..."

"Don't even think about blowing me off!"

Shit. "Okay, sure, but just for half an hour. I have a shed load of things to sort out before tomorrow." I waited, but she didn't reply. Perhaps she'd gone?

I turned off the water and peered around the shower stall. I nearly jumped out of my skin when Hilda handed me a towel, a scary-ass smile on her face.

"Bloody hell, Hilda! Give a guy some privacy!"

"You Brits are so adorable," she laughed. "I love all that shy guy stuff—it's cute."

"Yeah, whatever, just ... go, will you?!"

She was really getting on my nerves.

But when I left the locker room, Hilda's eyes had narrowed to slits and she was giving a death stare to someone on the other side of the room. I turned around and saw...

"Clare! Hiya! I didn't know you were coming here," *but thank God you did.*

I was pretty certain she'd saved me from a fate worse than death. I was such a wuss.

"Yeah, well, you ran out this morning before I'd finished my breakfast," she said, pointedly.

Hilda scowled, and for once I was quite happy to let another woman believe that I was dating Clare.

"Think I'll take a raincheck on our *date*, Miles," said Hilda. "I'll look you up when you get back to LA."

I half expected to see Clare disappear in a cloud of dust particles from the way Hilda was glaring at her.

"Um, right," I offered vaguely, and Hilda's lip curled.

She reminded me of an Alsatian that had lived next door to my mum when I was a kid. I actually took a step back in case she decided to bite. Hilda freaked me out.

She stalked out of the room, and I breathed a sigh of relief.

"Tell you what, Clare, you have great timing," I said.

She shook her head in disbelief.

"Miles! When are you going to toughen up? She would have had you for breakfast and spat out a bunch of bones at the end!"

"I know," I said, hanging my head. "I'm pathetic. I just, you know, I hate being rude to people."

Clare looked at me evenly.

"Well, it's not really fair of you to leave it up in the air. All this time, she probably thought she had a chance with you."

"That's bullshit! I never gave her a single ounce of encouragement."

"Are you really that dim?" Clare snorted. "That's not enough—you have to be really clear. Just say something like, 'I'm flattered, but we're going to be keeping it professional'."

"Oh, that's good. Okay, I'll remember that one. Thanks, Clare."

She was right—I was an idiot. God, it would be nice to just meet an ordinary girl for a change, you know? Have a few dates, get to know her slowly. Not just some random hook up where you got a strange tongue rammed down your throat. Well, okay, sometimes that was good, too, but that had usually only happened when I was drunk, and it was almost always a mistake. Um, make that *always* a mistake. Except that night with the Swedish air stewardess—she was hot. And maybe one, er, two other times.

Clare was watching me curiously.

"Are we going, or what? You have a script to learn."

"Yes, boss."

We'd dissected the script so many times I could see Clare's eyes crossing at the thought of *yet another* read through. She didn't complain; she didn't have to—I could see it written all over her face.

It had been hard work, but it was getting easier. I didn't want to come over as near illiterate when I started rehearsals with Lilia and Jo-Anne, fumbling and fluffing my way through the lines. I just hoped that there weren't too many rewrites on set, or I was screwed.

I'd made a load of notes on the script, too—ideas about how I'd play the character—as well as thinking about some kind of back story for him, for Nuriel. Believe me, that wasn't easy. I mean, he was an angel—literally, wings, harp, Birkenstocks, the whole gig. Okay, well, not the Birkenstocks and I hadn't seen a harp mentioned, although the guy was supposed to play the guitar. I could just about fake that. I'd played guitar before I took up the sax. I was a bit rusty, but good enough to fake it in the movie. I hoped. I'd bought a cheap guitar from a guy I found on Craigslist, then spent a few days practicing. I'd forgotten how much I enjoyed it.

"Hey, play me that Sam Callahan song," said Clare, the first evening I'd brought the guitar home.

I'd met Sam when we were both gigging at the Venue in South East London one night. He was a cool guy—wrote some great lyrics.

"Yeah, okay. Which one?"

"The one about being crazy in love. That's my favorite."

I ran my fingers along the neck of the guitar, pulling the tune out of my memory, digging it from the dark matter that made up my brain cells, and started to play.

Sometimes alone, I felt so lost.
You were all that I wanted.
And it felt like everyone thought it was wrong being together.

But we can do most anything.
Whatever we want to.
Just lean on me and I'll rely on you.

I know, know it sounds insane,
But girl, girl, you do something to me.

You gotta know I'm crazy for you,
And if you're crazy for me,
We can be crazy together,
Baby, there'll be no in-between.

I tell you there's no holding back,
and I'll only say words that I mean.
I wanna be crazy forever,
So say you wanna be crazy with me?

Clare's eyes had this sort of drowsy look about them when I finished. I think that meant she liked it, even though I was pretty rusty.

"I love that song," she sighed. "It's so sweet. And Sam's pretty hot, too."

"Yeah, whatever," I mumbled.

But it didn't matter what I really sounded like when I played in those scenes for the movie—they'd add the soundtrack later anyway. Whatever I could do to prepare seemed like a good idea.

At least I wasn't so nervous about taking my shirt off on camera now. Jo-Anne had said that there'd be a personal trainer available to help me from blobbing out on the shoot. Not Hilda, thank God, although I had to admit she'd really whipped me into shape. Yeah, it was the whips that worried me. Actually, no, that wasn't true. Just being alone with Hilda scared the shit out of me.

Thank God for Clare.

The next morning I felt strangely calm as we packed our bags ready to go on location. I could see Clare watching me out of the corner of my eye, waiting for me to freak out. But I didn't. Maybe because it felt like there wasn't anything more I could do. I was as prepared as I could be. I knew my lines, I was in shape, and my head was in a good place. For the first time I felt like I could do this.

Yeah, that lasted until the studio car arrived.

I wished it was Earl who was driving us, but he preferred to stick to jobs in LA. He said he didn't like being away from his family. It made me feel guilty for not phoning Mum more often. I made a mental note to do that as soon as I could.

The new driver didn't speak much. I was even considering the possibility he was mute, but then I heard him talking on his cell phone, so I guess he just didn't want to talk to me. Or Clare. She was enjoying herself, looking out of the window and chatting away.

"We definitely have to do this drive when you finish filming. It would be unreal: you, me, a car, and miles of California highway to cruise. Imagine the mayhem!"

That didn't sound half bad, and I hoped we could make it happen. Clare had missed out on the summer beer fest circuit around Europe with Nazzer and Paul—I hoped that a trip down the Californian coast would make it up to her. And it did look damn beautiful. I was surprised how wild the landscape was, just a few miles out of LA.

We arrived at Petaluma late in the afternoon and I was looking forward to having a cold beer at the hotel when we got there. It was hard to remember that I was still underage here, and I really hoped that the staff at the hotel would turn a blind eye.

I eyed the driver, wondering if he was the kind of guy I could ask to buy beer for me—I mean, if I gave him the money. He wasn't the friendliest ever, but it was worth a try.

We'd turned into a long, private driveway that led to the hotel when Clare nudged my elbow.

"Hey, look at that," she said.

There must have been more than fifty young girls standing in the boiling sun. They were all carrying homemade posters with 'Nuriel ♥ Esther' printed on them in crayon and decorated with glitter, and I could see several of the older ones were carrying copies of the book *Dazzled*.

As our car approached, they started shouting and waving.

The driver had a determined look on his face and started to speed up.

"Hey, careful!" gasped Clare, and her eyes were pleading.

Yeah, she totally knew what that would do to me. Besides, I agreed with her. I couldn't just ignore those kids, and I wondered how long they'd been standing there—it must have been 95°F outside.

"Just stop for a minute," I said.

"Sir, my instructions are to..."

"Just for a minute."

"It's not safe, sir..."

"Oh, for goodness sake!" snapped Clare. "They're only kids!"

With a sour expression, he pulled the car to the side of the road. We were surrounded in seconds, and I wondered briefly if it had been a good idea.

The driver eased himself out of the car and worked his way around to my side, but I was already opening the door.

The shrieking nearly punctured an eardrum, and I was pretty sure every dog within a ten mile radius must have pricked up its ears.

I felt like a real fraud when they all started screaming 'Nuriel' because hell, I hadn't even shot so much as one frame of film yet.

But someone pushed a pen into my hand and I started signing my name. I nearly bust a gut laughing when I saw that Clare was being asked to autograph stuff, too.

"No, no!" she whimpered, sounding alarmed. "I'm not an actress, honest!"

But she didn't get away with it, so she was standing next to me signing away. It was pretty damn funny.

Then we got our photos taken with all of the kids and some of their mums, and I was fairly certain it was one of the mothers who copped a feel while I wasn't looking—I was damn sure there was a hand on my ass that wasn't mine. Then Clare took over camera duties, and I smiled until my face was aching.

All the kids were really sweet and one little girl gave me a teddy bear wearing a t-shirt that said 'Somebody in Sonoma Loves You!'.

"Wow! Thank you!" I said. "I haven't had a teddy bear in ages—and this is a really brilliant one."

I smiled at her, and she burst into tears.

Shit!

"Hey, don't cry!"

"It's okay," said a woman, who I assumed was her mum. "She's just excited to meet you. We've been waiting here since after lunch. Yours is the first car that's stopped. Thank you so much. You've really made her day."

"What's your name, sweetheart?" Clare asked, gently.

"Reese," came the answer, as the girl wiped her sleeve across her nose.

"Well, Reese, would you like to get a hug from Nuriel?"

She nodded slowly, so I knelt down beside her and put my arm loosely around her shoulders. She giggled and got all shy, which was so damn cute. Then Clare took a ton of pictures with her mum's camera.

It felt good, doing something so simple that made a little girl smile.

Fuck, I was turning into a real sap! Not that I cared. Well, it was definitely worth it. My bear was cool.

Even Clare got some swag, because I saw her stuffing a chocolate brownie in her mouth that she'd been given by another mum. I tried to trade with her when we were back in the car, but I was too slow.

"Wow, that was amazing!" she said, as we drove away. "They were so nice! And they'd been standing there for four hours! Did you hear what that girl said? She only looked like she was about eight."

"Yeah, it's pretty humbling, but I know it's to do with the book—not me."

Clare rolled her eyes. "I wouldn't bet on it." Then she grabbed my bear. "Come to mummy!"

Clare was laughing at me. Well, that was nothing new, but I had to admit her impersonation was pretty damn spot on.

"Can someone wipe the sweat off Miles' brow, please! Can someone get Miles a coffee? Can someone wipe your ass, Miles?"

We'd been on location for two days, and I had to admit, the whole 'being waited on hand and foot' was pretty easy to get used to. But Clare was making me pay for it.

"Don't worry," she laughed, "I'll keep it 'real' for you. I won't let you get big-headed."

"Thanks, I think."

But she was right, about the hierarchy on the set, I mean. I hadn't really expected that—or thought about it much. On the few TV jobs I'd had, I'd been little more than a walk-on, so had just kind of faded into the background. But now I was one of 'the principals' (that included me, Lilia, and the actors playing her parents), and the background artists—the extras —weren't supposed to talk to us unless we approached them. The first morning I lined up at the lunch truck like the rest of the crew, and one of the Production Assistants had to bring me back to my trailer. It was embarrassing, but apparently I was cramping everyone else's style by trying to hang out with them. I felt like such a douche bag.

I could see how it might turn your head, all the attention, I mean. But also, I wasn't allowed to do anything that wasn't on my call sheet. And no one could even move a chair if they weren't in the right union—I nearly caused a strike when I tried to help move a light.

For the six weeks of the shoot, I wouldn't have to lift a finger. No laundry, no washing up, living in a cocoon.

Easy.

"You missed the fucking mark again, Miles! Jesus Christ, what is this? Amateur half hour? Goddamnit! Everyone take five before we do fuckin' Take 947!"

Jerk.

I tried not to show how humiliated I was by the comment, but when Merv the cameraman couldn't meet my eye, I felt even worse.

I risked glancing toward Clare—I could see the rage burning in her eyes and I felt a little better. She cared. I knew she cared.

The first few days of filming had been amazing—I felt like I was flying.

Lilia had been sweet and really helpful. She'd even made an effort to get to know Clare, although that hadn't gone quite so well. I was pissed at Clare for not even trying but I knew she wouldn't change. God, she was stubborn.

Jo-Anne had made me feel relaxed, like I could really do this, and watching the rushes at the end of the day had been brilliant. I mean, yeah, it was excruciating watching myself on screen, but I could see that Lilia and I really had something—chemistry or whatever.

But the shit hit the fan at the end of the first week. Jo-Anne got rear ended on the freeway and was in hospital with whiplash, internal bruising, and concussion. Apparently, she'd screamed blue murder when she was told she had to stay in hospital, but had been silenced when the studio said that the whole film's insurance would be invalidated if she came back to the set before the docs signed her off.

They'd made the decision to hire another director rather than close down the shoot until Jo-Anne was well.

I wasn't too sure about their choice, because Ron Paulini was known more for his *wham-bam-thank-you-ma'am shoot 'em ups* than sensitive teenage angst shit. I mean, the guy could nail a car chase and an explosion, but emotions—not so much. Maybe he was all they could find at short notice.

And he *really* hated me.

I wasn't entirely sure why: because I was British, maybe, and pretty obviously inexperienced, although Jo-Anne had never made an issue of it.

The first day with him had been shit. And then it got worse. Whatever I did, he yelled at me. Not in private, but in front of the whole crew. I was in fucking pieces by the end of that day. Clare was already simmering with fury when Lilia came over to my trailer—she'd backed me up all the way, which helped. She even managed to get Clare onside, so maybe it was worth it—they were the two most important women in my life right now.

The bullying had become worse, and I didn't know what to do.

"You've got to tell Rhonda," said Clare. "She should know what this wanker is doing. I mean, bloody hell, you're the leading man. He can't do this!"

"Guy seriously has a God-complex," agreed Lilia. "I've been doing movies and commercials since I was nine, and I've *never* seen anything like this before. I don't know how you stay so calm."

Her comment surprised me. I didn't feel calm—I felt like I was drowning.

A PA tapped on the door, throwing me a sympathetic look.

"Five minutes, Miss Purcell, Mr. Stephens."

"Yeah, all right," I mumbled, before slumping into a chair.

Lilia waited until the PA had gone, and spoke quietly.

"Clare's right. Call your agent. She won't put up with this shit."

Then she leaned down to kiss my cheek. My skin heated up at the touch of her lips and I felt my dick twitch. I ignored Clare's scowl and took a deep breath, ready to go out and face the wrath of Pencil Dick Paulini. Yeah, I knew the nickname was childish, but it was all I could come up with. Besides, it suited him.

The scene we'd been working on during the morning was set in the desert, but there was a lot of SFX stuff—dry ice and a burning bush. A magical waterfall was going to be CGIed in later.

I watched, intrigued, as Paulini personally adjusted everything in minute detail: cameras, lights, amount of smoke. It was obvious he was pissing off the crew by trying to do their jobs or checking up on them as if they didn't know what they were doing. At least it wasn't just me. But hell, he even had the sand on the ground brushed *twice* before the shot. Guy seriously had a broom up his arse.

"Okay, that's good," he finally admitted, surveying the handiwork of his fiefdom. "Quiet on set. Roll cameras..."

Someone called out, "Speed."

Paulini squinted, then called, "Mark ... And action..."

One of the braver PAs interrupted him quietly. "Um, Mr. Paulini, don't we need the actors for this scene?"

I wanted to laugh at the expression of fury on his face.

"Fucking actors!" he snarled.

What a tosser. *Yeah, suck it up, Adolf! You still need us.*

He only made me do seven takes, which was rubbish, but a hell of a lot better than earlier that day. He even yelled at Lilia, and I thought we'd be seeing his guts hanging out through his stupid Hawaiian shirt. But she simply said the heat was making her feel faint, and retired to her trailer.

"I'd really like to make a film without actors," he snarled.

He was stuffed now—he couldn't get the shot, and he couldn't order her back on set if she was ill. And he needed the film in the can. He'd just messed with the wrong woman. For the first time, it occurred to me that I wasn't quite as powerless as I thought either.

Except for the fact that I was still expecting to get fired.

Clare

I swear I wasn't doing anything stupid. Not really. I mean, it was 90 degree heat out there. All I did was bend down to pick up my water bottle.

"What the fuck are you doing, you stupid bitch?!" roared Paulini.

At me! Bloody hell!

I had no idea what I'd done wrong, and I stood there clutching my water, while everyone else tried to work out what had happened.

Miles stared at me in confusion and Lilia tapped her foot, looking irritated. A couple of the crew raced over to shade the actors with umbrellas, keeping the scorching sun from frying their brains. It was too late for Pencil Dick.

"You're in my fucking eyeline!" he yelled at me, spittle shooting from his ugly mug. "Are you so fucking stupid that you can't comprehend that?"

I opened my mouth to tell him to go to hell, but with two long strides, Miles was in his face.

"Don't you bloody talk to her like that, you bullying bastard!" he shouted. "Apologize!"

Everyone looked shocked. Miles had been nothing but quietly spoken and polite on the set, despite extreme provocation by the dickless wonder who was currently calling himself director.

"Oh, just great," snarled Paulini. "Now the fucking fag actor has his panties in a bunch about his lesbo girlfriend."

Excuse me, what?

I suppose everyone has their breaking point, and Miles had just reached his. Because that's when he hit him.

Suddenly, Paulini was on his arse in the dust and I heard an ironic cheer go up from the crew. They didn't like him either.

Paulini's face went purple, and I thought he was going to

spontaneously combust. I'd seen a TV program about that once and wondered if it was really possible. Not in this case, unfortunately.

Paulini pulled out his phone and stabbed the keypad three times in quick succession.

"You're history, buddy!" he mumbled, through a lip that was swelling faster than a porn star in a brothel.

Miles ignored him and walked over to me.

"You all right?" he asked, his voice quiet and calm.

"Uh, yeah," I said, slightly shocked that Miles had come over all macho. And defending my honour, too. It made me want to hump his leg, or something. You know, 90 degrees—bitch in heat.

Miles just handed me my water bottle—I hadn't even realized I'd dropped it—then he put his arm around my shoulders and led me toward his trailer.

God, it was so romantic! I mean, in front of everyone, too. Maybe if I pretended to trip, he'd carry me in his arms, just like Richard Gere in *An Officer and a Gentleman*.

But we were back at his trailer before I had time to hunt for a gopher hole.

And then the police arrived.

The dipshit dickhead director had actually called the cops! Un-fucking-believable!

But then again ... *oh, shit*.

Miles didn't even complain when the cops cuffed him. I could tell they were embarrassed but it wasn't like Miles could deny hitting the ugly wanker. Paulini was still looking like an extra from a horror movie, and Miles had a cut across the knuckles of his left hand. Plus, you know, at least 50 witnesses.

He just gave me a small smile and said, "I think you'd better call Rhonda."

And out of all that chaos, all those people yelling into their cell phones and snapping photos of Miles being taken away, Lilia just stood there, as if she was watching an interesting science demonstration. Her look of calculation was chilling. I didn't like it, and I didn't trust the sleazy sow.

But by then I was feeling a bit panicky and tearful, too. I called Rhonda.

Of course, I got her snotty PA.

"Ms Weitz is in a meeting," she sniffed.

"Yeah, well, this is an emergency," I yelled, "so put her on the bloody phone."

"Who did you say you are?"

"Clare Milt ... Miles Stephens' personal assistant. So shuffle your bony backside and get Rhonda!"

"Ma'am, there's no need to be offensive. I would be within my rights to terminate this call."

I'll terminate you in a minute, you titless braindead bint!

I took a deep breath, knowing that losing my cool (or whatever hold on my temper I had left) would definitely not help Miles.

"Then perhaps you would be so kind as to inform Ms Weitz," I said, sweetly, "that her star client has just been arrested, and if she doesn't do something about it, the whole film production is going to be stuffed up quicker than a tutu at a bishop's picnic!"

I mean, come on! How much more plainly could I put it?

There was a pause. A really long pause. What was she doing? Polishing her fangs?

"I'll get Ms Weitz."

"Good idea, luv," I replied, not at all sarcastically. For me.

I thought I'd perforated an eardrum when Rhonda's gazillion decibel shriek pierced the airwaves.

"Who is this? Is this a freakin' joke?"

"Bloody hell, Rhonda! It's not a flaming joke. And this is Clare. Miles has been arrested for thumping Paulini."

"Are you shittin' me?"

Charming.

"I'm serious. That Paulini bloke has been a right bastard since he got here. It's about time somebody pasted one on him—it just happened to be Miles. The dickless wonder called the cops and *I'm* calling *you*."

I had to hold the phone away from my ear for several seconds but eventually Rhonda got a grip.

"Listen, sweetheart," she snapped, "this is what you do. Get down to the precinct and try and get a message to Miles. Tell him not to talk to anyone, you hear me, *anyone*. The studio's lawyers will catch the next flight out and be there ... in about three hours."

I could tell she was about to end the call.

"Um, Rhonda, there's something else."

"What now?"

"Er, well, people on set were taking photos of Miles on their cell phones. Um, you know, with the police and with, er, handcuffs on."

"What the fuck were security doing? There aren't supposed to be any cell phones on the set."

Huh. That was news to me.

"Well, there were. So..."

She didn't need me to finish the sentence—the news would be all over the internet by now.

We were screwed.

Chapter Nine

COOL HAND PUKE

Miles

Just in case it happens to you—and you're a bloke—try not to get arrested while you're wearing makeup. Seriously. It just makes things a lot tougher.

The policemen who'd carted me off from the film set were pretty nice, considering. Watching Paulini ranting and frothing at the mouth, one of them had muttered that he felt like clobbering him, too. Okay, he may not have said 'clobbering'—he actually said something like, 'I'm going to hit that fat fucker onto his candy ass if he tells me how to do my job again'.

They told me that the cuffs were routine and I didn't feel like arguing. I wasn't sorry I'd hit the bald git—bastard totally deserved the fat lip I'd given him, but the repercussions of what I'd done were beginning to sink in. I'd blown it. And it was only a matter of time before I got fired. I wouldn't blame them either.

When we got to the police station, I had my fingerprints and mugshot taken, and was stuffed into a cell with a couple of really fucking enormous biker guys with more ink than a tattooed lady. And I was there in skinny jeans, a white silk shirt, foundation, lipstick, eyeliner and mascara.

And they were stumbling around drunk.

Fun times.

"What the fuck are you?"

I tried ignoring them.

"He sure is purty, huh, Floyd?"

And they laughed like it was the funniest thing ever. I hoped they didn't try a career in stand-up or they'd starve.

"Yeah, I think he's been playing with his mommy's makeup. Come on pretty boy, kissy kiss kiss."

Bastard had breath like the bottom of a parrot's cage. I stood up straight and looked him in the eye but didn't reply.

"I'm talking to you, mother fucker!" he slurred.

I really should have kept my mouth shut.

But I didn't.

"Yeah, I think I remember your mum."

His eyes widened for a moment and then he charged. Damn—250 pounds of mean bastard getting ready to spread my internal organs all over the cell until it looked like a Pollock original.

I dodged out of his way, and the stupid arse ran head first into the wall. It was like watching one of those cartoon characters, and I expected someone to yell out 'Timberrrr!' as he fell.

Then his friend swung a punch and when I blocked it, I thought it was going to snap my arm in half. That shit hurt! But I wasn't going to risk breaking my hand on a jaw that looked like it had been set in concrete, so I went for his bulging gut instead. I got in two quick punches, where my fists sank in up to my wrist. He gasped ... and then he puked.

I got caught in the splatter pattern even though I'd jumped back. It was like the scene from *Cool Hand Luke* where Paul Newman had eaten all the boiled eggs. Bloody hell, it even *smelled* like eggs—rotten ones.

I felt my stomach dry heave just looking at the mess.

I backed away from both of them and kept an eye open in case they looked like they were capable of having another go at me. Then I heard feet pounding down the corridor outside, and a couple of cops yanked open the cell door.

"Um, I don't think they were feeling well," I said, hoping to hell I wouldn't be done for assault twice in one day.

The older cop tried to hide a smile. "We may not be the big city here, son, but we've got CCTV."

He pointed up to the corner, and I saw the leery red eye of a camera winking at me.

"Oh." *Yeah, not a lot I could say to that.*

"You've got some nice moves," he said, "for a movie actor."

"Um, thanks?"

He smiled and shook his head.

"We'll move you to a quieter holding cell that's just been vacated, son. And we've had a call—your people are on their way."

He was good to his word. They moved me to an empty cell that didn't smell of vomit. Although I did, thanks to Dumb and Dumber down the corridor.

I rinsed off my shoes in the tiny sink, and rubbed at the bottom of my jeans with a paper towel. It helped a bit.

I couldn't help thinking about what the cop had said: my 'people' were on their way. That had to mean the studio. Oh well, it had been fun. I just hoped they wouldn't make me give back what I'd been paid so far. Because I didn't have it. I mean, I had some of it, but I'd had to cough up for the apartment, and I'd given a load to Mum. I *couldn't* ask for that back.

Four hours later I was bored out of my brain, hungry, and wondering if I'd made it into the Guinness record books for the shortest film career in history.

I heard the cell door clang open and looked up to see Rhonda staring down at me. Honestly, she scared me more than the two biker guys, although there was a resemblance.

"Well, this is a fucked up situation," she said.

Her voice was surprisingly calm, and I eyed her warily. I was *really* glad that the cell had CCTV, because I was afraid she was going to castrate me with her bare hands.

"Chill out, Miles," she said. "You're free to go."

"Really?"

"Yeah, really. Paulini's dropped the charges."

It was hard work getting that concept to connect with my mouth.

"But why? I mean, that's great ... but why? That effing bastard hates me."

"That is true, but one of the cameramen emailed footage of the asshat in action. The studio fat cats won't stand for that abusive shit ... the backers don't like controversy. Plus, Lilia threatened to walk if she had to work with him. Basically, Miles, the crew—and Lilia—saved your ass. Guess they like you."

"Blimey."

"You said it. Now let's get you back to your hotel. You look like shit and smell worse."

"But ... I mean, that's brilliant, but I did hit him."

"Yeah, I've seen the footage. Nice left hook, by the way." She sighed. "Basically, he was paid to drop the charges. It wasn't a lot, bearing in mind how much he'd pissed off Lilia..."

"Am I in trouble with the studio? Am I going to get fired, as well?"

For a moment she pinned me with her fierce gaze, and then she smiled. That was pretty frightening, too.

"No, you're not. The whole section of footage—Paulini yelling at Clare, you punching him—it got *accidentally* released to the press. Turns out the public really like a guy who'll stand up for a damsel in distress. The publicity people are pissing themselves with pleasure."

"Oh."

"Yeah."

And that was that.

Clare

When Miles was taken away, I was in a complete panic. The only time something like that had happened before was when he'd passed out in his mum's garden, drunk on cheap cider after my 16th birthday. He'd lost his key, didn't want to wake his mum, so planned on sleeping it off in the garden.

In December.

Twit.

The police had found him and taken him away to keep him safe. He got a rap on the knuckles but nothing more serious.

But this business with Paulini, that was *very* bloody serious.

Then Merv the Perv wandered over and gave me a one-armed hug. His nickname was just because he was the lead cameraman and spent the whole day looking down a long lens —he was actually a really nice guy.

"Don't stress it, Clare, honey," he said. "Paulini is history —we're gonna fix his wagon-butt good."

Or he may have said, "We're going to fix his wagon, but good."

I wasn't sure—but he told me not to worry. *Of course I was worrying!*

"Seriously, honey, Paulini can't pull this shit. A certain someone," and here he tapped his nose, "has sent the footage of him flipping out at you to the pap websites. No one likes a bully—your guy will be fine. Promise."

I got a ride to the police station with Polly, one of the PAs that I'd become friendly with, but once we got there I still wasn't allowed to see Miles. I didn't even know if he'd been told I was in the building. And I couldn't give him Rhonda's message. I just hoped he'd be sensible. *Oh God, this was Miles I was talking about.*

It was a real relief when Rhonda turned up, breathing smoke and farting fire. She paraded in some suits that I guessed were lawyers from the studio, and 30 minutes later Miles was released.

He was grinning like a crazy person when I walked up and smacked his arm, hard.

"Don't you ever get arrested on me again, you dope! I'm too young to get white hairs!"

He pulled me into a hug, and damn if his hard chest didn't feel good against me.

"Yeah, but it was worth it," he said, smiling broadly

"Thanks," I mumbled.

"You're welcome," he whispered against my cheek.

But he let go too soon. *He always let go too soon.*

Before we got a chance to really talk, Rhonda swept him off in her limo, and I rode back with Polly.

"You're quiet, Clare. Are you okay?"

I nodded and clapped a hand over my mouth as I yawned.

"Yeah, long day."

She smiled. "Yup, it sure was. But I think someone's got more than a li'l crush on our leading man."

My head snapped up. "Who? Who's got a crush on him?"

She laughed out loud. "You, honey! It's written all over your face. Can't say I blame you. Does he know?"

I was flummoxed. In all the years I'd known Miles no one had *ever* called me on being totally and utterly in love with him.

I glanced over at Polly, but her smile was sympathetic, and I felt my whole body sag.

"No. He has absolutely no clue. We've been friends since we were kids. That's all he sees me as—a friend. It's so frustrating."

She nodded. "Yeah, I get that. But it's also obvious that he cares about you. I mean, wow! If some guy punched out an asshat for me, I wouldn't be holding back anything. I think you should tell him how you feel."

"But that'll just make everything weird. I don't want to lose my best friend. And anyway, he's ... well ... gorgeous, and I'm just ... me."

She didn't argue so I knew she agreed with me.

"Tough one," she said, and shrugged.

Too right.

But I couldn't help thinking ... maybe, just maybe she was

right. Miles had risked everything with that punch, just because some tosser with a bald bonce had yelled at me.

I decided that maybe I *should* tell Miles how I felt. I was just afraid of what I had to lose.

I needed a drink. Maybe several. Not enough to make me pass out, just enough to give me the courage I was sorely lacking. And if things went horribly wrong, I'd just laugh it off and say it was the whiskey talking.

Brave, Milton. Brave.

There was a party atmosphere when we drove up to the private hotel where we were staying.

Since the working day had ended early, the crew were sitting on the back lawn, beers in hand, enjoying the stunning view into the valley, and the peace that came with having slain the wicked whacko of the west.

Miles was nowhere to be seen and neither was Rhonda. I assumed they were talking business and I wondered if I should be there with him. But Merv shoved a beer into my hand and wouldn't take no for an answer.

"We're celebrating, little lady," he said. "Your boy done good."

Just then a cheer went up, and I couldn't help smiling as Jo-Anne limped toward us. She had a sling supporting her right arm, a brace around her neck, and the biggest smile I'd seen outside of a toothpaste advert.

"Yo, Jo!" shouted Merv. "Where you been, honey!"

"Oh, chilln', you know!" she laughed. "Sounds like I've missed the real action."

"Yeah, but I got it on slo-mo," snorted Merv. "You'll love this shit!"

He flipped open his laptop and we all crowded around, watching Paulini bite the dust in close-up. I was a bit annoyed that the picture had caught me with my mouth hanging open like a sad cod, but it was cool seeing Miles in action again. And again. And again.

A shiver went through me. Yes, he did that for me. I *had* to tell him how I felt.

As soon as he got here, I'd tell him and...

He walked out, blinking at the brightness of the sun, his hair glinting gold. And that flaming fleabag floozie *Lilia* was hanging onto his arm.

I could tell by the glazed expression on his face that I was too damn late. The bitch-face had staked a claim.

I had no chance.

"Hey, slugger!" yelled Jo-Anne. "I never knew you missed me so much! Ya didn't have to break Paulini's face—all you had to do was ask nicely and I'd have come back anyways!"

Everyone laughed. Everyone who wasn't currently me.

"Next time we'll try to choreograph the fight scene!"

My face was frozen, my upper lip curled in a snarl. *Bitch-face was touching him!*

Then I let the disappointment wash over me. He was with *her* now. Not me. It was never going to be me. And I couldn't blame him.

Miles

Rhonda chewed my ear off all the way back from the police station. I knew I owed her big time for getting Paulini to drop the charges, but I just couldn't listen to the whole speech she was giving me about how to 'spin' the story.

I was slightly annoyed that Clare wasn't with us, but she'd just shrugged and said she was getting a ride with Polly, one of the PAs. I wasn't sure if that was her decision or Rhonda's.

I couldn't wait to get a shower and feel clean again. Having someone else's puke on your clothes—as well as being seriously gross—really puts a downer on the day.

The limo drew up at the hotel, and once we'd climbed out, Rhonda grabbed my arm.

"Don't fuck up again, Miles," she ordered, jabbing her stubby finger into my chest. "Your Get Out Of Jail Free card has now expired. Do we understand each other?"

"Yeah, sure, Rhonda. Thanks for coming up here. I really appreciate it."

I gave her a quick kiss on the cheek, and ran up the stairs to my room.

The shower felt amazing and I was reluctant to leave, but I was hungry, too. I wondered what Clare was doing.

I was only half dressed in a pair of jeans when I heard her knocking on my door. I yanked it open, a huge grin on my face. But it wasn't Clare—it was Lilia. And she was crying.

She launched herself at me and started sobbing into my chest.

"Lilia, what's wrong? Are you okay? Did someone hurt you?"

"I was so w-w-worried," she spluttered. "Were you okay in prison?"

She'd been worried about me? Wow.

"Yeah, I'm fine, and it was just the police station. Maybe if I'd murdered Paulini I'd be in prison." My joke bombed, and it seemed to make her cry harder. "Hey, it's okay, I'm fine. Really."

I wrapped my arms around her slim shoulders, and rocked her gently. She smelled so good, I couldn't help dropping a soft kiss into her long hair.

And that's when it happened.

She smiled up at me, and tightened her arms around my neck. Her lips just looked so damn kissable, I couldn't help myself.

She gave this little gasp and I felt her lips open, her tongue pushing into my mouth, sliding against mine.

And bloody hell! Suddenly, her hands were all over me, scratching down my back, stroking my chest, and when she hitched her left leg over my hip, I automatically reached down to hold it in place.

Her short skirt rode up her thigh, and as I palmed her leg she made these little whimpering moans. The sound went straight to my dick, and I was grinding against her before I knew what I was doing.

She pulled away abruptly, but her smile was blinding.

"We have to stop, Miles," she breathed. "Everyone's

waiting for you downstairs. If we don't make an appearance soon, everyone will assume we're ... you know."

I knew she was speaking, but the words weren't connecting with my brain, and my arms refused to let her go.

She gave this little giggle and pushed against my chest.

"Miles!"

"Oh, shit, sorry! Oh, God, I'm so sorry, Lilia!"

I sprang away from her like I'd been electrocuted. *What the fuck was I thinking?* Oh right, I hadn't been thinking. Not with my brain.

I'd already grabbed a t-shirt and was tugging it over my head, when I heard her soft voice.

"I'm not sorry. I liked it."

I turned around and gaped at her.

"You ... you did?"

"Sure," she said, her eyes sweeping up and down me. "And if it weren't for the fact that the whole crew wants to shake your hand and buy you a drink, you wouldn't be putting clothes *on* right now."

A slow smile crept across my face.

"Is that right?"

"Yes, that's right," she said, the challenge slipping from her face as I took two quick paces toward her again.

This time I kissed her the way I wanted to, and I wasn't the only one getting carried away. She rubbed her hand over my crotch so hard, I was glad I was wearing jeans, otherwise she'd have done some serious damage. But, yeah, it felt good.

I hadn't been with a woman since, jeez, Melissa, and that was five months ago. Maybe more.

My hands slipped down to Lilia's glorious arse, and she squealed when I picked her up so her legs were wrapped around my waist, and walked backward to the bed.

We fell in a heap with Lilia underneath, but I was careful not to crush her with my weight. I felt her hands fisting in the back of my t-shirt and her teeth grazing my neck.

"We can't!" she gasped. "Everyone is waiting!"

"Screw 'em," I mumbled into her hair, kissing my way down her neck.

She pushed my shoulders, and very reluctantly, I rolled onto my back.

"I ... I don't want to rush things," she said, quietly.

I sighed. That was fair enough. And anyway, there was no point making it obvious to the crew. Whatever this was. Her life was tough enough already.

She took a deep breath. "I think we should join the others."

"Yeah, okay, give me a minute."

But lying on the bed with her next to me wasn't really helping with the whole cucumber stuffed down the pants look. I tried to adjust myself but gave up. I pushed off the bed, staggered into the bathroom and stuck my head under the cold tap.

The sudden shock of water helped cool me down.

I toweled dry and watched as Lilia sent a text on her phone.

"Ready to go?"

She looked up, surprised to see me watching her.

"Oh, sure," she said, flushing slightly.

We rode the elevator to the ground floor in uncomfortable silence. I didn't know what to say to her—it was almost like I'd imagined the last ten minutes.

Eventually she spoke.

"Don't say anything to anyone, will you, Miles?"

I frowned. "Course I won't."

"Not even Clare."

"What? Nah, you don't need to worry about her—she's cool, Lilia."

She made a little huffing noise, and I glanced down to see her scowling. She looked gorgeous when she did that.

But after her speech, I was more than a little surprised when she suddenly grabbed hold of my arm as we went outside to catch up with the rest of the crew.

I was so fucking happy when I realized Jo-Anne was there, and clearly intending to get back to directing duties.

"Hey, Slugger!" she called, a shit eating grin on her face.

"Blimey, Jo-Anne! How are you?"

She pointed to her sling with her good hand, and raised her eyebrows. "Better than you by the sound of it."

I shook my head.

"Nah, I'm fine now. But I'm going to cover you in bubble wrap so you can't get hurt again."

"I didn't know you were into kinky shit, Miles."

I gave her a big smile and winked at her. I saw Clare watching us out of the corner of my eye.

"Hey, Milton! What's up?"

"Nothing much, you tosser. Hanging around police stations—same shit, different day."

She threw her arms around me, and I lifted her off the floor in a tight hug. "Admit it—you missed me!"

"Never did!" she snorted. "I just didn't have anywhere else to be—it was either the beauty salon or the police station. I chose the path of least resistance. At least you don't smell of vomit now."

"You missed me," I insisted.

"Might have," she muttered.

I gave her a big sloppy kiss and no matter how hard she tried, she couldn't help smiling.

Chapter Ten

WORKING GIRL

Miles

The rest of the shoot was fucking fantastic. After my run-in with Pencil Dick, I was even more appreciative of Jo-Anne. But it was still tiring so Lilia and I couldn't spend as much time together as I'd have liked.

I'm not saying that acting isn't a pretty cushy number, because it is compared to my mum working 45 hours in a supermarket each week, but after a day on set, which could include night shooting—a form of torture in itself—I was too tired to even watch TV.

When we had nearly a week of night shoots, I lived off espresso shots. I think if I could have mainlined the caffeine I would have. I didn't say anything, but I had a feeling that Lilia might have done some speed to keep her awake. But hell, it could have just been killer quantities of Red Bull, so I kept my mouth shut.

Clare was her usual grumpy self, but it was a hard week for everyone, and trying to sleep when it was bright sunshine and 90°F outside was almost impossible. We were all totally wasted by the weekend.

"Oh my God, I'm so tired," yawned Clare. Everything aches. Even my backside is tired and all I've done is sit on it."

"Want me to rub it better?"

She blinked then flipped me off.

"What, no answer?" I grinned at her. "No sassy come back?"

"You should worry!"

"Why's that?"

"When I tell you to bugger off, it's a sign that I care, but when I'm quiet..."

"What?"

"It's a sign that I'm plotting your death."

"Aw, don't say that—you love me really!"

"You're skating on thin ice, Stephens."

"Now, now you two!" laughed Jo-Anne. "You can't beat him up until we've finished principal photography and the film is a wrap."

Clare raised an eyebrow. "Then I can beat him up?"

"He's all yours," smiled Jo-Anne.

Everyone laughed, even though we were exhausted. Clare was great at keeping the mood positive.

Even once the night shoot was over, it was tiring as well as boring—with all the hanging around. Luckily, I had a stand-in for all the lighting set ups, camera angles and stuff. I struggled a bit with having to be able to turn the character on immediately after a long wait—I could see why some actors stayed in character, because it was hard to switch it on and off. But honestly, what sort of a dick would I have sounded like if I insisted on being called 'Nuriel'? Clare did it sometimes, but that was just to piss me off.

And I ate my food from a different truck—going to the front of the queue, which I really hated—so mostly someone would get me a drink or a sandwich. It was usually Clare.

She said she didn't mind, and that as my personal assistant it was her job. But it was useful, too. She picked up a load of gossip as she wandered around the set—who was sleeping with who, and who wasn't but wanted to.

Despite all the adjustments, the weirdness, and the long hours—I loved it. But what surprised me the most was that Clare seemed to love it, too.

"I can see why you like this, Miles, I sort of get it now. It's like..." and she chewed on a thumbnail while she searched for the words, "it's like the connection of ... people, of being human or something. Does that make any sort of sense whatsoever?"

"I think I know what you mean: it's belonging, but it's an escape, too."

She sighed. "If it weren't for all the other stuff," and she waved her hand around, "you know, the media crap, stylists, and all that—yeah, I sort of get it now."

I shook my head. "That's just a distraction. I love that we're creating something here. Everyone coming together—what we create is greater than the sum of what we put in individually."

Clare stared at me.

"What? I'm not allowed to have deep thoughts because I'm just a shallow actor?"

"I never thought you were shallow," she said, and a strange expression crossed her face and was rapidly gone. "So, are you ready with the new dialogue?"

Without telling anyone, Jo-Anne and Clare had been tweaking my speech on one of the key scenes in the film—the one where Nuriel tells Esther that he's in love with her. I'd been stressing over it, because it just didn't work in rehearsals. Clare had made some suggestions and they were brilliant, but we'd had to keep it quiet because there was a writers' strike going on, and Jo-Anne would have been in the shit if anyone had found out that the work wasn't hers.

I was sitting in my trailer, going over the scene again, when I was called to the set. Lilia's dialogue would be filmed separately and cut in later, so for now, I had to deliver my epic speech declaring undying love straight into a camera lens. I think that's what they call acting. Yeah, I know, but I needed somebody to react to.

"Um, Jo-Anne, could ... um ... you know, it would really help me if Lilia was standing behind the camera reading her lines, just so..."

She frowned. "She's getting into costume, Miles. You'll have to make do with Clare."

Shit. That was going to be weird, declaring my undying love to Clare. If she laughed at me, it would be so fucking humiliating.

"Clare, can you stand behind camera one, please? Do you have the script?"

I was surprised to see that Clare looked almost as embarrassed as me, but she took her place and gave me a thumbs up.

Okay. I could do this.

"Mark it ... cameras rolling... action!"

Clare's voice came out in a dull monotone. *"What do you want to say that's so darned important, Nuriel?"*

"I think I understand now—I really do."

"What do you understand?"

"God wasn't punishing me, when he sent me to Earth, I mean. I thought that was his reason, but I was wrong. How could he have been punishing me when I met you? I've learned—so much. Because of you. You. You're the reason this all makes sense. You're everything. You're my forever. I love you."

There was a long silence then Jo-Anne cleared her throat. "Wow, Miles. In one take. That was awesome."

"Really?"

I glanced over at Clare. She looked like she was about to cry. I had no idea why. Was it that bad?

Clare

The rest of the shoot was going well. If you didn't count the unseasonal torrential rain that washed away half the set, of course. Oh, and Bitch-face drooling all over Miles in the most obvious and disgusting way. But at least no one else had been arrested, although I was still contemplating assault on her scraggy arse.

And there was this writers' strike that meant there wasn't anyone available for rewrites on the set. Apparently that happens quite a lot. I mean, the rewrites, not the strikes. We didn't say anything, but Jo-Anne had helped me to tinker with some of Miles' dialogue on a couple of the scenes. As far as everyone else was concerned, Jo-Anne had made the changes. It was easier that way.

And it was obvious to *everyone* that Miles and Lilia were screwing. I mean, soooo obvious.

I knew Miles well enough to read the signs, but that wasn't necessary because the way that crotch-faced slut draped herself all over him, it made me sick to my gut. I wanted to bitch-slap her from the moment I woke up in the morning, to the moment I fell asleep at night. As well as in my dreams. Obviously.

I couldn't believe that Miles had fallen for her act. Okay, I *could* believe it, because Miles never thought anything bad about anyone. But I knew, *I knew* that it was all part of the career game to her. *I knew* she didn't really care about him.

And oh dear, just look at all those photographs of the two of them that just happened to have been leaked to the press. Well, goodness gracious, how did that happen? *Coincidence, my arse!*

I was pretty certain that Lilia was behind the photographs and gossip that they were an item, but she must have had help from somebody—I just wish I knew who it was. Despite the fact that cameras had been banned from the set after the Pencil Dick incident, along with all cell phones, the pictures kept on appearing. Jo-Anne was furious, and security was tightened, but it didn't seem to make much difference. The gossip mill was grinding away at full speed.

The headlines said things like:

Lilia in Love
Heavenly Bodies
Divine Intervention.

And one particularly nauseating header: *Angel wings and butterfly kisses.*

Jeez. Who wrote this rubbish?

But now it was the day I'd been dreading—*the sex scene.*

Filming was going to take place on a closed set, so I wouldn't even get to see what was happening until the rushes were shown in the evening. And I wasn't sure if I was pleased about that or not. Did I really want to see Miles pretending to make love to that skank? No, not really, but at the same time I didn't trust her skinny butt any further than I could spit.

Miles was hyped up and anxious as we sat in Mildred's makeup trailer.

He'd had to take his clothes off an hour beforehand to eliminate any red marks. I mean, sock lines just aren't sexy—not even David Gandy can get away with that. Although I probably wouldn't be looking at his ankles, should the opportunity arise.

The CGI people could get rid of any imperfections later, but it was expensive to do—or so I was told. Which was the reason why Miles was wearing a thin, cotton robe that was open to his waist, and Mildred—who was almost old enough to be his grandmother—was drooling onto her makeup brushes.

"This is going to be seriously weird," he muttered. "Fuck, what if I get, you know ... what if I get a boner?"

Oh, just shoot me now.

"Honey, all you've got to worry about is if you don't," said Mildred.

"What?" croaked Miles, sounding shocked.

"What?" I echoed, sounding homicidal.

Mildred smiled.

"Actresses have huge egos along with huge inferiority complexes—if you don't plant a redwood while you're thrusting, she'll take it as a rejection."

"Please tell me you're joking, Mildred!" begged Miles.

"Sorry, sweet cheeks," she said, not sounding sorry at all.

I wanted to shove her makeup brushes where the sun don't necessarily shine.

Luckily for her, Mildred snuck out to get a coffee, and I was left trying to calm Miles.

"This is going to be so weird," he said again. "Um, because, um..." he rubbed the back of his neck and threw me a nervous glance, "um because, well, Lilia and I, we've kinda, um ... like..."

"Oh, give me a break, Miles! You're boning her. I know."

"What?" he said, sounding surprised. "How did you know?"

"Are you serious?! Everyone knows. I mean, could she be any more obvious. So, yeah, it's common knowledge." *And how could you?*

He hung his head and scrunched up his eyes. I had to grab his hand to stop him rubbing his face and ruining all Mildred's work.

"I ... I really like her, Clare. She's so amazing. And she's really helped me, with the film and everything."

Yeah, yeah, heard it all before. I wanted to yell at him, *You always fall in love with your leading ladies, you idiot!* But I didn't. Of course I didn't.

He shook his head. "But this ... today ... it'll be like showing everyone something ... private, you know?"

Not really, no.

"And if I do get a hard-on—it'll be so fucking humiliating. But what Mildred said..."

"She's a shriveled old hag, don't worry about her. She's just jealous." *Like me.* "I tell you what, when you're on top of Lilia," *ugh, ugh, ugh,* "just imagine that you're screwing Mildred. That should reduce your testicles to the size of acorns."

He looked like he was going to vomit.

"You think?"

"Ha! It's working already, isn't it?"

"Bloody hell," he mumbled. "Thanks, Clare."

One of the PAs that I didn't know very well knocked on the door.

"You're wanted in the costume trailer."

"Oh shit," whispered Miles.

I was confused. "What costume?"

Miles closed his eyes. "It's for the merkin."

"The what?"

"Like an athletic cup... you know, to cover up the meat and two veg."

Oh?

Oh!

Ouch.

"I'll, um, I'll wander over with you," I said, trying to sound casual, although it wasn't easy, not with the thought of someone getting up close and personal with Miles' equipment —someone who wasn't me. Again.

He shuffled his feet into a pair of flip flops, reluctance oozing from every pore. Most days, it was evident that he loved what he did, the whole acting thing. Today wasn't one of those days.

We walked solemnly to the costume trailer, and I couldn't stand the silence. So it ended up with me talking non-stop about some of the things we planned to do once we got back to LA, and our hopes to get in a quick visit to San Francisco when he had a day free. I was trying to take his mind off things, but I don't think it helped.

I left him at the door, but he stopped and grabbed my hand, desperation in his voice.

"Don't leave me, Clare!"

"Miles, I love you loads, but I truly don't want to watch you getting your tackle taped up."

He almost smiled. "Me neither! I'm not asking you to. You could look the other way or ... just stay, please?"

I couldn't say no to him. Sigh.

The merkin man was a guy called Leon. He'd handled todgers for a number of movie stars. Maybe it was his specialty. I couldn't help wondering what he put on his business cards: *Chunk your Junk—Jewel Handler to the Stars?*

I sat at his table, examining the weird-looking thing. It was halfway between a single bra cup and a jockstrap—except there were no ties or elastic.

Leon picked up the merkin from my sweaty hands, and I turned my back while the business was concluded.

"First time, Miles?" the guy asked.

I didn't hear a reply. Perhaps Miles nodded. Perhaps he'd lost the power of speech—or maybe just the will to live.

"Okay, relax, man. It'll feel a bit weird as the glue goes on."

"Glue?!" My voice had gone up a couple of octaves.

Leon chuckled. "Yeah, it works better if the area has been, um, shaved. This'll hurt like hell when you take it off."

"Great," muttered Miles, sounding even more miserable.

Maybe thinking about the pain would take his mind off the arising situation.

"Wow, weird," said Miles after a few moments of rustling.

"Yeah, it's the GI Joe doll look," agreed Leon. "Just one thing: the glue tends to loosen up if you get hot or if you get a stiffy. Get one of the PAs to give me a call and I'll come fix you up."

I heard Miles take a deep breath.

"Got it," he said.

As we made our way to the set, Miles threw me a panicked look.

"Well, um, break a leg," I said, cheerfully. *Preferably hers.*

"Aren't you coming in?"

"Can't. Closed set."

At that moment Jo-Anne breezed past us, a clipboard shoved under her good arm.

"Where the hell's Polly?" she snapped.

"Working with the second unit," somebody answered.

"Ah hell, I forgot that. Clare, you busy? No? Good. Come with me."

I didn't have time to say a single word before she thrust the clipboard at me, and I was ushered inside.

Boy, it was hot, and they hadn't even got the lights on yet. The studio was tiny, crammed with bodies and... The Bed.

The Bed was large and white—very comfortable looking,

except for all the cables and spotlights that surrounded it. All a bit BDSM for a PG13 film, I thought.

Despite the fact it was supposed to be a closed set, there were a surprising number of people squeezing their way into the crowded space. As well as Jo-Anne, there was the gaffer—that's the electrician; the woman holding the boom mike; two cameramen; another sound guy; the script supervisor, who was in charge of continuity; and a prop woman—ready with her pre-prepared, spray on sweat, made from rosewater and glycerin.

Oh, and me, acting as Jo-Anne's gofer and note taker, because her writing hand was still in a sling.

Looking like a condemned man, Miles dragged himself toward the bed.

"Yeah, just drop the robe and make yourself comfortable," said Jo-Anne, sounding calm and relaxed.

Her easy-going attitude was going to make this a lot more bearable for everyone. I couldn't imagine the levels of ghastliness if that slimeball Paulini was still involved.

Miles shrugged out of his robe, and dropped it by his side of the bed. Most people averted their eyes to give him some privacy. Most. What can I say? If no one wanted me to see, they should have given me blinkers, you know, like on a carthorse's bridle.

My eyes watered just looking at that delicious V-shape, those rippling abs and, well, just, yum. But jeez, that jerkin, I mean merkin, was weird. But kind of hard to take your eyes off it, too.

Lilia swanned in a minute later, looking cool. *Yeah, you could probably freeze helium on her pointy arse.*

"Ready for a bit of horizontal Fred and Ginger?" said Jo-Anne, and everyone laughed quietly. "Yeah, it'll be about as sexy as a game of Twister—probably less so," she smiled.

She sat on the bed with Miles and Lilia, talking quietly. I could see them listening intently, nodding from time to time, a small frown of concentration on Miles' lovely face.

And then they got into position.

Miles was lying on his back and Lilia was straddling him, her bony carcass on display. Hell, I could have played *Bohemian Rhapsody* on her spine.

Then the cameras whirred.

Lilia ran her fingers down Miles' bare arm—I wanted to snap them off.

She let her long hair sweep across his fine, fine chest—I wanted to yank it out by the roots.

And when she kissed him, it was all I could do not to leap out of my chair, grab her by the windpipe and choke the ever living crap out of her.

But I didn't.

Jo-Anne called a temporary halt while the camera positions were adjusted, and I took a much needed gulp of water. Vodka would have been better. Miles threw me an anxious look, and I returned a tight smile, but then the she-devil whispered something in his ear and I wanted to wipe that look off her face with a cold kipper wrapped around my fist.

How could he stand it? When she puckered her lips she looked like a fish on the end of a hook. *Trout-faced trollop.*

Once the cameras angles were altered, I endured an unendurable ten minutes watching Miles run his hand down Lilia's arm. It was a sweet, sensual, loving movement. So tender, it hurt.

And if that wasn't bad enough, Jo-Anne had them switch positions, and there was another horrendous ten minutes while his body was on top of her, and she ran her hand down his chest to his waist. I nearly vomited on my brand new Vans.

But it got worse, because for the next 25 minutes, and what seemed like a thousand takes, Miles pretended to thrust, with her leg hitched over his hip—I thought I was going to have a meltdown. I was definitely having a hot flush. I mean, *25 minutes of thrusting!*

There was only so much a girl could take.

But when there were quite a few mutterings from the

cameraman about a problem with 'shadowing', we had a 20 minute break while the lights were adjusted.

Miles and Lilia sat back against the headboard, the sheet covering her non-existent tits. They looked so post-coital, I couldn't even look Miles in the face.

Then they started again, Miles thrusting, Lilia moaning, and his tight arse pistoning up and down like a pumpjack at an oil well. *Oh God, for a different image.*

I wanted to scream. I wanted to put my foot through the camera's lens, and dance on the shattered glass. I wanted to claw Lilia's rolling eyes out of her lollipop head and laugh like a hyena while I did it.

But damn it, Miles looked so unbelievably perfect.

I could see all the muscles in his back as he braced himself above her, holding his weight on his arms, staring into her eyes. And I wished it was me. So badly. In what universe was it fair that she got to have him? Just because she was beautiful and talented? Was I so awful? So hideous that he would never choose me? What if I wore a paper bag? What was wrong with *me?*

They changed the camera angles, and there was more thrusting, more moaning. Then a lot more stroking and long, meaningful looks.

Suddenly, Miles swore.

"Problem?" said Jo-Anne.

"The fuckin' merkin's dropped off," he said, cursing freely.

"As long as that's the only thing that's dropped off," said Jo-Anne, with a smile.

Everyone chuckled, and it relieved some of the mounting tension.

"Clare, can you go get Leon, please?" said Jo-Anne.

I was more than happy to leave that sweaty studio and find the merkin man. I knocked on his trailer and listened to a lot of scuffling and some swearing before the door jerked open.

Yeah, and Mildred was standing behind him, looking sort

of, well, sunburned. I couldn't help smirkin' at the merkin man.

"Jo-Anne wants you," I said, pretending nonchalance. "There's been a merkin emergency—Code Red."

He mumbled something to Mildred, who couldn't look me in the eye as she scuttled back to her own trailer. Then Leon picked up his merkin First Aid kit (glue, string, something that looked like an old sock), and we headed back to the studio.

Lilia had slipped back into her robe, and Miles was sitting on the edge of the bed, a sheet draped strategically. He leaned back on his hands and closed his eyes as Leon fiddled about, his head somewhere near Miles' knees.

Oh.

My.

God.

I really can't repeat the images that were pulsing through my brain at that moment, although I fully intended to write them all in my diary later.

After a lot of swearing (from Leon), and a pained expression and several sharp intakes of breath (from Miles), the merkin misadventure was resolved and we were good to go again.

Thrusting, moaning, eye-rolling, heavy breathing, yadda yadda yadda. The sex scene was finished.

Or so we thought.

For the first time, Miles refused to watch the rushes that evening, but a couple of guys in snazzy suits were sitting next to Jo-Anne, watching the images roll over the small screen.

"Don't worry about the sound," she said. "We'll dub in the effects later."

Oh, really? Well, I suppose that there wasn't exactly a convenient place to mike up Miles and Lilia—although I had a thought about where Lilia's microphone could have been hidden.

One of the suits shook his head.

"You're going to have to tone that down, Ms Moody. The MPAA will never pass that. We *need* PG13."

"It hasn't been edited yet," she said, between gritted teeth. "We can fix it in post-production."

Suit number two shook his head. "We'll need some more footage—less ... explicit. We can definitely see some of his ass-crack, and there was nipple action in one section."

"It can be fixed," Jo-Anne insisted.

But the suits weren't listening.

I guess Miles' thrusting was too convincing.

The end result was that a second day of watching sex between Miles and the minging floozy was scheduled for the following day. Believe me, *no one* was happy about that scenario.

Once the suits had left, Jo-Anne was free to vent.

"What the hell do they want?" she fumed. "Do they want to choreograph every thrust themselves?"

I shrugged. "Probably. Or maybe they just want to have a go with Lilia. You know, throw some moves, get in a quick grope."

Jo-Anne laughed. "Oh, hell, yeah! I can really see Lilia going for that—she'd beat the crap out of anyone who tried."

Her shoulders slumped a little, and she covered up a yawn.

"I hate getting this sort of interference from the studio— it's why I mostly stick to working with independents. They trust me to make it the best film I can. But with these guys, they've got the marketing people blowing smoke up their ass, telling them they need this shot or that shot to sell the film. But that doesn't give them license to order my actors around —or me."

She shook her head. "I love this business, I do. But it all comes down to money in the end. It's not even like this is a particularly expensive production—for Hollywood. Damn it, I'm not wasting a day of the schedule just to placate those idiots. I'll see what Trina can do in the edit suite. If I'm not happy, maybe they'll get their reshoot."

Then Jo-Anne looked at me. "But keep that to yourself, Clare. I haven't made a decision yet. Capiche?"

I saluted. "Yup. Message received and understood."

She gave a quick laugh. "And good work on those rewrites, by the way. Something you should think about taking further, honey."

Huh?

I was left with my mouth hanging open unattractively.

Later that evening, Miles met me for a drink in the bar. It was the first time we'd really had any chance to talk since he'd hooked up with the scuzzy ho. She was off meeting with her publicist, probably plotting and stirring her cauldron at the same time. At least it meant I could spend time with my best —sigh—friend.

"I can't believe the studio are making us do all *that* again," he complained.

"Well, it won't be so bad the second time, will it? At least you'll know what to expect." I paused, wondering if he'd drunk enough alcohol to tell me the truth. "So did you? You know, get a chubbie?"

He choked on his beer.

"Oh, hell, Clare!"

"Whoa! You did, didn't you? Is that what caused the merkin mishap?"

"Clare, please! I'm fucking begging you! Never, *never* speak to me of this again."

"Are you kidding? Just think of all the free drinks I could get telling *that* story."

"You wouldn't."

"Well..."

"Clare!"

"No, of course I wouldn't. Chill out, Miles."

"Bloody hell."

"God, the look on your face!"

"You're evil."

I laughed. "You say that like it's something new. You know

I love to torture you. By the way, what did Lilia say? If she noticed, that is."

"You're a bitch," he muttered. "And yeah—she noticed."

Polly walked over to join us. "Hard day?"

I dissolved into laughter, while Miles just closed his eyes and looked like he was praying.

"What did I say?" asked Polly, but from the look on her face, I'd guess she knew *exactly* what she'd said.

"Oh, you know," I wheezed between giggles, "Miles was finding it *hard* to concentrate. In fact I'd say the competition for worst day so far was *stiff*, not to mention that the acting was a little *wooden*."

Polly collapsed onto the bench next to us, tears running down her face at the look Miles was giving me. She patted his knee, which certainly caught my attention.

"Never mind, honey," she said. "Maybe we'll see your sweet face on the Adult Video News awards. Although I don't think they call it an 'Oscar'."

By now, I sounded like I was gurgling, and had spit beer down my t-shirt.

"Yeah, yeah," Miles mumbled. "Laugh it up. I should fire your arse. Yeah, I think I'll do that." He pointed his finger at my chest. "Clare—you're fired."

"'S'all right," I snorted, "you weren't paying me anyway, but you *have* given me plenty of blackmail material—we're good."

He sighed and rubbed his face. "Whatever. Anyway, my mum would kill me if I fired you—and *your* mum would help her bury the body."

Polly chuckled. "You've known Clare forever—you must have some dirt on her!"

Miles' head snapped up, and a wicked grin spread across his face.

"Yeah, I do! *Eli Grant* and his 'tiny todger'." He made air quotes as he said it.

"Don't. You. Dare!" I shouted, making Polly jump.

Miles laughed and leaned back in his seat looking relaxed. "You can dish it out, Clare, but you can't take it."

"Fine," I sulked. "I won't say anything about your *erection on set!*"

Okay, I may have spoken those words *slightly* louder than I meant, because several sets of eyes swiveled in our direction, and Miles groaned.

"Never mind," said Polly, standing and stretching tiredly. "From what I hear, it was nothing to be ashamed of. Keep up the good, um, work, Miles."

"Why are we friends again?" he said to me once she'd gone.

"Aw, you love me really," I said, wrapping my arms around his waist, and planting a squeaky kiss on his cheek.

"Nah," he said. "You're more like a bad habit."

He was joking. I knew he was joking. But I wanted to cry.

Chapter Eleven

CLUELESS

Miles

Clare's time in California was running out. In a couple of weeks, she'd be going home.

It had been a shitty few days, so having her around had been pretty much the only thing that kept me sane.

We'd been sitting in my trailer during a break in filming, and suddenly Rhonda turned up.

She charged in, eyes flashing. She reminded me of Taz, the cartoon Tasmanian Devil—in other words damn scary. I was waiting for smoke to come out of her nose or something.

"Miles!" she snapped, brandishing a newspaper in my face. "Something you forgot to tell me? I have gone *over and over* the importance of *image* with you. And then I get blindsided by this shit! What gives?"

Clare grabbed the newspaper from her and paled slightly as her eyes scanned down the sheet.

"Miles, it's ... about your dad."

What the fuck did that bastard have to do with anything?

She passed me the paper in silence, and I could feel Rhonda's eyes burning into me as I read.

When I'd finished, I pushed the newspaper away from me and looked up.

"Yeah, so?"

Rhonda looked like she was going to explode.

"So?! So?! Miles—this is *serious*! I've got the studio crawling up my ass and I really don't appreciate the view. Talk to me!"

The gist of it was that my bastard of a father had contacted some tabloid newspaper back home, giving them all this crap about how I was living it up in Hollywood, while he was half starving and trying to survive off state handouts, and I wouldn't give him the time of day, and he was in debt and going to get thrown out of his apartment. Blah blah blah.

Like I could give a shit. Bastard hadn't done an honest day's work in his life, and had never once paid Mum any child support. When he walked out, he took every fucking thing that was worth anything, even our TV. And now he was selling this trashy, made-up version of his so-called life.

It made me sick.

"What do you want me to say, Rhonda? He was a shitty father and a git of a husband to my mum. I haven't seen the bastard since I was eight."

Her face softened slightly.

"You've had no contact with him *at all* since then?"

"No."

"Okay ... well ... good. The studio PR people will have to deal. They'll probably pay him to keep his mouth shut and..."

My head snapped up. "What?"

"Miles, this is how it works: the studio don't want this sort of negative publicity. They'll pay him off and..."

"NO!" I yelled, making her stop mid sentence. Okay, so I didn't yell much generally but this shit was *way* out of order. "Rhonda, you don't get it. You *can't* pay that bastard off—he'll just keep on coming back. I *know* him. He won't care what contract you get him to sign—he'll break it. Yeah, you can sue him but it'll be too late and the money will be gone—women, drink, horse races. That's what he does. That's what he's *always* done. Let him sell his hard luck story once. After that, no one will be interested."

She peered over her glasses at me. "You sure about this, Miles?"

"Yeah."

I saw Clare give a staccato nod of her head, and felt relieved that she agreed with me, and she backed me up all the way. She hated him almost as much as I did.

Telling Mum was worse, and because she didn't Skype, I had to do it over the phone.

"Hi, Mum. It's me."

"Miles! Hello, luv, this is a nice surprise. How are you? How's Clare?"

"Yeah, yeah, she's good. How are you?"

"Oh, nothing to complain about. But tell me everything. How's the film going?"

"Um, well..."

She paused, and I could hear the anxiety creeping into her voice.

"Has something happened?"

"Sort of, yeah. It's not ... I don't know..."

"Spit it out, luv."

"It's Dad."

I could practically feel the ice creeping down the phone.

"Your father? What about him?"

"Mum, have you seen the *Daily Mirror* today?"

"No. Why?"

"They've published a story about me ... and him."

I waited for her to respond, but there was nothing. I couldn't even hear her breathing.

"Mum?"

"I'm still here. What did they say?"

"A load of crap and his hard luck story."

"Hard luck! He's lucky he's not in prison. What lies has he been spinning this time?"

"Like I said, just crap. About how I'm making all this money, and he's been frozen out, and is living off benefits. About to evicted. You know, the usual."

"Well, we both know he's a liar, so you mustn't let it worry you, Miles."

"I'm not worried, Mum. Honestly. But the chances are you'll have reporters knocking at your door. Rhonda spoke to Melody in London, and they'll send someone to help you if it gets to be a problem."

She gave a humorless laugh.

"Don't worry about me. Any reporter that comes knocking on my door, I'll send 'em off with a flea in their ear."

"Yeah, I can imagine. But it's probably best if you say 'no comment' to anything anyone says. Or just ignore them."

"Well, if you say so. But I'd love to give them a piece of my mind."

"Yeah, I know."

There was an even longer pause.

"I'm so sorry, luv."

I didn't understand what she meant.

"Why are you sorry? You didn't do anything."

"I'm sorry you didn't have a better father."

I didn't know what to say to that. What could I say? I barely knew the man. We only heard from him when bailiffs came knocking on the door because of some debt he'd run up in mum's name.

"Nah, better off just you and me, Mum."

"You're a good boy, Miles. Look after yourself. Give Clare a hug for me."

"Yeah, thanks, Mum. Bye."

She never liked talking on the phone much.

Clare stood next to me, having heard my half of the conversation.

"How'd it go?"

"She was upset. Apologized for *him* being a fucking awful father." I rubbed my eyes, tiredly. "And she told me to give you a hug."

"Pay up then," she said, wrapping her soft arms around me.

I pulled her closer and rested my head against her neck while she held me.

That had been a bad day, leading to a bad week. The story had been all over the internet, too. The worst thing was that reporters started hounding my mum at work and coming by the house. Luckily, she had some good friends who protected her from the worst of it, and even Melody sent someone to help her, which I thought was pretty decent—even if it was in the agency's best interests, too. I was angry that there wasn't a damn thing I could do about it.

Maybe I'd look him up when I got back to London. Pay that fucker a personal visit. Yeah, I really liked the idea of that.

After a few days, the stories began to disappear as other news took over. Things began to calm down, and the couple of reporters who came to the location went away with a few grainy shots and nothing else.

I was allowed to get on with the shoot, and get on with my life.

But I wasn't going to forget what that bastard had done.

Today had been the last day of location shooting and all the principal photography had been finished without going a day over schedule. Jo-Anne had been amazing, and I was in awe of how she'd managed to get everything completed in time, on budget, and without yelling even once.

She told me to expect a couple of days in the studio once Lilia and I were back in LA, plus three or four days of dubbing some of the dialogue. But otherwise I was done. I'd finished my first—and probably last—Hollywood movie. I kept waiting to feel something, anything, but I just felt hollow.

I was going to miss Clare like hell.

Things were going well with Lilia, I thought, and the sex was pretty good. It was irritating to keep seeing photographs of us together on the internet, but I figured that would ease up once we were back in LA.

I wasn't really sure what I was going to do next. Rhonda was keen to keep some momentum, as she put it, and send me for more auditions, but she wasn't pushing anything, which was cool of her. Melody had been in touch, too, saying that a stage job had come up back in London, but when I wasn't able to commit to the long rehearsals because of the publicity schedule for *Dazzled*, I had to pass. She said there'd be other opportunities, but it made me nervous to turn down work.

And Clare had to get back for the final year of her university course—a large part of me wanted to go with her, away from all of the crazy.

She'd been just so fucking fantastic, coming out here to support me. Yeah, the best friend a guy could have. I wanted to do something to show her how much I appreciated it—I just wasn't sure what.

Although I had to admit, it was kind of hard to juggle having a girlfriend and a girl *friend* who hated each other. I mean, seriously—glaring, ignoring, cold-shouldering, and making all these bitchy, barbed comments. I didn't understand why they couldn't get on.

"What are you thinking?"

Lilia's soft voice interrupted my thoughts. I hadn't wanted to wake her, so I'd been lying in bed, staring at the ceiling for the last half hour.

"Hey, beautiful!"

I leaned over and kissed her shoulder. She had a thing about morning breath fucking 24/7. Maybe it sounds gross, but it didn't bother me. I loved everything about her—well, except the way she treated Clare.

She ran her hand down my chest and tugged playfully at the sheet by my waist.

"So ... what were you thinking about?"

Looking back, the smart thing would have been to lie.

"I was just thinking about Clare."

As soon as the words were out of my mouth, I could have cheerfully punched myself in the head.

"Oh!" she snapped, her eyes flashing dangerously. "Well, as you think about *her* so often, maybe you shouldn't be here!"

"Um, we're in my room, Lilia."

Yeah, another wrong answer.

"Fine!" she snarled. "I can fix that!"

I knew I had about two seconds to dig myself out of my newly dug crater before Lilia went postal.

The brain to mouth chain reaction hadn't done me much good in the last ten seconds, so I didn't risk speaking. Instead, I held her arm gently and leaned over, pressing her into the bed, showing her with my body reasons not to be mad at me.

Sometime later, I nudged her with my shoulder.

"Hey, we have to get up."

Lilia groaned and pulled the sheet more tightly over her body. "No, I'm staying here."

"Nah, we got to. It's the wrap party."

"Oh, that," she sniffed. "Those things are always a waste of time—everyone stands around drinking and making small talk. Duh—bor-ing!"

I shrugged. "Sounds all right to me. Besides, everyone's leaving in the morning—it's our last chance to see the crew together."

"Whatever," she yawned.

"Come on, baby," I said, kissing her hair. "It's my first time—you just gotta promise to be gentle with me."

She brushed me off and rolled over.

"Okay, not forcing you," I said, but inside I was irritated.

I showered quickly and hunted around for a clean pair of jeans in the hotel's laundry bag. *God, I loved room service.*

"Where are you going?" said Lilia, as I pulled on a t-shirt.

"The wrap party."

"What? I said I wasn't going!"

"And I said I wasn't forcing you. But I want to go and see everyone."

"You ... you're just going to leave me here?"

I could tell she was really angry. Well, that was tough.

"Pretty much, yeah."

"If you walk out of that door, don't expect me to be here when you get back!" she hissed.

Ah, hell.

"Lilia, I don't know why you're making a big deal about this. I just want to go and have a few drinks and say thanks to all the people who've helped me."

"Oh, stop being so goddamn *nice*," she snarled.

Like I hadn't heard that before. Did women *want* guys to act like pricks? Did they *want* to be treated badly?

"Come with me. I'll wait for you."

"Fuck off, Miles!"

Fair enough.

And I opened the door and walked out.

Huh. That didn't feel so bad.

Everyone from the cast and crew was in the hotel lounge when I came down the stairs. I felt like a bit of a dick for not being there sooner.

Polly staggered over, hooked her arm around my waist and put a beer in my hand. From the way she leaned against me, I could tell she was well on her way to a grade 'A' hangover in about 10 hours.

"You're so pretty," she sighed. "Why are you so pretty?"

"How are those beer goggles working for you, Pol?" I said, with a laugh.

"Noooo!" she wailed. "You're beautiful. Let's have babies. Lots of pretty, *pretty* babies."

I couldn't help going a bit red, but I eased her into a chair and gave her a kiss on the cheek.

"Don't forget me when you're famous," she slurred.

Jo-Anne gave a huge laugh. "Trust me, Polly, he won't forget you in a hurry."

Which was true.

How could I forget any of them? They'd been with me on this amazing ride.

I scanned the room, feeling uncharacteristically sentimental, and then Clare's eyes met mine. She raised her glass in an ironic salute, and I took my beer and went to sit next to her. She was at a table with Mildred and Leon.

"Where you been, like I couldn't guess," she said, answering her own question and rolling her eyes at the same time.

I winked at her and chugged half the bottle of beer.

"Young love," sighed Mildred, and Clare pulled a face. She was so cute when she did that—it made me smile.

"What about slightly less young love?" Clare shot back, raising an eyebrow.

I caught the embarrassed glance that bounced between Mildred and Leon.

"Oh, wow! Are you guys together? That's great! Really something to celebrate," I said.

"Yup," nodded Leon, "she's it for me. Does things with a brush that I've just never seen before."

"Oh, God! Too much information!" snorted Clare, making me laugh—even though I had to agree.

But it was pretty cool seeing them together, holding hands and all that loved-up shit. I mean, they were knocking on a bit, like 40 or something, but they hadn't given up on love. I hoped I'd be like that. Except I didn't want to wait until I was 40 to meet The One.

Hell, maybe I already had, I just didn't know it yet.

Even as I was wondering if Lilia would bother to make an appearance, I saw her walk into the room.

In just a plain t-shirt—*huh, one of mine*—she was beautiful.

I crossed my fingers that she was in a better mood, but then she gave me this huge smile and small shrug, so I relaxed.

"Hi, guys," she said, to the room in general. "Drinks on me tonight. Go crazy." Then Polly's slumped form caught her eye. "Looks like someone already did."

"Yeah, well, we've been here for a couple of hours," said Clare, pointedly.

Oh, great.

Luckily, Lilia ignored her. Instead, she leaned down and kissed me full on the lips. Guess that meant I was forgiven.

"Mmm, I like this seat," she purred, pouring herself onto my lap.

It was kind of sweet, but it made it hard to talk to anyone else.

"Can I get you a drink, baby?"

"Yeah, a bucket of cold water," Clare whisper-shouted, and a few people laughed.

Lilia gave a little hiss of annoyance, and I stifled a groan.

I sent up a quick prayer of thanks when Jo-Anne interrupted whatever was going to be said next.

"Well, as we're all together, I'd like to just say a big thank you to everyone. This has been one of the best and easiest shoots I've ever been on. You know, except for the floods, hurricane, car wreck, actor getting arrested—all of that."

"Thanks for reminding me, Jo-Anne!" I grouched.

"Aw, honey, it was a cute mugshot!"

I took a swig of beer and smiled sheepishly, as everyone laughed.

"But seriously, you guys, you've been great, and it's been a pleasure working with y'all. Let's hope this movie *dazzles* them at the box office. Mazel Tov!"

Lilia swiped my beer, and everyone joined in the toast.

"Here," said Clare, passing me another bottle.

Even that seemed to irritate Lilia.

I turned the conversation back to Mildred and Leon, before the evening was spoiled.

"So, when are you guys going to do the deed?"

Mildred blushed bright red, and I choked on my beer.

"I mean, um, when are you getting married?"

Clare laughed out loud, and even Lilia cracked the ghost of a smile. Oh well, at least they weren't sharpening their claws on each other.

Yeah, spoke too soon.

Because then Clare downed her Corona and stood up. "Anyone want another—seeing as Lilia's buying?"

"Did you know beer makes you fat, Clare?" sniped Lilia. "Or maybe you just don't care."

Uh oh.

Clare smiled sweetly. "I could lose weight, but how would that be fair to all the skinny girls if I was this smart, funny *and* thin?"

Mildred coughed and tried to hide her smile.

But Lilia wasn't taking that lying down. "Intelligent and funny? That would be okay, but how would *you* know?"

"Well, gee, Lilia, probably because you're about as funny as a case of herpes."

Lilia narrowed her eyes and opened her mouth to reply, but I'd had enough.

"Stow it—both of you." I pushed Lilia off my knee and stood up. "This is a party—try and behave like fucking ladies."

And I headed off to find someone to talk to who wasn't going to give me grievous bodily harm of the ears.

Clare

He was right, of course. It was probably the four bottles of beer I'd had to drown my sorrows, but I'd just had enough of Lilia's bullshit. *And the way she'd sat on his knee, letting everyone know that she was staking a claim on her property.*

I hated to admit that I was impressed, too, because she'd batted my snarkiness right back at me. *Miserable harpy.*

She sashayed off to sit with the producers, and I wandered away to talk to the rest of the crew.

Half an hour later, I found Miles shooting pool with Merv. His arse looked biteable bent over the pool table like that. Miles' arse, not Merv's. I liked Merv, but his backside could have covered the national debt.

I wished I was in between Miles and the pool table, bent over it, while he lined up his cue. Phew, it was getting hot in that room.

He stood up and fixed me with a look.

"Why d'you have to piss her off? You know how I feel about her."

"She started it," I said, guiltily.

"Bloody hell, Clare! We're not in kindergarten now!"

He had a point.

"Um, sorry and all that."

He blew out a long breath and sighed. "Yeah, well, don't worry about it."

Then he dragged his hands over his hair and threw me a small smile. One thing about Miles, he couldn't hold a grudge.

I, on the other hand, was the queen of grudges. Flippin' spectacular at holding them.

"I am sorry. Really. I don't want to screw things up for you," *but I really hate your girlfriend.*

"I know. Forget it, like I said." He shook his head and his smile got wider. "Life would be bloody dull without you, Clare."

"Yeah, you'll miss me when I'm gone."

"I will," he said, and I could hear in his voice that he was serious.

"So, when do you think you'll come home?"

He shrugged. "I dunno. Rhonda wants me to audition for some other roles. I guess I'll stay out here for a while, see what happens."

"But you'll be home for Christmas?"

"Maybe, I don't know."

He glanced in Lilia's direction, and my heart gave an unhappy little sigh.

"Your mum will miss you."

"Yeah, I know." He frowned.

"She'll be okay. My mum and dad are keeping an eye on her. I'll drop in and say hi when I get back."

He leaned down to give me a quick kiss.

"Thanks, Clare. You're a good friend. Pain in the backside, sometimes, but a good friend."

The next two weeks were fantastic. And awful, too, because I was counting down to saying goodbye. And this time I didn't know for how long.

Miles rented a car and we took the long way back to LA. We had a couple of days in San Francisco, and Miles laughed while he drove us over the Golden Gate Bridge, and I closed my eyes and refused to look. We stayed one night in a tiny lodge on the coast road, and even saw a school of dolphins playing in the surf while we watched from the beach.

It was perfect.

Almost.

I tried to ignore the times he got calls from *her*, or the way his phone buzzed constantly with a stream of texts. I couldn't really blame Lilia. I mean, I knew that Miles was 100% trustworthy, but she didn't. It must sort of suck to have a boyfriend whose best friend was a girl. You'd always wonder, wouldn't you? But not Miles, no matter how much I hoped. He didn't have a cheating bone in his body.

Too soon, he was driving me out to LAX.

"I'll find somewhere to park and..."

"No, don't. Just drop me off here."

"But I was going to come in and wait with you," he protested, frowning behind his sunglasses.

"No, here's fine. No long goodbyes, Miles. Just chuck me out here and I'll email you when I get back."

"God, I'm going to miss you, Clare. It'll be weird being here without you."

"Ah, you'll lap it up. You'll be fine."

"Yeah, thanks." He paused. "Tell Mum I'm sending her my best girl to look after her."

"Ha! Okay."

"And say hi to Paul and Nazzer." He smiled. "On second thought, tell them they're a bunch of lazy toe rags."

"Will do. Come home soon." *Please.*

"Love you, Clare!"

He kissed me quickly and gave me an awkward, one armed hug. Then I jumped out and dragged my case from the back seat, ignoring the honking of horns behind us. I waved quickly, but he was already pulling away.

I watched until his car was out of sight.

Chapter Twelve

MOTES ON A SCANDAL

Clare

I'd been busy since I got back to London. Going to classes, working in the pub most evenings and at weekends. You know, trying to keep too busy to think.

I missed my best friend.

He emailed occasionally, and we'd managed to Skype once, but the bitch-faced floozie had torpedoed that by suddenly 'remembering' that they were supposed to be meeting friends. *Yeah, right.*

I guess I'd thought that once filming was finished, she'd lose interest in him. But she was still hanging around like a bad smell.

At least, for most of the Autumn, Miles had been away from her, filming on location in Texas. He wasn't the lead in *Lifers*, but it was a strong supporting role, playing a guy who'd just got out of prison after getting drunk and killing his brother in a car wreck. The film was about how their parents coped, but Miles was pleased with his part, and he was working with actors he admired.

He sounded happy.

The good news was that *Dazzled* was going to get a premiere in the UK—and I was invited. Seriously—posh frock, red carpet, the works. It wasn't until mid January, a month after the LA launch, and Miles would only be in London for two nights, but it was something to look forward to. Lilia would be there, of course, but Miles had promised me we'd catch up properly—just the two of us.

I was mopping up spilled beer, and stank like a brewery when my phone buzzed with an email.

This email.

To: CMilton93
From: Milesb4isleep
Sent: Friday 10 PM
Subject: Life and other jokes
Hey Clare!

Yup Im actually writing you—are you shocked?

Hows life in London? Enjoying the rain? :) How are your exams going? Hard to believe your (sp?) you're doing you're finals already. Good luck with them all— sure youll ace em.

I spoke to mum to a coupla weeks ago and she said she was ok. Is she? I no you see her every couple weeks, so thanx for that.

Ive been bumming around the last few days, well doing publicity for Dazzled an stuff. I got to hang out with Earl and his mates at the music shop, and did some jamming with the guys. That was cool. I even miss Nazzer and Paul. Have you seen those 2 freaks? How are they?

I decided to get a new place to live. I couldn't get a longer lease on the other, and I think I'll be staying out here for a while. I even got a car! Nothing fancy—just an old beater, but it makes a helluva lot easier for getting around.

Im getting better at not shoving my foot in my mouth during interviews. At least I think I am. Check youtube and let me know, will ya?

We had Thanksgiving this weekend and that was pretty good. I didnt realize what a big deal it is. I do now! We went to see Lilias family. I dont think they liked me much. I think they were expecting like a Duke or something. They nearly passed out when I said mum worked in a supermarket (hopefully not for much longer—but she says she likes working).

I've got a new PA!!! And she's called Honey, which took some getting used to, you know—'Can you do this for me, Honey?' It sounded weird. But shes really organized and whips my ass into shape. I like her, so it works out ok. But shes not you.

So anyway, the publicity people have been going kinda crazy with the premier and Da Silva has got some more freakin siuts for me. I know you have exams and stuff but if I sent you a plane ticket would you come? It would be amazing if you could. Let me know. Its December 7ᵗʰ. We could celebrate your birthday, as well? And Christmas, maybe?

Love ya loads,
Mx

I sat and stared at my phone for a long time. God, his spelling was awful, and I had no idea how he managed to get through 13 years of school without knowing how to use an apostrophe.

And I really wasn't sure how to feel about his email either.

He was putting down roots in Los Angeles, that much was clear. My throat felt tight and my cheeks got hot. I didn't want to cry because he sounded so upbeat, so happy. But it made it real. His life was there now. Not here. Not with me. Not anymore.

I wasn't sure I wanted to go to some glitzy LA premiere—I knew from experience how out of place I'd feel. But on the other hand, it might be my last chance to say goodbye to him because when he came to the London premiere it would be for just two days. This visit, me back in LA—it would be our swansong, so to speak.

I thought about it for the rest of the day, the email

burning a metaphorical hole in my pocket—or maybe it was burning a hole metaphorically—I was too tired to work it out.

When I went home for my dinner, and before I went back out to work the late shift, I casually mentioned to Mum that Miles had invited me out there for Christmas.

"Well, that was nice of him. Give him our best when you write back, won't you, love."

"Um, well, I haven't decided that I'm definitely going."

There was a short pause as she looked up from her magazine.

"Why wouldn't you? Your dad and I won't mind, and it'll be nice for you to get a bit of sun during the winter."

"Yeah, but it's Christmas. I'd feel sort of ... weird leaving you."

She gave a small snort of annoyance.

"We won't be alone. Prue will be coming to us for Christmas dinner as usual. I'm sure she'll feel much better knowing that you're out there looking after her boy." There was a long sigh. "She misses him. We all do. I keep expecting him to knock on the door with a big smile and a bag of dirty laundry like he always used to."

I fiddled around with the strap of my bag and looked up to see Mum watching me.

"I know you miss him, love. So take him up on his offer."

"I don't know," I said, putting off making a decision. "I can't stand his girlfriend. She's an obnoxious uptight bi ... cow."

"All the more reason for you to go, Clare," sniffed Mum. "He's always had dreadful taste in women—present company excepted."

I gave this empty little laugh. It didn't fool Mum. It never had.

"And what about my birthday? I mean, don't you mind?"

"You hate it when we make a fuss. Dad and I will celebrate your twenty-first when you get back. Go and enjoy yourself, love. Opportunities like this don't come around that often."

I resisted for about another 27 seconds, then I went up to my bedroom and opened my laptop.

I hesitated, wondering what to say. In the end, four words said it all.

 Book me a ticket! Cx

Miles

Some days Lilia really pissed me off with her bitchy attitude. Today was one of them. And damn it, it should have been one of the really good days. It was just four days before the LA premiere and for some reason Lilia was mad at me. That was nothing new. Pretty much everything I said or didn't say, did or didn't do, seemed to piss her off. I couldn't help wondering if it was worth it. But she could be really sweet and funny, too. I just wished I knew which Lilia was real.

When I'd first told her that Clare was coming over for the premiere she reamed me out.

"Why the hell have you invited *her*?" she yelled at full volume.

"Jeez, Lilia! Maybe because she's my best friend! Is that enough of a reason? Hell, she even worked on the film with us."

"Oh, please! She ran a few errands—that's hardly working on a movie."

"What the fuck ever. I've sent her a ticket. She's coming."

"You know she'll hate it. She's just not cut out for something like a premiere. It's about selling the look—she can't possibly do that."

What the...?

"That's such crap! You make her sound ... and you know what? Merv is no oil painting, but he'll still be there! I don't hear you complaining about him."

"Cinematographers are important," she snapped. "Clare is just..."

"Just what?"

"Insignificant," she said calmly, folding her arms.

It was her calm that finished me off. I walked out and didn't answer her texts or take her calls for two days. Then she'd come to my apartment and we ended up in bed. I thought our argument was over—but I was wrong.

Clare was flying in the day before the premiere. I'd hoped she could come earlier, but she'd had exams to do. I didn't want to mess with her degree, so I was planning on freeing up as much time as possible while she was here. Rhonda had me on a tight schedule with the dreaded round of interviews and press calls that seemed to be necessary for every film. I'd got a lot of them done before she flew in, so that was something.

Most of the interviewers were really nice, but it was still excruciating. Gayl's training helped—a bit—but when I got nervous, I had no control over my mouth whatsoever.

I'd just unclipped the mike from the latest debacle and found Rhonda waiting for me in the dressing room.

She shook her head with an amused expression on her face.

"I don't know why it works, but it just does," she said, nodding toward the live studio. "You sure can charm an audience, Miles, even when you're talking utter bullshit."

"Gee, Rhonda, you say the nicest things. Makes me feel all warm and fuzzy inside."

She laughed. "Yeah, yeah, don't do the cute thing on me, you're not my type."

"You're breaking my heart, Rhonda!" I said, pasting a wounded expression onto my face.

She slapped my arm.

"Shut up for a minute! Now, what's this I hear about you inviting your little friend to the premiere."

I frowned. "You mean Clare? Why the hell shouldn't I?"

"Whoa! Don't get all defensive on me, Miles, but doncha think you should have told me?"

"Um, no."

She rolled her eyes. "Well, have you even sorted an outfit for her?"

"What do you mean?"

"Jeez, Miles! Don't forget I've met Clare. She seems like a nice girl, but she's not going to win Model of the Year! She needs an evening dress, hair and makeup for your premiere! Look, get Honey to take care of it for you—that's her job."

So Lilia had been right about one thing—Clare needed a special dress for the premiere. Why didn't I think of that?

In desperation, I'd called Natalia Da Silva, seeing as she'd sorted me out with a suit and a load of other shit already.

I picked up my phone as soon as I got back to my apartment, and scrolled through to her office number. The call was answered immediately.

"Hi, could I speak to Natalia, um, Miss Da Silva, please? I was wondering if she could help a friend of mine get a dress for..."

I was interrupted immediately. "I'm sorry. Miss Da Silva only works with existing clients."

And suddenly the phone was dead in my hand. I wasn't sure what had just happened. So I tried again.

"Hi, I think I just got cut off. I'm a client of hers, um, Miles Stephens and..."

"I don't think so," the woman on the other end said, her voice rich with disdain. *And the bitch cut me off again.*

I realized that Honey was watching with an amused expression.

"What are you trying to do, Miles?"

"Fuck! I'm trying to get a dress for my friend Clare for the premiere. I thought I'd ask Natalia Da Silva but the bit ... the, um, receptionist keeps cutting me off!"

I knew I sounded pathetic, and Honey laughed at me.

"You know, Miles, that's *my* job, to do things like that for you, I mean."

"Yeah, but ... I just wanted to get her a nice dress," I said, plaintively.

"Let me know how that works out for you," she grinned. "Look, Miles, this is how it is: receptionists are programmed to be unable to grasp the concept that you are trying to make your own booking. Whether it's for a goji berry smoothie, for infrared fat wraps, or getting a table at Mr. Chow's—leave it to me."

"What's an infrared fat wrap?" I wondered, out loud.

She sighed theatrically, then winked. "Watch and learn, grasshopper."

I sat back, sort of hoping the same thing would happen to her so I wouldn't look totally inept.

"Yes, Honey Scholes calling on behalf of my client Miles Stephens. No, you will not put me on hold—I want to speak to Wendy immediately about the *Dazzled* premiere, so you will *not* make me look an asshole, got that?"

She was put through instantly.

Damn.

After a quick word of explanation to Wendy, she passed me the phone.

"Yeah, hi Wendy. I need an evening dress for the premiere, well, not for me, for a friend. You met her that first time ... I ... um..."

Don't remind her of that, you dick!

"Ah, the young lady who was with you? The British girl?"

"Yeah, yeah, my friend Clare."

"And what size is your friend?"

"Fu ... I mean, I'm not really sure ... uh, a British size 14 I'd guess. I don't know what that is in American..." I glanced desperately at Honey.

"Ten to 12," she whispered.

"Yeah, um, ten to 12."

"I see. Yes, well, it's rather short notice for such an *unusually large* sizing, but I'm sure Miss Da Silva can accommodate your request. There's an Alexander McQueen that might do?"

"Yeah, whatever you think. Just not yellow—she'll look like Big Bird."

Oh, shit! I'd spoken without connecting my mouth to my brain. Thankfully, Wendy just coughed to cover up her laughter.

"Of course, Mr. Stephens. Not yellow."

"Great, thanks. Um, do I need to come and pick it up or...?"

Honey rolled her eyes at me.

"No, Mr. Stephens," Wendy answered, patiently. "We'll send it with a couple of alternatives. Do you need one of our dressers, too? If you could let me know the name of your friend's hotel?"

"No, I mean, she's staying at my place. I can help her dress. I mean, um..."

There was a long pause and I cringed, realizing how that sounded. But Wendy was too professional to comment.

When we finished, I handed the phone back to Honey and dropped my head into my hands.

"I really suck at this."

She patted my shoulder sympathetically.

"It gets easier, Miles, but this brand of crazy isn't for everyone."

The dresses had arrived and were currently lying on the bed in the guestroom. I really hoped they were the right size and that Clare liked at least one of them. They looked all right to me. My favorite was a dark blue shiny number, with slits up the side. Clare's legs would look good in that.

Lilia didn't agree.

"You can put a bow on a pig and call it Mary, but at the end of the day it's still a pig."

"What the fuck is that supposed to mean?" *Although I could make a damn good guess.*

"Miles, I know she's your friend but the truth is she's *fat*. Whatever you put her in, she'll look *fat*."

"She's not fat, she's ... curvy. Anyway, I don't give a damn, she's my friend."

"You care more about her than you do about me."

"For fuck's sake! I just want her to enjoy the premiere! *You* were the one who said she needed to look the part."

"You have no concept of how this makes *me* look!" she ranted, her nostrils flaring.

"It's all about the *look* with you, Lilia! Why do you even care what other people think?"

"God! You're so naïve! This is *business*. Everything is *business*. The image is *business*. Am I getting through to you? Do you even understand what I'm saying?"

"I'm not stupid."

"Well, you're sure acting like you are."

"What, you think it's stupid for me to care more about my friends than what some anonymous stranger thinks? You need to sort out your fucking priorities, Lilia."

"Oh, you have no idea, do you?!"

We went a few more rounds after that, her yelling and hurling insults, me shouting back, and then we ended up fucking against the wall.

Clare

Holy shit! The flash of camera lights was nearly blinding! My heart was pounding in my chest and the noise felt like a physical assault—I half expected my eardrums to bleed. I could *feel* the pulsating energy of the crowd through every pore of my body. It was raw and uncontrolled and it scared the shit out of me. I glanced at the car doors to make sure they were locked and took a deep breath. Then my eyes darted upwards as twin beams of searchlights crisscrossed the night sky, reminding me of War films showing the London Blitz.

"How you doin', Miss Clare?"

Earl's drawl was deep with concern, but soothing at the same time.

"Just hyperventilating quietly," I choked. "Don't mind me."

183

He nodded and concentrated on following the slow moving line of limousines down West Sunset Boulevard, all heading toward the Cinerama Drome and the *Dazzled* premiere.

Somewhere in the traffic arcing out behind, Miles was traveling with Lilia. As they were the stars, they'd arrive last. Then, of course, they'd be spending time doing the whole red carpet thing, whereas I would be dropped off around the back somewhere. At one time that might have sounded kind of insulting, but I was glad a thousand times over that I didn't have to face the phalanx of surging fans. The police barricades barely restrained them, and I realized for the first time—I mean *really* understood—what Laura Dorien had said all those months ago about Miles being the new It Guy.

Thousands upon thousands of screaming girls were roaring at every car that passed them, posters and photographs of Miles and Lilia clutched in their hands, their mouths open in rabid Os, the shrieks and yells all blending together into one choking, blinding wall of noise.

I'd seen it a million times on TV, but experiencing it from *this* side—it was utterly terrifying. Walls made from flesh, staring eyes, open mouths, and a million starbursts flashing from handheld cameras.

As we neared the red carpet, the volume increased exponentially and the SUV seemed to shudder in sympathy. If we'd broken down there, I think that would have been the end of us. The phrase 'angry horde', so familiar from my history studies, actually meant something to me now. Thank God I hadn't drunk the whole bottle of champagne that Miles and I had opened before we'd left his apartment that evening, otherwise I'd have peed myself from fear. I'd have needed a canoe to paddle out of there.

The barricades and silk ropes flanking the red carpet were awfully flimsy. If the crowd surged, the police and security wouldn't be able to stop it.

My throat was dry and aching, my palms and armpits inexplicably sweaty. I tugged nervously at the beautiful blue dress Miles had arranged for me to wear. Touching the satiny material grounded me a little. I wanted to be beautiful tonight—okay so that was pushing it, but I wanted to look good, at least not like a complete scrubber. So I would try. I'd wear the heels, tolerate the makeup, and refuse to yank at the curls piled up on my head. Surprising myself, I looked okay. Mind you, that was the result of several hours work from the makeup artists that Miles had hired to do an Eliza Doolittle on me. Now if only I could remember to keep my traitorous gob firmly shut, otherwise I risked telling Lilia that she was a two-faced trollop with the personality of my grandmother's sideboard.

Passing the red carpet, I saw several Hollywood celebrities talking to fans, or rather, trying to hear and be heard above the viscous screams. A few were signing autographs. Lilia had told Miles that lots of stars turned out for these shindigs—some were supporting friends in the business, or as a favor, but others were just dolled up because their agent wanted them to be seen in the spotlight.

I was past being surprised by those sort of stunts now. Pretty much.

Miles

As we inched our way toward the Cinerama Drome, a line of black limousines in front of us, I caught a glimpse of the red carpet stretching out like a lolling tongue. Lilia grabbed my hand, her eyes glistening with excitement.

"Feel how fast my heart is beating," she gasped.

I didn't know if she meant me to grope her boob, or whether she just wanted to share her rush of adrenalin.

"You look so beautiful," I whispered into her neck. "It's hard to believe you're real."

She turned and stared at me, her glossed lips a tantalizing inch from mine.

"Why do you say such lovely things?" she said, and her voice sounded sad. "Why are you so nice to me?"

I didn't understand. "You're my girlfriend. Why wouldn't I be nice to you?"

She shook her head as if shaking off an unhappy thought. I wanted to ask her about it but didn't get the chance.

"Want a blow job?" she said, running her hands up my leg.

It took my brain a second to catch up, and I was sure my eyes bulged.

"What? Here and now? Hell, yes!"

She laughed. "I thought you'd say that. Too late—we're here. Game face on."

"Can I take a raincheck on the blow job?" I pleaded.

I thought she was going to answer but then the door to the limo was jerked open and I winced from the shock of noise. *I was going to be deaf after this.* I climbed out, smiled as instructed, even though it felt like I had to glue my lips into position. Then I leaned down and held my hand out to Lilia.

The camera flashes were blinding. I knew from experience that I was going to look stoned in the photographs. My pupils shrank to pinpoints and I tried very hard not to screw my eyes shut.

Lilia blinked a few times but otherwise seemed unfazed. Her hand rested lightly on my arm, and I wanted to grip onto her to protect her.

I was aware that the close protection squad that Rhonda had spoken about were following us, literally watching our backs.

We posed for photographs together, and then Rhonda's team split us up to answer questions from the six or seven selected TV crews.

I tried to remember Gayl's lessons: use their names; treat every question like it's the first time you've heard it; don't go off the reservation; keep foot out of mouth.

It seemed to go on forever.

Question 1: *Are you and Lilia dating?*

Answer 1: We're friends. It was great working on *Dazzled* with her. She's such an amazing actress.

Question 2: *Where did you get your suit?*

Answer 2: It's a Tom Ford. Pretty spiffy, isn't it!

Question 3: *Is there going to be a sequel?*

Answer 3: You'll have to ask Laura Dorien.

And on and on. *Keep smiling. Keep talking. Keep calm and carry on.*

Rhonda's staff closed down anyone who went over their allotted time, or anyone who pushed on the 'relationship' question.

It felt weird signing autographs. My brain was bleeding from the noise, and it was impossible to talk to anyone. So I just smiled, and pretended it was another role, which it was in a way. These people didn't know me—they just had a one-dimensional idea of me based on a book they'd read, and a TV trailer. It was so bizarre.

I felt Lilia's arm slide into mine and I couldn't help smiling down at her. As soon as she touched me, there was an increase in the decibels and the sky glowed from the number of camera flashes.

After a few more smiles and waves, she tugged at my arm and we walked inside to the relative peace of the cinema.

Thank fuck for that.

I felt exhausted and shaky as the adrenalin leached out of me. Even Lilia wasn't quite her cool, calm and collected self.

Jo-Anne Moody came barreling over, a glass of champagne in each hand.

"Hey, guys! Wasn't that a rush? Whoa, my nerves are screaming. How y'all doin'? I was just speaking to Laura Dorien and even she hadn't seen anything like it!"

Jo-Anne handed us each a glass, and I took a much needed gulp, shaking my head slowly.

"Un-fucking-believable. Is it always like that?"

Lilia nodded. "Yeah, that was something else." She looked up at me, still looking slightly dazed. "I've done 12 of these before and I've *never* heard it like that. Wow!"

She licked her lips and I couldn't help leaning down to kiss them, they looked so damn juicy.

She smiled, but I could tell she was irritated, and that smudging her lipstick was off the menu.

I saw Clare out of the corner of my eye. She was standing with Polly and Mildred and, damn, if she didn't look hot in that dress! I knew her legs would look great. She saw me and raised her glass, blowing a kiss at the same time.

I was so glad she was there.

Clare

Miles had looked drop-dead gorgeous, standing in his apartment in his made-to-measure tux. But seeing him on the red carpet, I realized he looked like he belonged there. It tore my heart a little more, because I knew he was slipping away from me—away from the world I lived in.

We didn't get the chance to talk either. Miles was completely monopolized all evening, the studio execs commandeering his attention, and Rhonda was busy introducing him to people. Important ones, I presumed.

I watched him from a distance while I chatted casually to members of the crew who'd been invited, which was most of them.

Lilia didn't come near me, although I caught her looking at me once. I smiled and raised my glass, but the miserable mare just sneered and turned her back. God, she was unbearable.

After more aimless talk, and drinking more champagne than was wise, we were ushered into the theater.

Miles was sitting at the front with Lilia on one side and Jo-Anne on the other. I was several rows back, sitting directly behind Merv, which meant I had to lean sideways to get a decent view.

I knew Miles had been to a screening and muttered something about it being "not too bad", but I'd never seen it all the way through.

I was utterly swept away. Seeing Miles' beautiful face in extreme close-up, twenty feet high, completely rendered me speechless, mute, thunderstruck, dumbstruck and wordless. Also slightly damp in the nether regions, if I was being honest.

And Lilia, damn her eyes, she was such a good actress. Why did she have to be such a first class megabitch as well?

I could see the real Miles sitting with his head hanging down. That didn't surprise me—I knew he wouldn't be able to look at himself. I saw Jo-Anne turn and whisper something to him and he shook his head, easing himself out of his seat and leaving by the nearest exit.

I counted to ten, then followed him.

I guessed he'd gone to the back of the building and wasn't surprised to see him standing by one of the fire doors that he'd propped open. Thank God he hadn't set off an alarm—that would have been embarrassing.

When I found him, his eyes were closed, although his face was tilted upwards, and he was taking deep breaths.

He opened his eyes and saw me.

"Bet you wish you hadn't given up smoking now, doncha?"

He smiled back at me. "God, yes. I think I'd kill for a cigarette."

I rooted around in my small bag. "Have a mint instead."

"Tease," he muttered.

"Says you, Mr. Movie Star. You looked good on screen," I said, honestly.

He shook his head. "It was fucking excruciating watching myself. I just couldn't. I know I'm being a whiny pussy, but that shit is just so embarrassing."

"Miles, you *love* acting, you know you do."

"Yeah, but it's the *process*—you know, getting into character, understanding ... no, *feeling* the character. The rest is all just ... this. It's not ... you know?"

My heart stuttered as I listened to him struggle to express himself. Why wasn't his *girlfriend* out here helping him with this? I was glad she wasn't, but she'd been through it—if anyone understood, surely she would?

He gave me a small smile. "Yeah, I know what you're

thinking. I've just got to grow a pair and get my ass back in there."

You have no idea what I'm thinking about your arse.

I just smiled and winked at him.

He surprised me by leaning down and letting a kiss whisper across my cheek.

"Thanks for being here, Clare. Love you, babe."

We made our way back to the theater and Miles went ahead first. I waited 30 seconds, then followed him. As I edged back to my seat, I saw Lilia's head tilt in my direction, and it felt like she was watching me out of the corner of her eye. *Ugh, creep much?!*

An hour later when the house lights came up, applause rang out. I studied the faces of people around me, and their adulation seemed genuine and unforced. Jo-Anne stood up and took a bow, grinning happily as the audience called out to her and cheered. I could see her bend down, presumably trying to persuade Lilia and Miles to share in the moment. Miles stood up first, and offered his hand to Lilia. She took it, smiling up at him.

God, it made me want to vomit. She smiled like a prom princess who'd never been kissed—if such a thing existed— when I really knew that she was a double hard bitch who chewed on iron bars and shat nails.

In my opinion. Of course.

Her white dress was stunning and she looked graceful, ethereal, with a beauty that matched Miles'—who was clearly not of this earth.

They looked great together, and the thought was acid in my brain.

My plan of action was to get mind-numbingly slaughtered, drinking myself to oblivion, and then pass out in the guest room of Miles' apartment.

He'd been vague on the details of where he'd be staying that night. I didn't ask.

The after-screening party was held at the Chateau Marmont. It was a bit weird seeing a place that looked like it belonged on the French Riviera, and its whitewashed walls gleamed from small spotlights positioned along the sides.

The paparazzi were out in numbers, looking for more candid shots than the rather formal and posed ones on the red carpet.

There was a fierce scrimmage as the limo with Miles and Lilia arrived. It was scary to see how viciously the paps elbowed each other, all hoping that theirs would be the money shot. I resented their intrusion, but it looked like a bloody hard way to earn a living. I could only assume that if they caught something scandalous enough, the rewards were great.

What a fucked-up world.

Polly patted my knee as I slumped down at a small table with her, Mildred, Leon, and Merv the Perv, who was sitting with a petite, black haired woman whom he clearly adored.

"Looks like you're my date for the night, Pol," I sighed.

She sniggered. "You are looking super hot tonight, Clare, baby, but you're still not my type."

I downed a glass of tequila that someone had thoughtfully placed near my right hand.

"I don't seem to be anyone's type," I complained.

"Aw, feeling a bit neglected?"

"If I don't get some action soon, my vagina will grow cobwebs."

Merv spat out a mouthful of wine and his wife/girlfriend/significant other looked shocked.

Polly laughed and Mildred looked at me sympathetically.

"Well, it doesn't help that your best friend looks like *that*," said Polly, jabbing her finger in Miles' direction. "What guy would want to compete with him?"

"There *isn't* any competition," I sighed. "Miles is just my friend."

God, I was sick of saying that. I was so boring, I bored myself.

"Wanna play a drinking game?" Polly asked.

"Will it mean I get legless in the shortest amount of time?" I questioned her.

"Probably."

"I'm in."

I didn't remember too much about the rest of the evening, except that Merv admitted that there was another reason for his nickname. *Too much information!*

So when I woke up lying face down on my bed, still in my posh dress and skyscraper heels, I wasn't exactly sure how I'd got there. I staggered into the bathroom and shuddered at the nightmarish vision in the mirror. I could have given Freddy Krueger a run for his money—no SFX makeup required. In fact, the makeup I had been wearing on my eyes was now smeared down my cheeks, and any trace of lipstick had long since fled. I wondered if the gravitational pull that had been in effect while I was asleep would one day drag my boobs down to my ankles. On the other hand, if I could shift the fat from my stomach up to my boobs and around to my backside, I might be able to achieve that hourglass figure. Mind you, it would probably be the kind of hourglass that would take a whole day to empty, being blessed with a fuller figure.

I realized that even as my mind was wandering and unable to corral my rambling thoughts, I badly needed a painkiller for the headache that was threatening to make my brain dribble out of my nose, in a manner not dissimilar to the way the Ancient Egyptians buried their dead. See what I mean? Bizarre rambling.

I wanted Tylenol and orange juice.

As I stumbled toward the kitchen, I couldn't help noticing that Miles' bedroom door was closed. I paused for a moment—in a totally non-stalkerish way—but couldn't hear anything. I knew he must be back, because his door was only ever closed when he was sleeping. I just didn't know if he was by himself.

God, the skank could be in his arms right now. Guess I'd find out later in the morning. And yeah, I was going to buy a whip so I could take my self-flagellation from the metaphorical to the literal. Or maybe I'd just use it to beat the shit out of her bony backside. That sounded more appealing.

When I went back to bed this time, I managed to wipe a washcloth around my face, and peel off the very expensive—and very crumpled—dress.

Sigh.

The next time I woke up, I felt a little better. I could imagine a gravelly voice saying, "She walks, she talks, she's nearly human."

The vision in the mirror hadn't improved much, but not having mascara over my face helped. And I was totally in love with the awesome shower in this new apartment. The four jets just about pinned me to the wall, and I had to fight my way back out when I'd finished. I was definitely awake after that.

I dressed thoughtlessly in a pair of jeans and one of Miles' old sweatshirts that was a gazillion sizes too big, but I loved it anyway. Of course I did. Oh, I had numerous ways to torture myself—each day I seemed to think of a new one.

There was still no sound or movement from Miles' room. I think I'd have thrown up in my mouth if I'd heard *bedroom* noises. Just thinking about it made me a little nauseous. It felt good to blame the skeaze, although, in truth, mixing tequila with champagne might have something to do with it, too.

I munched through some toast and made a pot of tea while I started Googling pictures from the premiere on my laptop.

But an unchewed piece of toast dropped out of my mouth at the photographs that I found.

I jumped when I heard Miles walk into the kitchen behind me, and I tried to close the website down, but I was too slow.

It hurt me to hear his strangled intake of breath.

He was standing next to me and I risked glancing up at him. His eyes were wide, and all the color drained from his face. He stared, shocked by the wave of images that scrolled across the screen.

Lilia doing a line of coke.

Lilia offering the coke to Joe Blow.

Lilia with her tongue stuck in another woman's throat, her hand groping her boob.

Lilia snogging some random guy.

Lilia with her head in Joe Blow's lap, his head thrown back and his mouth open.

And she was still wearing the white dress from the premiere. The pictures were just hours old.

Miles hurled my mug of tea at the wall.

I winced as the china shattered and the brown liquid splashed across his kitchen, staining the fresh, white paint, and dripping to the floor where it coalesced into an obscene puddle.

Shocked at the sudden violence, I tore my eyes away from the wall, but Miles had gone.

I didn't know what to do. I hated the evil bitch. I hated everything about her. But right now, I didn't want those pictures to be real.

I looked back at my laptop, wishing to see something different. But every gossip website and most of the serious news ones said the same thing: Lilia was a drug-taking cheat.

The slamming of the front door made me jump. I rushed to the window and was just in time to see Miles pounding down the road in his running shoes, sweats and a hoodie.

Chapter Thirteen

TRUE LIES

Clare

It was brutal. The Press couldn't get enough of Lilia's fall from grace. And yeah, they all used puns like that.

> *Forbidden Fruit*

> *Trouble in Paradise*

> *Fallen Angel*

They were generally sympathetic to Miles, describing him as the innocent victim, which he hated, but happened to be true. He'd got his heart stomped all over, and in the most public way possible. He'd been hurt and humiliated by someone he trusted.

The Press scented blood. I think they wanted to see him break down and crumble—preferably in public. Maximum meltdown.

The studio's publicity team didn't know whether to laugh or cry. On one hand, their precious movie was on everyone's lips, with rave reviews in a dozen newspapers and every website; but on the other, those damning photographs of Lilia had overwhelmed the movie's release. And, unsurprisingly, *that* story was whole-heartedly negative in the most prurient way—the image the movie sold failing to live up to the sordid reality.

Rhonda's agency was working overtime to deal with the increased interest in Miles. Less than an hour after I'd first opened my laptop, she'd been in touch. I wasn't sure what to expect from her, so when she phoned to demand a meeting with him, I was anxious and on the defensive. Miles just looked sad and tired, a little beaten—although I could also sense a deep anger simmering beneath the surface.

Thank God he'd returned quickly from his run, as soon as he realized he was being followed.

Because by then the vultures had descended. Paparazzi surrounded our building, and the phone was ringing off the hook. That was easy to handle—I simply unplugged it, but the mass of bodies beyond the concrete walls had trapped us inside. It was a siege.

I wondered if it was acceptable to throw buckets of cold water out of the window, seeing as spitballs wouldn't have reached far enough. I restrained myself, although it wasn't easy—you know, feeling so helpless and useless.

Rhonda obviously knew the score because she arrived with a team of four security guards, who started moving some of the reporters away from the building's entrance. At least she'd been able to get inside without being molested. But it was clear that we wouldn't be able to stay in hiding for much longer. The apartment was tainted—and it didn't feel safe.

I unlatched the door for her and stood well back. There was no way I wanted my picture in the newspapers. God knows what they'd make of that. I quailed at the thought. I didn't think reporters could get inside the building, but I didn't want to find out the hard way.

Rhonda shouldered her way inside and nodded briskly when she saw me lurking behind the door.

"Clare."

Her greeting was abrupt but not unfriendly.

"He's in the kitchen," I said, gesturing toward the back of the apartment.

I followed behind her slowly, not sure I wanted to hear whatever she had to say.

Miles was still slumped over a cup of coffee, which by now must have been stone cold.

"Hey, Rhonda," he said, starting to stand.

"Oh, sit, please," she said, waving a hand. "How you doing, Miles? You holding up okay?"

I'd never heard her sound so concerned.

"Yeah, I guess," he said, his answer convincing no one.

Rhonda looked around her. "Where's Honey? She should be here helping you manage … things."

Miles shrugged. "I didn't want her to fight her way through the sharks. She offered to come, but I thought it would be better if she stayed home."

He looked up as I hesitated by the doorway. I felt like I was intruding.

"I'll just wait in my room," I offered, pathetically.

Miles' eyes widened slightly and he looked panicky. "Please stay," he said, softly.

I glanced at Rhonda and she gave a small, discreet nod.

"Okay."

I walked over to the coffee machine and made a fresh pot, glad to have something useful to do.

"Well, this is a real bum fuck of a situation," she said.

Miles gave a small smile. "You're a poet, Rhonda."

"I'm not going to soft-soap you, Miles, so I'll tell you what options you've got. You can deal with it head on—put out a statement—give your side of the story…"

Miles looked at her in disbelief. "My side of the story? What the hell does that even mean? My girlfriend…" he seemed to choke on the word, "cheated on me. Fuck knows how many times, or for how long."

I narrowed my eyes as I looked at him. What did he mean, *for how long?* What wasn't he saying?

Rhonda sighed. "I have to ask, Miles: did you and Lilia

ever do coke together? Pop some pills? Smoke a joint? Anything?"

He shook his head tiredly. "No, but she had some coke with her once. I said I didn't want any because speed gives me headaches." He looked up at me and shrugged. "Jimmy—and me—we used to get high when we were in the flat in London. And drunk—a lot."

I wasn't really surprised.

Rhonda frowned. "Would this Jimmy guy say anything to the press, if he was approached?"

Miles looked startled, then an expression of resignation passed over his face.

"Probably. He'd say pretty much anything for twenty quid."

Rhonda sighed.

"So, basically, if reporters do some digging, your pal in London could make you look like a cokehead with a drinking problem ... who led Lilia astray."

I was furious—that was such an evil distortion of a limited amount of truth. But I knew Rhonda was right. You couldn't win against this shit—there was no way of fighting back. It was like wrestling with mist. The truth was whatever people wanted to believe.

"As I said, Miles, your options are to issue a statement distancing yourself from her..."

He shook his head, his eyes fierce.

"Or you keep your head down until it blows over. Which it will—eventually."

"I'm definitely preferring option two," said Miles, decisively.

Rhonda nodded. "Okay, but you have contractual obligations to market the movie—you have several interviews booked for next week and..."

"I'm not going on all those fucking talk shows!" he snapped at Rhonda.

"I didn't think you would," she said, calmly. "I was simply offering you the chance to make the decision yourself." She rubbed her forehead. "The studio is going to bring forward the London premiere to December 30, and hope things calm down after that so everyone can refocus on the movie. Between you and me," she continued, "they're hoping you and Lilia will sort things out—as a couple. But apart from anything else, they want you seen together."

He looked at her disbelievingly. "They've got to be fucking joking!"

"Stranger things have happened. Besides, they've got several million dollars riding on this so they don't give a shit about your personal life—only how it affects them."

"Yeah, well it's not going to happen," he growled, sitting back in his chair.

I felt a huge weight slide off my chest at his assertion that Lilia was history. And then I felt guilty for being relieved when Miles was so unhappy.

"But as I said, you're contracted to do several TV interviews with Lilia, too," Rhonda continued, looking straight at him.

His lips tightened and he shook his head.

"Not going to happen. They can sue the shit out of me—I won't fucking do it."

"Agreed," Rhonda conceded. "That would be best for now. Besides, Jo-Anne Moody has already offered to do your slots. I think everyone will accept that."

Miles looked relieved. "Really? Thanks, that's good to know. Tell Jo-Anne ... never mind. I'll text her. That's cool of her."

Rhonda gave a small smile. "She likes you. You've got a lot of goodwill out there, Miles." Then she took a deep breath and switched her twitching eye to me. "But it would be best if Clare wasn't here," she said, flatly.

"What? Why?" I gasped.

"Because," she continued, leveling me with a look, "everyone will assume that you're the reason for the breakup."

"But that's crap! I mean we're not ... we haven't..."

"It's how it'll look," she insisted. "Think about it: Lilia appears to go off the deep end, then the Press find out that Miles has a new woman who's been living with him for the last week. They'll go after him with long knives. You're not good for him right now, Clare."

I felt sick. And she was right, again.

I looked at Miles, horrified by the position I'd put him in.

He shook his head. "It's not your fault, Clare. And I don't care what they say about me."

Rhonda smacked her hand down on the table. "Do you care what they say about *her*?" she barked, pointing at me. "Because they'll say she's a homewrecker—splitting up Hollywood's golden couple."

I swallowed nervously, and Miles ran his hands through his hair in frustration.

"Now I can't even have friends? This is so fucked up!"

"So..." Rhonda let the word hang in the air. "What are you going to do?"

He gazed out of the window.

"What if I disappear for a while," he said suddenly. "Just take off."

Rhonda chewed over the idea. "Maybe," she said, at last. "Although you're damn recognizable at the moment—ironically *Dazzled* is turning out to be the hit that the studio was hoping for. Your face is on a lot of billboards, and what with the present coverage of..."

Her words trailed off, their meaning clear.

Miles shook his head. "It's gotta be worth trying."

"If you leave LA, you'll be on your own. I can't protect you out there."

He snorted and waved toward the front of the building.

"Anything's got to be better than being a fucking prisoner in my own home." Then he smiled—a real, genuine smile. "And I think I know what I'm going to do. I need to make a call."

He stood up quickly and pulled his phone out of his jeans.

I saw him delete about 20 messages, his eyebrows knit together in a frown as he walked out of the room.

"Do you know what this is about?" said Rhonda.

"Nope. No idea."

"Has Lilia called?" she asked quickly, making sure her voice didn't carry.

Just hearing her name made me want to commit violence on the soft furnishings, however innocent they were.

"He hasn't said anything, but the way his phone has been lighting up like Christmas, I'd guess she's been calling or texting non-stop. I don't think Miles has spoken to her, but I can't say for certain."

Rhonda sighed. "Well, despite what I said about you getting gone, I'm glad you're here."

I nearly fell off my stool, and stared at her disbelievingly.

She gave me a small smile. "Yes, it's better for the studio —and his career—if you're not seen with him, and I wouldn't be doing my job if I didn't point that out. But it's better for *him* that you're here. Miles is just too damn nice for his own good." She sighed. "He'll need his friends."

We both heard him walking back into the kitchen at the same time, which ended our conversation immediately.

"Sorted," he said, his face determined. "Rhonda, can you give us a ride to Earl's place? I don't want to use my car."

"Who the hell is Earl?"

"One of the studio drivers. He's a friend."

Rhonda shook her head, but a grudging smile crept across her face, too.

"Another friend, huh? What did you have in mind?"

Miles attempted a small grin. "Nothing much, but it's probably better that you don't know."

"Fine," said Rhonda, conceding defeat, "but let me get you out of here first."

"What about Clare?"

I was touched that his main concern was for me.

"Give it an hour and by then, I hope, all the paps will have left. Ten minutes down the road there's a cab company and..."

Miles started to protest but Rhonda was adamant.

"It'll be more discreet: better for her, better for you."

"It's fine," I said, quietly. "Just tell me where to meet you."

He scribbled down an address and I squinted, trying to decipher his horrible handwriting.

"Pack some clothes," he said. "Nothing fancy."

That I could do.

"And bring my sax."

Miles left with Rhonda shortly after that. It had taken him all of two minutes to toss some clothes into his gym bag.

Reverently, he had placed the black case containing his sax by the door, and I looked at him questioningly.

"I'll need my music," he said, softly.

I nodded my understanding, kissed him quickly, and watched him take a deep breath before opening the door.

Rhonda gave me a long, measured look. "Take care of him," she said.

A few seconds later the volume of noise increased tenfold. I could hear the assembled reporters yelling their questions in a heated frenzy. I didn't dare peek out of the window, but I could imagine Miles with his sunglasses pulled over his eyes, hoodie up, head down, being escorted into Rhonda's waiting car.

I knew it wasn't the smart thing to do, but I was desperate to see what was happening. I risked a quick peek out of the window as the car engine revved threateningly. I half expected to see bodies flung left and right like in some adventure movie. Instead, the tank-like SUV edged its nose through the massed bodies while photographers pressed their camera lenses up against the car's windows, hoping against hope that the tinted glass would reveal something.

Then Miles was gone. Almost instantly, the street in front of the building was empty. Only a few abandoned paper cups and cigarette butts showed that anyone had ever been there.

I waited 45 minutes, then headed out carrying Miles'

backpack stuffed with my spare jeans and a few t-shirts, and his precious sax.

Having it in my hands made me feel connected to him. And I knew why he'd wanted me to take it—he didn't want *them* to have that little extra piece of him that would have reminded them he was a musician. Maybe some other day, but not now. He was trying to hang on to himself—and I hoped he was strong enough to do it.

The cab office was only a short walk, as Rhonda had promised. Luckily, a driver was available immediately and he didn't give me a second look as I gave him Earl's address.

I climbed into the back seat and sent a text to Miles that I was on my way.

His reply was immediate.

Be safe. Mx

The cab driver made an illegal U-turn in the street and headed out to Earl's place in the quiet suburbs of Bellflower. The whole town was on a much smaller scale than anything I'd seen before in LA, and it felt like a real community, not just a bunch of people who happened to have bought a house in the same area. It reminded me a little of an English market town, as we passed farmland stretching out into the distance.

After a short journey, I climbed out and paid the driver, but before I could walk up to the front steps, a woman with a dignified air and warm smile opened the door.

"You must be Clare. I've heard so much about you. I'm Maureen. Welcome to our home."

"Thank you so, so much! Thank you for helping Miles," I babbled. "It's just so crap what's happened to him. Oh, sorry, I mean, it's just rubbish and..."

She smiled and her eyes sparkled.

"Don't worry, honey. I have two teenage children, plus I live with Earl. That man cusses like a walrus with toothache. Come on in."

Miles was waiting inside, still on edge and making sure there was no one waiting to snap a quick photograph.

"Clare," he breathed.

"It's okay, I wasn't followed."

Bloody hell—now I was sounding like some rubbish cop movie.

He pulled me into a tight hug and damn if he didn't smell just sooooo fantastic. I couldn't hug him back because I had my backpack in one hand and his sax in the other. I nearly dropped it on his foot because he'd cut off the blood supply to my arms.

"Umph! Suffocating here!" I gasped.

"Sorry! Sorry!" he muttered, loosening his grip a little. "I'm just so fucking glad to see you."

Maureen raised her eyebrows and gave me a conspiratorial smile.

Earl was in the living room, nodding along to some smooth jazz. I listened for a moment.

"Art Porter? 'Lake Shore Drive'?"

Earl looked up, surprise on his face, and Miles smiled at me with pride.

"Oh, come on!" I said, "I've known Miles since we shared our first pram together! He practically gives me a written test on anything to do with jazz!"

Earl snorted, and Maureen laughed out loud.

"Can I get you a coffee, Clare? Cream? Sugar?"

"Oh, yes, thank you! Just the cream, please."

She came back a few moments later and handed me a milky coffee, as well as a black one for Miles. Then I wondered how often he'd visited before because Maureen clearly knew how he took his coffee. Had he come here with Lilia?

Oh my God! Now I was getting jealous of a married woman who made him a cup of coffee! I seriously had to unbung my head from that dark pit of despair I called my arse.

Earl scowled. "Where's *my* darn coffee, woman?"

"You can have decaff or water, old man!" snapped Maureen.

Earl grumbled for a moment then agreed he'd have decaff. Maureen winked at me.

"So," I said, sitting back on the large couch. "What's the big plan?"

Earl grinned. "You want to tell her, son?"

Miles managed a small smile.

"Earl said we could borrow his campervan. Well, his son's campervan, so we can just take off. Road trip—what do you think?"

His expression showed excitement—mine probably showed horror.

"Camping? As in, not having a place to stay."

I wasn't too keen on the idea. I mean, you know, now showers and flushing toilets had been invented, I didn't really get the whole 'back to nature' vibe.

Miles rolled his eyes. "You were all up for doing the beer festivals in Germany last summer."

Yeah, not quite how my memory replayed that conversation.

"Besides," he said, quietly, "if I don't check into a hotel, there's less chance I'll be found."

There was no way I could refuse him after that—and he knew it. Git.

"Okay, but you'll owe me for this Stephens."

His smile was tinged with relief, and I felt bad for making such a song and dance about it. After all, it wasn't camping with tents—God, what a horrible thought—at least we'd have a roof over our heads, even if we'd be sleeping in a tin can instead.

"The things I do for you," I said, shaking my head.

He blew out a shuddering breath. "I know. Thanks," he said, quietly.

Maureen patted his shoulder, her eyes sympathetic.

"Did you call your mom yet?" she said.

My head snapped up, and Miles groaned.

"Shit, no, I haven't. Ah hell, I'd better go and do that." He looked at me. "What am I going to say to her?"

"The truth," I said. "That Lilia ... let you down. That you're okay and we're going to get out of town for a few days."

He nodded slowly.

"If you want to make your call in the backyard..." Maureen suggested, gently.

He nodded again and headed outside.

I sat listening to the soothing music, sipping my coffee. But inside, my emotions were still churning from the rollercoaster ride of the last couple of hours.

A few minutes later Miles returned, his face stony. My heavy heart sank a little further.

"How was it?"

He hitched one shoulder. "She cried."

I didn't know what to say after that, and the silence was profound.

We all jumped when music started pounding through the walls upstairs, and Maureen's voice could be heard yelling from the kitchen.

"Turn it down, Deena! Don't make me come up there and tell you!"

"My daughter," said Earl, his face glum. "She likes Justin Bieber."

"Oh, um, that's nice," I said, trying not to gag. "He's, um, very..."

"Popular," Miles suggested, raising his eyebrows at me.

"Yes, that's the word!" I agreed, brightly.

Wow! Miles' media training was really paying off.

Earl gave a small smile. "My boy, Freddy, he likes jazz."

"Oh, thank God," muttered Miles.

"You said it, son," agreed Earl, with a nod.

The music lessened by a fraction and we could hear loud thumps, as if someone was tossing heavy books onto the floor above us. Maureen's lips narrowed as she walked back in with Earl's decaff, and she muttered something under her breath that I couldn't hear.

"Excuse me a moment."

She stomped up the stairs loudly, and Earl grinned at our startled faces.

"God loves a feisty woman, and ya know, it sure does make life interesting."

He winked at me, and I wasn't certain if it was an insult or a compliment. But as the latter was rarer than hen's teeth, I just smiled back.

A few moments later we heard raised voices, then the music cut out suddenly.

Thundering footsteps were heard on the stairs as Maureen's voice sliced through the silence.

"Deena," she hissed. "We have guests!"

A sulky teenage girl sashayed into the room. She stood with one hand on her hip, surveying her realm. I was in awe— half a ton of attitude, a pound of opinion, and an ounce of concern caused the girl to frown at Earl. Then she saw me, and she looked taken aback. I smiled tentatively and she blinked.

But when she saw Miles, her jaw dropped open, and her eyebrows shot up so far that I thought her eyes would topple out of her head. Which was pretty much what happened with most females when they met Miles. And a few men.

"This is your daddy's friend Miles," said Maureen, with a hint of suppressed amusement in her voice, "and Miles' friend Clare."

"Hi," I said, trying not to laugh at the poor kid's reaction.

Hormones are just crap when you're a teenager. I remembered when I saw a guy I liked—I was so embarrassed, even my arse was blushing.

"Hi, Deena," said Miles, calmly. "It's nice to meet you at last."

I thought she was going to burst into tears, but she rallied quickly, and soon Maureen was busy taking photographs of the two of them. Deena chattered away about what a big fan she was of Laura Dorien and how she'd *just die* when she saw the movie, and she thought the trailer was *awesome* and *boom ting*, and the promotional posters *amazing*.

And even though it was the worst day of his life, and even though his private life was being dragged through the mud, Miles had smiled at a young girl so he could make her day.

I was so proud of him. And so in awe. *And so in love that it made me want to puke. If I had any balls, I'd have kneed myself in them.* God, pathetic much.

As soon as Deena had raced upstairs to post the photographs of Miles on her Facebook page, Earl took us out to the garage and showed us the campervan. It was a totally cool, beat-up old VW—the kind of thing my mum would have called 'a passion wagon'. God, I hoped she was right.

"Freddy will be home for the holidays, but you're welcome to keep the van for a couple of weeks," Earl said, stroking the rusty chrome logo. "She's got everything you want—pull out beds, two ring gas stove..."

"Shower and loo?" I muttered to myself.

"Oh, and he keeps his wetsuit in the closet. You could borrow that, too—you're about the same size."

Miles nodded. He looked a bit nervous at the thought of driving such a large vehicle. After all, he'd only got his license about seven months previously.

"So, you've got a full tank of gas..." said Earl.

"Half a pack of cigarettes?" I suggested.

Miles smiled. "It's dark and we're wearing sunglasses."

"Hit it!" we said together, and Miles laughed.

It was so damn good to hear that—*The Blues Brothers* was one of our favorite films. It reminded me of nights in, cheap beer and pizza.

We chucked our bags inside, well, I did the chucking; Miles tenderly placed his sax in a drawer under the seats where it wouldn't get thrown about.

The plan was to head north on the Pacific Highway, stop at one of the country park campsites west of Santa Barbara, chill for a few days, then go on to Saint Luis Obispo and a small jazz festival that Earl had recommended. If Miles got recognized, we'd just move on.

I had no idea how I was going to move on—from him, I mean.

Miles

My mood lifted when I saw the expanse of wide, yellow sand, and smooth, glassy waves breaking in the background.

I'd been driving for a couple of hours, just taking it easy, not in any particular hurry, letting the tension seep away. But seeing that beach, I really wanted to stop.

Clare said she didn't mind, so I pulled into the small, sandy parking site of a designated camping area and cut the engine. I could hear the waves crashing onto the shore below, and seagulls wheeling in the sky, their cry echoing the sound in my head every time I thought of Lilia. But it was peaceful here, too—no people.

"I'm going to go for a swim," I said, decisively. "Are you coming in?"

Clare shook her head, shivering as she imagined the cold water of the Pacific ocean.

"No bloody way! It's December."

"Uh huh, but they've invented wetsuits," I smiled, pointing at the sign that advertised rentals.

She folded her arms across her chest and shook her head again. I couldn't help noticing that when she crossed her arms, it pushed her tits up.

Yeah, well, I'm a guy, and I wasn't dead yet.

I dug through the small closet at the back of the van and pulled out the funky-smelling neoprene suit.

Clare wrinkled her nose. "No, thanks. You go ahead."

"What are you going to do?"

"Take a walk along the beach—see if I can find any driftwood to build a fire. We could toast some marshmallows."

She raised her eyebrows and winked. I couldn't help laughing. That sounded perfect. Clare always knew how to make me feel better.

"Fantastic! I'll see you in an hour or so."

"Have fun," she said, as if she couldn't believe that would be possible on a cool December morning.

The gray waves stretched toward the horizon, and I had the beach almost to myself. We'd passed a car parked about a quarter of a mile away, and I could see two surfers, tiny dots in the distance, but that was all. It was just what I wanted—emptiness. It matched how I felt inside. Thank God Clare was there, otherwise I might have seriously considered finding out if I could swim to Hawaii.

The beach was small, just a dip in the curve of a larger bay, with huge boulders jutting out through the soft sand. The contrast seemed significant, although I couldn't explain why.

It felt good to be in the sea, even though the water was damn cold. Jumping through waves and bodysurfing back to the beach, it was hard to think of anything else. I dived under some more waves and swam behind where they were breaking. The cold water made my head ache, but I didn't care—in fact I welcomed the physical pain.

After a while I realized that I was much nearer to the two surfers than when I'd started out. The current must have pulled me along without me noticing it. I caught a wave back to the beach, and watched as one of the surfers rode the wave behind me. As the figure got nearer, I saw that it was a woman. *There was definitely something to be said for skintight wetsuits*. Luckily, my dick was too shrunken with cold to pay much attention.

The blonde surfer smiled at me as she tucked her board under her arm and waded out of the foam.

"Hi there! Did ya forget your board?" she said, her tone amused.

"Damn it! I knew I was doing something wrong."

She giggled. "That's cute! And I just love your accent! Are you British?"

"Uh, yeah."

"I'm Sasha!"

Her brunette friend paddled over to join us, and threw a look that I recognized.

"And I'm Cameron. Wow, up close you really look like that actor guy," she said, suddenly.

"Who?" asked Sasha, frowning.

"You know ... the British guy from that film."

"British?" Sasha echoed, eyeing me narrowly. "Which film?"

"You know—the one with the angel. Um ... *Dazzled!*"

"Oh yeah! You totally do!" Sasha agreed, enthusiastically.

They looked at me expectantly, waiting for me to say something.

God, this was going to be awkward.

"So, what's *your* name?" said the one called Sasha.

"Miles."

There was a beat, then their mouths dropped open in synchronized surprise. It was almost funny.

"Ohmigod ohmigod ohmigod! You're *him!* You're really *him!*"

Great, just what I didn't want.

"Er, yeah, I guess."

I could see the exact moment that they connected me with all bullshit flying around about Lilia.

"Oh, God! I'm so sorry about your girlfriend!" breathed Sasha, her eyes wide and full of more bloody pity.

"Yes, she's such a freakin' ho!" Cameron added, her face severe. "I can't *believe* she did that to you! I mean, blowing that guy—and there are photos and everything!"

I couldn't help wincing. *I sooo didn't need to be reminded.* Jeez, it was like being back at school. Everyone knew you'd been dumped before you got through the door, and because your girlfriend hadn't got around to telling you herself, you were the last to know.

"Yeah, well... thanks," I mumbled.

"We're so sorry," whispered Sasha.

It was as if someone had died. But no, just my pride—and yet another relationship.

"Yeah, I'm going to head off now," I muttered, pathetically.

"What are you doing here?" said Cameron, breezily.

"Oh, just taking it easy. Chilling out." *Avoiding the press. Hiding, mostly.*

"Cool!" smiled Sasha. "Hey, we could teach you to surf if you like!"

Great—and then they could hold a pity party for me while they were at it.

"Thanks, that would have been good, but I, um, have to get going now. Gotta, you know, get going."

I started edging away from them and Sasha's face fell. I was half expecting her to unzip her wetsuit, whip out a notebook and pen, and ask for my autograph. But I managed to get away without them telling me how *sorry* they were again.

"It was nice meeting you!" Cameron called after me.

Yeah, memorable.

I waved, but didn't stop as I jogged up the beach.

By the time I got back to the campervan my good mood had entirely and predictably evaporated.

"What did those women want?"

As usual, Clare cut to the chase.

"To commiserate over Lilia," I spat out.

"Oh," said Clare, softly. "Want a cup of tea?"

I almost snapped at her, but managed to simply nod because, yeah, I was English, so a cup of tea fixed everything.

I pulled off the borrowed wetsuit and towelled myself dry in the chilly air. I hadn't really been thinking when I'd packed up my stuff, so I hadn't brought any underwear. Again. Maybe I should go back on *Ellen* after all, just for the free boxers.

There was no one in sight, so I dropped the towel and pulled on my jeans. When I turned around Clare was looking at me strangely.

"Yeah, I need to do some shopping," I said.

"What? Oh, yes, right. We should find somewhere soon."

She handed me a mug of tea and we sat side by side in the

doorway of the van, Clare's feet dangling, mine half buried in the cool sand.

"Uh, Miles—can I ask you something?"

Since when did Clare ask permission? I had a feeling this wasn't going to be good.

"S'pose so."

"What did you mean when you said you wondered *how long* Lilia had been cheating on you? What makes you think she'd done it before?"

Oh.

"You don't have to tell me..."

I shrugged. What difference did it make now?

"I don't know for sure—I don't know anything ... except what I've seen..." I stared into my tea. *Hell, I didn't know, maybe I was looking for some damn tealeaves to give me the answer.* "It's just that, the very first time we went out—to that awards dinner, before I'd even got the *Dazzled* job—I saw Joe Blow. I was going to the gents for a slash, and he was in there with this woman, getting his knob polished—real vacuum action."

"Bloody hell!"

"Yeah, that's about what I said. Anyway, I backed out pretty damn quick, and I bumped into Lilia. She was standing right there. I didn't think about it at the time, but why was she waiting outside the men's bogs? Then she said that getting blown was *his thing* and that he was *known for it*. I mean, how did she know? It's not all over the internet—not like now ... but *she knew*. So I've been wondering if she knew from personal experience."

"Oh..."

Her words ground to a halt, but mine kept pouring out, the most poisonous thoughts that I couldn't stop.

"Hell, for all I know she was thinking about him every time I had my dick inside her."

I could see that I'd shocked Clare, but I was really asking her.

"Do you think she was?"

She sighed and looked down. "I don't know."

"No. Neither do I. And that really fucks with my head, you know?" *Shit, this stuff was hard to talk about.* "She said it was a game. Lilia said that people like him did it to see how long they could get away with it. I guess that's all I was to her—a game."

Clare spoke slowly. "Well, now they know. No one gets away with it forever."

I shook my head impatiently.

"Didn't you listen to what Rhonda said? It would be easy enough for all this crap to get heaped on me. A couple of careful statements here and there, and I'll be the one at the bottom of the dungheap."

"That won't happen."

"Guarantee that, can you?" I said, viciously.

She fell silent, and I felt like a right bastard for taking it out on her.

She chewed a fingernail for a moment while we both took a minute.

"What did she say in her texts? I assume all those messages you deleted were from her?"

"I only read the first one. She said sorry."

"Was that all?"

I shrugged.

"I don't know. I didn't want to read the rest."

She nodded slowly.

"I think I'll swear off women," I said, staring into my tea. "I'm rubbish at relationships. Why do women cheat, Clare?"

I really wanted to know.

"Not all women cheat," she said, quickly.

I was sort of afraid she'd say that.

"No, you're right, I know. It's me—women always cheat on me. I must be a crappy boyfriend."

"That's not true! You're wonderful and caring and kind and..."

God, I loved that woman. She was so bloody loyal. I couldn't help laughing—at least I think that was the sound that came out of my throat.

"Yeah, that must be why I keep getting dumped."

"No!" she said, briskly. "You just have terrible taste in girlfriends."

Shit. She was right.

Clare

I could have slapped those dumb surfer broads for making Miles feel bad. He'd been almost happy when he left for his swim. But when he came back, he looked plain miserable.

I hadn't helped either. After my comment about him having terrible taste in girlfriends, he'd been quiet and withdrawn. I hated to think I'd hurt his feelings even more—but what I'd said was true, although I wasn't sure that was a good enough reason for saying it.

"Do you regret it?"

He stared at me, his gray eyes nearly black as the afternoon drifted into evening.

"I mean, do you regret coming to Hollywood, the film? All of it?"

He stared at his tea, now cold, then tossed the dregs onto the sandy ground.

"Honestly? Sometimes, yeah. I loved making the film and everyone was really great—helping me and that..."

"Except for Pencil Dick."

He managed a smile. "Yeah, except for him." He glanced over at me. "And it was great having you there. It felt good to know that I had a friend watching my back." He sighed again. "But the rest of it? No, that pretty much sucks. I hate talking about myself, so interviews are horrendous. I try and turn it around so I talk about the work—about the movie—as much as possible. It's weird, people acting like they know me. They recognize my face, but they believe the hype. I don't even feel like the person they're talking about is me—I don't know who he is—that guy. Does that make sense? I don't know. It makes me a little crazy, I guess."

"You could walk away."

He continued to stare at his empty mug.

"Yeah, I guess. I could be that guy who was in a hit movie once. That wouldn't bother me but..."

"But what?"

He looked up and met my eyes.

"It's not like I've got anything to go back home to in London, is it?"

I laughed lightly, even while my heart was screaming, *Me! What about me?*

He frowned. "I mean, apart from Mum, and your family. Bloody hell, if Nazzer and Paul are the best I've got going for me, I may as well stay here."

I nodded because I couldn't speak.

"Shit, sorry, Clare. I'm being a real emo bitch, aren't I. Let's find somewhere to get some food."

"Yeah," I choked. "Pity we can't buy any booze."

He gave a slight smile. "Actually, we don't have to. I gave Earl a hundred bucks to sort us out with beer and tequila for the road trip."

"Well, okay then! But we still have to buy marshmallows and then you can be all manly and build a fire."

"We could toast 's'mores.'"

"What the hell is a 's'more'?"

"Crackers with a marshmallow in the middle, I think. Oh, and with chocolate spread or something."

"How do you toast a cracker?"

"Buggered if I know."

"Think I'll stick to marshmallows."

"You're a lightweight, Milton. Let's get hammered."

Chapter Fourteen

A FUNNY THING HAPPENED ON THE WAY TO THE FORUM

Clare

"What's that rattling noise?" Miles said, quietly. "Can you hear that?"

"It's my t-t-t-teeth! I'm so c-c-c-cold! I thought C-C-California was supposed to be h-h-hot?"

I heard a shuffling sound, and suddenly Miles' arms were pulling me into his chest, his warmth radiating through me.

"It's December," he laughed, softly. "And night. C'mere. I'll warm you up."

Suddenly, I was wide awake. Even half frozen, I'd been only semi-conscious, but the moment Miles touched me, my whole body was on red alert. Or maybe it was on green, because it definitely wanted to go. I was primed and ready, almost breathless with desire. The fire shooting up from my belly was intense and instant. You'd think that having spent 24/7 with him for the last three days, I would have been somewhat desensitized, but no. I was like some supersonic radar, or giant satellite dish, tuned to his broadcast.

I held my breath as he moved closer, thanking every deity I could think of that the campervan had a system of seats and benches that could be turned into one reasonably large double bed at night.

Miles hadn't even so much as blinked when he set out our borrowed sleeping bags. But my heart was galloping as if I'd just run the Kentucky Derby on foot with my arse on fire.

As always, I played it cool, and slid down onto the improvised bed, trying to get warm.

Miles pulled me back into his chest and draped an arm over my body, languidly rubbing my shoulder.

"By the way," he said, sleepily. "I meant to say—you looked beautiful in that dress. Blue really suits you."

Oh, I really wanted to hear him say those words again.

"Sorry, what?"

"Mmm, hot," he mumbled.

I wanted to yell, *Speak up! Stop muttering!* What did he mean? That he was too hot, or that the dress was hot? Maybe he even meant that *I* was hot, which seemed less likely.

I wanted to beat him about the head and shoulders until he gave me a proper answer. Instead, his warm breaths stirred my hair softly and I realized he was asleep.

Bloody, bloody men! Just as they start saying something that we might actually want to hear, they bloody well fall asleep on us! Surely torture like that is prohibited under the Geneva Convention?

And then I wondered what would happen if I just jumped his bones. God, he was so clueless, he'd probably apologize for somehow falling underneath me! Maybe if I told him how I felt.

Miles, you're the most clueless man I've ever met. But you're also the sweetest, nicest, funniest, kindest person I've ever met. You're fuck hot, and every time I'm petting the poodle, I think about you launching your meat missile and sinking me with your pink torpedo.

God help me! If I actually came out and said that, it would be up there with, *I carried a watermelon.*

My own thoughts made me cringe. But at least the blushes were heated, and I drifted away, dreaming of the promised land that was currently breathing softly behind me.

When I woke up in the morning, I felt warm and almost comfortable. I realized with a start that I was lying across

Miles' chest and had my hand under his t-shirt, resting on his heart.

I shifted my leg, embarrassed when I noticed it was hooked over his hip. And, holy shit! That was some morning timber I could feel, even through two layers of sleeping bags.

My movement woke him up. *Damn! Damn! Damn!* I hadn't even had time to pull out my camera phone.

"Hi," he said sleepily, rubbing his eyes.

I tried to disentangle myself, dragging my hand down his firm chest and across his taut stomach. Suddenly, his eyes were wide open. His look was surprised then heart-stoppingly intense. And for a moment, for a brief, indescribable moment, I really thought he was going to do it—I really thought he was going to kiss me.

I felt my cheeks flush, and he blinked.

"Oh, sorry," he muttered, moving away from me. "Sorry, um..."

"No, no, it's fine," I squeaked. "Uh ... um ... I'll ... I'm going for a pee, and ... um ... and ... um ... I'll make some tea ... later."

"Yeah, okay," he said, looking toward his lap. "I'll ... uh ... just need a minute."

Oh by the love of all that's holy, STOP TALKING!

I kicked off the sleeping bag and pulled on my jeans, Miles' words running through my brain on repeat. I opened the door of the campervan, the sea breeze cooling my hot cheeks, and fell face first into a dune.

"I'm fine!" I shouted through a mouthful of sand, then crawled commando style so he wouldn't see me from the window. "I'm fine! Just ... fine!"

Please don't look! Please don't look!

He looked.

"Clare! Are you all right because I heard you..." he paused. "What are you doing down there?"

Looking for the center of the earth. Hoping a giant meteor will crash down right now. Wishing that Matt Bomer wasn't gay. Praying you're not looking at me!

"Um, nothing. Just dropped my toothbrush."

There was a short silence.

"You left it on the table. Do you want it?"

I stood up, brushed the sand off my knees and face, and looked him in the eye.

He was trying not to laugh. I scowled, and a huge smile lit up his face.

"Here's your toothbrush. And, um, happy birthday!"

I snatched my toothbrush out of his hand.

"Fuck off," I said.

His laughter followed me all the way to the washrooms. At least I made him laugh. I was good for something.

Despite the complete absence of anything approaching civilization, I had to admit the whole camping experience was more fun than I was expecting.

We took long walks, found small, out of season cafés to drink coffee and eat donuts. We talked a lot, and Miles tried to explain again why he loved acting, despite the tons of shit that seemed to accompany it. He told me about the house he'd seen online that he wanted to buy for his mum—just a few streets from where we all rented now, so she'd still be near her old , as well as my parents. He described some of the job offers that Rhonda texted him about on a daily basis. He offered to pay off my student loans, and although I was grateful, I declined. We argued a bit about that. He called me a "stubborn mare" and I called him a "patriarchal git". Fun times.

Plus, he'd insisted on paying for *everything*. I mean, I wasn't even allowed to pay for a cup of coffee. It was irritating —I'd always paid my way before. But Miles ignored me and my wallet. I teased him, calling him Mr. Moneybags.

But the truth was, it was just so hard to take in that Miles was, well, rich.

Mum and Dad phoned to wish me a happy birthday just before dinner. It was good to hear their voices, but I rushed them off, worried how much the call must be costing them.

I spent my birthday evening with Miles having a romantic meal in an Italian restaurant, improbably named 'Mama's Meatball'. When I say romantic, I mean the setting, you know? Candles on the table, low lighting, fantastic food, table for two, and the most beautiful man in the world sharing forkfuls of food with me across a starched linen tablecloth.

Our waitress did a double take when she saw us—well, when she saw him. I could see her wondering if it really was who she thought it was, but when she looked at me, it was like the sum didn't add up.

Him + her = ?

I could practically hear the cogs in her brain coming to a grinding halt. *Does not compute. Does not compute.*

I was resting my stomach after a wonderful starter of grilled mushrooms with gorgonzola, and a main course of penne al pesto, and was hoping I'd find room to fit in at least a taste of tiramisu from the dessert menu. Miles had already given up and was sitting back sipping his alcohol-free beer, as that was all he'd been allowed to order.

It was irritating that he'd got carded on my birthday, but he shrugged and said he'd make up for it later. I ordered half a carafe of red wine for myself. I offered to share it but he shook his head.

"Yeah, so I got you a present," he said, apropos of absolutely nothing.

"You did?"

He rolled his eyes.

"Of course! It's your twenty-first! I've had it for weeks." He looked slightly apprehensive. "I hope you like it."

"I'll love it whatever it is, you dope!"

He grinned and turned to dig something out of his jacket

pocket that was hanging on the chair back. At the same time his t-shirt rode up to reveal a hint of toned stomach.

I wanted to leap across the table and yell, *You! I'll have you for my birthday! On the table—now! And I'll smear tiramisu over your whole body and lick it off slowly!*

"What?" he said studying my face, which must have looked a picture. *Yeah, not that sort of picture.*

"Nothing."

He shook his head, bemused, then placed a small box on the table, the name *Harry Winston* inlaid in gold on the top.

"Wow! Seriously, Miles! What did you do?"

He laughed. "That's just the damn box—try opening it!"

I gave him an evil stare but he just rolled his eyes.

I popped the catch, giddy with anticipation, but when I opened it, all the breath froze in my lungs. I swear my heart stopped beating.

It was a small silver bracelet, like a charm bracelet, but every tiny charm was a heart. And in the center of each heart...

"Bloody hell, Miles! Are those diamonds? Real diamonds?"

He shrugged, trying to look casual but I could tell that my reaction had pleased him—and made him a bit uncomfortable.

"It's not just for your birthday," he said. "It's to say thank you for, well, everything. Coming out last summer when I was freaking out, you know. It meant a lot to me. So, yeah. Thanks."

Moving slowly, he lifted the delicate-looking bracelet out of the box and waited for me to hold out my left hand. Then he fastened it carefully around my wrist and sat back, a satisfied look on his face.

"Happy birthday, Clare."

"It's ... it's beautiful," I said, watching the diamonds glinting in the candlelight. "The silver is so delicate and ... what?"

He looked like he was trying not to laugh.

"What?" I said again, irritated.

"Um, it's not silver. It's platinum," he said.

My mouth dropped open with a soft pop.

"Oh."

"You deserve the best," he said, quietly.

I had no idea how much a bracelet like that cost. Probably enough to pay off my student loans.

Not that I'd sell it.

Ever.

Not that it would leave my wrist.

Ever.

"How did you get to be so smooth, Stephens?" I said.

"No idea, Milton," he batted back. "Are you impressed?"

"Well, um, it's really ... just ... thank you."

"You're welcome," he said, softly.

Yeah, it was perfect and romantic.

We walked back to the campervan, hand in hand, and shared a bottle of champagne that Miles had kept hidden away. I even got to snuggle up to him that night, our sleeping bags side by side. All that was missing was the knee-trembling, after dinner kiss—oh, and mind-blowing sex.

Yeah, that was all.

The following day we headed over to the jazz festival. It was small, friendly, and had some really talented musicians. Miles got to join in some jamming sessions, and he was only recognized a couple of times, but it was mellow and never got out of hand. He smiled, signed autographs and posed for pictures, but otherwise he was left alone.

He said himself that he could breathe out here, and that LA had been smothering him.

Of course, it couldn't last. Sooner, rather than later, we had to go back to reality. *His reality.*

Earl had been brilliant and picked up Miles' car from the garage in his building, so when we got back to Bellflower and handed over the VW, we had transport.

Maureen cooked us an amazing Tex Mex meal, and Deena told us that all her friends were green with envy.

Yeah, me, too, little girl.

Their son Freddy was back from Northwestern where he was a pre-med student, and more confusingly, he spent the evening flirting with me.

It took me a while to crack on to the fact that he was one of those guys who flirted with any female who had a pulse. And, as he was pre-med, probably some without a pulse, too. *Oh, God! Why did I have to think that?*

But he was cute and funny and made me laugh. I could have *sworn* Miles was sulking—but if Freddy's flirting made him jealous, then even better.

When we finally arrived back at Miles' apartment, we were both exhausted and kind of blue.

But that wasn't the worst of it.

Our little holiday for two was over, and that bubble of happiness was quick to burst.

It was Rhonda's fault.

She said that as he was back in town, Miles owed it to everyone to do at least one interview before the Christmas holidays started.

It was true that Jo-Anne had taken up the slack while he'd been away, but at the same time, Rhonda knew that suggesting he do it—virtually ordering him—it was going to be grim.

No one had talked about what would happen when Miles and Lilia were in the same room together again. The studio had tried to strong-arm Miles into seeing her, citing breach of contract and Lord knows what else. But he'd ignored them all, much to everyone's surprise, and was doing things his way. The studio backed down when they saw his determination.

"You've got to just pull off that band-aid, Miles," Rhonda said. "It's going to hurt like a bitch, but once you've done your first interview, the rest will seem like a breeze. Besides, Kimmel has been told not to ask you about Lilia."

"But you know he will!" I snapped.

She gave me a look that said, *butt out*, and for once I was talking to someone whose butt was bigger than mine.

"You can't hide forever," Rhonda reasoned.

No matter how much Miles might want to argue *that* particular point, we both knew she was right.

"Besides, it's Christmas Eve. You won't get many paps bothering you for a few days. I hope," she added, quietly.

Miles groaned and squeezed his eyes shut, his whole body filled with tension.

So much for the benefits of a vacation.

"I'm not ready," he said, looking down.

"Look, I can practice the questions with you."

"Like learning lines?" he smirked, opening one eye.

"Gotta roll with the punches, Miles," she said. "Because there's always someone itching to take you down. Grow up, grow a pair, and smell the coffee."

Rhonda really liked to mix her metaphors.

"Fine, if that's your advice, but I won't fucking like it."

"Not many do," she said, without a shred of sympathy in her voice. "Get over it."

So that was that.

I still wasn't sure it was a good idea, and Miles was acting weird. Weirder than usual. He'd been drinking more than usual since we'd been back. I mean, neither of us were exactly teetotalers, especially after our road trip—meaning we'd got through all the alcohol Earl had supplied us with and more— but over the last two days, Miles had been hitting the bottle harder than I'd ever seen him. And, instead of beer, he was drinking vodka.

If anyone ever tells you that vodka doesn't make your breath smell of alcohol, ignore them and get some better friends, because they're talking major league bullshit.

It was no different that night. Miles had a bottle of Sobieski in his dressing room.

"Take it easy with that," I said, my tone deliberately mild.

"Now you're my mother?" he sneered.

"Fuck off, Miles. You're being a dickhead."

He shrugged. "Why should I be different from everyone else?"

Before I had a chance to answer him, one of the APs knocked on the dressing room door and stuck her head inside.

"Five minutes, Mr. Stephens."

He didn't even bother to reply and that made me frown. Miles was never rude to people. *Never.*

He tossed another glass of vodka down his throat and belched loudly, grinning at me.

Then he stretched and stood up, at which point he fell over. He lay on the floor giggling.

"Bloody hell, Miles! Get up! You're going on air in about three minutes!"

"Who gives a shit," he mumbled, blinking up at me. "I mean, seriously, Clare, who cares?"

"I care!" I yelled.

His smile fell away. "You're the only one."

I knelt on the floor and helped him to sit up.

"I love you, Clare," he slurred.

"I love you, too, you big girl's blouse. Now get up and get your arse into gear."

"You love ordering me about, don't you? Is that what you're like in bed? All bossy. Cause I gotta say—that's hot!"

And he laughed again.

I felt my cheeks flame up, and I wasn't sure whether or not I hoped he'd remember saying that when he was sober. *He thought about me in bed?*

The AP knocked on the door again, and using strength I didn't know I had, I hauled Miles to his feet and shook him slightly.

"Get a grip and man up!" I growled at him.

He gave me a bleary smile and winked. "I'd like to man up with you, Clare."

Oh. My. God.

Then the AP opened the door and led him out. I had no idea how Miles managed to walk in a straight line.

I followed him to the wings of the theater and watched him glide toward his interview seat, as the audience exploded into rapturous applause.

Seeing him in close-up on the monitors, it was obvious to me that his eyes were unfocussed, but otherwise no one would have guessed that he'd been drinking. Yet.

Rhonda walked over and stood beside me, frowning slightly. It seemed to be a permanent feature with her these days.

After the initial welcoming questions, the interviewer dived right in.

"You're still only 20, Miles, but do you feel like you've matured since you've been here?"

"Maybe, but not until I've exhausted all other possibilities."

The audience laughed. I cringed.

"And how do you like living in LA?"

"I like California—especially if you're an orange."

Oh what? Now he was quoting Fred Allen?

The audience laughed again, and Miles grinned at them, looking happy and relaxed. *Too bloody relaxed.*

"What do you like most about America?"

"Freedom of speech."

"Really?"

"Yeah, I don't get to say anything I mean."

"Ha ha! Good answer!"

No, it's not, you clot! He's winding you up like you're clockwork!

"So, if you were President, Miles, what would you do?"

"Give the Colonies back to the Queen."

He smiled broadly. There was a communal intake of breath.

Oh God, Miles! You can't say things like that!

The interviewer was clearly taken aback, as was the audience. Miles smiled beatifically.

"Is he drunk?" Rhonda hissed at me.

I glanced at her nervously.

"Um, possibly."

"Why the hell did you let him go out there like that?!"

"It's not my fucking fault he decided to get blitzed! And, as he so charmingly reminded me, I'm not his bloody mother!"

She looked like she was going to rip me a new one, but I was *so* willing to punch her in the mouth if she said anything else.

"He *told* you he wasn't ready!" I snarled at her. "He loved that tramp, but *you* thought it was a good idea to put him on national TV 11 days after she was photographed with her mouth around another man's dick. What the hell did you expect?"

Since Miles' realization that Lilia had probably been cheating on him from the beginning, he'd refused to talk about her or even mention her name, and another few bricks had been put in the wall that he was slowly building up around himself. And I was on the other side of it.

"Christ," muttered Rhonda.

I turned back to watch the rest of the car crash interview.

"How do you respond when people—girls—scream at you.

Miles shrugged. "I leave my brain at the door."

A pickled brain at this rate.

"It's been a pretty wild ride for you since you came to Hollywood. How do you cope with that?"

"I dunno. It's like learning a new language, you know? Like if someone says to you, 'Oh yeah, that scene was great—it had an interesting stillness,' what they really mean is 'that was crap'."

Rhonda dropped her head into her hands.

"And how do you like being single again?" Kimmel said, a sly look on his face.

Miles smiled, although the humor didn't reach his eyes.

"I guess you could say it sucks."

. . .

Miles

It was entirely possible that my head had been separated from my body, then reattached using piano wire and a blunt knitting needle.

Opening one eyelid had a pain factor that was off the chart. I squinted up at the bastard bright light piercing through the thin material of the curtain.

Then I felt the bed move.

Shit! A woman with short, honey-colored hair and smeared mascara was smiling at me.

"Hi. Remember me?"

"Um?"

I opened the other eye.

"Sherry," she said, cheerfully.

"Oh," I croaked, relieved I had regained the power of speech.

She ran a finger down my chest and I realized I wasn't wearing a shirt. *Oh, shit. This was bad.* I couldn't remember a fucking thing since the interview. *Oh, God! The interview!* What the hell did I say? In fact, where the hell was I?

"Mmm," said the woman, "that's quite a tent you're pitching. Ready to go again, baby? Pretty wild night, hey?!"

Oh, fuck.

She was right. I was naked, hard ... and about to hurl. Any second ... *now.*

I managed to aim most of the vomit into a handy trashcan that was next to the bed. And even as I was throwing up, I couldn't help noticing that there were a number of used condoms in the bottom.

What the hell had I done last night?

The woman—Sherry—didn't look impressed. In fact, after my technicolor display, she looked a little green herself.

"Bathroom," she said, pointing to my left.

I shuffled inside, wincing at the sight of my face in her mirror. I rinsed my mouth out and debated whether or not to use her toothbrush. In the end I didn't. We may have fucked

—which seemed likely given the evidence—but I didn't know her *that* well.

I stuck my head under the tap and the shock of cold water woke me up more fully. All I had to do now was find my clothes, call a cab, and pray I had money in my wallet. *Shit.* And then I had to face Clare.

The fates were temporarily aligned in my favor, because when I slouched back into the bedroom, Sherry and the offending trashcan had gone. I heard someone moving around elsewhere in the apartment—*wherever the fuck I was*—but was relieved to find my clothes and phone in one piece.

I dressed slowly, hunting down each piece of clothing, wondering how the hell my shirt had ended up draped across the lightshade, and praying my head wouldn't actually explode or fall off. Then I took a deep breath and walked out of the bedroom.

Sherry was standing by the coffee machine in the kitchen. I had to admit she was cute, but at the same time, I never wanted to see her again in my whole life.

"Coffee?" she said, smiling.

"Uh, no I'm good, thanks. I should get going. I'll call a cab. Um, can you tell me where I am?" The cracks of my brain were starting to show.

Her smile slipped away and I felt even more shitty.

"North Hollywood, 27983 Victory Boulevard," she said, in a small voice.

"Thanks. And, um, you're beautiful."

A hard look crossed her face and she yawned.

I kissed her on the cheek and walked out, closing the door quietly behind me.

"Merry fucking Christmas!" she yelled behind the door.

Ah, hell.

The cab arrived a few minutes later, and it wasn't long before I was trudging up to the entrance of my apartment building. I closed my eyes and breathed deeply, knowing that the inquisition would start as soon as I walked in the door.

Clare was sitting on the couch fully dressed, her hands

wrapped around a mug of coffee. She looked up but she didn't speak and she didn't smile. I'm not even sure she blinked.

"I'm really sorry about last night," I started.

Her eyes narrowed, and mentally I began digging a trench.

"If I wanted to listen to an arsehole, I'd fart a tune," she said, her voice hard and clear.

Then she stood up, put her coffee cup on the table and went to the guestroom, slamming the door shut behind her.

Well, fuck.

I slumped down where she'd been sitting. Idly, I picked up her cup and took a drink. Ugh, milky coffee with no sugar. But it was liquid, and still warm. I drank it quickly, hoping that rehydration would help improve my brain function.

I had a horrible feeling that whatever Clare said to me, I probably deserved it.

Of course, first I had to get her to speak to me.

Feeling too tired and hung-over to make that sort of effort, I headed for my room. I reeked of vodka, sweat, and sex—a combination that was making me nauseous.

I stripped off my clothes, and let the shower wash away the wages of sin, if not the sin itself.

Feeling slightly more human, I debated the wisdom of speaking to Clare immediately, or sleeping on it and hoping I'd make more sense when less hung-over.

I almost opted for bed, cowardice seeming particularly attractive right there and then, but I *hated* fighting with Clare. It didn't happen very often. In fact, other than arguing over who was better at *Guitar Hero*, we hadn't really had any serious fights.

I took a deep breath and knocked on her door. I stopped in my tracks when I saw that she was packing her case.

"What are you doing?"

She wouldn't look at me.

"Going home."

"But ... but our flight isn't for another four days. For the London premiere. And it's Christmas..."

My words faded out as she ignored me, and continued throwing clothes in her case.

"I've phoned for a taxi," she said, her voice empty of emotion. "It'll be here in a few minutes."

I ran my hand through my hair in frustration. *I couldn't believe she was behaving like this!*

"Shit, Clare. Don't go. I know I've fucked up but..."

"Yeah, you did, Miles. Big time."

I started getting angry. It wasn't like I'd fucked one of her friends or something.

"Ah come on, give me a break. You know what I've been going through!"

"By the way, your Mum rang."

And the hits just keep on coming.

"What did she say?"

Clare straightened up and finally looked at me.

"She saw the interview."

"Shit!"

"She said you reminded her of your dad."

Fuck. That was like a knife in my chest—and she knew it.

"Look, I'm sorry, okay? It was dumb, getting drunk like that, and I'm an idiot, but I don't want you to go."

"Do you think my life is nothing?" she snapped.

"No!" *What?* "No, of course not!"

But she wouldn't let me finish.

Clare

After the interview last night, some of the groupies waiting outside had been happy to drag an inebriated Miles to a 'party'. I tried to make him come home with me but he wouldn't listen. He just sat and laughed at me, and went with the skanks. I'd waited up for hours, but he didn't come home.

My silent vigil gave me plenty of time to think about what I was doing. Or not doing. After hours of weighing up the pros and cons, of hoping against hope that Miles would finally come home—to me—something inside me broke. And even though I felt sick at the thought of it, my decision was to leave.

I knew it was unreasonable of me to be so upset. Miles and I weren't dating. We weren't anything. And that was the point. If I'd been a guy friend, I'd probably just have patted him on the back when he came home still drunk and smelling of sex and cheap perfume.

But I couldn't take it. I couldn't take being around him while he picked every woman under the sun, but he *never* picked me.

I phoned the airline to change my flight and packed up most of my stuff.

And now here he was, trying to persuade me that there was some reason for me to stay.

"Perhaps you thought that I'd just sit around waiting for you? I do have a life, Miles, it's not all about you!"

What a lie.

"I'm sorry! I didn't mean it like that. I..."

"No. You never do mean it. That's the problem."

We'd never had a fight like this before.

He stood watching me, his hands shoved into the pockets of his jeans. He looked tired and his eyes were red, but he was still so beautiful it made my heart ache.

I dropped the lid of my suitcase and tightened the straps. I was desperately hoping that he'd say something *real*. Anything. But he didn't. He just carried on watching me in silence. He wasn't even going to fight for me to stay. That about summed it up. I guess I'd stopped being *convenient*. I was the boring, fat friend who got in the way of him having a good time, and only served to make him feel guilty about it afterward.

I pulled on my coat and he still didn't speak.

"Goodbye, Miles," I whispered.

And I kissed his sweet face for the last time.

"Don't go. Stay with me. Please," he mumbled, his voice breaking.

I shook my head.

"Your world dazzles me but I don't fit in here—I have to go."

I left him standing in his apartment, his face shocked and pale.

And as I walked away I realized it wasn't his world—it was him. I'd been dazzled by him my whole life. And it wasn't enough. For either of us.

As half my heart withered with each passing moment, the other half felt light and free. I was going home.

Chapter Fifteen

CINEMA PARADISO

Miles

I couldn't believe that Clare had really gone. She'd really left me. At Christmas. And I only had myself to blame. I think.

Yeah, so did I do the smart thing and go after her? Find her at LAX and drag her back? No, I sat on my arse on the couch and drank half a bottle of vodka.

It was all that was left in the apartment. I guess I'd already drunk everything else.

I woke up about 14 hours later face down on her bed in the guestroom, clutching the shit-hot blue dress that she'd worn to the LA premiere. She was so sick of me, she didn't even want the dress to remind her.

Just to heap another layer of shit on my complete fucking misery, I watched the Kimmel interview clip on Youtube over and over, tormenting myself with the stinking heap of crap that seemed to be my life. I watched the audience laughing as I slurred my stupid answers, and I felt sick. At the time, I'd thought they were laughing because I was so damn funny— now I knew they were laughing *at* me.

Rhonda was furious, and sent me an email that made my eyeballs bleed just reading it. She also promised to drag me kicking and screaming to an AA meeting if I didn't get my shit together and quit drinking.

I really didn't like the idea of sitting around and sharing my *feelings* with a bunch of strangers, so I decided to shape up. Which was easier said than done when all I felt like doing was wallowing.

Talking to Mum on the phone had been another really fucking humiliating experience.

"And I've never been so ashamed of you! Making a fool of yourself like that on the telly! Drunk! So smug and full of yourself—just like *him*."

"Mum, I..."

"Don't you 'mum' me! It was a disgusting exhibition! And what the bloody hell have you done to Clare? That poor girl has done nothing but be a good friend to you, and she's been in tears ever since she got back. *In tears!*"

Shit! I'd only ever seen Clare cry once and that was when they shot Bambi's mum.

"I tried to call her today but she won't..."

"Of course she won't, and I don't blame her! Doesn't she mean *anything* to you? The way she's helped you and supported you!"

"I know, but..."

"Don't you 'but' me! You get your sorry arse over here and make it right! Do you hear me, Miles Fletcher Stephens? You sort it out!"

Yeah, so what does a grown man say when his mum reams him out like that?

"Yes, Mum."

But I had no idea how the hell I was going to make it right.

Clare

Christmas Day and I was back in London.

It had been a long and miserable flight, and even the wide, comfortable seat in first class didn't make me feel any better.

I stared at the bracelet of diamond hearts that Miles had given me just a week ago. I'd considered leaving it in LA, along with the fabulous blue dress that I'd worn to the premiere, but I couldn't be that cruel. Miles had given it to me in friendship, and despite everything, we had been good friends. Maybe we still were—sort of—although it seemed doubtful.

But last night had been a huge kick in the teeth and a much needed reality check.

I'd been through every possible negative emotion while I was waiting for him to come back to his apartment: anger, fear, loathing, grief. I also felt ridiculous, humiliated and utterly pathetic. It wasn't as if Miles had cheated on me; we'd never been together that way. I told myself that over and over again. *He hadn't cheated on me.*

It just felt like he had.

I took the bracelet off when I got home and put it away in its box.

Mum knew straight away that something was wrong. Probably the fact I was home four days early was one giant clue.

"Well, are you going to talk to me, Clare, or do I have to stand here trying to get blood out of a stone?"

I sighed and leaned back on my bed.

"We had a fight. That's all."

She sat down next to me, her eyes confused but sympathetic.

"It must have been a bad one for you to leave so suddenly."

"Yep. Pretty bad."

"Was it about the interview?"

I wondered how much of the truth to give her, because I really didn't feel like conducting a post-mortem on the pathetic excuse for a life that was my existence.

"Yeah. Mostly."

"But not completely?"

I looked up, seeing nothing judgmental in her eyes.

"I got tired of being in the way."

"What do you mean?"

I shrugged, unsure how to explain.

"But what that woman did to him," Mum pressed. "Surely you should be with him, Miles must be in pieces?"

"I know, Mum, he is. But it doesn't mean that I can fix him. In fact, I'm fairly certain I was making things worse."

"I don't see how."

I ground my teeth in frustration.

"I can't fix his relationship with another woman. I never could. It's up to him."

Mum nodded slowly, then sighed.

"Well, I'm sure you can sort it out when he's here for his premiere."

She frowned when I didn't answer. But I had no intention whatso-bloody-ever of going to that premiere. I would be quite happy to never see anything to do with *Dazzled* ever again.

I was relieved—I think—when I got a text from Paul and Nazzer saying that they were at the pub for a Boxing Day drink and did I want to meet them.

I'd already had a couple of beers—okay, four—while I was recovering from leftover turkey curry and Mum's dose of girl time. So I was feeling pleasantly buzzed when I waded through the unwashed humanity that made up the majority of drinkers at the *Stag Inn*. Also known to regulars as the *Stagger in and out*.

"Oi, Milton!" yelled Paul over the babble of people talking and drinking and enjoying themselves—selfish bastards. Didn't they know I wanted to be miserable? "Over here!"

They were sitting at a small table littered with empty bottles.

"Your round," said Nazzer, looking expectantly at me. "Get the beers in."

"How'd you figure that? I haven't seen you in weeks!"

"Well, Paul and me have bought two rounds each, so you're behind, you tightwad. Come on, get yer wallet out."

Grumbling, I forced my way to the bar and bought three bottles of Danish beer.

"So, how's our man in America?" said Paul, as I slammed the bottles onto the table. "Bet he's still crying into his beer over that slag. If I was him, I'd have tapped every bint I could by now."

I winced.

"Yeah," said Nazzer, sadly. "It's much harder to get women to talk to us now that Miles has cleared off."

"Like never," Paul agreed, sighing heavily.

"I'll talk to you," I said, rolling my eyes.

"But you don't count," Paul replied.

"Why the hell not?"

"Because," he said, drawing out the second syllable as if he were a dentist, "because you're off limits. I couldn't get it up —you're like my sister or something."

"Huh."

"I'll do you," offered Nazzer, after a short pause.

"Aw, Naz, would you?"

"Yeah, if you like. You scrub up okay—for a fat girl."

I must have been drunk because I was actually considering it for a moment.

Nazzer looked at his watch.

"So, we going to, or what?" he slurred through his lecherous smile.

"I dunno?" I said, yawning. "Is there anything good on telly tonight?"

"Yeah," said Paul. "A *Thunderbirds* marathon."

"Oh, cool!" said Nazzer, enthusiastically. "Let's get a kebab and go to your place. You coming, Milton?"

There are many low points in a woman's life, but when the bloke who's been within a hair's breadth of getting his hand down your knickers decides that he'd rather watch a children's sci-fi program made with puppets fifty years ago, you can't get much lower. Just saying.

I went home alone, and the boys went off to eat kebabs and watch TV.

If they'd cheered me up anymore, I'd currently be typing texts with my toes in a secure unit at Broadmoor hospital.

Three days later and two days before the delayed UK premiere of *Dazzled*, and I still hadn't returned any of Miles' calls or texts. He'd even emailed me, but I hadn't replied to those either.

The Press were getting their knickers in a twist about the premiere and the coverage had been relentless. They were still harping on about the irony of the film's theme of immortal love when Lilia hadn't been able to keep her sticky fingers to herself for, well, however long it had been.

Miles had originally planned to stay with his mum next door, but in the end it just wasn't possible. I wasn't sure whether or not to feel relieved that he wouldn't be so close to me.

In any case, it didn't matter because I'd decided not to go to the bloody premiere. When I'd refused to answer my phone yet again, Miles had called my parents' house on the landline. Mum had picked up the phone and tried to get me to speak to him. In the end, tired of her nagging, I'd taken the phone from her and simply replaced the receiver, cutting him off.

Dad buried his head in the paper and turned up the volume on the TV when me and Mum started yelling at each other.

But the truth was, I had nothing to say to Miles, and I wasn't ready to be friends with him either. It hurt too much.

It didn't take Mum long to send for reinforcements, so I wasn't surprised when I came home from work the next day to find Miles' mum, Prue, sitting at our kitchen table with a mug of tea and a plate of chocolate chip cookies.

"Hello, Clare! It's good to see you. How are you, love?"

"Yeah, fine, thanks, Prue. How are you?"

"I wanted to talk to you about Miles," she said, looking me in the eye, and ignoring my question.

I sighed. I'd been expecting this. I just hoped I'd have a bit more time to get my head straight first.

"He's really sorry, sweetheart, I know he is. He hates that you won't talk to him."

"Prue..."

She held up her hands.

"I know, love, it's none of my business, but you and Miles have been friends ever since you were nippers. It worries me to see you both like this—Miles is terribly upset."

Nice move, Prue. She was deliberately making me feel bad for upsetting *her.*

"He knows he was a first class idiot, getting drunk like that, and he's so sorry. Can't you forgive him? For me?"

"Prue... I *have* forgiven him. I just can't be around him ... when he's like that."

She looked slightly mollified.

"Well, will *you* tell him that you forgive him? He needs to hear it from you, love."

Emotional blackmail. She ought to do interrogations for MI5 or some other spooks.

"He said he's phoned and emailed you. If you could just give him a chance..."

Her face was so hopeful, I couldn't refuse.

"Fine. I'll email him. Happy?"

She smiled. "He'll like that. But it's his premiere tomorrow. I know he'll want you to be there."

Ugh!

"No, I don't think so..."

"Oh, come on, love, it's his big night! I know you wouldn't want to miss that. Now Sheila and Graham can't come, you'll be representing the Miltons."

I threw Mum a jaundiced look. "You're not going either?"

"It's your Aunt Paula's 25th wedding anniversary that night, so we're double-booked," said Mum. "When they changed the date of the premiere, there was nothing we could do."

"Don't worry, love," said Prue, patting Mum's hand. "I'm sure Clare won't let us down. Besides," she said, turning to face me, "these things are always best fixed face-to-face."

I wasn't sure it was something that *could* be fixed, face-to-face or otherwise. But as Prue didn't know the real reason for me not wanting to see Miles, it was impossible to explain how I felt.

Wow. I didn't want to see him. The knowledge hurt my chest.

"No, Prue. It's not the right place ... to talk."

"So you will talk to him?"

Jeez, she was relentless.

"Give him a chance, love," she said, as she gripped my hand and pressed home her advantage. "It's not like you to be angry with him. I'd always thought that you two ... well, I'm sure whatever he said to upset you, he didn't mean it. He's a man—he can't help it."

My phone beeped in my pocket, but I resisted the urge to see who the text was from.

"Is that him?" asked Prue, an eager expression on her face.

Fuming quietly, I pulled the phone out and looked at the message. My traitorous, hopeful heart plunged again. It wasn't from Miles.

"Nope. It's from Polly. She worked on the film with ... us."

"That's nice, dear," said Mum. "What does she say?"

"Nosy much!" I snorted.

What was with these two?! If they set up their own detective agency, they'd be solving mysteries from Jimmy Hoffa to the Loch Ness Monster.

"I didn't know it was a secret," said Mum, sharply.

Rolling my eyes, I opened the message.

"She says she's coming to the premiere and wants to meet up. Happy now?"

"That'll be nice," said Prue. "You two can go to the premiere together."

"I'm. Not. Going. To. The. Premiere!" I said, gritting my teeth.

Yeah, that was the plan, but after another 45 minutes of having my brain dragged out through my nostrils by Glinda and the Wicked Witch of West, um, North London, I would have given them my firstborn just to shut them up.

They hovered over me while I sent a text to Polly agreeing to meet at her hotel, so we could go to the premiere together.

I thought I'd probably be safe doing that. For one thing, if it was at all like the last premiere, I wouldn't even get a chance to talk to him.

Prue winked at me as I pressed 'send', and Mum just looked smug.

Harpies.

Then the Press descended.

The first we knew about it was an hour later when a couple of cars and a van pulled up outside, and I saw the telltale long black lenses of cameras pointed at Prue's house next door.

"They're here," I said, in an eerie sing-song voice.

'Poltergeist' had scared the hell out of me the first time I saw it.

"Who's here?"

"The press. Reporters. They're waiting for Miles," I added, quietly.

Prue peeped out through the net curtains and went pale.

"Is this what it's like for Miles?" breathed Mum.

I pulled a face. "Worse."

She shook her head in disbelief.

"I think you'd better go out through the backdoor," Mum said to Prue.

"And you should call Melody," I said. "You know, Miles' agent? Tell her what's happened. He won't be able to stay here now."

Prue looked shaken but she promised she'd make the call as soon as she got next door.

She slipped out through the back, clutching her cardigan around her like a security blanket. I understood how that felt.

Before Miles' plane had even touched the tarmac at Heathrow airport, the whole of our road was mobbed with press.

All the neighbors had their noses pressed to the windows, waiting to see a guy that they'd seen a hundred thousand times before, and had grown up playing in that street.

Thirty minutes later, Prue phoned Mum to say that Melody had booked her and Miles into the Dorchester, a hotel used to handling the security needed by celebrities, and that a limousine had been sent to pick her up.

We watched through the curtains as an enormous black car swept up to the pavement—or as near as it could get with 30 reporters and a dozen TV crews milling around. A pair of burly security guards cleared a route through the heaving bodies for Prue to exit safely, and she was whisked away into the night.

Mum threw me a nervous glance. I didn't need to ask what she was thinking.

I already knew.

But it didn't let me off the hook either. Mum insisted that I still had to go to the darn premiere, "because you promised".

God, it was so irritating when she was right.

And I had to buy a dress. One I could afford, bearing in mind the size of my student loans.

I felt a momentary pang of regret for the beautiful dress I'd left behind in Miles' apartment. I knew it wasn't the thing to wear the same dress twice, but it wasn't like anyone would have noticed.

A morning traipsing up and down Oxford Street, right in

the middle of the winter sales, was a miserable experience. You needed a sharp pair of elbows and language like a docker to even get near the clothes rails.

Running out of time, and loooong out of patience, I found something cheap that I thought would do in *Top Shop*.

Which was why, one hour, two donuts and a bottle of champagne later, I was standing in Polly's hotel room just off Leicester Square, wondering why the hell I'd thought magenta would do anything for my complexion. Or my boobs. Or any part of me, in fact.

"I look like a friggin' Quality Street," I grumbled.

"Yeah, you're quality, honey," she said, absentmindedly.

I rolled my eyes. "No! A Quality Street is a chocolate—one of those wrapped in colored cellophane and ... you know what, never mind."

She wasn't listening anyway.

"Does my butt look big in this?" she said, tugging at the day-glo orange frill around her hips.

"Yes," I said, honestly. "Enormous."

"You're a bitch."

"You say that like it's a bad thing."

She smirked. "Get used to it, honey, you'll be hearing that a lot."

Huh?

"Any particular reason?"

"Well, Lilia hates your guts."

"The feeling is mutual—but why in particular?"

"Because." She waved her arms around helplessly.

"Okay, you're going to have to be more specific. Because, what?"

"You've got Miles and she hasn't."

"I haven't 'got' Miles," I snapped, tetchily. "We're friends." *I think.* "That's all."

"Hmm," she said, a knowing look on her face. "Well, that's more than she has right now."

I scowled, wishing it were true.

"It's her own damn fault. If she wasn't such a cheating hag, she'd still have him."

"Maybe. I'm kinda surprised she bothered coming to the UK—the Press here hate her."

"The Press hate her everywhere—it's unifying. Maybe she should try world peace next."

Polly sniggered. "She probably will. A spell as a UN Goodwill Ambassador would look right for her *charidee* work."

I laughed then flicked my eyes toward Polly's ginormous suitcase.

"You sure you're not going to wear the black dress?"

She shook her head. "Nope, but you can wear it if you want."

With huge relief, I peeled off the pink monstrosity and tossed it onto her bed. You can't beat the ole LBD when you want to feel confident. At least, that's what I thought.

Unfortunately, Polly was half a size smaller than me and one of the seams tore as I forced the borrowed dress over my hips.

"Oops."

The champagne we'd shared had definitely mellowed Polly because she just shrugged her shoulders.

"Um, what do Americans call safety pins?" I said.

Polly rolled her eyes. "Safety pins."

"Oh. Have you got any?"

"No, sorry. Maybe they'll have some at the reception desk. Or failing that, you could staple it?"

Great. I was going to a film premiere where *he* would be there with *her*, in a dress held together with staples. *Isn't that life's way of saying you should have stayed in bed?*

But then my phone beeped with a text.

Don't get too excited—it was from my mum.

Is it there yet?

God, she was rubbish at texting.

I sent a message back.

> I'm with Polly. We're just leaving. Speak to you later.

Just as I was about to head down to get my dress stapled, there was a knock on the door.

I looked at Polly, who shrugged her shoulders.

A guy in the hotel's uniform was standing there with a suit carrier.

"Miss Milton?"

"Yes?"

"This is for you, madam."

Madam?

"I didn't order anything."

"For Miss Clare Milton."

I nodded, bemused.

"Sent by courier, madam."

He pushed the bag toward me, waited for a moment, presumably hoping for a tip, then huffed and stalked off down the corridor.

"Thanks!" I called after him.

"What is it?" asked Polly.

"Dunno. But it says it's for me."

Just then my phone rang.

"Hi, Mum."

"Has it arrived yet?"

"Oh! It's from you? Yeah! What is it?"

"Open it," she said, her voice excited. "I'll wait."

I pulled open the carrier and forgot how to breathe.

Inside was a gorgeous, floor-length, emerald green gown. You couldn't call it a dress. *This* was a *gown*.

"Holy shit!"

I wasn't sure whether I said that or it was Polly. Either way, we were both thinking the same thing.

I picked up the phone, stunned.

"Mum! Where did you get it? It's beautiful! It must have cost you an arm and a leg. Thanks so much! Wow!"

Her happy laugh echoed down the line.

"No, silly! Miles sent it—except he sent it to our house. I had to run around trying to find a courier to get it to you in time."

Miles sent it.

I didn't hear much of what she said after that.

"Are you going to try it on?" Polly whispered, reverently stroking the silky material.

"Uh, I suppose so."

"Wow!" she said, peering at the label. "Versace! This must have cost ... hell! I have no idea how much a dress like this would cost." She smiled at me eagerly. "You're so lucky, Clare!"

I didn't know what to feel. *Miles had sent me a dress?* Maybe it was a peace offering.

It fit perfectly. Of course.

I loved it. Of course.

We decided to walk from our hotel as it was only about 300 yards from the cinema where the premiere was being held.

Polly had insisted that we shouldn't wear coats because they'd look rubbish in photographs, and that Versace shouldn't be covered with a coat from Walmart.

"Nobody's going to take pictures of us!" I said, frowning.

"Ya never know," she grinned at me.

"Fine, whatever. But we'll freeze our arses off." Then a thought struck me. "But at least our nipples will look sensational."

"You're weird."

"What, you're only noticing that now?"

As soon as we left the hotel, we were fighting our way through hordes of screaming girls. It was a scrum just to get anywhere near the red carpet, and some slapper tried to pinch the silver invitations I was holding that showed we were legitimate premiere guests.

She was a couple of years younger than me, but taller, scraggier, and showing more flesh than a stripper in a Soho revue.

"Oi, get off," I snarled, snatching the invitation out of her filthy claws.

"Get over yourself," she laughed, completely unabashed at having been caught. "Nice dress, by the way. More Asda than Prada, love!"

"Oh, go and play with the traffic," I muttered, and pushed on through the crowd.

We showed our invitations to the security guards, who examined them at insolent length. I almost expected them to do a body search in case I'd got a weapon shoved down my cleavage. But that dress fitted like a glove, and trust me when I say *nothing* was getting down the front of there. *Unless Miles' hand happened to slip, in which case all bets were off.* No! Mustn't think like that.

I gave myself a mental slap.

It was a relief to be inside the warmth of the cinema. I'd been there many, many times before, and quite a few times with Miles. But not like this. It was familiar, but completely different.

For one thing, they'd gone to town with the decorations. I think it was supposed to be sort of heavenly, with swaths of silvery fabric drifting down the atrium.

Waiters, dressed completely in white, slid through the small knots of guests, offering English champagne (*seriously*), and funny little white canapés that I didn't fancy the look of. I was glad Polly and I had shared a box of donuts before we'd come out. The food at these things was rubbish.

I recognized two of the producers who were standing off to one side, looking a little nervous, but self-satisfied at the same time. That took some doing. Either that, or they were just constipated. Yeah, I'd probably better brush up on reading body language.

Polly and I clung together, trying to look relaxed, but we didn't recognize anyone else, and nobody spoke to us. It was like the first day of high school all over again. Except this time, Miles wasn't with me.

Gradually, the number of guests increased, and the excitement began to ramp up. When the actors who'd played Esther's parents arrived, the crowd outside started going crazy. It was only a matter of minutes now before Miles made his entrance, followed by Lilia.

They were traveling in separate limos, of course, but they'd be close together. It was the best compromise the producers could rightfully expect.

Jo-Anne Moody arrived looking happy and excited. She saw us immediately and walked straight over. That's what I liked about Jo-Anne—she wasn't always rubbernecking to see if there was someone more important to talk to.

"How ya doing, ladies!" she said. "Awesome, isn't it? Great dress, Clare. Bet I can guess where that came from," and she winked at me.

We chatted for a while, catching up on mutual friends, what she was working on next, gossip about the Biz, and some of the other cast members came over, whiling the time away until the real action started.

When the screams reached an unbelievable level, I knew Miles was on his way.

I stood by the door, and saw Prue stagger inside, ashen and shaking. I knew she'd come as his 'date' for the evening. She'd been nervous about it, but now she looked shell-shocked.

"Oh my God!" she said, as she stumbled into my hug. "That ... that ... bloody hell!"

"I know. Mad, isn't it?"

"Thank God for your friendly face, love."

I introduced her to Polly, then casually asked, "How's Miles?"

She smiled and patted my cheek. "Looking forward to seeing you, love."

Polly and Prue yakked away like old friends. I left them to it and watched Miles' slow progression up the red carpet. He was stopping to talk to as many fans as possible, and had obviously become adept at using their camera phones to take pictures of himself with them. He smiled and smiled and smiled, then stopped to do sound bite interviews with at least seven different sets of reporters.

I could tell that he was on edge, but whether that was because of the noise, the crowds, the fact of being blinded by camera flashes, or his dread of being asked something personal, I couldn't tell. Probably all of the above.

God, he looked gorgeous. He was wearing a severe, black suit that emphasized his lean body and angular face. It was the sort of beauty that didn't seem destined for us mere mortals—even ones dressed in Versace. I couldn't help dying just a little bit inside, wondering who his next actress love would be.

When he finally made it through the entrance, Prue pulled him into a tight hug, and I could see him smiling as she whispered in his ear. He kissed her cheek then straightened up.

I thought he was going to say something to me, but Melody got to him first.

"Well done," she said, and he gave her a tired smile.

"I managed to keep my foot out of my mouth, Melody. Do I get a prize?"

She laughed. "Yes, a big, fat pay check for your next film. Don't push it, buster."

Then she strolled off to do some grip and grin with the producers, and we were left staring at each other.

"Hi," he said, quietly.

"Hi. You look well."

"You, too."

"Thanks for the dress."

A smile lit up his face. "Do you like it? I thought it would really suit you—it does."

"Yeah, um, it was a nice surprise. Thanks."

I snagged an extra glass of bubbly from a passing waiter and handed it to Miles.

"God, thanks, Clare. I need that!" he said, emptying almost the whole glass in one go.

"Steady," said his mum, her voice a gentle warning.

He laughed and gave her a bright smile.

"Have you met my mum, Polly?" he said. "She wants someone else to boss around, so watch your back."

"You're not too old to put over my knee!" Prue threatened, wagging her finger.

I was the only one who heard Polly murmur, "Oh, I'd do that for you." And she sighed heavily.

I became aware that the sounds outside had changed. The screams and shrieks had changed to something deeper, more sinister.

I listened for a moment, trying to work out what was happening. And then it hit me—the crowd was booing. They were booing Lilia.

"Can you hear that?" I said, in a shocked voice.

Silence flowed out across the guests inside the cinema, and all eyes automatically swiveled to Miles.

But he didn't see everyone scrutinizing his face, waiting for his reaction—he was staring out of the window. He looked really angry. Furious, in fact.

"That shit is just wrong," he growled.

I couldn't help agreeing. The noise outside sounded like it could turn into a mob at any moment, and a shiver passed down my spine.

Before anyone realized what was he was doing, before his security team had a chance to react, Miles had pulled the door open and shouldered his way through the baying crowd, fighting his way back up the red carpet. To her. To Lilia.

Prue gripped my arm, the fear apparent on her face. But the crowd fell back, the booing and catcalls giving way to angry murmurs, then sullen silence. I could see Lilia's shocked face and her desperate relief when Miles put a protective arm around her shoulders and guided her toward the cinema's sanctuary, while her security team faced down the crowd.

It started with just one person, the sound echoing through the plaza, but a few more people began clapping, then full-blown applause rang out. Lilia whispered something to Miles and I saw him lean down to listen, her lips just inches from his ear.

I felt sorry for her. And really fucking annoyed that she'd managed to get Miles' attention, and his arms around her, *again*.

They turned in unison, glancing briefly at the crowd, and stepped inside.

He was still talking to her quietly, and she was nodding and smiling up at him.

The producers looked ecstatic and swept over to greet them, smiling, shaking hands, giving air-kisses, as if there had never been a moment's disquiet.

Polly raised her eyebrows as she looked at me.

I shook my head and poured the cheap, fizzy wine straight down my throat, draining my champagne flute. I emptied Miles' abandoned glass, too.

Then I hurried to the ladies' room before I made my mascara run.

I stood by the sink, splashing cold water onto my face, hoping it would help. It did. A bit. Enough for me to give myself a stiff talking to.

You are one stupid cow, Clare Milton! You're as thick as the floor. You keep going back for more punishment. Why not just have the word 'doormat' tattooed on your backside and ...

The door opened and I looked up. I was eyeball to eyeball with *her*—Lilia I'm-a-fucking-cheating-slag Purcell.

"You!" she snapped. "What the hell are you doing here?"

"Oh, just chilling. Checking out the scenery. Thought I'd go and look in the shop window for 'Slags R Us', but now I don't need to, seeing as you're here."

"You bitch!"

"That's so lacking in originality, Lilia, I'm disappointed. But as you mentioned it, yes, I am a bitch, I'm just not *your* bitch. You, however, are a skinny, mean-minded, pointy arsed, two-timing, dick breath bint. Have a nice day."

Wow, that felt good.

I heard her gasp, and it made me smile.

"You know," I couldn't help adding, "you're lucky Miles is even talking to you. You're lucky he's such a nice guy. But he doesn't like cheats. Boy, you really fucked up badly."

"It was an accident!" she hissed.

"Falling over in the street is an accident. Falling onto someone's dick seems premeditated."

"Fuck you!"

"No, thanks. I have standards."

She folded her arms over her scraggy tits and clamped her lips in a tight line.

"You're just jealous—because I fucked Miles and you never have and never will. Why would he want old ham when he can have steak?"

"You're entitled to your opinion, Lilia. It's just hilarious that you think yours actually matters to me."

She smirked. "Yeah, you're jealous."

"You must still be on drugs if you think I'm jealous of you, you frowzy tart."

Her eyes shrank to tiny points as her anger mounted. "You're a fat, ugly, sarcastic little bitch!"

"I should deduct points for repetition."

"Do you think you're funny?"

"No, I'm just allergic to cheating trollops—it makes me break out in sarcasm."

I thought she was going to hit me, and part of me really hoped she would, because my fingers were just itching to slap the shit out of her.

Her lip curled. "Let's see who's laughing when Miles is back in *my* bed." And she swept out of there like the Queen of fucking Sheba.

Damn.

Chapter Sixteen

LOVE ACTUALLY

Miles

I was so amped up I could barely remember my own name.

Not about the premiere, about seeing Clare.

I *had* to make this right between us. I felt sick at the thought of losing my best friend just because I'd been a stupid, selfish, navel-gazing dickhead. I was relieved when Mum told me that Clare would definitely be attending the premiere, because it wouldn't have surprised me if she'd refused to go.

Then it occurred to me that she probably wouldn't have anything to wear, so maybe that was a way back—a peace offering.

I got Honey to phone Natalia Da Silva, and *she* used her contacts to get something special for Clare. I'd had three dresses sent to my suite at the Dorchester, and had picked the dark green one. Then I had it couriered to her house. I hoped she might send me a text when she got it, but I heard nothing.

Of course, I was too dumb to get rid of the surplus dresses quickly. *That* was an interesting conversation when my mum saw them.

"Oh, love! Why didn't you tell me?"

I frowned at her.

"Tell you what?"

"Not that it matters. I'll love you whatever you do."

"Thanks, Mum. Any particular reason you're telling me this now?"

"Well, I don't think magenta is your color, love."

"What?"

"You know. Your, er, dress."

What?

"Bloody hell, Mum! Those dresses aren't for *me!* I got them for Clare."

The relief on her face was more than a little apparent.

"Oh. Oh, well that's all right then. I just thought, you know, now you're a proper actor..."

"Yeah, thanks, Mum. Please stop talking."

"Don't you be cheeky!"

"Whatever."

"Mind your lip! And while I'm at it, have you planned what you're going to say to Clare?"

"Other than 'sorry'. Not really."

"For goodness sake, Miles! You need to come up with something better than that. Can't you, you know, act it or something?"

"Yeah, well, I need a script for that, and I don't think that would work with Clare."

She sighed. "No, probably not. Just sort it out, will you. I hate seeing you both so miserable."

"Is it that obvious?"

"Of course it is, love. I'm your mother."

The screaming crowd, followed by the walk up the red carpet, had been a real head spin, but it was worth it just to see Clare waiting for me, looking really fucking hot. I'd definitely picked the right dress.

And then the moment, the very fucking second that we started talking, I heard the crowd booing Lilia.

I couldn't leave her to deal with that by herself—it was a mob out there, and they sounded like they were out for her blood. I wouldn't wish that on anyone. Whatever they'd done. *Or whoever they'd done.* And I hadn't forgotten how gut-wrenchingly horrible it had felt the first time I'd gone on *Ellen*, and the audience had yelled things at me.

But once I'd got Lilia inside the cinema, the producers were all over us like a rash. I suppose they were just happy to see us in the same room without lobbing rotten fruit at each other.

Lilia disappeared to the bathroom, and before I could get back to Clare, Donald Hyde grabbed my arm.

"Goddamn freakin' masterstroke, Miles! You couldn't have planned it better."

"I didn't *plan* it at all."

"No, sure, sure, but it'll play real well. The fans loved it!"

I wrenched my arm free, trying to calm the fuck down before I did something he'd regret.

"Is that all you care about? Why on earth wasn't there more security? It could have turned really nasty out there—nastier."

He waved a hand.

"I'll deal, don't sweat it. Look, kid, enjoy tonight, and we'll talk about the sequel when you get back to LA."

"The what?"

But he was already sliding away, oily bastard that he was, and then I heard Lilia's soft voice behind me.

"Miles. Darling, can we talk?"

I was aware that people were staring and hoping to eavesdrop on our conversation, but more than that, I *really* didn't want to talk to her.

"There's nothing to say, Lilia."

"Please, Miles. Just a minute, please? I can't ... not here ... please?"

I should have been expecting this, but for some reason I thought she'd just ignore me, or pretend nothing had happened.

Ah hell. "Fine. You can have one minute."

She pouted. I used to find that hot.

"Somewhere private," she whispered. "Everyone's watching us."

Against my better judgment, but curious as to what the hell she could possibly say, I let her lead me to a small room next to the cinema's booking office.

I leaned against the desk, and she closed the door behind her.

"You look good," she said, with a small smile. "But then again you always did. Right from that first day."

Seriously? She wanted to do small talk?

"Just say what you've got to say, Lilia."

"Don't be angry with me, Miles," she gasped, her voice breaking.

God, I hated it when women cried. It always made me feel like such a shit.

"I'm not angry—now," I replied, watching as she bit her lip. "I just don't particularly want to talk to you."

She took a step closer.

"I'm sorry about what happened. I ... I love you."

"I doubt that very fucking much, Lilia. You don't fucking cheat on someone you love."

A sob escaped her chest, and she dabbed at her eyes with a tissue.

I tried really hard not to care what she said, but I kept seeing the images of her with Joe Blow. I closed my eyes, but the pictures were still there.

"Miles? Please, baby?"

"Why? Why did you do it?" I couldn't help the words spilling out. "Were you with him ... the whole time we were together?"

"No, of course not!" she cried, even managing to sound upset. "I ... I was drunk ... It was just that once."

I studied her face. She seemed so sincere. If nothing else, Lilia was a brilliant actress. She'd win an Oscar some day.

"And the woman—the other guy? Was that just once, as well? Are there any other 'just one times' that you want to tell me about?"

"You're being hateful!"

She was crazy if she thought I'd feel bad about saying that. And she hadn't answered my question.

"How can I believe a word you're saying?"

"It's true, Miles. I promise."

"Yeah, well, I don't believe you."

"Then what can I say? What can I do to make it right?"

Her voice was pleading, but there was a hint of calculation in her eyes, and I remembered that Clare had never liked her —or trusted her.

"That first evening, when we went to the Metron Awards ... do you remember that?"

"Of course," she smiled, relaxing a little. "You were so nervous." She giggled, and placed a quick kiss on my cheek.

I leaned away from her touch, and she looked irritated. Well, screw her! We were going to finish this conversation she'd been so desperate to start.

"And do you remember when I saw ... when I saw *him* with that woman in the men's bathroom."

"Oh," she said, softly, lowering her eyes.

"How did you know?"

She looked up and frowned.

"How did I know what?"

"You said, *He does that. It's his thing.* But how did you know? Unless you already..."

I couldn't finish the sentence because I was afraid I'd vomit.

There was a long, heavy silence.

"You don't know what it's like," she said at last, her voice crisper, harder.

"What? What are you talking about?"

"*The business!*" she snarled, all pretence falling away, all acting finished. "You don't know what it's like!"

I stared at her in disbelief. "I think I've got a pretty fucking good idea!"

She snorted.

"You've done it for eight months. You've been a *star* for just a few weeks."

The bitch actually used air quotes when she said 'star'.

"Do you really think you know how it works? I've been in this business since I was seven years old. Seven! Have you any idea how difficult it is for a *child* star to be taken seriously? To win real, adult roles? Do you think anyone actually cares about you? Because they don't. It's all about money. It's all about *who* you know."

"So, you just thought ... what? Give some head to get ahead?"

"You bastard!"

"Yeah? Well, *I* took you seriously, Lilia. *I* cared about you! But that wasn't important. You just ripped my fucking heart out like it was worthless, like it meant nothing."

I was struggling to get the words out, and I tugged roughly at my bow tie before I managed to undo it and loosen a few buttons on my shirt, allowing air into my lungs.

"I've had hate mail," she said quietly, her lip trembling.

"Yeah?" I said, harshly. "It's probably from my mum."

"Miles, please."

"Please *what*, Lilia? What do you want from me?"

She took another step closer, and her hand drifted down my arm, coming to a rest on my waistband.

I flicked her hand away.

"Can't we be friends?" she pleaded.

"No. I've got all the friends I need."

"Like Clare!" she hissed, her face twisting with an ugly sneer.

"What the fuck has Clare got to do with anything?"

"She was always there—always in the way!"

I couldn't believe she was spouting this shit.

"We went to that fucking premiere together, Lilia. You and me. Remember? You offered to blow me in the limo. Maybe you remember that, or were you confusing me with him already? You left the party without a word. You got high.

You got laid. I wasn't there. Your responsibility, Lilia. No one else's."

I was *so* finished with that conversation. I brushed past her and got the fuck out of the room.

As I walked back to the party, my heart was racing and anger was firing jets of fury through my veins. I took several deep breaths and tried to look like I wasn't about to smash something or hit someone.

Clare was talking to Mum and Polly, and I felt better seeing her there, calm and assured as ever. She pushed her hand through her hair and another wave of sudden anger washed over me. She wasn't wearing the bracelet I'd given her.

And then I realized what had happened.

She hadn't wanted to come tonight. In all likelihood Mum had talked her into it. A sick, hollow feeling squeezed my heart. *How had I let this happen?* And, more importantly, could I make it right?

I walked up to Mum, trying to smile.

Clare's eyes narrowed as she looked at me. Then she turned her back. My smile died on my face and I was going to say something to her but Mum grabbed my arm.

"Let me fix your bow tie," she said, tugging me toward her. "You look a mess. And you have lipstick on your cheek," she hissed, scrubbing furiously at my face with a tissue.

Before I had a chance to say anything, Hyde stood up to give a quick speech, thanking everyone on some ridiculously long list, including God, and then we were all ushered into the theater. Mum was sitting next to me, and Jo-Anne was on my other side, with Lilia next to her. I couldn't see where Clare was sitting and I slumped down in my seat, knowing it would be another two hours before I could talk to her.

I sat through that fucking movie, hating every minute of it.

I was amused and embarrassed when the sex scene came on, and Mum watched it through her fingers.

"That's not something I ever wanted to see," she

whispered. "I saw enough of your backside when you were a little baby!"

"Didn't mean anything," I muttered.

Although that wasn't strictly true: at the time, Lilia and I had been together. That was one of the things that had made filming that scene so hard. Probably what had made *me* so hard that day. Now, the thought left me cold.

I wondered what Hyde had meant about a sequel. As far as I knew, Laura Dorien hadn't written a second book, although that didn't mean much in Hollywood. *Fuck!* I realized I'd better get Melody or Rhonda to check my contract—I might have signed up for a sequel without knowing it. That would just be my fucking luck.

I was glad Mum's house purchase was going through. If the studio sued the pants off me for breach of contract—refusing do a sequel—she'd be protected.

The theater lights came back on and I was only vaguely aware of the applause. Mum was crying and hugging me, and people were standing up wanting to shake my hand, but I was looking for Clare. I couldn't see her through the crowds of people who surrounded me.

Lilia caught my eye, and gave me a small, hopeful smile.

Shit. She just didn't give up.

The premiere party was being held in the Palm Court of the Langham Hotel, near Regent's Park. You know, palm trees, piano and harpist, Gothic charm that film studios loved. Whatever.

Everyone wanted to stop and talk and smile—except I still couldn't see Clare.

After an hour of smiling and being polite—and avoiding Lilia at every turn—I'd had enough. Even Mum, who loved a good party, had already left, complaining that her new shoes hurt her feet.

I craned my neck, trying to find anyone that looked green, well, wearing green. Luckily, I spotted Polly and strolled over. *Wow. Orange was not her color.*

She was pasted, and when she wrapped her arms around

me and started crying and warbling on about pretty babies and cherubs, I smiled my first real smile for hours.

"Pol, put a lid on the waterworks! Have you seen, Clare?"

"She went home, but I'll keep you company."

"Home?"

Clare had gone. Again.

Shit.

This time, I didn't hesitate. I got my arse out of there and grabbed the first taxi I could find.

It took ten minutes to get to Clare's house. Ten damn minutes too long.

I thumped on the door and rang the bell.

Clare

Mum and Dad were out at Aunt Paula's party, so I had the house to myself.

I was glad of that, because I wanted to wallow. Preferably with chocolate. I got lucky when I found a Black Forest gateau that Mum had bought to celebrate with Prue, and proceeded to stuff my face. I ate well over half of it. A generous half. The kind of half that a miserable sod might call three-quarters. Whatever. I felt full and nauseous. All I needed now was a sappy love story on the TV, and I was all set for a classic wallow in the time honored tradition.

The evening had been a complete and utter nightmare. From the moment Lilia had arrived, everything had gone wrong. And then she'd dragged him off to her lair, and when he came out again his shirt and tie were undone, and he had lipstick on his cheek. It was soooo obvious what they'd been doing. Especially when she followed him out, a smug smile pasted across her ugly trout pout.

She'd told me she'd get him back—it looked as though she was right. I really didn't think he would have succumbed that quickly. I hated being proved wrong.

So I was as irritated as all hell when some bastard rang the bell *and* knocked on the door.

The last person I expected to see was Miles waiting on the other side, looking ridiculously beautiful and debonair in his tailor-made tux.

I, on the other hand, had changed into sweatpants and an old t-shirt. One of his. Oh, and I had crumbs down my cleavage.

The cold air rushed in as I stood in the hallway, my mouth open more widely than the front door.

"You left," he said.

"You were busy."

He frowned. "Can I come in?"

"If you want."

I let the door hang open, then turned my back and headed into the warmth of the cozy living room.

I heard him close the front door and follow me inside. It had been a long time since we'd been in this house together.

He stood awkwardly while I gestured for him to come in, my eyes fixed on the TV.

After a moment's hesitation, he pushed the living room door shut and hovered near one of the armchairs. We were alone together at last.

"I missed you," he said, softly.

And I didn't know if he meant tonight, or the last few days.

I folded my arms tightly in front of me and tried to smile.

"Yeah, me, too."

He rubbed his head as if it ached, and took a step toward me.

I backed away, knowing that I'd crumble if I let him touch me. And I *couldn't* go back to living like that.

He looked hurt and bewildered as I moved to the other side of the room, and slumped down onto the couch.

"You didn't wear your bracelet," he said, quietly.

"What?"

The pain in his voice tore my eyes away from the TV screen that I was pretending to watch.

"The bracelet I gave you—you're not wearing it."

"Oh..."

I couldn't meet his eyes.

"Clare, I know I've been an idiot..."

"Yeah, you have. But that's okay, I'm used to it."

I was letting him off the hook, and he knew it. He gave a small smile.

"Around you I just seem to open my mouth to change feet," he agreed.

There was an awkward silence. We'd *never* been uncomfortable sharing the same space, but everything had changed.

"So," he said, shoving his hands in his pockets, "how've you been?"

"Bloody hell, Miles! You make it sound like you haven't seen me for a year. I saw you a couple of hours ago."

"Feels longer."

True.

When I didn't respond, he sighed heavily and went to lean against the wall by the window, staring at the wintry street outside.

I fiddled nervously with the hem of my ... his ... my t-shirt.

I didn't want him here.

Except I did. And I didn't.

"Why did you leave like that?" he said, his voice soft and a little husky.

So fucking clueless!

I felt a spike of anger. "You don't get it, do you?"

He shrugged helplessly.

"No, I don't. Not really."

In that moment, I realized we were never going to square this circle. There was no point prolonging the agony.

"Well, it doesn't matter anyway. I just ... I think you should go now."

I hated saying the words and Miles looked stunned, but a tiny germ of self-preservation was forcing its way to the surface.

"What? Now? But..." his words ended abruptly, and he rubbed the back of his neck in a familiar gesture of frustration. "Please, Clare, I'm trying here."

I held back a sigh.

"I know. It's just ... better if you go."

His expression morphed into one of anger.

"Why did you even bother coming tonight if you don't want to talk to me?"

Fury, long held back, flared inside me, and I pointed an accusing finger at him.

"Because *your* mum and *my* mum nagged me until I said I would."

"You weren't going to come at all?"

"No."

He shook his head, tiredly. "I don't get it."

"I know you don't."

"Then please give me a fucking clue!" he shouted.

"I'm sick of it!" I yelled back. "All of it! I'm sick of being in the way! I'm sick of being second best!"

I could see from his face that he *still* didn't understand. Frustrated, angry, and on the verge of tears, I stood up and headed for the door.

He blocked my way.

"Christ, Clare, I'm fucking begging you now. Please don't. Talk to me!"

I shook my head, my eyes stinging and my throat aching too much to reply.

I reached out for the door handle and started to open it, but Miles was quicker. He slammed it shut, trapping me in the room.

"Let me go," I sniffed.

"No. If you go, I'm going with you."

"You can't."

"Why not?"

"I'm going to bed. I'm tired and I've got a headache."

"Is that the only reason you don't want me to come?"

No.

"Mostly, yes."

His eyes narrowed but I think he knew that if pushed me now, he'd get the opposite reaction from the one he wanted.

"Let's both get out of here," he said, trying to sound calm. "Find a pub and just ... have a couple of drinks. Okay?"

"I don't feel like going out again."

He tugged his hair in frustration and swore softly.

"Look," I said sighing, giving in grudgingly, "dad's got some beer in the fridge if you want a drink."

He smiled uncertainly. "Okay. Sounds good. Thanks."

I pulled myself away from him, grabbed two cans of lager from the kitchen, and handed one to him.

He sank down into an armchair and popped the tab.

Suddenly, he stood up again.

"Fuck this!" he said, and came to sit next to me on the couch.

I looked at him in surprise. There was a determined look on his face.

"Clare, I'm not with Lilia, no matter what you think you saw."

My heart started to pound.

"You had lipstick on your face."

"Yeah, she kissed my cheek. That's all. She said she wanted to apologize."

"Did she?"

"Sort of. Not really. Mostly, she was trying to make excuses for what happened."

He rubbed his eyebrow with his index finger.

"I don't want to talk about her," he said. "She's history. She means nothing to me. But you..." he hesitated... "You're my best friend. I miss you. You mean more to me than all that shit. I miss you so much."

He stared into my eyes and slowly his expression changed. I watched as his gaze dropped to my mouth, and he licked his lips.

I swear I was holding my breath, feeling the electric pull of the tension mounting between us.

And then he leaned over and kissed me.

His lips were soft and gentle, the kiss so tender and loving, it took my breath away.

I sat there, unmoving, as if a taxidermist had managed to yank out my guts and stuff me in the last ten seconds.

He pulled back slightly as I remained frozen.

"Sorry," he whispered. "I thought ... I guess I was wrong. Sorry."

He started to move away, and that's when I launched myself at him.

I heard his sharp intake of breath, and then we were all lips and tongues and teeth, panting and breathing hard as we caught up on years of sexual frustration—certainly on my side.

His mouth was hot and wet against my neck and I moaned like a maiden aunt at a Chippendales party.

He wrapped his arms around my hips and dragged me onto his lap, and I could feel how hard he was beneath me.

Bloody hell! That felt gooood!

"I want to make love to you," he snarled against my throat, his fingers digging into my waist. "Right now, Clare. Right fucking now!"

"Upstairs!" I gasped.

He stood up quickly, even though I was still in his arms. *Jeez, I was definitely going to send a thank you card to Hilda the Nazi fitness trainer, because Miles could hoist me around like a delicate elf, instead of my 140 pound, five foot nothing carcass.*

He knew the way to my bedroom—we'd spent enough innocent hours in there over the years. He slammed the door shut with his foot, dropped me onto my bed and flung his jacket on my chair. Slowly, he loosened his bow tie as he prowled toward me.

My lady parts were celebrating, so heady with anticipation, that they were practically singing the Hallelujah chorus.

"I want you so badly," he whispered, his voice hoarse with desire and need.

Holy hell!

I thought I was going to combust on the spot. It would be just my luck if I passed out or died before we got to the really good part...

...And just as my brain is about to seize up, he lunges at me and pulls me to him, kissing me hot and heavy.

Oh my God! Oh my God! His body feels so amazing! Jeez, all those hours in the gym have really ... mmm, ooh, oh the way his tongue feels on my neck. Oh, God, he's kissing me, really kissing me. And his hair feels so soft and...

Oh my God he feels so hard! That's for me! He feels that for me! I'm in so much trouble here.

Fuck, she's so hot. I never thought ... uhh, that feels... oh, fuck...

Don't break my heart, Miles. You know I love you. I've always loved you. Those other creeps—no one could compare. Oh my God, he's got his hand under my t-shirt. When was the last time I shaved? Oh, hell, I'm wearing that old bra. I've been meaning to throw that out and... Oh my God! He just touched my nipple. Damn, that feels so ... oh, yes ... oh, yes.

Fuck, she's got great tits.

Oh Miles, I know I'm not in your league; I've never been in your league, but no one will ever love you as much as I do. And I know you ... I really know you. All your insecurities, your shyness, your bizarre sense of humor. Oh my God, he's trying to unhook my bra. Huh, where did my t-shirt go? When did he take that off?

What if he's expecting me to be bare? I mean, that Brazilian grew back ages ago and no way was I going to go through that again. That was sheer Hell with a capital H. I don't care if that's how they do things in Hollywood. Okay, well, maybe if Miles likes it like that ... oh my God, he's got his hand down the back of my knickers. My arse is huge. Oh, don't stop, that just feels ... oh wow! I'm going to do it—I'm going to stick my hand down the front of his trousers.

Oh my God! It just jumped! I swear it jumped at me! Mmm, it's so hot and ... blimey ... that's big! I mean, bloody hell, I can hardly get my hand around it. Wow, supersize me!

Fuck, she's feeling me up. Oh fuck.

Oh God, the light's still on. I wonder if I can turn it off without it being too obvious? I shouldn't have eaten that gateau. Okay, not quite the whole gateau, but most of it. Will he think I'm fat? I *am* fat compared to all those stick insect actresses he knows—I'm *enormous* compared to *her*. Oh God, I'm so fat.

Fuck, she's got the most amazing arse—full and round, so soft and ... oh fuck, I'm going to come in my pants if I'm not careful. One times one is one ... one times two is ... oh fuck.

Oh God, I just love his body. I mean, look at that chest. I *am* looking at that chest. He's so bloody sexy. I can't believe after all these years we're finally going to do it. I love you I love you I love you!

Fuck, look at the size of those knickers! They're huge! That's hot

He's taken his trousers off. Oh boxer briefs—swoon. Yummy! Mmm, ooh that feels good. Oh my God, that feels so good! How did he know ... ohh ... mmmm...

Shit, she's so wet. Oh God, I hope she comes quickly. I really want to be inside her. Hold it together, Stephens, you owe her this. One times one is one. One times two is two. Land of Hope and Glory, Mother of the Free ... Oh, thank God...

Oh my God! Oh my God! Oh my God! Oh. My. God! Oh! Ooooh! OOOOOH! AAAH! "Miiiiiiiiles!" Oh, God, I said that out loud. Oh wow. That was ah-may-zing! He is a stud, a sex god! I am a goddess! I am all powerful. Oh, what's he doing? Oh, ouch! Oh, wow, wow, wow! Oh my God—I think he's pushed it all the way into my spine! OH GOD!

Fuck. Shit. God. Oh God. Hold it. Hold it. Hold it. Can't. Can't. Can't. UH! UHHH! MMM. Damn, she feels so good. Sooo good. Goooooood! Oh, God. I can't. I can't. Shit. Fuck. Uh. Uh. Uh. Uh. Uh.

What's happening? Again? What? No! Again?!! I mean ... oh, wow. Oh wow. OH WOW! Uh. Uh. Uh. Uh. Uh. "Miiiiiiiiiiles!"

He shoots. He scores. Gooooooooal! *"Fuck, Claaaare!"*

Clare

I can't believe it. I didn't know sex could be like that: what I felt, what I still feel. *Two orgasms*, I mean: *two!* How the hell did he do that? Oh, God, I really don't want to think about where he's been practicing—and who on. Oh, why do I have to have all these thoughts? That was so wonderful, making love with Miles. Was it making love for him, too, or just me? Oh, just look at him lying there; he looks so, so fine. Just think, women all over the world want what I've just had —that's so weird. I mean, they want the character he plays— Nuriel—in the film, not Miles. Okay, some of them want Miles; okay, most of them, but I'm the one who's had him.

God, I can't believe I'm thinking about him like some sort of trophy: he's *Miles*—my friend. My best friend. And tonight has been the best night of my life.

Miles

Oh God, have I just made a horrible mistake? She doesn't look happy. I *know* Clare—she's thinking it over, she's regretting it, I can just tell. God, she looks so gorgeous, all sort of heated and with the most fantastic, soft curves. Shit, I could get hard again just looking at her. But she's got *thinking face*: that's not good. Oh hell, I hope I haven't just gone and lost my best friend for good this time. I know Clare's not the kind of girl who could be a fuck buddy, and I wouldn't want her to be that. If I'm honest, I don't want her to be with anyone but me.

She's having second thoughts, I can tell. *Shit, shit, shit!* I couldn't blame her: these days I live on one fucked up merry-go-round. Why would she want to be part of all this craziness? I mean, she has a life—a good life. She's clever and funny and loyal and really cute—she could have any guy she wanted.

And she knows me—she knows I'm not the image that they're selling. I can't believe she's here with me. She knows all the shit that went down with Lilia—hell, she saw most of it. So why is she with me? Maybe she was just trying to make me feel better; yeah, that would be like Clare, always trying to make me feel better.

Oh, shit, is that all this was? Her trying to cheer me up? A mercy fuck? That's not what I want! *Is that what I want?* No, it felt so amazing with Clare—it felt *right*.

Oh, God, she's turned away from me. She doesn't want this; she's regretting it already. Fuck, what do I do?

Maybe it wasn't good for her? I mean, it felt amazing to me, but she obviously doesn't think the same. It couldn't have been that bad, could it? She had two orgasms. Oh, God, she was faking it—obviously—moron. They didn't feel fake, though; it felt pretty damn real. Yeah, because I wanted it to be real, obviously.

So what do I do? I guess all I can do is to make it easy for her; easy for her to leave me. Damn it, Clare.

Clare

Oh, he looks so serious. I can't look at him. It felt so amazing but now it's so awkward. I just want to snuggle into him; I want to fall asleep in his arms and wake up with him in the morning. He probably just wants to go. I should let him go. *I don't want him to go.*

"Clare, are you okay?"

"I'm fine." *I'm not fine!* I'm confused—and still kind of turned on.

I feel his warm hand drift down my arm and I swear the skin tingles, as if he's just trailed an ice cube across me, or passed an electric current up my arm. *Oh, Miles, don't stop touching me!* He's stopped touching me. Oh no.

"Um, I guess I should go?"

Is that a question? No, of course not. He's just being polite. He knows this was a mistake. Oh God, I can't speak. If

I try to speak, I'll cry, I know I will.

The mattress moves underneath me and I know he's sitting up. I can't help looking; one last look. Oh, God! Look at that back! How did I miss that before? Oh, right, because he was on top of me. Look at those muscles; and, oh my God! He's really got that triangular shape. I never noticed before— not from the back. Broad shoulders, going down to a slim waist. He's so gorgeous—and so out of my league.

What's he doing? Why isn't he going?

I really want him to go now. *I don't want him to go now!*

"Clare?"

"Yes?"

Say something, Miles! Say something!

Miles

Oh God, I should say something. What should I say? Does she want me to go? I should just go. *I don't want to go.*

"Clare?"

"Yes?"

"Um, I know this is kinda weird..."

She's sighing. *Oh shit.*

"It's okay, Miles, don't worry about it."

She's brushing me off. She wants me to go.

"Um, I'll just go then?"

"Okay."

Okay? No! It's not okay!

"Right. Um, thanks for having me. Oh God, I don't mean *having* me like that. I meant ... er ... thanks ... um ... I'll be next door at Mum's."

"Okay."

This is the worst day of my life.

Clare

He gets up and dresses in silence. I can't bear it. I can't bear *him*. How could he do this? How could he sleep with me and then be so cold? I don't understand. Did I do something wrong? Maybe I was bad in bed. That must be it: I'm crap in bed. I'm a lousy lover—a lousy lay. He's seen me naked with the light on, that's it. He's seen all my wobbly bits—on both sides. He's repulsed; my body repulses him.

Oh God, I'm so embarrassed. No, it's worse than that—I'm breaking apart. I can't let him see me breaking apart. I've got to hold it together. Just another minute and he'll be gone. Gone. I don't want him to go.

Miles, don't go! I love you!

Miles

Oh God, she's so quiet. I've really screwed it up this time. My best friend. *My best friend!* What the fuck was I thinking? I wasn't thinking. Okay, I was thinking with my man parts—Miles Junior. I can't help that. Little bastard led and I followed. No, that's not true.

Clare, I think I love you!

She won't want to hear that. She'll just laugh at me. She'd probably think I was joking anyway.

Hey! Maybe I can say it to her and if she thinks it's a joke, I'll just laugh it off.

Fucking coward. *Yeah, yeah.*

"Um, Clare?"

"What now?"

Oh wow, she sounds really angry. Maybe this isn't the best time to say anything.

Say it! Say it!

"Um, I think I love you."

"What?"

"Nothing."

"You said something."

"No, I didn't."

"Yes, you did—I heard you."

"No, you didn't."

"Yes, I bloody well did, Miles! You said ... you said you thought you loved me. What does that even mean?"

"Um ... that I love you?"

"Well, do you or don't you?"

Is that a trick question?

"I do?"

"You do?"

"Yes."

"Really?"

"Yes." *And more than you'll ever know.*

"Oh, okay. I just wanted to be clear."

"Yeah."

She's not laughing. Does that mean...?

"Just so you know..."

"Yeah?"

"I love you too, Miles."

"You do?"

"Of course, you moron."

Oh wow! I thought she was mad at me. She loves me?

And then I pull her into my arms and kiss her like there's no tomorrow.

Chapter Seventeen

THE DAY AFTER TOMORROW

Clare

Bugger me, it was hot in my bedroom.

I woke up sweating and wondering if Mum had left the central heating on all night again. She did that sometimes. She said it was by accident; funny that it always seemed to happen on really cold nights.

But it wasn't the radiator in my small bedroom that was making me hot—it was the man lying next to me. *Definitely hot.*

One arm was thrown behind his head, and the other was draped around my shoulder. My face was squished up against his fab-u-lous chest and I probably looked like Miss Piggy. His eyes were closed, the lids trembling, and I thought he was dreaming. I was pretty certain I was, too. The sheet was pushed down to his hips, and his chest and stomach rose rhythmically. I could practically count every muscle of his abs. I could write poetry about them. I lay there composing my ode while the soft breaths ebbed and flowed through his beautiful, flawless body.

Ode to an Abdominal Oblique

Thou newly ravish'd groom of stillness
Thou descending stone-like sternum,
Child of Nazi Hilda.
A vivid valley between moreish mounds.
The faultless form of your Pectoralis,
Crowned with rosy buds.
A golden trail of happiness
Leading to the Promised Land.
Such wild ecstasy.

And the memories flooded back. His touch, his kiss, his arms around me.

And the sex!

I mean, I was an English literature student and you'd really think I could have come up with a better word than 'wow'. But right there and then, 'wow' covered a lot of ground.

After that amazing first time, and the horrible awkwardness that had followed, we'd made love again and again.

We'd even been, um, busy when Mum and Dad got back and slammed the front door. Okay, so I was 21 and had been having sex for more years than my parents would like to believe, but that didn't mean to say I wanted them to interruptus the coitus. Boy, it had been soooo hard to keep quiet. In the end, Miles stuck his tongue in my mouth just to shut me up. Well, it may not have been the *only* reason, but it worked just as well.

And now, lying here next to him with the cool morning light edging between the curtains, I felt a deep sense of peace. And excitement. Peace, because we'd finally said everything we needed to say to each other. Oddly enough, it was a short conversation.

It went like this.

"I've loved you forever, you twerp!" I said.

Miles blinked at me. "Yeah, me, too."

I shook my head. "No, I mean I've r-e-a-l-l-y loved you—like forever!"

Miles looked annoyed. "Well, why the hell didn't you tell me?!"

"Oops."

He rolled his eyes. "No more 'oops', okay?"

"Okay."

So, yeah, that had been a bit of an 'oops' moment. (I really was going to have to get some better vocabulary after the holidays were over, and I was back studying.)

I admitted that I'd always loved him. He admitted that he had no clue, but that I'd always been his best friend, and he'd always compared other women to me.

He told me a little bit about what the evil witch had said to him last night, but refused to give details on the grounds that he couldn't think about her while he was lying between my naked thighs. Sigh.

And did I mention excitement? Because we were finally together, and he said he didn't want it to end once he went back to LA.

He said he'd wait for me, until I finished my degree in five months time. And then I'd go out to join him in Kalifornication. God, I couldn't wait.

We'd talked in whispers most of the night, and made love again and again. *Wow—stamina! I really should send a thank you note to Hilda.* Although, maybe not. She seemed like the stalker type.

But wow! I hadn't had that much sex in, blimey, ever. *Ever, ever, ever!*

Unfortunately, I was now desperate to pee. And from the way my flora and fauna was feeling down under, I was afraid that all the sexing was going to give me cystitis.

I suddenly realized his eyes had opened and he was watching me.

"Hi!" I said, my voice unnaturally high.

A slow, sexy smile spread across his face, and he brushed his hand down my arm.

"Clare."

The way he spoke my name—like the answer to a question, like a promise.

A shuddering breath left my body, and he grinned at me. I watched, my eyes about to dribble out of my head, as his big top rose down below, ready for the greatest show on earth.

And then I heard it.

Footsteps in the hall, and Mum yelling up the stairs. "Clare! Are you coming down for breakfast? I'm making bacon sandwiches!"

Miles groaned. "I love your mum's bacon sandwiches."

"Huh. More than you love me?"

"It's about 50/50 at the moment."

"Sod off."

He laughed, and his eyes crinkled happily.

But now that I thought about it, this could be a tad awkward. You know, the whole Mum-and-Dad-don't-know-I-have-a-fuck-hot-guy-in-my-bed-and-might-actually-think-I'm-still-a-virgin. Yeah, that sort of awkward.

"I guess we'd better get dressed then," said Miles, trying to hide a smile. "Go and face the music."

"Easy for you to say. My mum loves you. In fact I think she probably loves you more than she loves me."

He planted a kiss on the tip of my nose. "Yeah, probably, but your dad is going to have my balls."

"No way! I need those! The only person who's having your balls is *me*."

"So, what do you want me to do? Climb out of the window? Live in your attic? Pretend I've got amnesia? Hope *they* have amnesia?"

"Are there any other options?" I asked, chewing on a broken fingernail.

"I could just come down and say hi," he suggested.

"I don't know. That sounds complicated. Do you think it will work?"

He smirked at me. "One way to find out."

I sighed heavily. "Okay, but if my dad kills you, I'm going to be really pissed off."

"Just pissed off? Not wildly heartbroken? Not utterly bereft and going bonkers in a Mrs. Rochester sort of way."

"Don't push your luck, Stephens."

"Can I push something else?" he said, rocking his hips against me.

"That is such a cheesy line! I can't believe you said that!"

"Is that a no?" he asked, a wicked grin on his face.

"Yes. That's a no. Maybe later."

"Only maybe? Did I tell you I have a Jacuzzi in my hotel room?"

"Oh."

"Yeah."

"Well, if my dad doesn't kill you, I wouldn't be averse to shagging your brains out in a Jacuzzi. Does it have jets?"

He laughed quietly and his eyes softened.

"God, I love you," he said.

There was really only one comeback to that.

"I love you, too."

I found my pajamas which had somehow ended up under the bed, pulled them on and tramped off to the bathroom, leaving Miles to follow me if it seemed safe.

The bathroom mirror hated me.

When I saw myself, I nearly passed out from shock. Not only did I have horrendous sex hair (small print: bird's nest), my face was far too flushed to look normal, and I had a small bite mark on the top of my left breast. Yeah, well my parents definitely wouldn't be seeing *that*. Even though it meant I'd have to fasten my pajama top up to my neckline and risk looking like my Great Aunt Sally.

I dragged a brush through my hair, had a very satisfying pee, flushed the loo, washed my hands, and wondered if I could smuggle Miles out in the laundry basket.

Hmm. Probably not.

He was quite big.

Swoon.

I made my way down to the kitchen. Dad was reading the Sunday papers, and Mum was making the aforementioned haute cuisine bacon sandwiches.

"Hello, love. Did you have a good time last night?"

Oooh. There were so many ways to answer that question. None of which my mum would want to hear.

"Yeah, it was good. How was your party?"

"Oh, same old faces—it was all right. But I want to hear all about the premiere. How was Miles?"

At that moment, the upstairs toilet flushed again.

Dad looked up, a frown on his face.

Mum looked at me, a frown on her face.

I looked at the floor. Wow. How come I'd never noticed how fascinating our kitchen floor was before?

"Clare?"

"Um, yeah?"

"Is there somebody up there?"

"Technically ... yes."

Mum narrowed her eyes. "Have you got a *man* up there? A yes or no answer will do."

"Um, yes?"

Then Miles poked his head around the door, a huge smile on his face.

"Morning, Sheila. Morning, Graham."

God, he looked edible. He was wearing the tux and white shirt, and his bow tie was hanging out of his pocket. Forget the bacon sandwiches—I wanted to eat *him*.

"Morning, Miles," said Mum, faintly. "Bacon sandwich?"

"Oh, brilliant! Thanks, Sheila. I've missed your bacon sandwiches. I haven't had anything like that in forever."

He sat at the table, just like he had so many times before, except this time he picked up my hand from my lap and kissed my fingers. *In front of Mum and Dad!*

My face exploded with color, and Mum dropped the frying pan back onto the cooker with a loud clang.

"Hey, baby," he said to me. "You look beautiful this morning."

Dad choked on his tea. We all knew I looked like the back of a bus that had broken down. I *prayed* that Miles would never lose his rose-tinted glasses. They suited him so well.

Unsurprisingly, we ate in silence after that. Well, the three members of the Milton household did. Miles chatted away, asking questions about mutual friends, and catching up on all the local gossip. As much as was possible, given our single syllable answers.

At the end of the meal, Dad stood up and cleared his throat.

"I'd like to have a word with you, please, Miles," he said. "If you'd like to come through to my study."

"Dad! You haven't got a study!" I snapped. "It's the garden shed—and it'll be freezing!"

He ignored me with a dignified silence. Miles grinned and winked, then leaned down to kiss me.

"Don't worry, baby," he whispered. "I'll tell him that my intentions are strictly honorable ... even if they aren't."

And then he followed Dad into our tiny back garden.

"Well!" said Mum.

"Yeah," I said, chewing on yet another fingernail.

"So, you and Miles?"

"Yeah."

"At last."

"Yeah."

She smiled. "How does it feel?"

I closed my eyes. "Wonderful."

She leaned over and gave me a hug.

"I'm so happy for you both."

"Thanks, Mum."

Dad and Miles didn't stay in the shed very long. Well, it was December. But I think they'd been at the sherry, because Dad was swaying slightly as he walked back up the garden path.

When I finally got Miles alone, he told me that the conversation had been okay.

Just okay?! It made me crazy that he wouldn't tell me what had been said!

Miles

Waking up with Clare was the best fucking way to start the day. I wanted every day to start like that from now on.

Last night had been one hell of an emotional rollercoaster —actually dodgems would be a better metaphor. Bloody Lilia had nearly trashed the whole evening, but the ending was better than I could ever have imagined.

Clare. My best friend, my best girl. My *girlfriend*. It was kind of hard to get my head around the idea, but damn, it made me happy.

And the sex!

Jeez, what I'd been missing out on all these years! Just thinking about that made me a bit crazy. Hot, wet, tight; all soft curves and silky skin; flesh a man could sink his fingers into—or his teeth. So passionate. I felt like my lungs weren't big enough to breathe her in, and my heart couldn't beat fast enough to love her the way I wanted to.

I couldn't get enough of her.

I hoped she'd forgive me for behaving like such a fucking animal all night, but seriously—I could not get enough of this woman.

How had I been so blind? All this time, my dream woman had been right in front of me and I hadn't seen it.

I blamed her.

I'd always thought she wasn't interested in me. She was forever laughing at me, for one thing, and she was so smart— book smart and street smart—so I'd always figured she'd end up with some brainy guy from her university, someone who was as clever as her. I never thought she'd settle for me. Damn, I was happy that her standards were crashing.

Now, it was my job to make sure I did my best to live up to what a woman like her deserved. To try and deserve her. Because I sure as hell hadn't *earned* her.

I wasn't entirely certain how I was going to keep Miles Junior in check around her either. And seeing her cum! I'd never seen anything so fucking hot in my entire life. And I'd watched *a lot* of porn. Well, Jim the Unwashed, the guy that I used to share a house with, he'd insisted we got cable just so he could have access to porn 24 hours a day. But a real flesh and blood woman—there was no comparison.

And now I could close my eyes and have my own private porn show running in my head whenever I wanted it. Yeah, probably best not to do that around her parents. I mean, they liked me well enough, but no father wants to think that some guy is getting it on with his little girl, right?

It was hilarious seeing Clare so flustered this morning. For a moment, I really thought she was going to have me shinning down the drainpipe or something, just so I could avoid her parents. I'd stayed at her place hundreds of times—true, most times it was on the couch—but a couple of times we'd ended up in bed together, even though nothing had ever happened. It pissed me off to think about all the lost opportunities.

I let her go ahead, so she could break the happy news to Sheila and Graham that she'd been shagging the next door neighbor, but from the look on their faces when I walked into the kitchen, I realized that she'd left out that detail.

I could tell that Sheila was okay about it, but Graham wasn't quite sure what to think. I guess he thought he needed to have 'the talk' with me, because after I'd eaten three of the most fuck-tastic bacon sandwiches ever, he took me aside for a 'man to man' conversation.

I didn't know what to expect, but I wasn't too worried either. I could run pretty fast.

It was fucking freezing outside, and his shed was no barrier against frost.

We sat on a couple of old deckchairs, and he poured me a glass of sweet sherry. God, I hated that stuff.

"So, Miles," he said. "It's good to see you again, son."

"Thanks, Graham."

We both took a sip of that God-awful syrup, and I felt my tongue disintegrate from the contact. *Damn.* I'd had plans for that. *Licking Clare's soft, round stomach; licking her warm thighs; licking her full breasts and ...* oh, shit. This was getting awkward.

I shifted around on the deckchair trying to get comfortable. It was a losing battle.

"Ahem."

My head snapped up as Graham cleared his throat.

"I want to know what your intentions are toward my daughter, to our Clare."

I squared my shoulders and looked him in the eye.

"I love her, Graham. I want to marry her. I just haven't told her. Well, I've told her I love her—I haven't asked her to marry me—yet. But I will."

"I see. Right. Well..."

There was a long pause while I waited for the axe to fall, to be told that I wasn't good enough for his daughter. I wouldn't have disagreed.

"So," he said at last, "what do you think about Tottenham's chances against Manchester United?"

We didn't stay outside, I mean, in the shed, much longer after that, thank fuck. I was freezing my balls off in there, and I was pretty sure I'd need them later. In fact, I was hoping that Clare had plans for my balls. Wow, that sounds really bad, but you know what I mean.

Yeah, it's probably not cool to be thinking about shagging a man's daughter while you're sitting in his shed drinking his sherry.

Graham popped a breath mint before we went back in. Sheila probably didn't approve of sherry at that time of the day. It was so fucking disgusting, I didn't approve of it either, whatever time it was.

Actually, I had no clue whether it was still morning or afternoon already. Not that I cared much either. My only plan for the day was to make up for lost time. With Clare.

When we got back to the kitchen, Clare was waiting for me with a tense expression on her face. I don't know what she thought Graham was going to do to me—maybe hit me with a shovel and bury me in the back garden. She looked relieved when I walked in and sat next to her.

"Wow, your hands are freezing!" she said, as I touched her fingers.

"Yeah. December. Shed. But I can think of a few ways that you can warm me up..."

She blinked a couple of times and then gave this sweet, shy little smile. It was so un-Clare, but I liked it.

"Can you?"

"Yeah."

"Um, okay. But I thought you had that interview thing to do."

Shit. She was right. I'd forgotten about that. Melody would have my ass, and not in a good way.

"Crap! What time is it?"

"Just after 12."

"Damn. I have to go. I told Mum I'd see her this morning as well."

Clare's face fell.

"But we still have a date for the Jacuzzi, right?" I said, praying she hadn't changed her mind.

Her smile made my cock sigh with anticipation.

"Yeah, sure. What time will you be finished?"

"About four, I think. Come by after then? Room 607."

"Okay. Have fun."

I couldn't help rolling my eyes. She knew I'd rather chew my foot off up to my elbow than sit and talk about myself for two hours.

The only person I wanted to spend time with was her.

"And, ah, stay the night with me, please, baby?"

"At the Dorchester?"

"Yeah. Please?"

"Wild horses doing a clog dance couldn't stop me."

She stood up to say goodbye to me, and a quick peck on the cheek turned into something much, *much* hotter. I barely heard Sheila's embarrassed cough, but then Clare was pushing me away.

"I'll see you later," she whispered.

I didn't think any paps were watching the house, but I went out through the backdoor just in case.

Mum was standing at the sink. Yeah, and smoking a cigarette! *Busted!*

I tapped on the door and she jumped. I couldn't help laughing as I saw her stub the butt out and wave her hands around, trying to dispel the smoke. Believe me when I say that doesn't work—I tried that shit when I was 15 and I didn't get away with it then.

She unbolted the backdoor, a guilty expression on her face.

"Mum! You were smoking!" I said in an accusing voice, looking sternly at her.

"It was just one," she said. "It's been a stressful few days."

"You nearly killed me when you caught me smoking!"

"You were 15—and it's a horrible habit to start. Besides, I'm your mother. Come here and give me a hug."

"I don't know, Mum, you smell all smoky."

She slapped my arm. "Don't be cheeky!"

I laughed and she pulled me into a real bone crusher.

"I was so proud of you last night," she said, into my chest. "So proud. Not just the film, but the way you looked after that awful girl, too."

She looked up at me, and I felt my lungs tighten at the mention of Lilia.

"I know, love, I do. Believe me, but it was the right thing to do." There was a pause as she looked me up and down. "I take it you've come from next door."

I nodded.

"From Clare?"

I couldn't help grinning when she gave an excited squeak.

"Really? You and Clare?"

"Yeah. I know it's weird and..."

"Rubbish!" she snorted. "The only weird thing is that it's taken you two all this time to work it out."

I wasn't quite sure what to say to that.

"You're happy."

It wasn't a question.

"Yeah, really happy. She's just..."

I didn't know what words to use to describe Clare or how I felt about her. My admiration for scriptwriters grew by the second—they always knew what to say.

I stayed for a quick coffee, and Mum filled me in on what the lawyers had said about a likely moving date to her new house.

"I don't think I'll be able to get back for that, Mum. There's a whole load of publicity stuff I'm contracted to do. I mean, maybe, but..."

"Don't worry, love. I don't expect you to. Sheila and Graham have already offered to help. So has Clare. I'll be fine."

That made me feel worse. Not that they were helping, but they were doing what I should be there to do.

Yeah, I was a lucky bastard in so many ways, but some things—like missing your mum's big day—that sucked.

I got a few odd looks as I walked to the tube station. Probably the fact that I was still wearing my tux, or maybe the fact that I didn't have a coat. Or it could have been because there was a bloody great nine foot high poster advertising *Dazzled* at the station's entrance. It still felt strange. It didn't feel like the guy in that photograph was me.

The train was crowded with people standing, but not really busy like it could get—not so close that you had your back shoved against somebody's rancid armpit. Trust me, for the London underground in summer, you need a biohazard suit.

My mind drifted back to Clare, and I knew I had this huge, goofy smile on my face. I couldn't help it.

Then I saw the newspaper that the guy standing next to me was reading. The front page had a photograph of the crowd at the premiere and close-ups of people yelling at Lilia. It looked bad in the stills photograph; it had been a helluva lot worse to be there. The headline said, 'Angel to Devil— Lilia Under Fire'.

The guy flipped the page over, and inside there was a strip of photographs showing the whole event, moment by moment, shot by shot. This time the headline had my name in it: 'White Knight Miles Better'.

Fun-nee.

The guy probably felt me reading the paper over his shoulder because he glanced up, an irritated expression on his face. Then his eyes crossed and he did this comic double take. I knew I had about two seconds before he said something. Thank God the train was pulling into the station at Hyde Park Corner.

I pushed my way to the doors and had just managed to jump off when I heard him call out, "Hey, man!"

Too slow, sucker.

The winter afternoon sun felt bright compared to the gloom of the underground station, and I walked briskly through the park, my breath weaving like smoke through the winter air. *Jeez, it was cold.* I'd gotten, um, become so used to LA weather, I'd forgotten that London in December was cold enough to freeze the balls off a brass monkey. I shoved my hands in my pockets and picked up the pace, then risked life and limb crossing the busy road in front of the hotel...

...And walked straight into an ambush of photographers.

"It's him! Miles! Miles! Over here!" *Bloody hell!*

"Are you and Lilia together again?" *Fuck, no!*

"Are you in love with Lilia?" *NO!*

"Is it true she's pregnant?" *What the fuck?*

"How do you like London?" *Seriously?*

"Have you forgiven her, Miles?" *Fuck off.*

"How does it feel to be a hero?" *Arsehole.*

"When are you filming the sequel?" *Who gives a flying fuck?*

"What do you think of British girls, Miles?" *Tosser.*

"Have you been with Lilia? Did you spend the night?" *Mind your own fucking business.*

"Where were you last night?" *Sod off.*

"What do you think of the new Prime Minister of Australia?" *What?!*

Fucking hell!

I put my head down and tried to get through without punching anyone, as they pushed their cameras right into my face. Some of them were deliberately shoving into me and trying to get a rise. Pictures like that would have been worth a lot more.

The doorman tried to clear the entrance with one arm and create a space with the other as I inched toward him.

Finally, I fell into the lobby, breathing hard, and feeling like I'd been mugged.

The door swung shut behind me, but I could still hear the calls and yells, softened by the barrier of glass.

"Are you all right, sir?" the doorman asked, looking genuinely concerned.

"Shit! That was ... thanks, mate. I mean it, thank you."

He gave a small smile. "That's quite all right, sir. Just doing my job."

I was definitely making sure he had a fucking fantastic after-Christmas bonus.

As my heart rate started to return to something like normal, I realized that everyone in the lobby was staring at me, although several discreetly turned away when I caught their gaze.

Then I saw Melody walking toward me—she didn't look happy. She jerked her head quickly and took my elbow, steering me behind a pillar and into a small alcove furnished with a plush settee and an aspidistra.

"Are you okay?"

"Yeah, fine," I said, rubbing the back of my neck to relieve some of the tension. "I just wasn't expecting *that*."

"Well, yes," and she paused. "Have you seen the papers? You've made quite an impression: hence the welcoming committee."

I threw her an irritated glance.

"You weren't answering your phone," she said, a slight note of accusation in her voice.

"I left it in my room before the premiere."

I'd answered automatically before it occurred to me how much information I'd just given her, bearing in mind I was still dressed in last night's clothes.

"I see," she said shortly, glancing up and down at my wrinkled tux. "Well, your interview will be in the Park Suite Right, ground floor. One hour. They've been told not to ask about your private life or who you're dating, but you'd better be prepared to talk about last night. We need to rehearse."

"Yeah, yeah, sure. Just give me 20 minutes."

She nodded. "Twenty minutes. And Miles ... wear a clean shirt."

Her mouth hinted at the ghost of a smile, and I grinned back at her.

"Yeah, that I can do."

The shower was just what I needed to calm down, but it would have been a thousand times better if Clare had been there, too.

I couldn't stop thinking about her. The more time that passed, the more dreamlike the whole night seemed. A small pinch of concern made my heart rate spike. I hoped like hell she wasn't going to change her mind once she'd had time to think about it. I wouldn't blame her if she did.

I resented having to do another round of goddamn interviews, but I reminded myself it was part of the job, and beat being unemployed and living off baked beans and instant soup. Something I remembered all too well.

Even so, I didn't bother shaving but in deference to

Melody, I dug out a clean shirt, as instructed, and found a pair of jeans that seemed presentable. Anyway, they'd be filming me above the waist—I could have worn lederhosen and no one would notice. Well, the interviewers might.

I'd just run some gel through my hair when Melody knocked on my door. And, God bless her, she'd brought room service with her and a caffetiere of coffee.

"I thought you'd need it and I damn well know I do," she said.

"Have I told you how bloody wonderful you are?"

She smiled. "No, but I'll remind you on my next invoice."

Melody went through the list of probable questions based on the topics provided for the interviewers. Then she helped me prepare answers and, finally, escorted me to the room where the interviews were being held. Hell, maybe she was even going to sit there and hold my hand, or get ready to hoick my foot out of my mouth, should the need arise. She probably sensed that my personal safety catch was on the verge of being released, and she didn't know whether or not my trigger finger was getting twitchy.

Cameras, lights and recording equipment were already in place, and the first interviewer was touching up her lipstick when we walked in. She gave me a killer smile and licked her lips.

Shit.

It was going to be a long afternoon.

Clare

As soon as Miles left, I went back to bed and slept for three hours. I was knackered, exhausted, worn out, used up, fatigued, tuckered out and just plain tired.

But looking on the positive side, my vocabulary was in better shape.

Frankly, if I was going to be having sex with Miles on a regular basis, (and I couldn't help looking around for a black cat so it could accidentally on purpose run across my path),

I was going to have to do something about my level of fitness. Not that I had a level. A couple of basements, perhaps.

I mean, I'd been flat on my back most of the night, although not the *entire* time, but I was still weary beyond words. Miles, on the other hand, looked like he'd just had eight hours of uninterrupted beauty sleep when he walked into my parents' kitchen.

But you know—so what if I was five foot nothing and weighed 140 pounds? Miles was beautiful enough for both of us.

He could have had a supermodel. Hell, he probably *had* had a couple of supermodels—maybe at the same time. But he'd chosen me—and after waiting all these years, I was *not* letting him go. If the world ended tomorrow, they'd have to pry me off him with a grappling hook.

Hmm. Grappling with Miles.

Yeah, sorry. Hard to stay on track.

The point was, he was *mine*.

Of course, that wasn't what the newspapers were saying. Most of them were carrying front page pictures of Miles charging into the crowd to save Lilia, and they'd all leapfrogged to the same conclusion.

The online accounts were even more fanciful.

"A source close to the couple said, 'They're in a really good place right now. He's forgiven Lilia, and they're more in love than ever before'."

Ugh. Vomit.

What 'source'? How did they make up this crap and keep a straight face? It was such bollocks! Sheer fabrication, because nobody knew the truth except me and Miles. Oh, and Mum and Dad. Probably Prue, too. But that was all. Oh, and Lilia—she knew how he really felt.

But then I saw something that made my stomach drop into my shoes, by way of my bed socks.

"They're really looking forward to working together again on the sequel to 'Dazzled'. They met making the first film, and that was a

very special time for them. They're hoping that they'll rekindle their magic on set."

A sequel?! That was the first I'd heard of it. Miles hadn't mentioned a sequel. Why the hell hadn't he said anything about that to me? How could he face working with that cheating chav again?

I tried not to stay angry, but I was upset.

I was the last to know, and that hurt.

Miles

It was nearly four o'clock and I'd had enough of talking. Besides, the questions were all the same:

"How did you enjoy the premiere?"

"What made you walk into the crowd like that?"

"What do you think of your fans now?"

"How's Lilia this morning?"

"What will it be like working on the sequel with her?"

"What else are you working on?"

The answers were all the same, too...

Good.

It seemed the right thing to do.

Great.

Fine, I think.

A sequel hasn't been confirmed.

Nothing definite.

...but with a lot more smiling, and a few dumb jokes like they expected from me.

I'd done so many of these short interviews now that I was practically on autopilot.

But the last question of the day threw me.

"So, Miles, I hear you're getting married. What can you tell me about that?"

How the fuck did she know? I hadn't even asked Clare yet?

She must have seen the shock on my face, and the bint smiled, pleased with herself.

And then I realized that she hadn't got a clue about Clare

—the stupid bitch was trying to get some shock value out of her pathetic question.

"I think that's enough questions for today," Melody said, quickly.

I appreciated her help, but I was putting the fucking lid on *that* line of questioning.

"No, I'd like to answer that one," I interrupted.

The interviewer looked like she was having an orgasm.

"I don't know where you heard that, Carmel," I said, my voice controlled and level, "but it's completely wrong. I'm not even dating anyone at the moment. Anyone."

She looked faintly disappointed and then a look of calculation followed it.

"Well, that was a great interview. Thanks, Miles. Maybe you and I can go ... somewhere and grab a cup of coffee?"

"Sorry, no can do. I've got wall to wall meetings, but thanks, Carmel."

She looked annoyed—not that I gave a flying fuck.

"Maybe next time you're in London."

"I always like being interviewed by you, Carmel," I said, a huge fake smile on my face.

Stupid cow believed it, fluttering her eyelashes and pouting.

Even Melody raised her eyebrows and shook her head in amusement.

"Well, that was entertaining," she said, once we left the room. "You're getting good at this, Miles." Then, more sincerely, "How are you holding up?"

I was tired of people asking me that, but yeah, I understood why they did it. And I knew Melody wasn't just being nosy. I trusted her—she'd given me my break.

"I'm okay. It's just when people say crap like that, it pisses me off. But yeah, I'm fine."

"And how *are* things with Lilia?"

I pulled a face.

"That good?"

"Ha, well ... I'd be happy if I never had to have anything to do with her ever again."

"But you know you have to—for publicity?"

"Yeah, I get that, Melody, believe me. And I don't want to make your job harder... actually, there was something I've been meaning to ask you?"

"Oh? I'm intrigued."

"The contract with the studio?"

"Yes?"

"Do I have to do it if there's a sequel to *Dazzled*?"

She gave me a shrewd look.

"Well, I've seen the contract, obviously, but I'd have to check the fine print. I would suggest, however, that even if you're not locked into a sequel—and I'd be surprised if you weren't—you should think *very* carefully before you turned it down, simply because of ... *personal* issues. Miles, you're a young actor and you have great potential—that much is clear. But you're at the beginning of your career, and you should think *very* hard about making a bad decision at this point."

"You think it would be a bad decision?"

She leaned against the wall and sighed heavily.

"Financially, yes. Professionally, that's less clear-cut. The reviews for *Dazzled* are all good, particularly for your role. But part of my answer will depend on how your next project *Lifers* is perceived. It's a tougher sell, but people need to know you can do more than fantasy and romance."

She was right, I knew she was right. But the thought of having to work with Lilia again—that sucked.

"Do you still want me to investigate the contract?"

"Yeah, please. Just so I know where I stand."

She smiled. "You're learning, Miles."

I'd only been back in my room a couple of minutes when there was a knock at the door.

I pulled it open, excited and, in all honesty, a bit nervous.

Clare was standing there with a little scowl on her face that made me smile.

When she stormed into the room, I felt my smile slip.

"I suppose you were going to tell me that there was a sequel to *Dazzled*?" she snapped, her eyes sparking, and her mouth clamped into a hard line. "Perhaps it just slipped your mind?"

"Well..."

"Because it really pisses me off that I had to read in a bloody newspaper rather than to hear it from you!"

"Hey, wait a minute!"

"No, you wait! If we're going to do this whole dating lark, then..."

I was so happy to hear that she still wanted to date me that I shut her up the only way I could think of.

I kissed her.

As soon as our lips met, my body went into overdrive. I wanted to *touch* her everywhere. I wanted to *feel* her everywhere.

Her hands flew up to my neck and gripped me hard.

Then she pushed me away abruptly, leaving me panting like a dog.

"You can't distract me that easily!" she barked.

I couldn't help grinning at her, and before you roll your eyes, I *know* that was a really dumb thing to do.

Clare

I was furious. You know, the whole red mist, ready to do some violence sort of fury.

I stormed into that hotel room, prepared to give Mr. Oops There's Something Important I Forget To Tell My Girlfriend a piece of my mind. A really sharp piece.

But then he kissed me. And I almost let him get away with it. But just because my heart was thundering like a 300 pound sprinter going over the hurdles, and my blood was about to superheat to the temperature of a solar flare, I wasn't letting him get away with that.

I pushed him off.

And he *grinned* at me! That was *so* out of order.

"I am seriously pissed here, Miles! Don't you dare grin at me or you'll be needing the services of a Hollywood dentist after all."

"Okay, okay! I get it. But, shit, Clare, you're so hot when you're angry."

I gaped at him. I was standing there yelling at him and *that* was turning him on?

I was so screwed.

"Be careful what you say next, Stephens! You do realize my vagina has an on—off switch linked directly to whatever comes out of your mouth?"

He gave a dark laugh.

"Are you sure?"

"Yup, pretty sure."

"Are we talking about just the *words* that come out of my mouth?" he asked, flicking his tongue over his lips as I imagined it licking between my breasts and toward my stomach. Or a bit lower.

"Um..."

"Nothing else of interest?"

"Um..."

He took a pace toward me so his body was flush against mine. He leaned down very slowly, pushed a strand of hair behind my ear, and placed his lips against my ear.

"Sorry," he whispered.

He tugged my earlobe with his teeth and kissed his way down my throat to my collar bone. Wrapping his arms around my waist, he walked me back toward the bed.

"This is coming off," he said, tugging at the hem of my sweater. "And this *definitely* has no business covering up those fan-fucking-tastic tits," he continued, peeling off my t-shirt. He unhooked my bra with one hand, and started massaging my breasts with the other, pinching the nipples lightly.

He unzipped my jeans and pulled them down slowly. I lay on the bed, splayed out like a baby whale while he stood, fully clothed, gazing down.

Moving lazily, he removed his t-shirt and jeans with

teasing slowness, and slid down until he was level with my side. He kissed my lips softly, then scooted further down the bed and kissed his way from my knees back up to the top of my thighs.

"Still mad at me?" he said.

"Um..."

"Still want to tell me off?" he murmured against my skin.

"Um..."

"Go on, Clare," and he bit my neck. "Tell me how *bad* I've been."

"Um..."

Yeah, I'm not sure who won that conversation.

Chapter Eighteen

DEEP THROAT

Clare

Miles was yelling at me—and I was yelling back.

"You were going to sleep with Nazzer! He's a complete tosser!"

"Yeah, but he's *your* friend!"

"That's how I know what I'm talking about!"

His eyes flashed and he was breathing fast, his hard chest rising and falling rapidly.

How dare he look so damn hot when he was shouting at me.

I was considering storming off, but it's hard to make a dramatic exit when you're sitting naked in a Jacuzzi, let alone flounce. I was not a flouncer—it would have just looked wrong.

"Yeah, well I didn't sleep with him," I pointed out, trying to sound calmer.

Telling Miles about that night in the pub with Paul and Nazzer was not the smartest thing I'd ever done, but honestly, I thought he'd laugh.

Instead, I'd got a very different reaction.

"It's not like you and me were even talking to each other," I said, "let alone, um, dating."

"Yeah, but *Nazzer!* Couldn't you do better than that?"

"Actually, no!" I snarled, my cheeks flushing, "And if you

have to know, he turned me down for a *Thunderbirds* marathon."

"Thank fuck for that," Miles said, quietly. Then he looked up. "He what? A *Thunderbirds* marathon ... what channel was it on?"

I felt my eyes cross with anger and humiliation, then I saw the suppressed smile that lifted the corner of his mouth slightly.

"You smug bastard!" I shouted. "I totally believed you then!"

He shrugged and sighed.

"I'm still pissed off that you thought of sleeping with Nazzer."

"And I'm still pissed off that I had to watch you bump uglies with Lilia for two whole days of filming!" I fired back. "Let alone knowing you were doing it for real when the cameras stopped rolling."

He winced and looked away.

"Sorry," I said, quietly. "That was below the belt. I mean ... um ... sorry."

He still couldn't look at me, and I felt bad for making him feel that way. I wasn't being fair.

"Hey," I said softly, shifting across so I could lean against him. "I didn't mean that."

"Yeah, I know," he sighed, running a hand through his wet hair. "Can we just *not* do this. I hate arguing with you."

"Okay."

"Thanks."

"Um ... but don't get upset. I want to ask about the sequel. Why didn't you tell me?"

He rolled his eyes.

"I only found out about it last night," he grumbled. "Hyde came up to me at the premiere and said we should talk about the sequel when I got back to LA. It was the first I'd heard of it. I mean, Laura Dorien hasn't even written a second book. But, I guess because this movie is making money for the studio, it's a no-brainer decision."

"So you're going to do it."

"Maybe."

"Maybe?" I felt hopeful but a little confused.

"Well, Melody is going to check my contract to see if I'm locked into it, but even if I'm not, she said I should think about it anyway."

"Oh."

He put his arm around my shoulders and tugged me closer.

"What do you think? Do you think I should do it?"

"Oh, no way, Miles! You are *not* putting the responsibility of that decision in my lap!"

He looked annoyed. "I'm not trying to! I'm just asking my *girlfriend* what she thinks about something that will affect us both."

"Oh, sorry," I mumbled. "I can't get used to that—you know, discussing things—couples stuff."

I sucked on my teeth as I thought about it, and Miles smiled when I blew out a long breath that made me sound like a tired carthorse.

"Melody thinks you should?"

"She says I shouldn't dismiss it just because of..."

"Because of Lilia?"

"Well, yeah."

"She's right."

"She is?"

"Look, it's only six weeks of filming. You're a professional —you can do that."

He frowned. "Yeah, but there's still months of promotional stuff that we'd have to do together. I might not be able to come back to London for a while."

"Maybe you could make a film in Britain?"

He frowned.

"That would be great, but the UK film industry needs a life-support system right now."

"Well, you never know. It could happen. It would be cool

if you used your own voice for a change—not always having to do an American accent."

He frowned again. "I'm so used to that now, I don't know if it would make it harder or easier. Doing an accent, it gives me something to hide behind, you know?"

I felt sad that he still felt like that. But that was probably what made him such a brilliant actor, feeling everything so much, living without that extra layer of skin that most people needed.

"Well, it would be brilliant if you did film in the UK. Hey! Maybe they'd shoot a period piece. You could wear breeches. Your arse would look so hot in breeches."

Even the word was turning me on ... bree-ches. Yes, and a loose white shirt—a wet shirt—clinging to every muscle. Look, I *know* that's been done, but come on! You have to admit that's hot!

He laughed, but I was serious.

"Anyway," he continued, "I'll have to see her—Lilia—on Monday when we do the New York junket. I wish you could be there for that."

"I know. Me, too."

His face suddenly brightened.

"So, come with me! You don't have to be back at university for a few days yet. Come with me."

"What, fly all the way to New York just for a weekend?!"

"Sure!"

"Get you, Mr. Jet Set!" I paused. "Are you serious?"

"One hundred per cent. I'll book your ticket now if you say yes."

Wow! He was just sooooo smooth. When did that happen?

"Well," I said, slowly, "I could try out my kung fu moves on Lilia."

He laughed, delightedly.

"You haven't got any kung fu moves!"

"I so have! I used to love Bruce Lee films, and Jackie Chan."

He grabbed my wrists as he pulled me onto his lap.

"Go on then. Show me some moves."

So I did. Just not the ones he was expecting.

We finally fell into bed to sleep a couple of hours after midnight.

The Jacuzzi sex had been amazing—a bit weird, sort of squelchy, and we made a hell of a mess on the bathroom floor —but amazing. And for future reference, reverse cowgirl is definitely the way to go.

We both felt guilty about that—the spilled water, not the amazing sex, obviously—so we'd tried to mop it up with towels. We got through a lot of towels.

But hey, this was the Dorchester—they'd probably had a lot worse things happen. Didn't one of those rock bands bring back a live goat? Or maybe I was imagining it, which is pretty scary in itself.

And have you any idea *how much I loved room service?!* Food, drinks, whatever and whenever you wanted it. I felt sort of awkward having people jumping every time I snapped my fingers, metaphorically speaking, but Miles said he wasn't going to feel guilty about it anymore, because the suits from the studio once had him working 64 days with only one short break, plus he'd worked Christmas Eve (which I didn't like to remember), and all the days between Christmas and New Year. So if we wanted toast at midnight, we should just go ahead and order it. But hold the caviar. Neither of us liked that bizarre stuff.

For the last half hour, we'd been arguing—well, having a lively discussion—about what to do for New Year's Eve. Miles said he wanted us to stay in and, you know, do *couples* stuff. It wasn't that I was averse to his suggestion, but I had promised Nazzer and Paul that we'd go out, and Miles hadn't seen his friends since April.

He was also irritated that I'd been Googling his name to see what the gossip sites were saying about him.

"I don't know why you read that rubbish," he complained. "You know they make it up when they don't have a clue. You'll just turn into a moody cow if you see something about Lilia."

Which was true. But it didn't stop me. I wasn't deliberately being a masochist, but I thought it was a good idea to see what lies the harlot was putting about—when she wasn't putting herself about. You know, forewarned is forearmed.

What I wasn't expecting to see was a clip from one of yesterday's interviews.

"He's single, ladies! In an exclusive interview with rising star Miles Stephens, I can exclusively reveal that the shy hunk is not dating at all. In an intimate one-on-one, Miles said, 'I'm not even dating anyone at the moment. Anyone.' Hasta la vista, Lilia! So line up ladies, because this man is open for business. And I'm first in the queue. This is Carmel McConnell reporting..."

"What the hell is this, Miles?" I yelped, spinning the laptop around to face him.

He looked at the screen and frowned.

"That's from one of the interviews I did yesterday. What about it?"

"What about it? You lied! You flat out lied! You said you weren't—and I quote—that you 'weren't dating anyone'. How is that supposed to make me feel?"

"I don't know, Clare," he snapped, pressing his lips together in a thin line. "Protected? Safe? Why the hell would I want to give some stranger the details of our private life to broadcast wherever the fuck she likes?"

Oh.

"You *know* that isn't real," he said, pointing at the laptop. Then he gestured between us, "This ... this here is what's real."

I felt like such an idiot.

"Sorry. I am—I'm really sorry. I don't mean to be all paranoid, but you're going back to LA soon and I don't know when I'll see you again. It freaks me out a bit."

His head hung forward. "I know. I get it. But you have to trust me. I don't go around dipping my wick into anything that has a pulse. I'm not like that—I never have been. Jeez, you *know* that."

"I do know. I'm just being stupid."

He pulled me into a hug.

"Promise me you won't believe any of that shit," he mumbled into my hair.

I blew out a long breath. "Okay."

His grip tightened.

"Do we really have to go out tonight?"

"Yeah, you lightweight—it's New Year's Eve. Besides, Nazzer and Paul will be waiting."

An hour later and halfway across London, I was regretting insisting that we meet up with the tosser twins, because the first thing Paul said when he saw Miles holding my hand was,

"Huh, so you've tapped that now, you dog!"

I thought Miles was going to go nuclear, and actually I kind of wanted him to, but he just acted cool.

"Yeah, well, you lost your chance, dickhead," he said, his voice quiet and even. "She's *mine*, so keep your fucking hands to yourself or I'll break them off. That goes double for you, Naz."

Seeing Miles getting all protective and territorial had a strange effect on me. Well, obviously it was a huge turn on, but it made me feel delicate and girly, like I should take up embroidery or flower arranging. And it made me feel loved. No guy had ever made me feel that way before.

The look on their faces was priceless. Paul actually seemed slightly scared. Nazzer looked like he was having trouble understanding the English language.

"Um, happy New Year?" I said.

It was tense and uncomfortable for a few minutes, but then we started talking like old times. Almost like old times, because that night Miles kept a hold of my hand the whole time, his thumb rubbing small circles over my palm.

Miles

I hadn't seen Nazzer and Paul in nearly eight months, but my first reaction to Paul's dumbass comment was to beat the living shit out of him for talking about Clare like that.

She must have felt me tense up, because she was clinging onto my arm with both hands.

After she pulled me onto the seat next to her and we got some drinks in, I started to calm down a bit. I don't even know why I was surprised that Paul was such a prick—I'd always known his brains were in his backside, especially when it came to women.

Not that I thought of myself as an expert or anything—hell, no! But when a guy's best chat-up line is, "Oi, love, do you want to feel my shirt? 'Cause it's boyfriend material," you see the problem.

Yep, he actually said that. Of course, he got his ass handed to him because the woman's reply was something like, "What? Go with you while there are dogs in the street?"

I guess I was just feeling sort of protective, and things that I would have laughed at a year ago, now just irritated me.

Despite that initial hiccup, it was good to see the guys. They didn't give a shit about what I'd been doing, except to ask if Lilia was as hot in bed as she looked.

Clare answered that one for me.

"What difference would it make to you? You couldn't even find your dick with a map."

I was still slightly taken aback when Nazzer told me that they'd found a replacement sax player for the trio. I've got to say that stung. I don't know why really, it wasn't like I was expecting them to wait around—they had lives, too. I suppose it was just the reality of knowing that the old part of my life was over.

Of course, they totally loved it when this woman came

over to get my autograph. They asked if she wanted me to sign her tits. I told them to shut the fuck up and had to buy her a drink to apologize.

As it happened, she *did* want me to sign her tits, but Clare vetoed that one.

In fact, I thought she was going to toss the woman out onto the street by her hair extensions, especially when she said her vajazzle was inspired by the angel imagery from *Dazzled*.

We all laughed—well, I cringed—then Paul took me to one side and asked what a vajazzle was. I told him to Google it, but he probably thought that Googling was something porn actors did. And now I think about it, he did suggest I got into making porn films because, "That's where the big bucks are—and big bazookas!" And he could watch them being made.

So, all in all, it was kind of a fun evening, but it felt like I was saying goodbye.

I suppose that's exactly what it was.

We left the pub well after midnight, but it was impossible to get a cab. We tried waiting for a bus, but some drunk guys started giving me hassle, and Clare mouthed off to them, so we had to leg it. I was soooo glad that Clare wasn't the kind of girl who wore high heels when she went out. Now if she wore them in bed, yeah, I could totally get into that.

But we didn't want to wait for any more buses after that—I was kind of afraid of the trouble Clare's mouth would get me into if we stood at a bus stop. And I really didn't want to find out if training for a fake fight with a Hollywood stuntman would make a difference when four bricklayers from Essex threatened to rearrange my face.

So we walked. Well, I walked—Clare rode piggyback most of the way.

We finally crawled into the hotel and had about two hours' sleep before getting up for the flight to New York—8 AM on New Year's Day. That was *brutal*. I didn't even get a chance to say goodbye to Mum. I called her from the airport to wish her a happy New Year. I couldn't even say when I'd see her again.

On the plus side, the plane was nearly empty and we slept most of the way.

We were staying at the Bowery Hotel on Manhattan's Lower East Side. Honey had liaised with the studio to book me a room, but I didn't know where they'd stashed Lilia. I didn't care much either, I just didn't want to run into her by accident.

Clare laughed.

"Are you kidding me? I'd *love* to run into her by accident!" and she flexed her biceps. At least, I think that's what she was doing.

Yeah, even though Clare was a Literature student, I don't think she understood the whole concept of 'accident' and 'deliberate'. I guess it was kind of easy to get them confused.

But when we turned up for the press junket the next day, Clare got her wish.

I was standing backstage, I mean, in another room, waiting for everything to kick off, when Lilia swept in looking like she owned the damn place.

I had to hand it to her, she had style.

"Happy New Year, darling!" she said, a beaming smile lighting up her face.

She really was beautiful.

I didn't mean to be rude, but when she tried to kiss my cheek, I craned my head away from her.

She looked angry, but then covered it up with a playful pout. Instead, she linked her arm through mine and smiled up at me.

"Did you have a wonderful New Year? Mine was fun, but I missed you. What did you do?"

"He went out with his girlfriend!" came an icy voice from behind me.

Who needed the cavalry when Clare was around?

. . .

Clare

Lilia practically growled at me. Enough barbs were shooting from her eyes to have ventilated me severely.

"What are you doing here?" she snarled.

"I invited her," said Miles, calmly. "Like she said, we're together now. Clare's my girlfriend."

Lilia tore her arm free and marched off without a word.

"Wow," said Miles, an amused smile lifting the corners of his mouth, "you pissed her off in less than three seconds. I think that's a record."

I rolled my eyes. "I piss her off by breathing. *You're* the one who pissed her off in less than three seconds."

He leaned down to kiss me. "Yeah, we make a great team."

At that moment, they were all called onto the platform in the conference room. Jo-Anne led the way, followed by Lilia, Miles and Donald Hyde.

I was getting sick of seeing his shiny, botoxed face, and I think it was mutual because his lip always curled when he looked at me. Although that might have been from the plastic surgery. I hadn't said anything to Miles about how Hyde behaved around me, because I didn't want him to get arrested for thumping someone again.

Rhonda was there, too, and gave me a quick head nod. Wow, that was the most effusive she'd been with me—progress. Well, to be fair, we'd sort of reached an entente when the scandal about Lilia first broke and after the interview debacle. Whatever, she seemed to be coming around to my presence. *Yeah, well, she'd bloody have to!*

The journalists' questions were fairly benign and straightforward, asking about the possibility of a sequel, asking about how it felt to be in a hit movie, and so on and so on.

Miles was funny and charming; Lilia smiled a lot, but managed to say absolutely nothing when she spoke; and Jo-Anne was warm and thoughtful in her answers. Hyde just sounded like a prick in a good suit.

I may have been biased.

I was kind of zoning out for most of the interview, the late nights and five hour time difference getting to me, when one question to Miles had me pinning my ears back and listening intently.

"Bearing in mind Nuriel is an angel, is there any part of the character that you identified with?"

Miles looked uncharacteristically serious as he answered.

"Yeah, I really liked his capacity to learn." He shook his head slightly. "I don't mean because he was smart and had been God's go-to guy," a ripple of laughter drifted around the room, "the opposite in fact. He thought he knew everything, but when he fell to Earth, when he fell in love, nothing made sense any more—it's then he's at his most honest. Love doesn't make sense—until it does. When he finally realizes that he knows *nothing*, he can finally start to learn." He paused again. "Kind of levels the playing field for us mortals."

Again, the massed reporters chuckled. The questioner gave Miles a shrewd look.

"Is that your experience of love, that nothing makes sense?"

There was a collective intake of breath, and Rhonda looked irritated. I wondered if she was going to pull the plug.

Miles just smiled.

"I think that's every guy's experience of love," he said, looking toward me, a small smile threatening to break out. "It doesn't make sense, until it does."

I didn't think it was possible to love him any more than I already did. Turned out I was wrong.

My biggest mistake of the afternoon was to go to the bathroom.

Now, generally speaking, going to the bathroom is usually viewed as a good thing—you know, saves you from having an embarrassing incident in public. In this case, it meant having an embarrassing incident in private.

I'd just availed myself of the facilities and was washing my hands, when Lilia slunk through the door.

I couldn't help wondering if she made a habit of skulking in bathrooms just waiting to piss me off. Maybe it was one of her many talents—that and being able to blow a guy while being photographed for *People* magazine.

"I know why you're here," she said. "I know why you're with Miles."

"Is it a multiple choice answer, or were you hoping your hot air would help with global cooling?"

"You're just with him now because he's famous—and he's got money."

The accusation stung, but I was determined not to let *her* see that.

"Coffee, chocolate, men ... some things are just better rich. I would have thought you'd appreciate that, Lilia."

"You're just a mercy fuck," she continued, scathingly. "It's obvious Miles feels sorry for you."

"Yeah? Well, it's obvious he loathes your bony ass. I guess that makes us even."

"Not even nearly!" she hissed, losing her composure. "How long was it going on—you and him?"

I was filled with contempt.

"If you really think Miles is capable of cheating, you don't know him at all. He loathes cheats, and he's not capable of being one. You're on your own with that."

She changed tack faster than a politician at an Elton John concert.

"Well, if you really cared about your *friend*, you'd realize how bad it'll look if word gets out that he's dating a Wisconsin skinny."

"A what?"

"An o-beast! A fugly, overweight bitch."

"Well, at least your vocabulary is improving. And, frankly, however you describe me, people will still think it's an improvement over a cokehead prima donna with knobbly knees, sagging tits and an arse you could sharpen your pencil on."

I fixed her with my thousand-yard stare that I learned in the Marines, (not really), and poked a finger at her bony chest.

"Girls like you make me sick, Lilia. You always have to blame everyone else when something goes wrong. I mean, you're rich, famous, and even I can see that you're a good actress—hell, you had Miles fooled when he thought you really cared for him—but that part of your life is over. So thank your lucky stars that you still have a career and leave him the fuck alone."

"Or what?"

"I'll find you."

"Are you threatening me?"

"You're not totally stupid then."

And if only I could have swept out of there with my head held high. Well, actually, that's exactly what I did—and walked straight into the door.

My nose exploded, and the pain was so bad, I think I saw stars. I know that had already happened a few times due to Miles' mega orgasmathons, but as this was from being smacked in the face, believe me when I say it's different.

"Ow! Fug! Crab! Ship!"

Which translates as, "Ow! Fuck! Crap! Shit!" because, come on, I had blood pouring out of my nose.

Lilia just laughed at me and walked away, leaving me in tears with a pool of blood gathering on the floor.

"Classy ... not," she called over her shoulder.

Half blinded with pain, I staggered toward the sink and watched as blood dripped down. Worse still, both my eyes were swelling up into slits. I filled the sink with cold water, grabbed a handful of paper towels and wadded them up to make a cold compress.

Then my phone rang. Miles! Thank God! But as I picked it up, I dropped it into the water. It bleeped unhappily once, then died.

I collapsed into a heap on the floor and cried my eyes out.

Which was how Bette found me, a sweet old lady who was visiting from Oklahoma City. She probably thought I was a druggie who'd been mugged, because she backed out of there so fast, I was afraid she'd meet herself coming back. But when she returned a few minutes later, she'd brought the hotel security with her.

"Do we have a problem here, ma'am?"

"Ob caws theb's a fuggin' publum! I'b brogen by fuggin' dose!"

"Do you speak English, ma'am? Do you need a doctor? Doc-tor? Doc-tor? Med-ic? Hos-pit-al?"

"I wan' Biles!"

"I think she said she's got piles," Bette added, helpfully.

"Yeah, probably from sitting on the marble floor," said the security guard. "That sure won't help. We'd better get you up, ma'am!"

"Doh! I wan' Biles! Biles Steebun! The ackdor!"

"She's saying something about the backdoor. Do you think that's how she got in?"

"Probably," said the security guard. "We get a lot of crack whores shooting up in the alley. Pardon my French, ma'am."

"Oh by Gud!"

"What was that, dear?"

"Let me handle this, ma'am," said the security guard. "She could be dangerous."

"She doesn't look dangerous," said Bette.

"Appearances can be deceptive," intoned the dickwad.

"No need to be a smart-ass," snapped Bette, which made the dickwad blink. She pointed at my shoulder bag. "Why don't you do your job and see if she's got ID?"

"Huh, probably stolen," muttered dickwad.

"Photo ID will prove you right then, won't it?" she stated. "I'm Bette by the way, dear. Visiting from Oklahoma City. It's so exciting to walk right into a crime scene. It's just like on NCIS—even down to the fresh blood. I wonder what the spatter pattern will tell us?"

"I gob hid id the dose." I held out my hand. "By dame ib Clem."

"Did you say your name is Clem, dear?"

Dickwad pulled out my passport. "According to this her name is Clare Milton from England."

"How exciting," said Bette. "Do you know the Queen?"

It was only when Miles sent Rhonda to look for me that I was found.

He nearly freaked out when he saw me covered in blood, sitting in the dickwad's office, with two NYPD specials in attendance.

"Jesus Christ, Clare! What the hell happened to you, baby?"

"Had an argubent wib a door," I mumbled.

"What? You did all that by walking into a door?"

"Yeb."

"Can you vouch for this person, sir?" said one of the cops.

Miles looked annoyed. "Of course I can! She's my girlfriend!"

They all did the usual double take. They looked at him ... they looked at me ... they looked at him. It was like watching a tennis match in slow motion. And every single one of them was thinking the same thing: *what the hell is he doing with her?*

Although they might also have been thinking about recommending him a good optician.

"Yeah!" said Miles, angrily. "And she's a guest in this hotel and she needs a fucking doctor, not the police!"

It's amazing what you can get when you're famous.

We were whisked off by limo to some private clinic, all paid for by the hotel, who were desperate for me not to sue, or for Miles to give them a bad review—which, financially, probably amounted to the same thing. They had a reputation to uphold for cool, hip people to stay there, and although that didn't apply to the girl who was dimmer than an eclipse at night who walked into doors, Miles was definitely someone they wanted to come back again.

It turned out that my nose wasn't broken, thank God, but I did have two amazing black eyes.

Miles bought me a pair of ridiculously expensive Gucci sunglasses to cover them, but I still looked like a giant panda after a bad night out.

He cancelled everything else he was supposed to do that day, and we hung out in our room eating pizza, drinking beer, and watching TV.

Clips from the junket were shown later that evening. Jo-Anne was being interviewed on 'Letterman', and they were running it as a trailer.

I had to admit, there was something sexy about seeing my boyfriend on TV, especially as it wasn't *Crimewatch*.

It was just my friggin' luck. I was in a fantastic hotel room, overlooking the city that never sleeps, with a bona fide film star sex god, and my libido had taken a one-way ticket to a nunnery.

Worse still, I was going back to London the next day, and we didn't know when we'd be able to see each other again.

Miles held my hand, and fed me pieces of pizza, which made him officially perfect in my book.

And then we sat back to enjoy Jo-Anne's interview.

But just before they brought her on, a picture of Miles was shown on the screen.

"Hollywood insiders are trying to confirm a sighting of 'Dazzled' star Miles Stephens' new girlfriend. Ever since costar Lilia Purcell was photographed in a compromising position with an unknown male and female, as well as—it is alleged—Golden Globe winner Charlie Sheehan, relations have been strained between the two stars. Today it seems the angelic actor has found love again in an unlikely place."

And then they showed a photograph of me and him when we arrived at the hotel the day before—and Miles had his arm around me and was whispering something in my ear.

I remembered exactly what he'd said, because it had made me laugh.

"One day I'm going to buy you your own chocolate fountain—and then I'm going to dip my dick in it and see how much you really like chocolate."

Yeah, that had made me laugh. But I wasn't laughing now. Our secret was out.

Someone had talked.

Chapter Nineteen

TRULY, MADLY, DEEPLY

Miles

The press coverage was wholly negative. I was described as a cheating bastard who'd led Lilia astray then pushed her off the deep end. Clare was a manipulative, social-climbing home-wrecker.

Lilia was looking pretty damn squeaky clean. It was amazing how quickly people 'forgot' those damn photographs, even though Joe Blow was in rehab and being divorced by his wife. Rumors, half-truths and blackwhite newspeak were enough. That's what it felt like. I didn't give a shit what they said about me, and I was starting to think that pretty much anything could be forgiven and forgotten with the right spin. It was a depressing thought.

And it was everything Rhonda had warned us could happen. I made a mental note to listen very carefully next time she told me something—the woman was a goddamn soothsayer.

Apart from the sheer fabrication of the whole thing, I think what hurt the most were the vicious attacks on Clare personally, based on one, blurry photograph: too fat, too ugly, what did I see in her, yadda, yadda, yadda. It made me want to come out of our corner fighting. Of course, Rhonda advised against that. Strongly.

"Miles, honey, you've just got to suck it up," she said.

"But how can they get away with this? It's all such bullshit!"

"Yep, got the memo on that. But I recommend that you do what you did last time—keep your head down and your mouth shut. And the same goes for you, Clare."

"Will this affect his career?" Clare asked, carefully.

"I don't give a fuck about that!" I shouted, unable to control my voice.

"Well, you should care," Clare replied, forcefully, "because if you give up now, what's been the point of it all? And Lilia wins." She sighed and stared at her fingers. "I can't even blame her."

"What the...?"

"We don't know for sure that she was the one who said anything—it could have been the hotel security, or people from the clinic. Hell, it could have been dear, sweet Bette from Oklahoma City for all we know. Lilia is just working to save her own skin."

"Well, I never thought I'd say this," said Rhonda, dryly, "but Clare's right. Say nothing. Do nothing."

"Fuck!" I couldn't help snarling the word. "I'm surprised they haven't said I've been beating her up as well!"

Rhonda tsked loudly. "Yes, well, you're not going to like what I say next—either of you—but you've got to send Clare home, to avoid *exactly* that scenario. So far, the Press only have a grainy photograph of Clare, but if they see her bruised like this, they'll have a field day." She looked firmly at me. "And that *will* finish you."

"Bloody hell," breathed Clare. "She's right. I've got to leave as soon as possible."

"No, baby," I pleaded with her, but her jaw tightened and she got that really stubborn look on her face.

"I'm going, Miles. I was going to head back tomorrow anyway. I'll just change the flight for this evening—or sooner, if I can."

I felt beaten. I didn't know who the winner was—Lilia or the gossip sites. It certainly wasn't me—or Clare.

"Look, it's only five months until I graduate," she said. "We'll be fine. We'll email and write ... okay, well *I'll* email and write, you can Skype me."

"Maybe you could come out for my birthday?" I said, feeling hopeful.

"Um, I don't think so. It's right before my finals and..."

"No, of course, sorry. I wasn't thinking. That's way more important."

Rhonda cleared her throat.

"Okay, kids, I'll leave you to it. Nice to see you again, Clare. It's been ... eventful."

They shook hands and risked a tentative smile at each other. I was glad that they seemed to be getting along better —it made things easier. Yeah, in the huge pit of chaos that surrounded me, it made things easier. A bit.

But when the time came, Clare wouldn't even let me go to JFK with her.

"It would be just our friggin' luck to get photographed with me looking like I've gone ten rounds with Mike Tyson," she said. "We'll just say goodbye here. In private."

She was trying to be tough and I loved her for it. I was missing her already and she hadn't even left yet.

"This sucks," she mumbled into my chest as I wrapped my arms around her, feeling her soft curves pressing against me.

"Yeah, big time."

"I love you," she said, her voice so quiet I could hardly hear her.

"Love you, too, Clare. All the way. You're ... perfect."

She laughed quietly.

"I am *so* going to remind you of that the next time I piss you off, or when I eat the last mini donut in the box."

A knock at the door interrupted any reply I might have choked out. The airport car had arrived, and the valet was there to collect her suitcase.

We shared one more desperate kiss, and then she pulled away from me.

"By the way, I left you a present," she said, as she stood at the door.

"You did?"

"Yeah, just something small. Read it and think of me."

"Read it?"

"Yes, you know—black marks on the page that make up words."

"Funny."

She winked and blew me a kiss.

Then she was gone.

I realized she hadn't told me where she'd put this present —or what it was.

Clare

God, I was going to miss him.

I left my 'gift' in an envelope marked *Private* and put it in his messenger bag, in the same pocket where his iPod charger lived. I knew that way he'd find it sooner rather than later once he got back to LA and I was in London. I wanted to leave him something funny and silly—something that would remind him of me.

I knew that it was going to be a very long five months. It was the most we'd been apart *ever*. I was dreading it, so it seemed important to leave something that would make him laugh. At least I hoped it would.

I'd written a résumé that summed up our sexcapades over the last few days—or rather, Miles Junior's exploits. It may have been the only dick in the world to have its own CV— well, along with Mark Wahlberg's equipment, perhaps.

Nationality: *British*
Driver's license: *stick shift*
Work Experience: *varied (blondes, brunettes, redheads)*

Previous Employment: *bathrooms, school library,*
theater, restaurant restroom, on flight bathroom,
sometimes bedrooms

Personal Attributes: *nine inches long, impressive*
girth; circumcised; liberal (dresses to the Left)

Always rises to the occasion and is good at thinking
for himself. Dresses suitably for all events and
knows how to behave in public private.

Thoughtful, passionate and not dissimilar to an
Eveready battery (keeps going longer).

Qualifications: *Masters degree in Physiology and*
Anatomy

Hobbies: *making surprise appearances, and*
attending charity events

Current Employment: *contented girlfriend*

And I attached a close-up photograph of the prospective job applicant in his pink, rubber interview suit. I'd used my camera phone to take the photograph when we were messing about. I thought it would make Miles laugh.

It had been a mad few months, and a crazy week. My best friend was on his way to becoming an international movie star—but best of all, my best friend had become my lover.

Yeah, and now I was traveling First Class!

JFK was busy when I arrived, but the British Airways VIP lounge for first class passengers—excuse me the *Concorde Room*—was quiet. I liked the idea that I was considered first class, especially after having been dragged through the proverbial primordial slime by certain gossip websites and magazines. So yeah, first class was suiting me very well, even if it meant Miles had to pay to have a first class girlfriend.

Oh, who the hell was I kidding? I was so low rent, I would have made a reality TV show look classy.

And I have to admit that I was slightly intimidated by the sheer opulence of the first class lounge. Who knew that airport terminals had chandeliers? Oh, and complimentary champagne, which was probably a bad idea, but getting sloshed when I felt so miserable seemed like a sensible option. Yes, I know. Alcohol when you're flying just dehydrates you and makes the jetlag worse. Whatever. But some situations can only be improved by administering industrial doses of alcohol or chocolate.

But then I discovered the real jewel in the crown of the Concorde Room: the spa!

With an hour to kill, I opted for a shoulder rub and flying feet. No, really, that's what they called it. I suppose someone thought it was witty. But, wow, that was some foot treatment. It was almost as good as sex. Well, not quite, but if they'd given me a bar of dark chocolate to go with the free champagne, it would have been pretty darn close.

The masseuse, Marla from Detroit, put these weird glove things on my feet that smelled of lime. I've never been a toe sucker—*ever*—but I swear, the aroma was so heavenly, it made me want to lick my own feet. God knows what I'd have done if Miles had been there—mount him on the ergonomic chair or give him a foot job? It would have been even money, either way.

Then Marla used hot stones to massage the soles of my feet—it was unbelievably wonderful and amazing, and I stopped feeling ticklish after the first 30 or 40 passes.

It was supposed to make my feet 'feel lighter'. I wondered if it would work on the rest of my body. Yes, I was a curvy kind of gal (okay, chubby—well, hefty), but I'd always thought if I could just push the fat from my stomach up to my boobs, I'd have the perfect figure. I may have mentioned it before— I really should look into patenting that idea.

"I suppose you've met lots of famous people?" I said to Marla, by way of starting a conversation.

"Oh, you know it, ma'am! They all stop by here on their way to London. My magic hands are spoken of on five continents."

Marla was brimming with humility as well as being

fabulously indiscreet. Once I got her started, she couldn't stop spilling the beans.

Celebrity A was a groper—never kept his hands to himself. Groped guys, too. "He's not fussy," she said.

Celebrity B had bad breath. "He could have stunned a buffalo at a thousand yards. I needed an oxygen mask just to give him a massage."

Celebrity C had a fungal infection in her toenails. "I thought I was gonna hurl my chicken burrito when I started working on those trotters."

Me, too, Marla. Me, too.

I would have *loved* to tell you which celebrities she was referring to, but you could probably Google it for yourself. Or use your imagination—that would work.

"I hope I'm not being indiscreet," she giggled.

I wanted to channel my inner Oscar Wilde and say, "No, but your answers are." Instead, I just smiled and pumped her for more dirt.

"Did you ever meet that actress, oh, what's her name ... skinny, small tits ... you know... the one who got caught blowing that guy?"

"Oh! You mean Lilia Purcell. Sure, she's been in here a few times." Marla leaned down to lower her voice, and I couldn't help craning my neck to hear her. "She's a lousy tipper," she whispered, conspiratorially.

Damn! Marla had totally backed me into a corner! If I didn't give her a humungous tip now, I'd be lumped in with Lilia—she of the airtight wallet.

I'd been shafted royally. Even so, I had to admit that I was in awe of Marla from Detroit, and I wondered how much of what she'd said was true, and how much was simply the equivalent of onboard entertainment.

But then my flight was called, and I had to leave Marla and her magic hands.

"Have a safe journey," she said. "Thanks for the tip. Hey! You never did tell me your name?"

"Oh," I said, quietly. "I'm no one."

It was a long and dreary flight home. Worse still, the house was empty when I got in because Mum and Dad were both out at work.

I trudged up the stairs and dumped my suitcase next to the bed. The last time I'd slept there, Miles had been in it. I sniffed his pillow, but his scent had already faded. Oh, my God, I'd turned into a pillow sniffer! And that night already seemed a long time ago.

When my phone rang, I knew without looking at the caller ID that it would be Miles. Apart from anything else, I'd programmed an alarm call on his cell phone to remind him to call me the minute he got home. He said he wouldn't need reminding, but although he was just about perfect, he was still a guy.

"Hey Clare," he whispered, his voice tinged with sadness. "Are you at home?"

"Yeah, just got here."

"Me, too."

"I know. I programmed your phone."

There was a long pause.

"I miss you."

"I miss you, too. It feels weird here."

"Weird, how?"

Weird because you're not here and I feel like my body has been ripped in half.

"I wish you were here, that's all."

He sighed.

"Yeah, me, too."

"So, how's it going? How's does it feel to be back ... home?"

It hurt to think that LA was his home and that London was just somewhere he'd lived once.

I could hear a rustle in the background and I knew he was pulling his t-shirt over his head. The thought of those fabulous abs that I was missing already, sculpted by long hours with the gym Nazi, made my mouth water—and other parts.

"Yeah, just been looking at my schedule," he murmured. "I've gotta do a couple of days dubbing some of the scenes from *Lifers*—you know, the one I shot in Texas. That's all. Then some publicity stuff on *Dazzled*."

"How's Lilia behaving?"

I could practically hear him rolling his eyes.

"Like Lilia. She's still spinning this line like we're an item. I don't know—it's taken some of the heat off since … you know. So Rhonda says. Who knows, maybe it's a good thing. At least they're not slagging you off as much."

What was Lilia's game? There was no way that bitch would do me any favors. I felt my body stiffen with sudden anger. And now I wasn't even there to put the skanky ho in her place this time. Maybe I should write a book: *The Teflon Tart—Making Sure that Shit Don't Stick.* Could be a bestseller. Or not.

Miles could tell how I was feeling because he carried on speaking hurriedly.

"Don't worry about it—you know I don't think of her like that. But the studio bosses really get off on it. They think it'll help sell the film and if Laura Dorien agrees to the sequel … you know, if people believe the romance. Everyone wants a happy ending, right?"

I knew I did.

Then his voice changed. Regret and irritation were replaced with pure sex.

"I found your letter," he said, his voice low and husky. "I mean, the CV. It was a great … job reference. And I was wondering if you had, um, *an opening*, because Miles Junior seems to be out of work at the moment."

I couldn't help smiling.

"Really? Is he looking for a job?"

"He's feeling kind of redundant."

"That's odd. I thought he would have taken himself in hand by now."

"You think he should?"

"Definitely. It's important to keep your *skills* up to scratch."

"There's this audition I'd like to try out for," he said, his voice rough with need.

"Do you want to run through your, um, lines with me?"

"Yeah, I'd love to do a run-through with you. Right now."

His words made me feel warm all over.

"Have you got everything you need to hand, Miles?"

"Yeah."

"Is it an action scene—or is it a love scene?"

He hesitated for almost a whole second.

"Both."

"Perhaps you'd better describe the setting, just so I can picture it."

"It's set in a bedroom."

"Uh-huh."

"There's a guy."

"A guy—got it."

"He's lying on his big, empty bed. He's lonely."

"Why is he lonely."

"He misses his hot girlfriend."

He called me hot!

"How much does he miss her?"

"Too fucking much."

"And I'm guessing she misses him, too."

"Yeah, I think that's in the script."

"Well, it should be ... so what does he do, being all lonely and stuff?"

"He's thinking about her."

"Is he doing anything while he's thinking about her?"

"Yeah. He's remembering how good she makes him feel."

"How does he do that?"

"He imagines her hands on him. All of him."

"Is he imagining her hands on his chest?"

"Lower."

"His stomach?"

"Lower."

I swallowed, imagining exactly what he was telling me.

"Is he stroking himself?"

"Yeah."

His voice came out in a long sigh, and I sat down on my bed, feeling heated and really turned on.

Miles' voice brought me back to myself.

"Do you think his girlfriend is doing the same thing—thinking of him—because it doesn't say in the script?"

"I'm sure she is. In fact, I'd guess she's imagining his hands on her—in her—right now."

He groaned, and I slipped my hand inside my decidedly damp knickers.

"W-what happens next?" I said, my voice shaky.

"This is where the action scene starts."

"What, like guns?"

"No, but there is a weapon."

I couldn't help laughing, even if it did come out as a breathy gasp. "So, the action speeds up?"

"God, I miss you, Clare."

My lungs gave a painful squeeze as Miles dropped all pretence, playfulness peeled away. *He misses me.*

His breath was coming faster now and I slid onto my back to take care of myself, missing his hands, his body, his beautiful eyes staring down at me as we made love.

I screwed my eyes shut and tried to convince myself that he was near, and that he loved me. Only one was true.

Three minutes later, I concluded that the Miles Junior CV had been a great idea. Miles Senior seemed to agree with me, if the grunting sounds coming through the speakerphone were anything to go by.

"Clare? Baby?"

His voice seemed a long way away.

I scrabbled around the rucked up duvet and finally found the source of his voice.

"Sorry!" I gasped. "I dropped the phone."

His dry chuckle made me smile. "Yeah, me, too."

We spoke for a while longer but then he had to go—some publicity thing—even though he'd only been back less than an hour. He didn't elaborate; he just sounded tired and more than a little blue.

After he ended the call, I decided to email him daily 'job advertisements' until he came back to London, or until I flew out to join him in LA, in the hope that they'd result in more hot, steamy phone sex.

But five days later, I concluded that the Miles Junior CV was a really, really, fucking awful idea.

Because it ended up on the internet.

LA was eight hours behind London time, so I was really surprised when Miles called me while I was eating my lunchtime sandwich on the grass in front of the British Museum.

"Hey! Have you been out partying because I know it's only 4 AM and..."

He interrupted me.

"Clare, have you been online this morning?"

"I checked my emails, but..."

He sighed. "I think you'd better look at the Hollywood Life website. Or just Google my name."

I pulled out my phone and connected to the internet. It took me less than 15 seconds to see what he was talking about.

"Holy fuck!"

A photograph of the Miles Junior CV was sitting on the gossip website's homepage—along with an enlarged photograph of Miles' very erect dick.

The breath left my body, and I felt sick.

"How the hell did they get hold of that?"

"I'm guessing it was someone who worked in my building," he said, his voice full of tension. "Or it could have been someone at the gym. I, um, I've been kind of carrying it around with me."

"Shit, Miles, you idiot!"

"I know. Rhonda is going crazy."

"Hey, it's okay," I stammered, trying to calm him—and myself. "It could be a photograph of anyone's di ... I mean, a photograph of some random guy. It doesn't prove anything."

He sighed again, and I damned camera phones to hell and back.

"I'm so sick of this shit," he spat out. "It's just relentless. Why does anyone care?" He swore softly, and I felt like such a fool for putting him in this position—for screwing things up for him, yet again.

"It means I'll have to be more careful," he said, "and ... oh, fuck. Rhonda's calling me on the other line. I'll talk to you later, okay?"

He rang off before I could answer.

My sandwich didn't seem so appealing now. Trying to eat would have choked me, so I pulled it to pieces and fed it to some pigeons that were keeping an eye on me a few feet away. One of them looked kind of tousled, with ruffled feathers and a bad foot. I threw most of the crumbs in his direction—or it could have been a her.

I definitely felt kinship with the scraggy bird.

Feeling all kinds of sorry for myself, I dragged my weary backside to my next lecture: 'Dissembling in Austen's England: a study of delicacy and disillusion'.

What would Jane Austen have said about my sorry arse? I imagined her gimlet eye and no-nonsense attitude pinning me with a bright gaze: "a very obstinate, ungrateful girl—very ungrateful indeed, considering *who* and *what* she is."

Yeah, I cut that lecture, went home, ate two magnum Snickers, drank a four pack of Heineken, and fell asleep on my bed.

Problem solved.

I was woken by the sound of my phone ringing. What bastard was calling in the middle of the night?

I opened one, bleary eye. Huh. It was only 10 PM. And it was Miles.

"Hi!" I croaked. "How are you? Are you okay?"

I could hear him breathing softly on the other end of the line.

"Yeah, I'm okay."

"You don't sound okay—you sound like you've got two broken legs and your dog just died."

He chuckled quietly but I could tell his heart wasn't in it.

"How's it going? What did Rhonda say?"

"She's pissed at me."

"No surprise there."

"No, I guess not. But it feels like I can't get a break—the hits just keep on coming."

"I know. And I'm really sorry. I feel like such a bloody idiot!"

He sighed. "It's not your fault, Clare. I'm the flaming tosser who carried that picture around with him. I should have just put your photograph in my wallet like a normal guy."

We both laughed at that, although it had a hollow sound.

"Oh well. At least it's given you the night off."

"What do you mean?"

"Well, you were booked to do *Ellen* again, weren't you?"

"Yeah."

I counted to three before I understood his meaning.

"Shit, no! You're not really going to go ahead and do the interview, are you? Not after—well, not after what's happened?"

"Yep. That's pretty much it."

"Bloody hell, Miles! Is that really a good idea?"

"I don't know. Rhonda seems to think it would be best to face this one head-on."

"Is that a joke?"

"Oh … it wasn't meant to be. I think it'll be okay. Ellen's cool. She'll have a laugh and we'll move on."

"Are you going to say it's not you?"

"You mean lie? Maybe. I'll try and laugh it off, but if she asks me outright, yeah, I'll probably lie. Like you said, no one can prove it one way or another."

"Wow."

"Yeah."

He took a deep breath. "So, we're live on tape, and it'll air at about seven. I'm not sure what time it'll be on cable. It could be pretty late…"

"I don't care—I'll find out and set my alarm."

Which is what I did.

"Okay," he said, softly. "I love you. Wish me luck."

"Good luck. I love you, too."

At 3:55 AM, my alarm rang. Normally, I'd have wanted to hurl it across the room, but in truth, I was so wound up, I'd hardly slept anyway.

Miles' interview was trailed for nearly the full hour before he was finally introduced.

He strode onto the stage and bounced in his seat as the applause died down. At least they didn't heckle him this time.

Ellen: Miles! How are you? I'm so glad to see you—I thought I'd catch you off guard and you'd still be in your underwear!

Miles: It was close—but it was your underwear anyway. Well, not *your* underwear, because that would just be freaky, [*laughter*] but *Ellen* underwear. I should probably stop talking now.

Ellen: No, don't do that—it's an interview.

Miles: Oh, I always forget that bit. [*laughter*]

Ellen: So, how have you been?

Miles: Good, thanks.

Ellen: Doing any interesting jobs at the moment? [*Audience noise*] Because that's a pretty impressive, uh, résumé you've got there. [*Audience laughs*]

Miles: Thank you very much.

Ellen: I hear they're remaking *Nine and a Half Weeks*, and that you're going to be in it.

Miles: That's news to me.

Ellen: I think they're going to call it *Nine Inches*, I mean *Nine weeks*. [*Audience laughs*]

Miles: Ha ha! I loved that movie. Kim Basinger is so hot.

Ellen: Seriously, man, it's been an interesting couple of days for you.

Miles: I think the Chinese use that as a curse: 'May you live in interesting times'.

Ellen: Do you feel cursed? Because it seems like the gossip sites are on your case a lot at the moment.

Miles: It is what it is. I can't do anything about it. You've just got to have a sense of humor about it. I liked the whole CV thing—it made me laugh.

Ellen: Really? You can just laugh it off?

Miles: Sure.

Ellen: Wow! That's pretty amazing.

Miles: Mind you, I haven't spoken to my mum yet.

Ellen: Will she be mad?

Miles: Pretty much, yeah. She's great though.

Ellen: Wow, we don't want Miles' mad mom coming over here and kicking some butts!

Miles: No, she's awesome.

Ellen: And I guess it's not like anything she hasn't seen before. [*Audience laughs, Miles just smiles*]

Ellen: Seriously, how do you cope with the intrusion into your personal life?

Miles: [*shrugs*] What people think of me isn't

really any of my business. The fans are great
—that's all that matters.

[*Audience applauds*]

He was so smoooooth. Gayl Lemon would have been
proud of him. But I sort of missed the guy who only opened
his mouth to change feet. I guess we were both growing up.

Chapter Twenty

THE END OF THE AFFAIR

Miles

It felt weird being back in LA without Clare.

We'd waited so long to be together. I was still kind of mad at her for not saying something sooner—about us. I wasn't sure I understood her reasons. I mean, she'd wittered on about feeling inadequate and 'not being good enough', whatever the fuck that meant. It was so damn obvious that it was the other way around.

But, whatever, I was just glad that we'd got there in the end. So it really sucked to be apart *again*. I knew it was only for a few months, and then we could be together permanently. At least, I hoped that's what it would be. She was my everything: my best friend, my lover, my yesterday and today, my tomorrow.

Cock-gate had been embarrassing, but as most people seemed to think it was a spoof, I'd got off pretty lightly. The experience, coming on top of all the other dungheap worth of shit, had made me a hell of a lot more careful. I started locking my phone when I wasn't using it, and didn't carry anything personal around with me except my driver's license and credit cards. I was more wary of the people around me, too.

Hilda had tried to hook up, but I'd blown her off and

found myself a new personal trainer. I was surprised to find that working out was addictive. Who'd have thought I'd like that shit?!

But I hated, really fucking hated, what they were still saying about Clare. Lilia had come up smelling of roses. Some people were even suggesting that the photographs of her and Joe Blow were fakes, which was even more irritating. I tried not to care, but I did. I really did.

At least Clare was away from the worst of it, and she hadn't got papped back in the UK. No one was sure whether or not she was the 'mystery brunette' from New York, and as we hadn't seen each other in months, she was safe. I was followed and photographed everywhere I went. But the only shots they got were of me going to the gym, buying groceries, and hanging out with Earl at the Sam Ash music store.

I was also having to rethink where I lived. Several times, I'd come home to find teenage girls waiting outside. That wasn't too bad, even if it annoyed the other residents, but once a couple of girls had got inside and were waiting at the door of my apartment. I don't know how they got there, but it wouldn't have been that hard to wait until someone was going out, or to press all the entry buttons and see if someone buzzed them in. I'd had to call the supervisor when they'd refused to leave after getting the usual autographs and photos.

Honey had helped me find a place to buy that had better security. It was strange to think that I was going to be a homeowner. Mum had moved into her new house a few weeks ago, and she said she was happy. I loved the idea that no one could ever make her leave that place: it was hers. I'd tried to get her to come out here, but the only time she'd been on a plane was a package holiday to Malaga when I was 12. She'd said Hail Mary's for the entire flight—and she wasn't even Catholic. So as for her coming out to LA to visit, I was still working on that.

My new place was a Spanish style bungalow, with five bedrooms and a swimming pool. Bloody hell! I would be a homeowner with a swimming pool. It took some getting my head around that. But as soon as I'd seen it, I knew that Clare would love it.

I couldn't wait for her to come out here and be part of this new life with me. I didn't want to do it without her.

I missed her.

Clare

I was in a filthy mood, but what was new?

I hadn't seen my boyfriend, the love of my life, in five, long, lonely, celibate months. I'd been studying between ten and fourteen hours a day for the last six weeks, and now I was being dressed up in a cap and gown that made me look like a mortician at an Addam's Family makeover party.

Mum and Dad were disgustingly happy, so proud that their only child was the first person in the family to leave university with a degree. Yeah, and I was pretty pleased, too, especially as I'd been awarded a double first, but I'd worked hard for that. I'd sacrificed a lot: money, sanity, and a social life being the key things.

But what really had me channeling my inner Hulk was that I hadn't been able to talk to Miles *on my special friggin' day!* He'd sent me a text while I was still asleep apologizing like mad, but saying that he was filming somewhere remote where there was no cell phone signal, and he'd call me tomorrow.

That was a real bummer and explained the bad temper.

I knew I'd see him in a couple of days when I flew out to LA, but it still wouldn't be the same. I know, I know. I was being a whiny emo bitch. I should just be grateful that Mum and Dad hadn't disowned me and sent me to an orphanage like a chunkier, better fed version of Oliver Twist, but I was still moaning and asking, "Please, sir, may I have some more."

Prue was coming to my graduation ceremony, too, so I'd be surrounded by family. Paul and Nazzer thought they might come along to the after-party in the pub, but as I'd told them there was no free bar, I had my doubts as to whether or not they'd show.

The academic gown was black, of course, with a purple hood—a strip of material hanging around the back of the robe, making it look like a monk's cowl. Which was not inappropriate bearing in mind my solitary sexual pleasures of the last five months. The mortar board was the typical square cap with a tassel hanging in your eyes. I kept trying to push it to one side, but it insisted on falling to the front, like a third eyebrow. Apparently, the mortar board was supposed to mimic a Roman Catholic biretta, but I wasn't feeling very Godly, and I'd been swearing under my breath all morning.

"For goodness sake, Clare!" snorted Mum. "You sound like a cross between a docker and a navvy! Is that language really necessary?"

"Yes," I said, sullenly. "I have Tourette's. Didn't I mention that?"

"Don't be flippant. You're spoiling a special day. Me and your dad are very proud of you."

I sighed. "I know. Sorry, Mum. Just wishing ... you know."

She smiled. "Ah well, only a couple of days to go. Then *I'll* be the one missing you."

I felt a stab of guilt. I'd been wallowing so much, I hadn't stopped to think how Mum and Dad would feel, what with me moving 6,000 miles away. I *should* have considered it: I knew how much Prue missed Miles. And he was a bloke, and rubbish at staying in touch. Except with me. He texted or phoned every day. Sometimes, if our schedules were compatible, we Skyped, too. (And, as a side note, Skype-sex is even better than phone sex. Just saying.)

In the end, Miles had come out of the various scandals pretty well. In fact, the denting of his 'angelic' image had brought him some interesting work. For the last two months, he'd been filming a thriller up in Toronto, and had been playing the part of a rookie cop who'd got involved with the Mob.

Lilia was still a pain in the rectum. She'd signed on for a

sequel to *Dazzled* and, after long and tense negotiations, Miles had decided to do the same. He was still doubtful it was the right thing to do, but he felt he should show some gratitude to Laura Dorien, and to Jo-Anne, who had also signed on for directing duties. Filming would start in September. At least I'd be around to keep Lilia's sticky paws away from Miles.

I'd officially be his PA. So I'd be paid to be with the man I loved and to have wild, abandoned sex with my boss every night. I couldn't see a downside.

Honey was still on the team, but she spent more time with Rhonda these days—the agency had become increasingly busy because of the success of *Dazzled*, and both women were now working exclusively for Miles. I also wondered if there wasn't a little bit of a love interest *thang* going on there. But I'd recently developed an aversion to gossip, so I didn't ask questions.

Polly had also signed up for the sequel, and I was looking forward to hanging out with her in LA. And we'd all been invited to Mildred and Leon's wedding—no merkins involved —which was taking place in Santa Monica in August.

I was starting a new life—and I couldn't wait.

I'd be living in LA with the man I loved. And I fully intended that we'd spend as much time as possible shagging like bunnies. It was good to have ambition.

But first, I had to graduate.

So, as a graduand of University College London, I sat with my peers for two hours, and listened to the Provost's address and various other speeches. I was already feeling nostalgic for the end of my academic career but I still didn't think it had been necessary to order the DVD of the event. But Miles had insisted, as he wasn't able to attend in person.

The Royal Festival Hall was filled with students in their robes, and friends and family in their best clothes. I wasn't sure where the parentals were sitting, but I knew they'd be able to see me when I picked up my degree certificate. Except it wasn't even the real thing—I had to pose for my graduation photograph with something that looked like a wooden rolling pin, and was told that the certificate would be posted to me within the next six months! That was rubbish!

The ceremony finished, having moved with the speed of an arthritic snail, and at last I joined the academic procession as everyone started shuffling out of the hall. I'd arranged to meet Mum, Dad and Prue at the graduation reception for the kind of wine you could cheerfully put on your fries if the vinegar ran out, and canapés that could chip your teeth, but when I turned my phone back on, Mum called me immediately.

"Oh, Clare, love! I've left my purse under my seat. I was in row 33F. Can you go and get it for me? I can't leave your father—you know how he gets at these things."

I grumbled a bit, but hurried back into the hall, worried that her credit cards might currently be paying the bar bill for some other cheapskate UCL student—not that I wanted to think badly of my fellow graduates.

But as I made my way through the auditorium, my heart began to beat faster.

Someone was sitting in the exact seat Mum had sent me to.

He turned his face toward me, and my heart leapt and flopped around like a newly landed cod. He smiled, and I swear the lights dimmed in comparison as my eyes met his.

"Hey, baby," he said, softly. "Did you miss me?"

My voice got tangled on the way out of my throat.

"What are you doing here?" I spluttered.

His smile got even wider. "Surprise," he whispered, as his arms wrapped around my waist.

His warmth, his touch, his lips against my neck. I was beyond words, choked by the joy that flooded through me.

And then he sank to one knee, and I stopped breathing.

"Clare: you've been my best friend my whole life. I love you. And I want to tell you that every day for the rest of your life. Will you marry me?"

In his hand rested a small, aquamarine box with the words *Tiffany & Co* inscribed on the lid. He opened it, and nestled there in the silk was a solitaire diamond ring that threw rainbows around the hall.

I looked down into his beautiful gray eyes. He looked so nervous. Did he really think I'd say no?

"You want to marry me?"

He nodded, his expression tense.

"But I'm a complete cow. I nag you all the time. I'm moody and bad-tempered, and I can eat a whole box of chocolate éclairs in a single sitting. I watch daytime TV, and eat toast in bed so it's full of crumbs. I eat kebabs with cabbage and chili sauce, and use all the hot water in the shower."

"I know," he said, smiling. "And you leave wet towels on the bathroom floor, and eat KitKats by biting off the chocolate and sucking the biscuit. You steal my t-shirts, and don't appreciate the genius that is modal jazz. You suck your teeth and roll your eyes when someone irritates you, and…"

"Yeah, all right! No need to go on!"

"You clip your toenails on the balcony, and you fart in your sleep."

"Hey!"

"And I love you so fucking much. So will you? Will you marry me?"

What could I say to that undying declaration of love?

"Oh, okay then."

His eyelids fluttered closed for a second, then he blinked up at me. His eyes were glistening with tears.

"Thank you," he whispered, and slipped the ring onto my stubby, chubby finger.

He was beautiful, talented and famous—but that wasn't his fault. As for the rest, well, we were working on it.

And so I packed my bags to head to California—the sunshine state. Oh wait, I think that's Florida. Ah, you know what I mean—the state with a lot of sunshine. Land of a thousand stars. With him. My fiancé. With Miles. My own personal miracle.

Yeah, pretty mushy, but what did I care? I was in love.

And so was he :)

REVIEWS

Reviews are love! Honestly, they are! But it also helps other people to make an informed decision before buying my book.

So I'd really appreciate if you took a few seconds to do that.

Thank you!

MORE BOOKS BY JHB

Series Titles
The Education Series
An epic love story spanning the years, through war zones and more...
*The Education of Sebastian (Education series #1)
*The Education of Caroline (Education series #2)
*The Education of Sebastian & Caroline (combined edition, books 1 & 2)
Semper Fi: The Education of Caroline (Education series #3)

The Traveling Series
All the fun of the fair ... and two worlds collide
*The Traveling Man (Traveling series #1)
*The Traveling Woman (Traveling series #2)
*Roustabout (Traveling series #3)
*Carnival (Traveling series #4)
*Gypsy (Traveling series #5)

The Justin Trainer Series
The bodyguard and the billionaire
Guarding the Billionaire (Justin Trainer series #1)
Saving the Billionaire (Justin Trainer series #2)

The EOD Series
Blood, bombs and heartbreak
*Tick Tock (EOD series #1)
* Bombshell (EOD series #2)

The Rhythm Series
Blood, sweat, tears and dance
*Slave to the Rhythm (Rhythm series #1)
*Luka (Rhythm series #2)

Standalone Titles
Contemporary Romance
The Lilac Cadillac
Battle Scars
One Careful Owner
*Lifers
At Your Beck & Call
The New Samurai
Exposure

New Adult
*Dangerous to Know & Love
Dazzled
Summer of Seventeen

Paranormal
*The Dark Detective: Venator (Book #1)
*The Dark Detective: Paukúnnum (Book #2)

Novellas
Playing in the Rain
*Behind the Walls

Anthologies of Short Stories
*The Year Book Volume 1
*The Year Book Volume 2
*The Year Book Volume 3

Audio Books
One Careful Owner
(*narrated by Seth Clayton*)

On the Stage
Later, After: Playscript
Trailer

With Alana Albertson
Father Figure

* These titles are published in languages other than English. Please check Jane's website for details—and receive **a free short story every month** when you sign up for her newsletter :)

QR code for Jane's website

ROMANCE WITH STUART REARDON

My love co-author with these titles

Two book series - contemporary romance
*Undefeated
*Model Boyfriend

Three book series - romcom
*Gym Or Chocolate?
*The World According to Vince
*The Baby Game

Standalone
Survivor Love Island *(romcom)*
*Touch My Soul *(novella)*

WRITING AS BERRICK FORD

Police Thrillers, UK

Dead Water
Dead Man's Dive
Dead Reckoning
Dead Shore

www.berrickford.com